THE FAVOR

SUZANNE WRIGHT

The characters and events portrayed in this book are fictitious. Any similarity to real persons, living or dead, is coincidental and not intended by the author.

For D, I miss your brand of crazy.

PROLOGUE

Watching my ex pick himself up off the deck, I winced at the deep cut above his eye. *Ouch.* He'd need a few stitches for sure. But I wasn't feeling very sympathetic right then.

"Maybe you should do something, Vienna," said Melinda, sidling up to me.

I gave my foster mother a helpless shrug. No one with a brain would try to get between Dane Davenport and something he wanted. And right then, what he seemed to want was to pummel my ex-fiancé into the ground.

I would not at all be opposed to that.

Owen had been something of an asshole lately. Today, he'd gone too far. He might not have made himself as problematic as the others who were set on separating Dane and me, but he'd certainly had this coming.

Melinda turned to her husband. "We can't just stand here."

"Why not?" asked Wyatt. "Owen should have known better."

Why yes, yes, he should've. An uber-successful business mogul, Dane had a reputation for being someone you did *not* cross or underestimate. He was driven. Relentless. Assertive. Unforgiving. Intimidatingly intelligent. Richer than God. And, until several months ago, married to his job.

Now he was married to me.

He was also my boss.

He rarely lost his cool like this. Probably because he didn't waste emotional energy letting others get under his skin. But as others weren't supposed to know that our marriage was purely a business arrangement, he naturally had to play the role of possessive husband. And since there was no missing the blatant edge of danger he carried, he certainly had a menacing vibe going on right now.

Dane stared the prick down. "I warned you, didn't I? I warned you time and time again to stay away from her, but you didn't listen," he reprimanded, his tone soft. "Worse, you pulled *this* shit. For someone who claims to care for Vienna, you sure don't show it."

Owen clenched his fists. "I *do* care for her, she's—"

"Not yours," Dane finished. "They're *my* rings on her finger. It's *my* name she's taken. It's *my* bed she shares. She is mine. So whether you care for her or not isn't fucking relevant."

Owen swallowed. "She was mine first."

"And you should have held tight to her. You didn't. You let her go. That was your mistake."

"I did what was best for her."

"No, you did what was best for you. You might have cared for Vienna, but you didn't put her first. She was *never* your priority."

Owen nostrils flared. "I was young back then. A kid."

"A kid who wanted the space to pursue his ambitions. She gave that to you; she didn't curse you for it. And how do you repay that? By trying to break up her marriage. You think she'll thank you for that? That she'll *want* someone who'd do that to her?"

My ex's jaw hardened. "What I think ... is that Vienna deserves to be loved. You'll never love her—you don't have that in you."

Those words stabbed me right in the chest ... because they were true. Dane didn't love me. Never had. Never would.

I shouldn't care. I wasn't supposed to care. And I definitely didn't like that I did. But I'd gone and fallen for my fake husband. Yeah, I was *that* stupid.

Dane sighed. "So you've said before. I didn't care what you thought then; I still don't care now. You're of no interest to me. And you're of no interest *to her*. You need to man the hell up and accept it, because I won't have you playing these games with her. You're going to leave here, and you're going to stay away from her."

Owen jutted out his chin. "You don't get to dictate what I do."

"When it comes to my wife, I absolutely do."

"You won't keep her in the long-run, you know. She'll see that I'm right about you eventually. Then she'll leave you."

Dane tilted his head, looking at him curiously. "Now why would you think I'd let her do a thing like that?"

Owen's head jerked back. "You can't *force* someone to stay with you."

"Vienna knows I'd never let her go."

Damn, Dane was so good at acting that if he hadn't been so clear about not wanting a real marriage, I might have believed him.

"She's just a possession to you," Owen insisted.

"My most prized possession, as it happens," said Dane. "And I have every intention of keeping her. Deal with it. Accept it. Leave her alone. Get rid of this dream you have of winning her back. It won't happen."

"And if I *don't* stay away from her?"

Dane's mouth curved into a cruel, chilling smile that almost made me shiver. "I'll make you wish you had."

Owen's eyes flickered. "She can do better than you. You don't deserve her."

"And you think you do? You, who just behaved like a complete asshole, think you deserve her?"

Shame flickered across my ex's face. "Maybe neither of us do. But—"

"There are no 'buts.' You're mistaken in thinking that you'd be married to her now if you hadn't messed up. I'd have lured her away from you, even if it took me years. Don't think for one moment she would be yours if A, B, or C hadn't happened. I would have made her mine one way or another. You'd be wrong to think I don't mean that. I'm ruthless about going after what I want. Quit banking on me fucking up and losing her the way you did. I'd never let someone so important to me walk out of my life."

Owen narrowed his eyes, studying Dane hard. "Son of a bitch, I think you might just actually care for her in your own way."

Dane's gaze slid to me, burning with possession, impatience, and something … more. Something that made my pulse quicken and my breath catch. But Owen was wrong. Dane didn't care for me. There was no way he'd want this marriage to be real. He didn't even want a girlfriend, let alone a wife … right?

CHAPTER ONE

Six months earlier

Stopping at my desk, Hanna regarded me warily. "Uh-oh, your eyelid's twitching. What's wrong? Did someone mistake you for the model on the Syphilis Awareness billboard again?"

I narrowed my eyes at my friend and coworker. "No. And I don't look anything like her." We'd had this conversation already. But Hanna liked to poke at me in that way that only one of your closest friends would.

"You have the same pale blue eyes and high cheekbones. Her hair isn't *exactly* the same platinum blonde shade as yours, but it's close."

People always assumed my hair color came straight out of a bottle. In truth, I'd inherited it from my half-Swedish grandmother.

"But she doesn't have your blunt bangs or Jessica Alba-mouth," Hanna went on because, yeah, she was a pain in my ass when bored.

"Can we *not* talk about the model who looks nothing like me, please?"

"Of course."

"Great. If you've come to speak to Dane, he's not yet back from his lunch meeting, but he shouldn't be much longer."

"I came to check on you. A little birdie told me they saw Travis enter the building earlier. The last time the idiot came here, you almost had to call security to remove him."

And who was Travis? My boss's sly, smarmy, self-entitled brother.

I sighed. "I'm fine, just annoyed. He wanted to wait for Dane in his office. I said no. He tried flirting with me to get his way. I said no. He claimed he had a migraine and just needed a quiet place to sit. I said no. Then he got all mean and *demanded* I let him in. Again, I said no. We went around and around like that for a while until, finally, he stalked off—but not before threatening to have me fired."

Hanna shook her head. "He's such a weasel. Why do you think he wanted access to Dane's office?"

"He said he wanted to wait for him in there." It wouldn't have surprised me if he'd intended to nose around and sniff out some sensitive material that he could sell to Dane's competitors. Travis seemed to harbor a deep resentment for his brother. I suspected it was petty jealousy since—in total contrast to Dane—the only thing Travis appeared to be successful at was being an absolute tool.

Hanna tilted her head. "Although he's a boil on our butts, he generally doesn't send that eyelid of yours twitching. It usually takes more than that to set it off. Come on, tell me what's bothering you. You'll feel better for it. And I'm nosy—help a girl out."

"It's nothing, really. I just discovered something about myself that I don't like."

"Ooh, I do that daily. So, what'd you discover?"

I clasped my hands together and rested them on my desk. "I can be very petty. See, I'm going to bump into my high school sweetheart today—a guy I was briefly engaged to. He's rich and successful now. Although I don't want him back, I want him to look at me, see how much better my life is without him in it, and regret letting me go."

"Girl, pretty much everyone wants their exes to feel that way. It doesn't make you petty. It makes you human. And back up … you were *engaged* to this guy? How is it we've known each other for four years and I've never heard about this?" She propped her elbows on the desk. "Okay, walk me through how it all went down."

"Short version—"

"I want the long version."

"Well, you're getting the short one. Owen Redford and I grew up together. He was one of my closest friends. We dated during the last few years of high school, and he proposed to me after graduation—it was a gesture to show that him going away to college wasn't going to change anything between us. But he ended our relationship five months later. He said we'd rushed into getting engaged and that we were too young to make such a commitment."

Hanna's face went all soft and sympathetic. "That limp-dicked asshole crushed your teenage heart."

"Not quite, but he certainly dealt it a few kicks. People always used to talk about how he was made for bigger and better things than the life he'd been born into. We grew up in a real shady neighborhood. A part of me worried he'd leave me behind when his life officially took off … and he did. He asked to remain friends, but I never saw or heard from him again after that."

"Not even once?"

"No. I bumped into his aunt a few times over the years, so I know he's married, has a kid, owns a huge house, and has a cushy job." I sighed. "I'm glad things worked out so well for him. I really am. It's just made me painfully aware of how little my own life has changed since we last saw each other. Not that I don't *like* my life, it's just become sort of … stagnant."

I had my health, I had people who loved me, I had a well-paying job, and I never took any of it for granted. But I felt like I was stuck in one place, existing only to eat, sleep, and pay my bills. I didn't date, didn't go on vacations, didn't take much time for myself. I didn't really *have* time, since I worked a lot. Being the PA of a workaholic was murder on my personal life. I definitely needed to shake things up a bit.

"Is there no way you can get out of seeing Owen?" asked Hanna.

"Probably not. His boss arranged a meeting with Dane months ago. I had a brief chat with the guy's PA earlier via phone, and she told me that Charles would be bringing two of his 'rising stars' with him. I almost fell off my chair when she said Owen's name. And since Dane usually likes me to sit in on these sorts of meetings and take notes, it's highly unlikely that I can avoid seeing Owen."

"Shit." Straightening, Hanna waved a hand at me. "Well, you might not be married, rich, or live in a flashy house, but you're a smart, confident woman who anyone would respect purely for working as Dane Davenport's PA for a full four years. Not many people could work so closely with a corporate psychopath. At least not without having a breakdown."

I sighed. "Granted, Dane's … a little difficult at times, but he's not a psychopath."

"You've not noticed the power-hunger, lack of empathy, absence of a conscience, or that he is a control freak? None of his previous PAs lasted longer than six months—they were either fired or left in tears. Dane is *not* anyone's idea of a nice guy. Not that I'm complaining. There's something real yummy about a bad boy. The whole cold and ruthless thing works for him."

Okay, so he liked power. Didn't most CEOs? And, yes, he could be a little insensitive and careless with people's feelings. He was also ruthless, sure, but … "He's not cold or without a conscience. And he doesn't lack empathy." Well, not *totally* anyway. "He just doesn't always bother to call up any emotional tact."

"He made Gibson cry yesterday. Sweet, fresh-faced, quick-to-laugh Gibson. That's like kicking a puppy. Which is something Dane probably often did as a child—being mean to animals is textbook for psychopathic kids, you know."

I sighed again. "He's not a psychopath."

"Come on, he even has that hunter stare they're known for having. Look me in the eye and tell me it doesn't make you want to squirm. The hairs on my nape stand up every time."

Yeah, I didn't fare much better against it. There was always a dangerous glint in his dark, steely eyes. They could focus on you like a laser, pin you in place, and direct so much intensity at you that your personal space felt invaded.

Even after four years of working for him, I was not immune to that unflinching, relentless, apex-predator stare. Not at all. It was like being watched by a jungle cat. A big, badass jungle cat who wondered what an insignificant little thing like you was doing in its domain.

"Anyone can perfect a stare like that if they try hard enough," I said.

Hanna squinted, and her mouth curled into a smile. "You know something? I think you like him."

In all honesty, I'd had a harmless crush on my boss for years now. I didn't give myself a hard time about it. There was no way to remain unaffected by Dane Davenport. "Good-looking" was too tame a term for him. Tall, dark, and supremely male, he exuded a raw sex appeal that could shake any girl's equilibrium.

It wasn't just his appearance that made him so lethally seductive. It was the entire package—his powerful personality, innate aura of authority, unshakable self-assuredness, and the untamed air about him that spoke of danger.

He was effortlessly desirable, and he was very much aware of it. He didn't flaunt it, though. He did, however, make no bones of exploiting the impact he had on the female gender. He flitted from woman to woman, never taking the time to romance them. For Dane, nothing and no one came before work. He'd built a life that seemed designed to keep people out.

Sometimes, I couldn't help but feel that he had an empty spot inside him. One he tried so hard to fill with work but never quite succeeded.

Despite being offhand and rude at times, he'd secured himself a vast network of clients, partners, and allies. He had a sort of … cold charisma. A powerful, masculine, irresistible presence that wasn't tempered by warmth but still drew you into his orbit like a magnet. And I, sadly, was not at all immune to it.

I didn't pine for him, though, for two reasons. First, I was a realist. I knew there would never be anything between us, and that surety enabled me to box the whole thing into my mental fantasy drawer. A drawer I only ever opened when I was spending quality time with my vibrator.

Second, even if he wasn't too much of a workaholic to be fully invested in a relationship, he'd be too difficult a partner. In business, things were never good enough for Dane—he was always moving the marker, always driven to have "more," always finding imperfections. I suspected he'd be the same way with his partner; that he'd never feel truly satisfied. That kind of relationship did not appeal to me.

Really, Dane was far too professional to get involved with one of his employees anyway. Would I ever consider a one-night stand if he gave me any indication that he'd be up for it? No. I valued my job too much to lose it over an "indiscretion."

"You do have a thing for him, don't you?" pushed Hanna.

Like I'd share that with Hanna, who couldn't hold in her own pee. "It's not *that*, it's just … he gave me an opportunity that not a lot of people would have."

Understanding flashed across Hanna's face. "And so you'd feel disloyal saying anything negative about him, I get it."

Well, it *would* be disloyal. When I'd first come to work at o-Verve Pro Technologies, I'd been hired as a secretary for one of the low-level staff. Clint was an arrogant, egotistical, narcissistic chauvinist who was prone to throw tantrums and believed that everyone was out to sabotage him.

I'd been nothing short of mortified when I realized that the CEO had overheard me telling Clint to "*Stop being a precious little man-child and quit with the drama before you give yourself an ulcer. Oh, and don't think I'm going to clean up that mess—you swiped the stuff off the desk, you can put it all back.*"

It was not a great way to speak to your boss, no, but I'd found that Clint responded well to my teacher-addressing-an-unruly-student tone. It always snapped him right out of his tirades.

When I'd gotten called into Dane's office later that day, I'd been sure he meant to fire me. Instead, he'd informed me that he'd be moving me to another department within the building. Namely, his …

Shocked as all shit, I stared at him. "I don't understand."

"I need a new PA," he said, lounging in his leather chair. "I did a little digging after overhearing your … conversation with Clint. I learned a lot of things about you. You're meticulous. Dependable. Highly efficient. Hyper-organized. You don't balk at hard work, you have a positive attitude, you're good at multi-tasking, and you've been a great right-hand person for Clint. And I saw—or, more precisely, overheard—that you can handle difficult characters. I need all that in a PA."

"Don't you already have one?"

"Yes. She can't deal with the workload and would prefer to spend her time flirting with me. Needless to say, she doesn't have a future as my PA."

I licked my lower lip. "Not that I'm trying to talk myself out of a job but, well, my way of handling 'difficult characters' isn't always in a calm, professional manner."

"But if Clint could have been handled using a calm, professional manner, you'd have gone down that route, wouldn't you?"

"Yes."

"I don't need someone who's always polite. You'll come into contact with a lot of strong, demanding, self-entitled characters—me included. If you're sweet and agreeable and can't handle yourself, they'll eat you alive. I need someone who won't be railroaded."

He leaned forward and rested his elbows on his desk. "I'm good at recognizing talent and skills in people; at knowing where and how they'd be useful within my company. I believe this position would suit you. But, be warned, it isn't a dream job. I'm not an easy man to work for; I'm a perfectionist who has little room for error. By doing the amount of jobs—big and small—that I'll be requiring you to do, you'll be expected to be ten people at one time. I need someone who can keep on track with everything, who won't need any direct supervision, and who isn't going to start sniffling if I'm not nice to them. I believe that's you. So, care to take a chance and see if I'm right?"

I'd taken the chance. He hadn't lied. A lot of pressure came with the job, and he could be a nightmare to handle sometimes—mostly because he had very strict standards for others and himself, and he had no tolerance for anyone who couldn't keep up. He could also be inflexible and overly detail orientated. Any displays of laziness, inefficiency, or a bad work ethic from his employees were met with chillingly insensitive putdowns.

He also tended to forget that, unlike him, not everyone was married to their job. But in many other ways, he was a good boss. He paid well, looked after his employees, rewarded hard work, and didn't tolerate any workplace bullshit.

Moreover, he'd once been my fucking hero—he'd stepped in when I thought everything would come crumbling down around me and he'd fixed the situation without batting an eyelid. For that alone, I'd always be loyal to him. Of course, he'd made it clear that he hadn't done it to be "nice" and that he'd call in a favor one day but—

"Speak of the psychopath …"

At Hanna's words, I snapped back to attention. My gaze flew to the elevator and, sure enough, Dane came walking out with that purposeful, sexy as hell, alpha-male stride. He looked so self-possessed and implacable it made my pulse skitter and my hormones sigh in appreciation.

The dark tailored suit looked damn good on him, but no suit could hide the menace that seemed to lurk just beneath the very controlled surface he showed to the world. That menace occasionally flared in his eyes or deepened his voice.

"We'll talk later." Hanna pushed away from my desk. "I want to hear how it went with the ex." She hurried away, bidding Dane a good afternoon as she passed.

I was pretty sure he grunted by way of hello, but it was hard to tell from all the way over here. Taking in his default unimpressed expression, one might think he suffered from chronic indifference. It tended to make people nervous; they often seemed compelled to try to please or amuse him. The latter was truly a waste of time. In all the years I'd worked for him, I'd never heard him laugh. Not. Once.

I flashed him my receptionist smile as he neared me. "Afternoon, Dane."

He flicked up his brows ever so slightly—his usual way of greeting me. Well, it was more than a lot of people got.

Grabbing some papers from my desk, I followed him into his sleek, spacious, masculine office. The glossy, cognac-brown wooden flooring perfectly matched the ergonomic desk, the full-wall shelves, and the coffee table in the seating area at the far side of the room. Two black leather sofas framed the table, and I could attest that both were delightfully comfortable.

Dane sometimes held one-on-one meetings in the seating area, but he mostly used conference rooms. I got the sense that he didn't like having many people in his private sanctum. Not that anything in the room revealed much about him. There were no mementos, no knickknacks, no clutter. Even his kickass desk was surprisingly sparse. There was only his desktop computer, laptop, landline phone, nameplate, and a single coaster.

There were two things I envied about Dane's office. One, the private bathroom. Two, the floor-to-ceiling windows that boasted an incredible, skyline view.

"Coffee?" I asked once he'd settled in his chair.

"No."

In the beginning, I used to bristle at his curt manner. Now? I was used to it. I knew not to take his rudeness personally. Dane didn't put much effort into sparing the feelings of anyone.

After relaying some important messages to him, I placed the papers on the desk in front of him. "You need to sign these."

He only grunted.

I gave him a bright smile. "I like these little chats we have."

He gave me one of those droll looks I'd become accustomed to over the years.

I headed to the door. Reaching it, I looked over my shoulder as I said ever so casually, "Oh, and Travis turned up to see you."

Dane's eyes narrowed as he studied me hard. "What did he do?"

I blinked. "Who says he did anything?"

"What did he do, Vienna?" Dane repeated. He very rarely raised that smooth, low-pitched, authoritative voice ... as if never doubting that he had his conversationalist's full attention. From what I'd observed, he was right not to have such doubts.

I really didn't like tattling on people, but I figured Dane had a right to know that his brother might have been up to something. "Travis wanted to go into your office even though you weren't here. I wouldn't let him, so he kicked up a fuss. When it didn't get him anywhere, he left. He also wants you to call him."

"Define 'fuss.'"

"He whined and yelled and growled and promised he'd have me fired."

"Did he touch you?"

"No." But he *had* threatened to. I decided not to mention that, though. It would only piss Dane off, and he was even more of a pain when he was in a mood.

"Hmm." He made that sound far too often. It was infuriating, because it could mean everything or nothing.

Moving swiftly on … "Don't forget you have a meeting in an hour. The agenda is on your desk, and I emailed you the materials that you'll need to review for the meeting."

His gaze on the laptop screen, he said, "You'll attend it with me." An order.

"That's fine," I said, nothing in my voice betraying that it was *far* from okay.

He went very still, and his eyes flew back to mine. "Is that going to be a problem?"

Seriously, the guy was a *warlock* or something. It was next to impossible to get anything past him. "Of course not," I replied. "Are you sure you don't want coffee?"

He didn't answer. He just fixed me with that hunter stare. The only reason I didn't squirm or avert my gaze was that I'd had plenty of practice at acting unaffected.

The cell phone he'd placed on his desk began to ring.

"I'm sure," he finally replied, reaching for the chiming phone.

"Okay. Buzz me if you need anything." With that, I left the office and returned to my desk. It was clean and tidy but, unlike his, far from sparse with a computer, printer, landline, stationery, and the fake cactus that my foster mother gave me. Melinda knew I'd accidentally kill a real plant.

I didn't have time to dwell on the upcoming meeting—I had too much shit to do. As the founder and CEO of an incredibly successful analytical software company, Dane maintained a schedule that was never anything but hectic, and his workload was never anything but heavy. That meant *my* workload was just as heavy.

There was never a lull in the activity during the day. It started off at full throttle and remained that way until the business hours finally came to an end—and sometimes even longer than that. But I liked working in such a fast-paced environment. Each day was similar yet different.

Luckily, Dane wasn't one of those bosses who asked his PA to do ridiculous shit like buy him condoms or cater to diva-like whims. In fact, he never sent me on *any* personal errands, as if preferring to keep his personal life separate. He was an intensely private guy, and I'd long ago given up trying to get to know him.

He rarely sent me out of the office on errands, though he did occasionally ask me to courier sensitive documents to other buildings. He also used me as a sounding board on occasion, which I liked. Mostly, though—in a nutshell—I handled his calendar, kept things running smoothly, and freed up as much of his time as possible by taking care of tasks that didn't require his personal touch. I also made sure everyone else was in sync with his calendar of meetings, trips, and conferences.

The most trying part of my job was screening Dane's emails, calls, mail, and visitors. Everyone "needed" to speak to him, and everything was a "priority."

One of the things I most liked about being his PA was that I often accompanied him on business trips. They weren't necessarily fun, since my time was rarely mine during those trips—I ran on pretty much the same schedule as him. Still, I got to travel on private jets, stay in luxury hotels, and attend exclusive events.

I was part way through an expense report for his last business trip when Dane came striding out of his office, and I realized that almost an hour had gone by. My stomach sank. All too soon, he and I were heading to one of the conference rooms for the meeting.

I was so annoyed with myself for caring that Owen would be there. I didn't want it to matter. Didn't want *him* to matter. He didn't deserve to. Not that I was still hurting after what he'd done. But I didn't like being reminded of that time; of how small he'd made me feel when he'd not only dumped me but dropped me from his life like I was a bag of crack.

Maybe it wouldn't have hurt as much if we hadn't been friends for so long. I didn't trust easily, but I'd trusted Owen. I'd never thought he'd ever cut contact between us like that. And it stung that he'd so easily been able to do it.

As we reached the conference room, Dane stopped at the door and turned to me. "Is there something I should know?"

I blinked. "I'm sorry?"

"You're uncomfortable. Why?"

Yep, he was a warlock. "I could tell you, but it involves talk of feminine products—"

"I don't need to hear it."

I almost snickered.

Dane entered the room first. The three men gathered at the long table instantly rose to their feet. Once they'd all exchanged greetings and the visitors were done metaphorically kissing Dane's ass, he gestured at me and said, "This is my PA, Vienna."

A tall, well-groomed figure moved aside to get a better look at me. *Owen.* Karma clearly hadn't caught up with him yet, because he was even more good-looking than he'd been seven years ago. He had more muscle definition now and carried himself with more confidence, but he didn't make my heart skip a beat the way he used to.

He blinked. "Vee? Jesus." He stepped forward as if he might hug me, but Dane's body shifted *ever* so slightly to the side. It was enough to make Owen halt, though he didn't spare my boss a glance.

I gave him a professional, distant smile. "Owen, it's good to see you."

"You … you look great. It's been a long time. Too long. I didn't realize you worked at o-Verve."

Well, why would he?

One of the other men cut in, "You two have met?"

"We were childhood friends, but we lost touch." I shrugged. "It happens."

Dane quickly introduced me to Owen's companions and then said, "Shall we sit?" Really, it was an instruction, not a question.

As usual, I sat on Dane's side of the table and silently took notes on my tablet. During internal meetings, I often contributed. But when Dane met with people from outside the company, like other CEOs, stakeholders, or potential clients, I left the discussion and negotiations to them.

As the meeting went on, I pretended that Owen wasn't casting me way too many looks, just as I pretended that Dane wasn't watching both me and Owen very closely. If I focused hard enough on the screen of the tablet, I could even pretend I was alone and that their voices were coming over a speakerphone.

I couldn't help but note that the visitors seemed a little in awe of Dane. It wasn't unusual. In matters of business, he was *brilliant.* He was a master at getting to the heart of an issue. When seeking a solution, he never gave up and moved on. No, he rose to every challenge and pushed his goals forward.

What others would think of as a pipe dream he'd make a reality in a few precise, well-executed moves—overcoming any obstacles or setbacks. He was also hell-on-wheels in the boardroom. His reputation as someone who couldn't be pushed around by competitors was well-earned.

All things considered, I'd expected for it to feel as though the meeting lasted forever, but the time flew by. Soon, people were shaking hands and saying their goodbyes.

Owen gave me another smile. "It was real good seeing you again, Vee."

"Same to you," I lied.

Once we were alone, Dane pinned me with those steely eyes. "How well do you know Owen? There's more to it than you two being childhood friends. He made you uncomfortable. Why?"

Ugh. "We were engaged for five months when we were teenagers. It was a little awkward to see him again after all this time, that's all. Not that I'd expect *you* to understand, Mr. Dauntless. Has anyone ever made you feel uncomfortable?"

"No." He grabbed the door handle. "You and I need to talk later."

"Sounds ominous. Are you going to fire me?"

"Is there a reason I should fire you?"

A memory of me earlier flipping off his brother flashed in my mind. "Probably."

The corner of his mouth *almost* twitched. "Your job is safe. For now."

CHAPTER TWO

Later that day, I parked in the lot outside my apartment building and switched off the engine. It wasn't a very well-lit parking area, so I was glad that dusk hadn't yet completely fallen. There were many times I'd needed to stay late at the office to help Dane with one thing or another, so I often didn't make it home until it was super dark.

Slipping out of my car, I locked it with the remote fob and then dug the can of pepper spray out of my bag. It was only a short walk to my building, but a girl could never be too careful.

Crossing the crack-ridden pavement, I glanced around. There was no one hovering about. All I could hear were my heels clacking on the ground and the sounds of street traffic.

Reaching the footpath that led to the main entrance, I neatly sidestepped the cans, wrappers, and crinkled flyers that littered the ground near the overflowing trash can.

I could afford to live in a nicer neighborhood, I just preferred being near my family. Especially my father, Simon.

Inside the building, I took the elevator up to my floor and headed into my apartment. There, I tossed my coat on the back of the armchair and slipped off my shoes. After changing into my sweats, I shuffled into the kitchen and sighed at the sound of raised voices coming from next door. The walls of my apartment were annoyingly thin, so it was unfortunate that I had neighbors who screamed at each other loud enough to wake the dead.

They were actually super nice people. Ashley was a hoot and had become a close friend. Her boyfriend, Tucker, was one big teddy bear who was impossible to dislike. But when they argued, they *argued*. Ashley would always storm out, and she'd always come knocking on my door to complain about whatever he'd done.

At least the argument hadn't started until after I'd finished my bath. I'd needed the quiet time to wind down and relax before dinner.

Too tired to cook, I dug a microwavable mac and cheese meal out of the freezer. It might not be terribly healthy, but the meal would suit me just fine.

As I closed the freezer door, I almost knocked down one of the drawings I'd attached to it with magnets. I gently skimmed my fingers over the sheet of paper. There were five stick figures beneath which Freddie had written the names *Maggie, Simon, Freddie, Vienna,* and *Deacon* in his childish scrawl. The first four figures stood together, but the fifth stood alone—Deacon always did.

My heart squeezed. I wished I could do more to help them, particularly Simon, but I didn't have that power. And I damn well hated that.

Once my meal was ready, I sat at my small dining table and dug into my mac and cheese. My neighbors, sadly, continued to row. And said row got louder and louder.

I closed my eyes, wishing for silence, knowing from experience that it could always be worse. This area of Redwater City, Florida might not be glamorous, but it was nicer than most. My building was secure and stable. Although my apartment was small and cramped, it was clean and well-maintained … unlike the one I'd lived in as a child.

I could still remember the smells of stale air, spoiled food, cigarette smoke, and body odor that greeted me each morning. I could remember the taste of rusty water. Could remember how hot it would get when the air conditioning failed to switch on. Could remember the dirty dishware in the sink, the piles of unwashed laundry, and the rats … God, the rats.

More, I could remember the burn of a palm slapping my face so hard it felt like my eye exploded. I could remember hands shoving me hard, feet kicking my legs or ribs, and fingertips digging into my jaw as my mother screamed in my face. It would have been a relief that she left if my entire world hadn't then imploded. But I was grateful that I'd been fostered by Melinda and Wyatt—who'd always supported my contact with my father—even if my early years with them hadn't been smooth sailing.

A door banged shut as the arguing cut off abruptly. Moments later, knuckles rapped hard on my front door. I pushed out of my chair, left the tiny kitchen, and crossed the equally small living area. I opened the front door, and Ashley marched inside.

"That man thinks he can lie to me and get away with it," fumed Ashley, a flush staining her dark skin. "Nu-uh. Not as long as I've got a hole in my ass."

My mouth twitching, I followed her into the kitchen. She looked about to make herself some coffee, but then she spotted the mac and cheese. "Smells good." She sat at the table. "You done with this?" she asked, helping herself to the food.

I smiled. "I am now." Taking the chair opposite her, I tilted my head. "So, what happened?"

Ashley shoved a forkful of food into her mouth. "I dreamed he cheated on me."

I waited for her to expand. She didn't. "Okay."

"I told him about it. He said he'd never do that. But he *blinked* when he said it."

I would have chuckled if she didn't look so serious. "I don't think he'd ever cheat on you. He loves you." The guy worshipped her, and Ashley absolutely adored him in return. She might have a harder shell than he did, but she was a softie on the inside.

Ashley sniffed. "Hmm. He liked some bitch's photo on social media. When I confronted him, he accused me of cyberstalking him. Like I even have time to monitor his lying ass. He shouldn't have a problem with me logging into his account from time to time either. How *is* that a problem?"

"He's probably just hurt that you don't trust him."

"I trust him with my life. I just don't trust that he's not doing stupid shit online. Heaven knows he does it at home. He keeps denying that he turned the thermostat up. Like I can't see he did it."

Another knock came at the front door—this one gentler. "That's probably him," I said, pushing to my feet.

Ashley straightened in her seat and pasted an aloof look on her face. "Probably." But she didn't rise from the table.

I left the kitchen and made my way to the door. Opening it wide, I smiled at Tucker. The guy was at least six foot seven and built like a linebacker, but he was a gentle giant.

"Hi, Vienna," he greeted, polite as ever.

"Hey, Tucker."

"Is Ashley here?"

"She is. Come in." I closed the door once he'd stepped inside. "She's in the kitchen."

He thanked me and then headed to the kitchen, closing the door behind him. I sat on the sofa in the living room to give them some privacy. I could hear their muffled voices talking curtly, but then those voices softened. I had to smile. They reminded me a little of Melinda and Wyatt. My foster parents argued over the weirdest stuff sometimes, but they were a tight and happy couple.

My intercom buzzed. I frowned. Apparently, I was a popular girl today.

I headed to the wall-mounted control panel and jabbed the intercom button. "Hello?" I said into the microphone.

"It's me," rumbled a deep, distinctive voice that seemed to vibrate with testosterone.

I almost jerked back in surprise. Not once in the four years I'd worked for Dane had he ever come to my home. Ever. So, yeah, this was new.

"We need to talk," he quickly added.

Yeah, he'd informed me of that earlier, but I hadn't realized he'd meant we'd do it *here*. He'd left o-Verve at 4 p.m. and still hadn't returned by 6 p.m. Figuring that we could postpone the discussion until tomorrow, I hadn't lingered at the office.

Curious about what was so important that it couldn't wait, I pressed the button that would unlock the main door to the complex. It wasn't long before he arrived at my apartment. Spying him through the peephole, I opened the door.

"Dane," I greeted simply, ignoring how my feminine parts woke right up and did a cheer. It wasn't fair that this attraction I felt toward him was so damn unrelenting. I was too susceptible to him. Too helpless against the one-way chemistry that wouldn't back the hell down.

I'd read once that chemistry couldn't possibly *be* one-sided, but my situation was evidence that theory was complete bullshit. The undeniable, inexplicable force always pulsed in the air around me whenever I was near him; always made my nerve-endings tingle and my body feel so very *aware*. But it was abundantly clear that my boss was totally unaffected.

His eyes drifted over me, and I was suddenly unbearably conscious that I was dressed in my sweats with my hair tied up in an unruly knot. He'd never seen me in anything other than business attire, and I always styled my hair into a sleek, professional bun for work.

I stepped aside, allowing him to enter. His all-knowing eyes swept over our surroundings, and I fought a blush. At work, I was hyper-organized. At home? Not so much. Probably because I needed a little break *from* being hyper-organized throughout the majority of the day. I kept my home super clean, but no matter how many times I decluttered, I never managed to keep everything in their designated places.

Piles of unopened mail, books, and papers were untidily stacked on the coffee table. Change, receipts, and stray cosmetic items littered the fireplace mantel. Jackets had been tossed over the back of the armchair. My e-reader, blanket, and a half-eaten box of chocolates had been slung on one side of the sofa.

Dane took it all in and then lifted a brow at me.

I shrugged. "I was playing a game of Jumanji—it tends to get messy. So, why are you here? Is something wrong?"

Just then, my neighbors came strolling out of the kitchen hand in hand. They both halted at the sight of Dane. Tucker seemed to stand a little taller—he often did when men sniffed around me, like the protective big brother I'd never wanted.

"Dane, these are my friends and neighbors, Ashley and Tucker. Guys, this is my boss, Dane Davenport."

Tucker inclined his head, even as he narrowed his eyes. "Good to meet you."

Ashley fanned her face. "Vienna didn't tell me you were hot."

Tucker glared at his girlfriend. "I'm *right here.*"

"It was just an observation." Ashley smiled at me and wagged her fingers. "See you tomorrow, Vienna. Bye now, Dane."

He didn't respond, but I said my goodbyes and then locked the door shut behind them.

"You have coffee?" Dane asked when I turned to face him.

"Sure." I padded into the kitchen, conscious that he was close behind me. He settled at the table while I cleared its surface and then prepared our drinks. Once I'd set our coffees down, I took the chair opposite him. He was looking at the drawings on my fridge.

Before he could ask about them, I prompted, "So, you came here because ...?"

He slid his mug closer to him. "I have news."

"News?"

"I'm getting married."

My stomach plummeted and twisted painfully. A horrible pressure began to build in my chest, and I swallowed hard. "Really? Well, congrats." God, that couldn't have sounded faker. "I didn't realize you were seeing anyone."

"I'm not."

I felt my eyebrows squish together. "I don't understand."

"My paternal uncle was a very rich man who'd made a wide range of very lucrative investments. Hugh set up trust funds for me and my two brothers. He left each of us stocks, shares, money, properties, and even art. But there's a clause. Like my brothers, I can't access the trust fund ... until I'm married."

"But, why?"

Dane sipped his coffee. "Hugh never married. He was all about work. And it wasn't until later in life that he regretted it. He used to ask me what the point was in him having such a massive home when there was only him to live in it. The closest thing he had to children of his own was my brothers and me. He encouraged us to work hard and be successful but to not neglect our personal lives. He didn't want us to make the same mistakes that he did."

"Hence the clause."

"Yes. There's also another snag. If by the time I reach the age of thirty-eight I'm not married, the assets in my trust fund will be divided between my brothers."

Which, essentially, pressured him to do as his uncle wished. "Wow. He *really* wanted you guys to get married."

"More, he wanted to ensure that we didn't wait until late in our lives before we found someone to share that life with. It worked with Travis and Kent. They both married young."

"Is it normal for people to attach conditions to trust funds?"

"It's not uncommon. I know someone who couldn't access theirs unless they married someone of a certain religion. Hugh wasn't so much fussed about *who* we married as he was about *when* we married."

"You're thirty-seven now," I recalled.

"Yes. And I'm no more interested in marriage now than I ever have been. I don't even have any interest in a relationship."

"So you're getting married purely to gain access to your trust fund?"

Dane shrugged. "There are more fickle reasons to get married. It's not about the money, Vienna. Hugh left me things that have sentimental value to me. They're mine. And I don't like the idea of any of the assets ending up in Travis's hands. He'd gamble most of them away, and his wife, Hope, would squander the rest. Kent said he'd hand me his share since it's rightfully mine, but I can't be sure he truly would."

I nodded. "Okay. I get it." And it wasn't my stuff, so I wasn't in a position to say what the best way would be to deal with the situation, was I?

Watching me closely, Dane lifted his mug and took another sip of his coffee. "I want you to do something for me."

If he asked me to pick out wedding invitations or something, I *so* wouldn't be pleased. I could support him getting married, but I still didn't like the idea of him shacked up with someone else. Apparently, my measly crush hadn't been so measly after all. "What?"

"Marry me."

My lips parted, and I stared at him. "You're not joking, are you?" It wasn't a question; it was a shocked whisper. Dane did not joke.

"It'll only be for show. We won't need to stay married very long." He lifted his brow. "I warned you I'd one day call in my favor."

Yes, he had. But I hadn't ever imagined he'd ask *this* of me. My heart started to beat faster, and my ribs suddenly felt too tight. "Dane …"

"You said you'd return the favor when the time came."

I had, because I'd been so damn grateful to him. My asshole-ex, bitter after our separation, had secretly filmed us having sex, and he'd threatened to post the video online if I didn't do as he dictated. And what had he wanted? For me to either pay him a substantial sum of money I didn't have or to sexually perform in front of a videocam for him.

I'd heard that sextortion went on, but I hadn't believed I'd ever be a victim of it. I'd known that if the secret video he'd taken of us ever went live on the internet, I'd lose everything. I'd literally felt my world coming apart around me.

Dane had overheard me arguing with my ex-boyfriend on the phone. He'd demanded the details and promised me he'd "take care of it." A day later, he'd announced that the video no longer existed and that my ex would never bother me again. I'd asked Dane what exactly he'd done to fix the matter, but he'd been very vague. We hadn't spoken of it since.

"Are you going to go back on your word?" he asked.

I licked my lips. "Dane, you're a highly sought-after guy. You don't need to call in a favor to get a woman to marry you."

"I don't want the emotional complications of a real marriage. I like being alone. I want someone who'll play the part of my wife and then sign the divorce papers quietly when it's over. That's all. But it needs to look real, because Travis and Hope are salivating after my trust fund—they figure it's a done deal that they'll get his share of it. If they can prove the marriage is fake, they will."

"Has it occurred to you that I could be dating someone?"

"No, because you don't complain when I call you on weekends, no matter the hour. You don't tell me you have plans when I ask you to stay late or spring a late meeting or last-minute business event on you."

"Yeah, well, being your PA kind of eats up my time," I said, feeling a little defensive. "Why ask *me* to play the part of your wife?"

"I've never made any secret of my aversion to relationships. I rarely date the same woman twice, and I don't take the time to get to know them. People would never buy that I'm suddenly head over damn heels for a relative stranger. It would look especially suspicious to anyone who's aware of the strings that are attached to my trust fund, yes?"

I nodded. "Yes."

"You've been my PA for four years now. We see each other pretty much every day. It wouldn't be hard to sell a story that we grew close, fought our feelings for a while, finally acted on them, but kept it secret. It's not like it's something that hasn't happened to other couples."

Well that was true enough.

"You'd have been my first choice in any case, because I know I can trust you. Several of my business competitors have tried hiring you as a spy or luring you away from my company, but you remained loyal to me and to o-Verve. Plus, you have one of the best poker-faces I've ever seen, which we'll need if we're going to fool people."

I slumped in my seat. "This was *so* not how I expected my evening to go." I'd earlier decided that I needed to shake things up a bit, but this was *not* what I'd had in mind.

I took a sip of my coffee, but I barely tasted it. "You have a whole year before you need to be married. You could meet someone within that timeframe who makes you reconsider your views on marriage."

"I won't, nor would I want to." He leaned forward, resting his forearms on the table. "This isn't a spur of the moment thing, Vienna. I've thought it through. All the way through. You and I could pull this off."

I poked my tongue into the inside of my cheek. "If we *did* go through with it, how long would we need to stay married?"

"Twelve months, at the very least. Purely because I have to be married for an entire year before I'm allowed to touch my trust fund."

I felt my eyes widen. "Jesus, your uncle *really* covered his bases."

"He did," Dane agreed, a muscle in his cheek flexing. "I suppose he knew he couldn't be sure that neither me nor my brothers would marry solely to access our trust funds; he probably thought that if he could force us to stay married for a year, we might find some joy in the marriage and decide to make it real."

"I can see it pisses you off that he did this, but he meant it as a gift, Dane. He didn't want you to be alone."

"Yes, but he didn't consider that not everyone is the same as him. If I do, by some miracle, later in life decide I want to marry for real, I'll try it. But I don't foresee that happening. For now, it's definitely not what I want."

I inwardly sighed. I wanted to help him. I did. I also wanted to return the favor I owed him, just as I'd promised. But *marry* him? That wouldn't be a small thing.

Then again, taking care of the whole sextortion situation hadn't been a small thing either, had it?

I scratched at my head. "You said the marriage would be for show. So … no emotions, no expectations, no sex, no being anything other than a fake couple?"

He nodded. "Exactly."

"Honestly, I don't see how it would work. You're a highly sexual person, Dane. There's no way you'd stay celibate for the duration of a fake marriage—and trust me, you'd be *expected* to be celibate if I was playing wifey, because I won't be known as the poor woman being cheated on left, right, and center by a husband she 'loves.'"

His brows snapped together. "I'm not a slave to my impulses, Vienna. I can go without sex if need be. And I *would* need to go without it, because Travis will have me watched. You'll need to take a temporary vow of celibacy just the same."

Oh, wonderful. Not that I *had* a sex life. Unless the nights I spent with my vibrator counted. "I'm not sure if people will buy that we're a couple."

"Countless people already think we're sleeping together."

"They do? Why?"

"Because you've stuck around this long, and because I've never threatened to fire you." His eyes bore into mine, burning with intensity. "Say yes, Vienna."

I groaned. "I'd be walking around with a divorce under my belt at twenty-five. Well, I'd be twenty-six at the time we separated, wouldn't I?" More, if I ever remarried, I'd be unable to explain to my husband—a man I truly would love and adore—that my previous marriage had been fake. I'd never be able to tell my family the truth either.

Would I be able to fool them into believing I loved Dane? Probably. As he'd said, I had a good poker face. Even Wyatt struggled to sense when I was lying, and he had a tip-top bullshit meter. But … "I hate the thought of lying to the people I care for."

"So you told them about the sex video?"

Well, no.

"You keep absolutely no secrets from them? You believe *they* tell *you* everything? That they've never lied to you for one reason or another?"

I sighed. "I get your point—everyone lies sometimes, everyone has their secrets."

"I never told a soul about that sex video; I kept your secret for you. Would you really balk at keeping one for me? It's not like I'm asking you to do anything that you'd need to be ashamed of. If your family *could* be told the truth, they wouldn't vilify you for keeping your word and repaying a favor—especially if they knew the ins and outs of what happened with your ex. But no one besides you and me can know the marriage is fake, Vienna."

"My family wouldn't tell."

"Maybe not, but you'd have to ask them to lie for you to others—including people *they* may care for. You'd have to ask them to put on an act for you when they're around everyone else. Would you feel comfortable asking that of them?"

I exhaled heavily. "No. No, I wouldn't." It would be more unfair to ask them to play a part in the deception than it would be for me to lie to them.

"You needed my help two years ago, and I gave it to you."

"If you think back, I didn't actually *ask* for your help." It was a weak argument, yes, but it was all I had.

"No, but you were happy to let me take care of the problem for you. And I did. Thoroughly. Now I need something from you."

"Look, I want to help you—"

"This is the only way you can."

I closed my eyes. *Fuck.* It didn't seem wise to fake-marry a guy you had a crush on. Like *at all.* But whether I liked it or not, I *did* owe Dane. I never would have agreed to my ex's demands, which meant the sex video would have been plastered on the internet. Once something was on there, you could never get it off. Anyone could have seen it.

My family *definitely* would have seen it, because my ex had made it clear that he'd send it to each of my loved ones. He'd also promised to email it to my boss and other coworkers—it would have been easy enough for him to get their email addresses from o-Verve's website.

Even if Dane had been prepared to dismiss the matter, he couldn't have kept me as his PA—I'd have lost the respect of everyone at the company. I wouldn't have *wanted* to stay anyway for the simple reason that I couldn't have looked any of my coworkers in the eye.

Wherever I went, I'd have been paranoid that someone had seen the video and recognized me from it. And if they had, I'd have had to deal with people laughing, sneering, and maybe even coming onto me, demanding an "encore."

I wouldn't have been the only one affected. My father and foster parents would have stood by me, but they'd have suffered embarrassment from it, too. People might have made cruel or snarky comments to them—maybe even at their place of work, which would have led to them defending me and possibly losing their jobs.

Since I would definitely have lost my own job, I'd have had to find another. Dane might have allowed me to conceal from future potential employers *why* I'd lost the job. But, knowing my ex, he'd have been spiteful enough to send my new employer a damn copy. After all, he'd warned me that he'd send one to my landlord, neighbors, and any future boyfriends.

In short, the sex video had had the potential to not only wreck my life, but to fuck with the lives of the people I cared for. Dane, though, had stopped that from happening, and he'd done it without complaint. So, yes, I owed him.

I opened my eyes. "What if someone discovers that the marriage is fake?"

"They won't. Even if they did, you wouldn't face any repercussions. The only person who stands to lose anything here is me, and I'd lose a lot. But if I don't take this chance, I'll lose it all anyway."

"There's really no other way you can access the trust fund?"

"If there was, I wouldn't be here now." He paused. "I'm not asking you to make a lifelong commitment to me. The marriage won't be real. On paper, you'll be my wife for a year—that's it. Just say yes, Vienna. Help me like I helped you."

I groaned, knowing I had only myself to blame for this. I'd essentially made a deal with the devil. That kind of thing tended to come back and bite you on the ass. Hard. "Okay. I'll do it."

There was a glitter of satisfaction in his eyes. "Good." He took another sip of his coffee, casual as you please. Like we weren't discussing getting fucking married.

"So, what now? Do we elope?"

"Not out of the blue. That would scream 'fake.' We need to lay the groundwork first."

"Groundwork?"

"Yes." He sank back into his chair. "I didn't take a plus-one to any of the corporate events I attended in the last two months. It wasn't unnoticed. People asked if I was dating someone. I said no. But many of them are so sure I'm hiding something that you and I won't need to *look* cozy when we go on any dates; they'll read all sorts into what they see."

"So you'd already put your plan into motion before approaching me with your proposal. Why did you wait two months to ask me?" He hadn't originally asked someone else, had he? Had I been second choice? And what did it even matter?

"I needed to tend to some things first and ensure all my ducks were in a row," he replied. "If you have plans for Saturday evening, cancel them. That will be our first date."

My stomach flipped. "Will there need to be a lot of PDA? Public displays of affection?"

"I know what PDA stands for. And no, there won't need to be much of it. I don't want to shove our apparent relationship in people's faces—it wouldn't look realistic. I'm a private man. I want it to look as though we're trying to keep the relationship low-key for now."

Clever. "I take it that means we'll continue as we are at work."

"Yes. Don't mention our 'relationship' to anyone. Word will eventually get around o-Verve that we seem to be dating. People will ask you questions. Be vague and evasive."

"Don't confirm it but don't deny it?"

"Exactly."

"What about the, um, engagement? When will that become official?"

"July, while we're on a business trip in Vegas. We'll also marry while there, as if we saw no reason to wait. It'll be fast, yes, but I'm known for moving fast when going after what I want."

Six weeks. I had six weeks until I'd be walking down the aisle. My belly did a slow roll. There was an audible click when I swallowed. "Okay."

"And you'll need to move in with me once we're married."

"What about my apartment? I know it's nothing special, but it's mine."

"It would look odd if we didn't live together, Vienna. I'll buy you another apartment after this is over. No, don't argue, I won't see you homeless. Especially when you'll be giving me a year of your life. It's only fair that I ensure you have a home to go to when you leave mine. Think of it as the divorce settlement or compensation for losses incurred, whatever. We'll talk about it more when the time for the divorce approaches. For now, we'll concentrate on the upcoming dates and engagement."

I frowned as a thought crossed my mind. "You're not going to propose in public, are you?"

A smile briefly lit his eyes. "We'll see."

CHAPTER THREE

Pulling my black, skin-tight, off-the-shoulder dress out of my closet, I bit my lip. It was sexy yet elegant, even with the thigh slit, and I loved it. But I'd never worn anything like this before in front of Dane, *my boss*. It would feel weird.

My gaze flicked to the more formal dress further along the closet rail, but then I remembered what Dane had said to me yesterday before I left o-Verve …

Don't dress as my PA. Wear what you'd wear to go on a date, not what you'd wear to go to a business dinner.

I looked back at the black dress I was holding and gave it a firm nod. Yes, this would do. I'd throw on a light layer of makeup, add some jewelry, maybe curl the ends of my hair and leave it down. First, I needed to shower.

Blowing out a breath, I put a hand to my fluttering stomach. First dates were always nerve-wracking. But this wasn't a real date, so I technically had no need to feel nervous. There was no pressure to impress, no worry that this might end up being a waste of my time, no need to stress over whether or not my date would like how I looked. Plus, this wasn't a stranger. I knew him fairly well.

And yet, I was a bag of nerves.

Well, it wasn't every day that a girl went on a fake date with her soon-to-be fake husband.

It wouldn't require any acting skills on my part to seem attracted to him. I just hoped he believed it *was* an act, because I didn't want him knowing about the little crush that I'd done an amazing job of hiding so far. And how did I know he was clueless about it? He hadn't found a new PA. Dane did *not* keep women around who mooned over him.

Hopefully I'd do just as good a job of hiding it when we were living together. God, was I really going to marry Dane? Was I really going to stand in front of an officiant with him *in six weeks' time*? Was I really going to be his fake wife for an entire year?

Yes, apparently, I was.

Twelve months seemed like a long time but, really, a year could fly by. Every time Christmas came around, I often couldn't believe it was already—

A knock sounded at the door. Figuring it was most likely Ashley, since no one had buzzed me through the intercom, I carefully laid my dress on the bed, padded out of the room, and made my way to the front door. I looked through the peephole out of habit. Tension zipped through me, but I just kept on looking. Because I *had* to be hallucinating. I had to be. There was no way *he'd* have found out where I lived and then trudged over here.

Owen knocked again, adjusting his tie with his free hand.

I stepped back and raked my fingers through my hair. I couldn't imagine what would bring him here, and I wasn't sure I wanted to know. I could ignore him, of course, but he'd only come back. Owen was tenacious that way.

I unlocked the door and pulled it open.

Owen's mouth curved. "Hi, Vee."

"How did you get in the building?" I asked, not feeling all that welcoming.

"I was about to buzz you when someone opened the main door to leave the complex. I slipped inside before it could close." He took a slow step forward. "I was hoping we could talk."

"Talk?"

"Can I come in?"

"I have somewhere I need to be soon."

"Ten minutes. Please. Or maybe we could meet for lunch tomorrow."

Meet? Lunch? Fuck that. It seemed simpler to just find out now what had brought him here. I opened the door wider and stepped aside. "Ten minutes."

He walked in like he owned the place and glanced around. One corner of his mouth canted up. "So, you're still all about the clutter."

I gave him a Dane-like "Hmm." I gestured at the sofa and then sank into the armchair. "What can I do for you?"

He perched himself on the edge of the couch and braced his elbows on his thighs. "I just …" He licked his lips. "It was a shock seeing you again the other day. I had no idea that you worked at o-Verve. I deliberately didn't look you up over the years. I didn't want to know if you were married."

"I heard you are."

He pulled a face. "Tiffany and I have actually filed for a divorce. People change as they age. We grew into people who still get along well but who are more like housemates. Well, housemates and colleagues—we work at the same company."

"I see. Well, I'm sorry to hear you'll be divorcing. It can't be easy for your kid."

"She's a little spitfire," he said, his mouth curling into a genuine smile. "Five, but ready to take on the world." He pulled his phone out of his pocket and pressed a button at the side of the cell, making the screensaver pop up. "This is her."

I looked at the picture, feeling my own mouth tip up. She was cute as hell with her dimples and dark curls. "She looks like your mom."

"Yeah," he agreed, his eyes on the picture. "Her name's Vienna. I named her after the sweetest, strongest girl I ever met."

Maybe I should have felt touched or humbled. Instead, a cold anger fluttered through me. This fucker had dumped me, disappeared from my life, shit all over a friendship I'd cherished … and he'd named his kid after me? What in the everloving fuck had gone through his head?

"You don't think it's messed up—not to mention *seriously* unfair to her and to her mother—that you named your daughter after your ex-girlfriend?" I asked.

"Ex-fiancée," he corrected. Rubbing at his brow, he sighed. "I guess I didn't really see it that way. I just … Part of me wanted to honor you. A lot of people tried to put me down, told me I'd never get anywhere in life. You always supported and encouraged me, always told me to ignore those assholes. You'd say I could do and be whatever I wanted. You didn't even yell at me when I broke off the engagement."

I shrugged. "I figured it just wasn't meant to be."

"What if you're wrong? What if it *was* meant to be and I just forgot that for a while?"

He could *not* be serious. "Owen—"

"For me, you're the one that got away, Vee. It sounds cliché, I know, but it's true. Seeing you again … it just brought everything back. You still care for me. I know you do."

"No, Owen, I really don't."

He smiled. "Yes, you do. And I still care for you. You can't know how many times you popped into my head over the years. Hell, I even thought about you on my own damn wedding day." He shoved a hand through his hair. "I shouldn't have thrown away what we had. It was by far the stupidest thing I've ever done, and I'm so sorry I hurt you. It won't happen again. If you give me another chance—"

"I'm seeing someone," I blurted out.

He stilled, his eyes flickering. "Seeing someone?"

"Yes." It might have been a fake relationship, but I was still spoken for. And if I didn't state now that I was taken and he later heard I was dating Dane, it would seem weird to Owen that I didn't mention it.

He blinked rapidly. "Well, it can't be serious. You don't live with him. You're not with him on a Saturday evening."

"I'm meeting him later, which is why you really need to go." I pushed to my feet. "I have to get ready."

He stood slowly, watching my face closely. "Does he make you happy?"

"Yes."

"Do you love him?"

"Yes."

His eyes narrowed just a little. "I don't think that's true. Call it a gut feeling."

"Believe what you want," I said, crossing to the door. I opened it wide. "It was nice to see you again, Owen. I wish you well, I do. But I need you to leave, and I'd rather you didn't come back. The past is better off left where it belongs—far behind us."

Seconds ticked by as he stared at me, saying nothing. Then, finally, he strode out of the apartment. "I'm not giving up, Vee," he said just as I was about to close the door. "I fucked up once before. I know what I lost. I won't lose it again." Then he was gone.

Cursing under my breath, I shut the door, wishing I hadn't answered it in the first place.

Was I moved by his declaration? No. Not in the slightest.

It wasn't that I was an unforgiving person. I didn't hold grudges or refuse to accept apologies. But if a person ever sincerely screwed me over, it was like a mental wall slammed up between us. I didn't purposely put it there. It just happened. It was a self-defense mechanism, I supposed. It had protected me from my foster sister's hurtful words and actions for a long time.

A wall had popped up between Owen and me when he broke off the engagement, talking like I'd somehow conned him into proposing to me against his better judgement. He'd said he needed to concentrate on moving forward with his life, as if I would hold him back. And I'd known that what he really meant was that he wanted to put the early part of his life behind him, wanted to become someone new and make a fresh start.

I'd understood, so I hadn't vilified him for it. But I'd hated that he'd made me feel like I wasn't good enough to be part of the future he'd mapped out for himself, that I wouldn't fit with whatever new image he meant to create. Yeah, my defenses had slammed up in an instant. And I was glad of that, because it had numbed the pain and allowed me to move on from Owen faster than I otherwise might have done.

If he truly believed I still cared for him, he was dead wrong. I didn't wish him ill, but I wanted nothing to do with him. Nothing at all.

Determined to shove him out of my mind, I made my way to the bathroom. It was time to get ready for my fake date with my fake secret boyfriend.

Later on, I strolled out of my apartment complex and over to the sleek, fancy, black car that was parked at the curb. I smiled at the broad figure who opened the rear door for me. "Hi, Sam, how are you?" Nothing in my voice or expression gave away that I was still feeling twitchy with nerves.

"I'm well, Miss Stratton," replied Dane's driver. "And you?"

"Fine, thanks." I slid onto the warm, butter-soft leather seat and looked at the lethally sensual male beside me who was focused on his phone—no doubt responding to a business email.

My breath caught at the delicious sight of him in a perfectly fitted, charcoal shirt and black slacks that would no doubt hug his epic butt just right. I saw him in tailored suits every day, always looking effortlessly well-groomed, smelling *amazing*, and generally oozing raw sex appeal. But it never got old—he could still make my pulse spike.

"Dane," I greeted simply, going for blasé.

His piercing gaze snapped to me. If I hadn't been watching him so closely, I might not have noticed how he imperceptibly stiffened. His eyes raked over me, taking in everything from my loose, flowing hair to my strappy high heels; lingering a little on the thigh slit—it was a slow, blatant, thorough perusal. His gaze briefly glittered with something hot that made my skin prickle.

He nodded, as one would when appraising an object and then turned back to his phone. I almost snorted.

"So, where are we going?" I asked when Sam pulled onto the road.

His thumbs deftly flying over the screen of his cell, Dane named a prestigious, well-known restaurant. "Many people who I know and do business with frequent there. It's a place where we'll be recognized."

I didn't try to keep the conversation going—it was clear he was busy. The guy was always on the clock. I honestly didn't know how being in such high demand all the time didn't drive him insane.

Realizing that I was twirling my ankle madly enough to sprain it, I forced my leg to stay still. It wasn't just nerves that were pricking at me and making me restless. I still hadn't quite shaken off the annoyance I felt at Owen. He had no freaking right to turn up at my home and … No, I wasn't going to think about him. I wasn't going to fume about the things he'd had the nerve to say.

Turning to the window, I rested my loosely clasped hands on my lap and did my best to let all my edginess slip away. Yeah, it didn't work.

"What's bothering you?"

The question almost made me jump. I looked at Dane and shrugged. "Nothing."

"You're annoyed about something. What?"

"It's not important."

"But it's bugging you enough that you look ready to punch someone." He pocketed his phone and pressed a button that raised the privacy screen between us and the driver. "Tonight, I need you to be all about us. Your head can't be elsewhere. So, tell me what's wrong."

I sighed. "I had a brief visit from Owen earlier."

A slight hardness slid into Dane's expression. "What did he want?"

"To talk." Not wanting to go into any detail, I added vaguely, "He might be a problem."

"He wants you back," Dane guessed, his tone clipped. "I thought he was married."

"He and his wife have filed for a divorce, apparently. I told him that I'm involved with someone. I didn't say who," I hurried to add.

"Did it deter him?"

"No, but he'll back off eventually."

"If it comes to it, I'll deal with him." Dane adjusted his cufflink. "Who ended the engagement? You or him?"

"Him," I reluctantly admitted.

"Why?"

I inwardly groaned. "Do we have to talk about this?"

"It's the sort of thing I'll need to know if we're to pull off our act. A woman would normally tell her new partner why she separated from her ex, right?"

True. "He wanted to start afresh and reinvent himself. That meant leaving behind anything or anyone that was part of the old him."

"I see. Did you give him an earful?"

"No. I wished him well and then hung up."

Dane's brows snapped together. "He broke off the engagement by phone?"

I gave a curt nod. "I'm sure you can now understand why I really wasn't delighted to see him at o-Verve."

"Does he have a shot at winning you back?"

"Hell, no."

Dane's gaze pinned mine. "You need to be sure, Vienna. I can't have you backing out on me in a few months, declaring you can't go through with our plans because you've realized you still love him."

"That would never happen for two reasons. One, I don't love him. Two, I wouldn't leave you in the lurch like that."

"You're in this until the end? I have your word on that?"

"Yes. And you know I won't break it."

Just then, the car began to slow. I looked out of the window and saw the restaurant in the near distance.

When the vehicle stopped, Dane said, "The moment we step out of the car, it's—"

"Lights, camera, action?" I supplied.

"Yes. And we'll stay in character right up until the end of the night. I trust Sam, but not even he can know this isn't real. He doesn't have your poker face. If anyone questioned him about us, they'd see right through his lies."

"Understood."

My door was pulled open. I smiled at Sam as I slid out of the car. He escorted me to the other side, where Dane waited. As I turned to face the restaurant, I didn't miss Dane's swift intake of breath behind me. My back was mostly bare, due to the tasteful V dip in the dress.

That didn't stop him from splaying his hand on my lower back, resting his palm just above my butt. It was bold and proprietary and made my stomach all fluttery.

Casual and confident, he steered me into the restaurant. The pressure from his hand was light but very much firm and dominant as he, essentially, took control.

Inside, my brows lifted as I glanced around. This was no casual restaurant. There were no comfy booths, no wall-mounted TVs, no empty tables piled with dirty dishes, no waitresses in mini-skirts.

I also couldn't see a single kid anywhere. There were lots of classily dressed ladies and well-groomed men. The wait staff here were as smartly dressed as the patrons.

Voices murmured. Silverware clinked. Classical music played softly in the background. With its expensive décor, hanging chandeliers, and crystal dishware, the place was both charming and elegant. The dim lighting and flickering candles also gave it a cozy, intimate atmosphere and softened its snobby edges.

It wasn't the scents of various foods that dominated the air. It was perfume, cologne, fresh flowers, and burning candles.

My high heels click-clacked on the marble floor as we were led to a table near the large window. A prime spot for sure.

As Dane pulled out my chair for me, he lightly stroked my earlobe and said, "I like the earrings."

I almost startled at the subtly flirtatious touch. He was smooth, I'd give him that. Remembering to play my part, I made sure my smile was just a little on the flirtatious side as I replied, "Thank you." I sat on the padded seat, which he then smoothly slid toward the table.

No sooner had he settled on the seat opposite me than he ordered a bottle of red wine, probably remembering it was my drink of preference. He filed everything away in that incredibly perceptive brain.

The waiter handed us menus and then disappeared. Dane slightly adjusted the positioning of the small candles, the floral centerpiece, and the salt and pepper shakers. He wasn't fidgeting. It was more like he was claiming the space and making it his own.

I scanned the menu, unsurprised that the selections were all gourmet dishes. I'd probably go with the prime rib. Honestly, this wasn't really my scene. I preferred Italian food. Mostly pizza.

"I've never seen you with your hair down before," he said.

I lowered the menu. "It wouldn't have been professional to turn up at the office looking like this."

"Hmm." His eyes slowly skimmed the length of my hair from the roots to the curled ends. It felt like he'd stroked it.

"I didn't expect you to bring me here," I said.

"Why not?"

"I'm usually the one booking dinner reservations for you and your lady friends. This isn't where you take them."

"Which is why I brought you here. If this was truly a serious date, I'd take you somewhere different than I took the others, so you'd know I don't see you as a simple companion for the evening."

I nodded. "Gotcha."

The waiter appeared with our wine, took our food orders, and then left.

Dane picked up his glass. "Tell me about your family," he said.

My stomach twisted. "My family?"

His brow hitched up. "Couples tend to tell each other about their families, yes?"

Ugh. I smoothed a wrinkle out of the white tablecloth. "There's my dad, Simon—we're pretty close. I also have my foster parents, Wyatt and Melinda. I see them often."

"And your biological mother?"

I clenched my fists beneath the table. "I haven't seen her since I was taken away by social services as a kid. As for siblings, I'm an only child. Plenty came and went over the years I was in foster care, but none stuck around long enough for me to form a real bond with them."

"Your foster parents don't have any biological children?"

"They have one. A daughter. Heather's a few years older than me."

"But you don't think of her as a sister?"

After the things she'd done to me, *fuck*, no. "We've never really gotten along. But her son is a sweet kid." Heather had purposely gotten pregnant by a rich guy and now lived off her child support payments—she actually considered that sneaky move an achievement, like getting a college degree.

Dane raised his glass to me. "Impressive, Vienna."

"Excuse me?"

"You answered each of my questions without really giving me much information."

I shrugged one shoulder. "Just practicing being vague and evasive—I thought you'd appreciate it." I sipped my wine. "I know you have two siblings but no nieces or nephews, and I know you lived with your uncle for a short while, but that's pretty much it."

Dane was silent for a long moment. "My mother died of cancer when I was young. My father died when I was fifteen. My uncle then took in me and my siblings, but he died of heart failure some years ago."

I waited for him to expand, silently noting that he hadn't specified how his father died. But he didn't say another word. "Now who's being vague and evasive?"

"There's not much else to say."

Not much else he *wanted* to say, I thought. But I let it go, because there was plenty of information that I'd kept to myself about my own family.

It wasn't long before our food arrived. We talked as we ate. He didn't touch me, but he *really* didn't need to. Not when he was so wholly focused on me, like every sentence that came out of my mouth was a nugget of pure wisdom.

His gaze occasionally dropped to my lips as I talked, but then it would lock with mine again, alive with an electric intensity that almost took my breath away.

Sometimes his eyes would drift to my hair, as if fascinated by it. I could genuinely believe he wanted nothing more than to reach out and stroke it.

Honestly, I was getting a little hot under the collar. I knew none of this was real. I knew his attraction to me was faked. But my body didn't care about that. It was tipsy just from the intoxicating, sexual buzz in the air.

I found myself wondering … would a girl get a lazy, controlled seduction from Dane? Or would he allow himself to lose that control he clung to and then boldly *take* what he wanted? Both were questions for the ages.

Having finished my meal, I took a calming sip of my wine. I could feel the weight of many curious eyes. "I didn't think people would pay us much notice. We've eaten together before."

"At business lunches or dinners. Never alone."

"You don't date, so people might not automatically assume that that's what this is."

He gave me a look that questioned my intelligence. "They're looking at you in that fuck-me dress and they know for sure it's a date."

I felt my brow crease. "This is not a fuck-me dress."

He leaned forward. "No man who sees you in that is going to think about anything other than having you beneath him all night long. So yes, Vienna, it's a fuck-me dress."

I almost asked if he was including himself in that, but I knew it wouldn't be wise. It was important not to allow any lines to be blurred. "Whatever. If it helps us with our pretense, all the better." Deciding to play up to our audience, I reached over and stroked my finger along his watch, grazing his wrist slightly. "What time is it?"

He drank the last of his wine. "Almost time to leave."

He settled the bill, shooting me a glare when I offered to go halves with him on it. Like I was attempting to unman him or something.

I rose from the table and skirted around it. On his feet, he cupped my elbow and urged me to pass him. The featherlight graze of his lips over my temple made my pulse jump.

Again, he kept his hand on my lower back as he guided me across the large space. The feel of his warm fingers on my bare skin was a tease all by itself—my flesh was super-sensitive from the sexual buzz I couldn't quite shake off.

Noticing a familiar figure exit the restrooms, I almost groaned. "Hope's here," I whispered to him.

Travis's wife was beautiful. She had flawless skin, sleek black hair, a curvy figure, and a sweet face that was in *total* contrast to her personality. She was one of those people who'd never worked a day in their life yet looked down on anyone who didn't have a job that earned them six figures a year.

She smiled at Dane. But that smile dimmed when she caught sight of me. To Hope, assistants of any kind were inferior. "What a surprise," she said to Dane. "Travis has been trying to reach you for days. You didn't return his calls."

"I did," he told her. "He just didn't answer. I don't have the time to chase him. Is he with you?"

"No, I'm here with friends. You know, it's quite sad that you'd have a business dinner on a Saturday night. You never do anything but work. You should really try getting a life."

"I like the one I have."

Her eyes slid to me, and her lips thinned. "Hello, Vivienne."

I almost rolled my eyes. She knew damn well what my name was.

"If you're aiming to seduce my brother-in-law by dressing like that, it won't work. He never mixes business with pleasure."

"I appreciate the warning," I said.

"We're leaving now," said Dane as he skimmed his fingertips down my inner arm and then smoothly took my hand in his. "Enjoy your meal, Hope." With that, he gently pulled me toward the door. I could feel her watching us, and I knew she was probably getting a good look at us holding hands, but I didn't turn around.

Reaching the exit, Dane pushed open the glass door and guided me to the waiting car outside. I could only assume he'd texted Sam to pick us up.

Inside the car, I waited for Dane to put the privacy screen up before I asked, "Do you think Hope suspects we were on a date?"

"Yes. She'll no doubt call Travis and tell him all about it. He'll probably wave it off, too sure that his world is in order and that I'd never fall for a woman. It won't be until he hears about our second date that he'll sit up and take notice."

"When are we having our second date?"

"Next Saturday."

"Same time, same place?"

"Same time, different place. One where other people who I know often eat."

In other words, another pretentious restaurant. "I'd better tell my foster parents about our 'relationship' before our second date. The more time they have to get used to it before I announce we're engaged, the better chance of them buying it. I can't spring an engagement on them."

He nodded. "You'll also have to formally introduce me to them at some point. It might help if they see us together, looking happy and stable."

"I hate that I'll be lying to them. Won't you hate that you'll be lying to people?"

"No."

I blinked. "Just no?"

He shrugged.

"I know your relationship with Travis is strained, but I got the impression that you get along well with Kent."

"I do."

"But you're fine with lying to him?"

"My personal life isn't his business. Why I choose to get married isn't his business."

Since just thinking about the wedding had the potential to give me indigestion, I changed the subject. "I take it you don't want me to dress as your PA on our second date either."

A phone *pinged*. He fished his cell out of his pocket. "No, I don't," he replied, his eyes on the phone screen as his thumbs tapped it like crazy. "Wear another fuck-me dress."

I sighed. "It's not a fuck-me dress."

CHAPTER FOUR

Lifting her mug of coffee from the round patio table, Melinda blinked at me. "You're dating Dane? Dane as in your boss Dane?"

The rusty wrought-iron patio chair creaked as I squirmed a little in my seat. "Yes." I usually found it relaxing to sit in my foster parents' backyard and listen to the sound of wood snapping in the firepit. Today? Not so much. Because I had to lie to them. I knew they'd be disappointed in me for being so unprofessional as to get involved with my boss, but I couldn't tell them the truth.

I took a swig from my beer bottle, bracing myself for a "that's not smart, you could jeopardize your job" lecture. I wouldn't go on the defensive. Nope. Their concern would be well-warranted.

As if the dog sensed my tension, Ranger padded over to me. I stroked his short, coarse fur, becoming more and more uncomfortable as the silence dragged on.

I looked at Melinda just in time to see her shoot Wyatt a smug grin.

"*Told* you," she taunted him.

I felt my brow crease. "What?"

Wyatt shrugged. "We're not stupid, sweetheart. We worked out for ourselves that you two are interested in each other. I mean, you made it clear that he can be hell to work for at times, but you never once told us you were thinking of quitting."

Melinda nodded. "When you first got the job, you told us not to get too excited; that he'd probably fire you after a week or so. Weeks went by, and you were still there. Those weeks turned into months, and those months turned into years. Unless there's something I don't know, he's never threatened to fire you."

"I'm good at my job," I said.

"We don't doubt that," Wyatt assured me. "But we know our girl. We know you lose all tact if someone pushes your buttons hard enough. You can't tell us there were times when you didn't show him a little attitude."

Okay, so I'd *occasionally* flipped him off or called him a rude asshole. But I'd come to learn that Dane wanted to have at least a few people who'd be honest with him; who'd see past the CEO title and not pussyfoot around him. Of course, if I'd ever showed him attitude in the presence of others, he'd have probably fired me on the spot.

"Wyatt said that you and Dane wouldn't cross the platonic line," added Melinda. "But *I* said it would happen eventually. There's only so long you can fight what you feel for someone. So, who made the first move, you or him?"

I shook my head. "Oh no, I'm not giving you the ins and outs of how it all went down." I'd tell them as few lies as possible. "But I will say that it's serious."

"Serious to you or to both of you?" she asked.

"To both of us." I rubbed my arm as a cool breeze swept over my skin and rustled the dandelions and long grass. "I know you must be thinking it's too soon for me to be sure of that—"

"No, sweetie, I'm not," said Melinda. "You two have spent pretty much every day in each other's company for the past four years. You might not have been sleeping together, but your relationship probably hasn't been *emotionally* platonic for a while now. You've had a sort of workplace-partnership for a long time. If you care for each other, I can imagine it feels almost effortless for you to switch to a *real* partnership." She squeezed my hand. "I'm happy for you, and I hope it works out."

And now I felt *awful.* They were being so understanding and supportive, and I was being a big fat liar.

Standing, Wyatt grabbed some firewood from the pile and tossed it into the pit. "Have you told your dad yet?"

I sighed. "No. I will. I just … I worry he won't take it well. He doesn't like change."

"Your happiness is important to him, though." Retaking his seat, Wyatt grabbed his beer from the table. "He'll be pleased for you if he thinks Dane makes you happy."

"Yes, but if some part of Simon feels threatened or off-balance by my having a man in my life, I might find myself dealing with Deacon."

"I've never come face to face with Deacon—he doesn't seem interested in talking with me or Melinda. But from the things you've told me about him, I don't believe he would hurt you."

"He might try to hurt Dane, though." Deacon in a rage wasn't pretty. I'd seen him lash out at people and knock them down flat. "Then Simon, Freddie, and Maggie would be upset."

Melinda let out a long breath. "The situation breaks my heart, you know."

I nodded. "Yeah, mine, too."

"Does Dane know about it?" she asked.

I shook my head. "I'll tell him at some point. It's just such a hard situation to properly explain. And then questions will follow that won't be fun to answer."

Just then, the sound of a door shutting came from inside the house.

"Oh, that's probably Heather and Junior," said Melinda. "She called earlier to say she might visit."

I kept my groan of annoyance to myself. I knew it pained Melinda and Wyatt that Heather and I didn't see eye to eye. I wished, for their sake, that I could make it happen. But even if too much hadn't gone on between us, Heather would *never* be interested in us having a sisterly relationship.

I'd never quite worked out why she hated me so much. Maybe it was simply that all her parents' attention had been focused on her until I came along. I was the first child they'd fostered, and Heather had made me feel unwelcome from second one.

Okay, that was an understatement. She'd been an epic bitch who'd loved to sneakily bully and terrorize me.

She'd knocked me around, forced dog food in my mouth, bit me hard enough to mark, and pulled a knife on me several times. That wasn't even the worst of it.

When Melinda and Wyatt finally learned of it all, they'd been both horrified and devastated. They'd also cracked down hard on Heather. Their punishments hadn't been physical, but they'd been highly effective. The abuse had then stopped, but she'd continued with her bitchy ways.

Even now as an adult, Heather did petty and mean shit like flirt with my boyfriends, cause drama on my birthdays, or make belittling comments to me. She had a pathological need to feel superior to everyone else, particularly me.

Maybe she was just a fucking crank—I was pretty open to that theory. I mean, surely it wasn't normal to get a perverse joy out of causing drama and destruction; it was like it made Heather feel powerful.

I knew Melinda and Wyatt blamed themselves and often wondered where they went wrong with her. I hated that. They were good people, and they deserved better.

Junior came rushing out onto the deck, smiling wide. "Grandma!"

"Hey, mister." Melinda helped him climb onto her lap. "I've missed you." She pressed several kisses to his face, making him chuckle.

I smiled. "Hi, kiddo."

He gave me a shy wave, knowing better than to give me any affection in front of his mother—Heather didn't like it. I'd hug him when she wasn't looking.

He was always dressed in expensive designer clothes, much like Heather herself. In some ways, she treated him like a doll. An accessory, even. But at least she wasn't cruel to him. She fed him and kept him clean, which was more than my mother had done for me.

Strolling onto the deck like it was a catwalk, Heather gave me a long look but said nothing. Turning to her mother, she flicked her glossy brown hair over her shoulder. "Mom, I was hoping you and Dad could watch Junior for me for a few hours. I have a date."

"Of course we will," replied Melinda.

"We love having our little guy with us," added Wyatt.

It wasn't nice that she dumped Junior on them so often, but it was better for the kid that he was around people who'd openly show him love. I'd never once seen Heather kiss or hug him.

"Tell me about this man you're seeing," Melinda said to her.

Heather's red-painted lips curved. "I met him at a bar last week. His name's Thad Drummond. He's an attorney. Lives near the marina. You'd like him. I was originally going to meet up with him last night but, well … he had to rearrange."

Probably because the guy's wife wanted his company. I'd never met him, but I knew he was married. How? Single men held no appeal for Heather. She was only ever attracted to a man if he was taken. Once he'd left his wife, Heather lost interest in him and soon after moved on. But not before said man had lavished her with expensive gifts.

Her eyes darted to me. "Maybe I could ask him if he has a brother for you. You've been single for too long. You shouldn't give up just because you've so far struggled to hold a man."

"Heather," drawled Wyatt. It was a warning.

She widened her eyes. "What? I'm just saying."

"As it happens, Vienna has a man," Melinda cut in. She squeezed my hand. "I'm real pleased for you, sweetheart."

"And who is this man?" asked Heather, her gaze hard.

"His name is Dane Davenport," said Melinda. "I have to say, I love the name Dane. I'm really looking forward to meeting him."

"Wait, are you talking about her boss?" Heather looked at me. "You're dating your boss?"

"Yes," I said before sipping my drink.

"And here I was thinking you were smart." Heather snorted. "Sleeping with your boss is a sure-fire way to eventually lose your job."

"Not if they have serious feelings for each other, which they do," said Melinda. "Perhaps you could try being happy for her."

Heather's eyes flared. She drew a long breath through her nose and then shrugged. "Whatever. I'll be back in a few hours. Don't worry, I won't be trunk. I mean, *drunk*."

I narrowed my eyes. She'd said "trunk" on purpose, knowing the memories the word could spark—memories I quickly shoved back into their mental drawer.

"Heather," snapped Wyatt.

Smirking, the bitch swanned back into the house and then left.

The tension slipped from my shoulders and I took another swig of my drink. There was seriously a special place in hell reserved for that woman. "Junior, where are my cuddles?" After I'd spent a good few minutes talking with and making a fuss of him, I watched as he crawled into his tent at the back of the yard.

Melinda rested her hand on my arm. "I'm sorry about Heather, sweetheart."

"You don't need to apologize," I told her. "You didn't do anything wrong." Before the woman could insist that she was somehow at fault for Heather being the way she was, I added, "On another note, you should know that the dog's trying to dig his way under the fence again."

Wyatt cursed and stood. "Ranger, we've talked about this."

It really was astonishing how many women tried wrangling their way into Dane's office to either see or lie in wait for him. They'd probably wait naked—I'd never know for sure, because I never allowed them to go inside. *No one* entered his office unless he was there *and* okayed it. But the attractive, scantily dressed redhead in front of me just was not getting that.

Candace sighed. "I only need a minute of his time."

What people didn't seem to realize was that pretty much *every* minute of Dane's day was accounted for. He often went from meeting to meeting—some were internal, some were external, some were short, others went on for hours. Such was the life of many CEOs.

I always kept an hour of his day free in case there were any last-minute fires to put out or he needed a little "me" time to reflect. Today, there had been no fires, and he'd declared that he wanted to spend his free hour "undisturbed."

"If you'd like to leave a message, I will pass it on to Mr. Davenport," I said.

She gestured at his office. "Oh, come on, he's *right there.*"

"He made it clear to me that he wasn't to be disturbed."

Her mouth curved into a confident, sultry smile. "Trust me, he'll want to see me."

Ugh. "Then I'm sure he'll be more than happy to hear that you left him a message, and he'll get straight back to you."

She narrowed her eyes. "You know, Hope warned me that you might stop me from seeing him. She said she had a feeling that you want him all to yourself. Like you'd have a chance with him." Candace rested both hands on my desk. "I've tried to be nice about this, but I'm just about done with you. Go and tell him I'm here, and do it *now*, or I'll have you fired."

Oh, how original. "You'll have me fired?"

"I'm one of his sister-in-law's best friends. What do you think he's going to say if I tell him that you were being such a rude little bitch to me?"

I leaned toward her and pitched my voice low. "I think the real question is … what are *you* going to say when people ask why security guards dragged you out of o-Verve? You think I won't call them? I will. I do it, like, all the time. Seriously, this sort of shit happens so often they have this drill down to a science. You can become familiar with this drill, or you can leave a message for Mr. Davenport and *go*. I'll let you choose."

Twin flags of red stained her cheeks. "You are one snobby little whore."

"'Snobby' is a little harsh."

"I could ruin you in a hot second and—"

"I don't know why you're here," a voice cut in, calm yet dark with menace. "I also don't care. Get out of my building, or I'll have security put you out."

I briefly glanced over my shoulder at Dane. He was walking toward my desk, his eyes hard and flinty on Candace.

"Dane," she breathed, losing every ounce of bluster. She forced a smile. "I just came by to say hi—"

"You heard what I said." His tone was silky smooth but carried a chill.

Candace's face fell. "Why are you upset with me? I only wanted to see you. She wouldn't let me! Did you know she stops people from seeing you?"

Unreal. "It's sort of my job at times."

Dane took another step forward. "You don't get to come here and speak to my PA like shit."

"I didn't—"

"You called her a whore," he whispered, but there was enough venom in his tone to make the redhead flinch. "An insult to Vienna is something I won't tolerate."

Candace gave him a beseeching look. "Dane."

"A few calls, Candace. It would take only a few calls from me to have your carefully constructed world fall apart. Your drug habit would be unearthed. The affair you're having with your father's business partner would be outed. A very specific kink you like to hide would be made public."

Her eyes bulged. "No. No, you can't."

"I can. I will. Unless you apologize to Vienna and get the fuck out of my building."

Candace turned to me and swallowed hard. "I'm sorry. I am."

No, she wasn't. She was simply sorry that he'd overheard her.

With all the dignity that she could muster, Candace hurried over to the elevator.

Dane glanced down at me and said, "My office."

I followed him inside the large space and closed the door. "Does she really have a drug habit?"

"Yes." Dane settled in his leather chair. "She's been doing cocaine since she was fourteen."

"How do you know that? How do you know all that stuff about her?"

"We have a few mutual acquaintances who like to talk."

"She was super confident that you'd want to see her." Which made me wonder if they'd slept together.

"No, I haven't had sex with her."

I almost gaped. "I never said you did."

"But you were wondering."

See, he was a goddamn warlock.

"Despite Hope's strange belief that her friend and I have slept together, we haven't. Candace has made plenty of offers, but I don't go for 'clingy and desperate.'"

"I'm not so sure she's received that message yet."

"After what just happened, she won't be back." His gaze swept over my face. "Are you all right?"

"Fine. I've dealt with worse."

"Hope's not going to be happy when she hears the story from Candace. That was a test."

I blinked. "A test?"

"Hope urged her friend to come here. Her theory was probably that if I turned Candace away, there was a high chance that I was dating you."

I nodded. "Ah."

"Not only did I turn her away—something I would have done anyway, because I don't like her—I threatened to ruin her purely for insulting you. Hope will see that act of protectiveness as a definite sign that you and I are seeing each other."

I folded my arms and shrugged one shoulder. "You overdid it."

His brows snapped together. "I, what?"

"You threatened to expose all her dirty laundry to the world."

"And I wasn't kidding."

"She called me an ugly name, that's all."

"Doesn't matter. I'd never tolerate a verbal attack on someone who belonged to me."

I tilted my head. "You'd truly be prepared to ruin someone's reputation *just* for offending your girlfriend?"

He leaned back in his chair. "What do you think?"

I looked at him for a long moment. "I think you're a ruthless, unforgiving bastard who'd catapult anyone that crossed you into a boundless mountain of shit."

He nodded. "Then there you go."

Our second date was much like our first—all subtle touches and quiet conversation. Again, people looked and whispered. Again, I did my best to ignore it. Again, Dane paid me such intense attention that, honestly, it was like his world revolved around me.

One couple actually approached us, said hello to Dane, and asked him to introduce me. When he referred to me as his PA, they smiled … as if it was code for something else.

On the upside, the food was freaking divine.

Either someone from our building had been at the restaurant that night or they knew someone who had, because word quickly got around o-Verve that Dane and I went on a date—something I learned from Hanna, when she came to my desk, asking why I was seen having a meal with Dane.

"*Are you guys dating? Please tell me you guys are dating,*" she'd said, her hands clasped, looking far too excited.

I'd vaguely replied, "*Dane doesn't date.*"

"*According to my source,* you *were not dressed for a meeting. You were wearing a fuck-me dress, you had your hair down, and there was a lot of careful touching going on.*"

I'd sighed and said, "*It wasn't a fuck-me dress.*"

"*Is he a good kisser?*"

"*How would I know?*"

Hanna had pouted. "*Fine. Be that way. But I'm watching you two from here on out.*"

When I later told Dane about it, he'd seemed pleased that word of our "secret relationship" was beginning to spread around the teams. I wasn't so pleased, because eventually I'd have to deal with sneers and people accusing me of sleeping with my boss to get a raise or something. But I'd known in advance that it would happen, I'd metaphorically signed up for it, and I'd deal with it when the time came.

As the days went on, though, the workforce seemed mostly excited at the idea that "Dane's fallen for one of our own" instead of a socialite, heiress, or model. Oh, there was some general pettiness from a few women, but I'd expected that. I'd overlook it so long as they didn't start mouthing off. Hopefully people's fear of Dane would keep them on their best behavior.

When Saturday came around, he and I went on a third date. It was basically just a repeat of the previous two—posh restaurant, small but possessive touches, lots of eyes on us.

At work Monday morning, it was business as usual. I'd originally worried that the fake-dating lark would in some way bleed over onto our workplace dynamics, but it seemed that we both managed to compartmentalize everything just fine.

I was halfway through the process of sending some outbound emails when the office phone rang. Honestly, it rang so many times throughout the day, there'd been occasions when I'd woken at night, convinced I could hear it.

I lifted the receiver and said, "Good morning, you've rea—"

"Dane Davenport?" a familiar voice clipped. "That's the guy you're seeing? Dane Davenport?"

I balled up my hand. "I'm working, Owen."

"For a guy you're also dating, right?"

"What gave you that idea?" I asked airily.

"My boss saw you both having dinner on Saturday night. He said you looked *real* cozy."

"Dane and I often attend business dinners together."

"Don't try to blow me off, Vee. Jesus, I can't believe you're with Davenport. It doesn't make sense. You'd never be so unprofessional as to sleep with your boss."

No, I wouldn't. I'd simply have fun imagining it. Lots and lots of fun.

"He doesn't do relationships, Vee. Maybe he'll offer you a fling, but that's it. You're worth more. If he doesn't see that, he doesn't deserve you."

"And you do?"

He sighed. "No. I let you down. But don't you think we've both paid for my mistake long enough?"

I frowned. "You seem to have this insane idea that I've been holding a candle for you all these years."

"You loved me, Vee. You loved me enough to wear my ring. I think a part of you still does, even though you might not want to."

"You're wrong. Even if I wasn't happy with someone else, I wouldn't go back to you. Not ever. Don't call me again." I placed down the receiver.

"Problem?" a voice asked from behind.

My pulse spiked, but I managed not to jump. Slowly turning to face Dane, I folded my arms. "Just Owen."

Dane twisted his mouth and then tipped his chin toward his office. Only once I'd followed him inside and closed the door did he speak again. "What did he want?"

"He called to ask if you're the guy I told him I was seeing," I replied. "His boss saw us together on Saturday, apparently."

"And?"

"I didn't confirm or deny we're dating, but Owen seems sure we are. He doesn't believe you're serious about me, though. He thinks you'd only want a fling. He also can't make sense of me doing something as unprofessional as sleeping with my boss."

"Hmm." Dane leaned back against his desk. "We're going on another date this weekend."

"Another restaurant?" I asked.

"No. This time, you're going as my plus-one to a charity ball. *Not* as my PA, as my official date."

I lifted my brows. "So, we're 'coming out,' so to speak?"

"Yes. People at the event will ask questions, especially my brothers. We'll tell them that we've been a couple for a few months. I don't want them thinking we're idly dating. I want them to believe this is serious. So make sure you put on your best acting hat on Saturday at the gala—we'll have a hell of a show to put on."

CHAPTER FIVE

Butterflies frantically took wing in my stomach as we entered the ballroom of the opulent hotel. It was truly beautiful with vaulted ceilings, marble flooring, sparkling chandeliers, and intricate crown molding on the walls.

Thick, scarlet drapes framed the pretty French windows. A spiral staircase led to a second level, where I could just make out a few tables and chairs. I wondered if that was where they'd be holding the gala's dinner and auction.

Muted laughter and the murmur of voices flowed throughout the space. A lone male played soft, classical music on a grand piano. White-gloved waiters meandered through the ballroom, offering canapés and flutes of champagne to the many guests—all of whom were dressed in tuxedos or gowns, much like Dane and I were.

My floor-length, ruby red chiffon gown was gorgeous. Dane had tried giving me money to buy one, but I'd point-blank refused and lied that I already had one. In truth, I hadn't wanted to take any cash from him to buy clothes. It would have felt weird.

I'd originally intended to pin my hair up into an elaborate do, as many of the other female guests had done. Dane had asked me to wear it down. When I'd asked why, he'd merely replied, "Because I like it down." To be honest, I'd still had every intention of pinning it up, but I'd been running late so I hadn't had time.

My hand flexed around my satin clutch. "There's a whole lot of people here." I spotted several of Dane's business associates. There were also a few celebrities, including an English model, Jaxxon Carter, and her race-driver husband, Connor McKenzie.

Most of the attendees stood around in clusters, deep in conversation. Others breezed around the room, admiring the décor. The event organizers had used a beautiful combination of gold, silver, white, and copper tones that worked well in the large space. There were also floral arrangements here, there, and everywhere.

Dane grabbed two champagne flutes from a passing waiter and gave one to me. "Here."

"Thank you." I sipped at the bubbly liquid. "Are your brothers and their wives here yet?"

"Not that I've noticed." He curled an arm around my waist and cupped my hip, making my pulse jump. Jesus, he smelled good. His signature cologne was sensual, mysterious, and powerfully masculine. It made me want to lick him all up.

"Stay close to me," he added.

I took a steadying sip of my drink. "Will do."

I wasn't entirely sure why I was so nervous. It was just a fundraising gala ball, for heaven's sake. But, to be fair, I was under a lot of pressure tonight. Our fake dates were easier when we were seemingly exercising subtlety. My job this evening was to convince people I was enamored with Dane, but I had to be careful to not overdo it. *And* I'd need to stop my body from going into meltdown after a night of him touching me more openly than normal—which would be easier said than done.

If I couldn't get through this gala without losing my nerves, I'd never get through my upcoming, fake wedding. Just thinking of it made my stomach roll.

Reaching for humor to lighten my mood, I joked, "So, should I call you babycakes from now on or something?"

Dane gave me a droll look. "No."

"Shnookums? Dear one? Sugar lips? Light of my life? Ooh, I know—big daddy."

He sighed and shook his head, but his eyes were dancing. "Only you, Vienna. Only you." He guided me across the room to a group of people I didn't recognize.

One beamed at him. "Ah, Dane."

My fake date nodded. "Clint."

Clint's eyes drifted to me, gleaming with speculation. "And who is this beautiful guest of yours?"

"This is my Vienna," said Dane, his voice loaded with possession. And, yep, several sets of eyebrows lifted high.

Clint blinked. "*Your* Vienna? Like that, is it?"

"Wouldn't you claim such a stunning creature if you could?"

Clint grinned. "Oh, I sure would."

Dane looked down at me, one corner of his mouth kicking up into a warm, sexy smile that made me tingle in all the best places.

After the group asked us a few questions, such as how we met and how long we'd been dating, the conversation switched to business. No surprise there. A lot of networking went on at such events. But as that wasn't Dane's main purpose tonight, it wasn't long before he moved us on.

Over the next half hour, we walked from group to group. All were surprised to see he had an actual date, and many hit us with the same questions that the first group we'd spoken with had asked.

Some of the men treated their female companions like they were just pretty ornaments. Dane didn't do that to me. He included me in conversations, touched me constantly, kept me close, and would sometimes turn his full attention to me. Whenever he did the latter, my nerves went a little haywire. Being the center of his focus could be a heady thing.

Conscious of our audience, I made sure to occasionally touch him or cast him brief, soft smiles that held secrets. I was always rewarded—sometimes with a brush of his mouth to my temple, sometimes with a stroke of his hand over my hair, and sometimes with a slow, lazy smile I felt in my core.

It wasn't long before I caught a glimpse of his brothers and Hope watching us from the corner of the room. I was guessing Kent's guest was his wife. I'd never met her.

I expected them to approach, but they seemed intent on merely observing us for the moment. I gave them a little wave and then edged closer to Dane. Without pausing his conversation, he smoothed his hand up my back and rested it on the crook of my neck. His thumb brushed my nape, and the featherlight touch almost made me shiver.

A warm flush unfurled in my stomach and trickled through my system like honey. Torture. It was a delicious torture.

Soon enough, we were on the move again. As we walked over to the next cluster of people, the bottom fell out of my stomach. The arm that was curled around my waist tightened as Dane smoothly greeted the group, not even so much as stumbling over Owen's name.

My ex stared at us, his face hard. "Dane. Vienna."

The beautiful raven-haired woman at his side lifted her brows and smiled. "Vienna? Our little girl's name is Vienna. You don't hear it a lot."

My gut twisted. *Shit.* This had to be Owen's wife.

Owen's boss nudged him, a rakish grin on his face, and said, "Told you I was sure there was something going on between Dane and your friend."

"Friend?" Tiffany's smile faltered as she glanced from me to Owen. "You two know each other?"

"We went to school together," I said. Well, what else could I say? I certainly wouldn't spill the whole story, especially in front of so many people.

Dane's dark gaze met mine. "The dinner will be starting soon. Shall we go find our table?"

Eager to scamper, I nodded. "Sounds good to me."

He nodded at the group. "Enjoy your evening."

I echoed his sentiment and gladly allowed him to lead me to the spiral staircase. I wouldn't have to worry about slipping on the marble stairs, thanks to the carpet runner. "Did you know Owen would be here?" I whispered.

Dane put his mouth to my ear. "I suspected he might be. It's a good thing. He needs to believe you're off-limits. Needs to believe you mean something to me."

Reaching the second level, I took in the many tables. They were all beautifully presented. Floral centerpieces. Pure white tablecloths. Artfully arranged napkins. Fancy wine glasses. Gleaming silverware.

When we consulted the seating plan, I felt my nose wrinkle. "Your brothers have been seated at our table."

"I figured they would be."

We crossed to one of the large, round tables and sank into our allocated seats. A few people were already there, and they said their hellos.

Dane draped an arm over the back of my chair and leaned close. "Did you know that Owen had named his daughter 'Vienna?'" he asked, his voice low.

"Not until a few weeks ago when he turned up at my apartment," I quietly replied. "He said he wanted to 'honor' me because I'd always supported him. Still, it's just … weird. And wrong to everyone involved."

"I'll be surprised if his wife isn't asking herself if him choosing that name for their child had something to do with you. As she pointed out, it's not a common name. He might find that he has to answer a lot of uncomfortable questions later." Dane combed his fingers through my hair, admiring the blonde strands. "I like that you wore it down for me."

I felt my brow crease. "I only left it down because I didn't have the time to pin it up."

One corner of his mouth hitched up. "Ah, I see." He didn't sound as though he believed me. "Have you told your family about us yet?"

"I told my foster parents and their daughter." I lowered my voice, adding, "They bought the story a lot easier than I thought they would."

"It'll be best if you introduce me to them soon." *Before I propose,* he didn't add but I heard.

Spotting a mood-plummeting sight in my peripheral vision, I sighed. "Speaking of relatives …" I pasted a polite smile on my face when Kent, Travis, and their wives appeared at the table moments later.

Dane stood to shake hands with his brothers. Kent's greeting was one of genuine warmth, but Travis's was somewhat stilted. Hope merely smiled at Dane, but Kent's wife stepped forward and offered Dane her cheek. He gave it an obliging peck and went to introduce me, but she touched his arm to get his attention and tried drawing him into conversation. Rude.

Dane ignored her attempt and then offered me his hand. Once I took it and stood, he said, "Kent, Travis, Hope, I believe you've all already met Vienna." He looked at me. "Beside Kent is his wife, Jen."

Kent's genuine smile didn't falter. "It's a pleasure to see you again, Vienna."

"Same to you," I told him.

Travis merely inclined his head while Hope offered me a weak smile.

Jen lifted her chin and gave me a condescending head-to-toe look. "I don't often have the chance to meet one of Dane's women."

Dane stilled, seeming a little surprised by her attitude. He shifted closer to me and away from her. She noticed his withdrawal and didn't appear to like it. I had no idea what her deal was, but I suspected she'd voice it at some point. Snobs usually did.

Dane sank back into his chair and again hung his arm over the back of mine. The others took their own seats … which sadly placed Jen next to me. Ugh. A waiter quickly appeared and poured drinks before melting away.

Travis looked from me to Dane. "So, you two are an item now," he said, his voice carefully even. But I detected the hint of skepticism there.

"We are," confirmed Dane.

"How long has it been going on?" asked Kent, seeming rather pleased.

"A few months," replied Dane.

Travis's brows dipped. "Really? I wouldn't have guessed. You did well to keep that under wraps." His eyes slid to me. "No wonder you turned my friend down. You were secretly after my brother."

I'd turned down his friend because, like Travis, he was a fucking tool. And I wasn't "after" Dane at all.

Seeing that Dane had stiffened, Travis lifted a placatory hand. "I know, I know, I'm not supposed to let my friends hit on your employees. He and I were a little drunk at the bar that night."

"Wait," said Jen. "She works for you, Dane?"

"She's his PA," Hope told her.

Jen's brow furrowed as she stared at him. "I thought you didn't get involved with your employees."

"Obviously I made an exception," said Dane, picking up his champagne flute.

"Well," began Hope, "you should consider yourself lucky that Vienna's willing to overlook your many … exploits, Dane. I mean, she was the one who ordered the flowers for those women and booked your dinner reservations, so she knows you've been around the block quite a few times."

I almost rolled my eyes at the non-too-subtle reminder of Dane's past.

"Speaking of those exploits, some of them are here." Travis turned to me. "If they do anything petty like shoot you little smirks or try to flirt with him, just ignore them."

I hated that his comment twisted my gut, but I really did despise the idea of being around Dane's exes. They were all grace and elegance and chic designer clothes. Still, I didn't let Travis see that his verbal arrow had hit its mark. "Petty people are easy to ignore." Him included.

He narrowed his eyes, clearly picking up on my insinuation.

"Enough, Travis," said Dane, dancing his fingers over the side of my upper arm.

Travis lifted his shoulders, all innocence. "What?"

"You're trying to make Vienna feel uncomfortable—I don't fucking like it," said Dane, his voice low and dripping with frost.

"How about a change of subject?" proposed Kent.

How about if Travis and Hope went the fuck home?

The conversation was a little awkward after that, so Dane and I mostly talked between ourselves. The waiter soon returned, poured more drinks, and took orders for the upcoming dinner.

"I hope they hurry with the food," I told Dane. "I'm starving."

"They'll hold the auction first," he said.

"You planning to bid on anything?"

"I'm planning to *win*."

"And you're so sure you'll procure whatever you bid on?"

He gave me a pitying look, as if I was dumb as a rock for thinking differently. He also managed to later win the two pieces of art he bid on. Well, of course he did.

Once the auction was over, the meals arrived. Talk flowed easily around our table as people ate, although both Dane and Kent mostly ignored Travis, who became increasingly obnoxious the more he drank.

After the dinner was over and soft music began to play, Dane took my hand. "Dance with me." It wasn't a request.

On the dance floor, he drew me so close I was pressed up against him. Which basically sent my nerve-endings into a frenzy. Standing tall, he splayed one hand on my lower back as we swayed—slow, sensual, intimate.

Other couples danced around us, but I paid them no attention. I was far too caught up in the way Dane's dark eyes stared into mine, as soft and warm as hot chocolate. God, he should have been an actor.

"You didn't tell me Travis's friend came onto you," he said, his voice so low and smooth I almost missed the anger there. "When did that happen?"

"A month or so ago."

"And I didn't learn of this why?"

I shrugged. "It wasn't worth reporting. He asked me out. I said no. Get rid of the frown. You're supposed to look happy."

His mouth twitched into a smile. "That's right, I am." He stroked the pads of his fingers along my back. "If someone puts any moves on you again, I want to hear about it."

I gave a slow nod. "All right. So, I know why Travis and Hope don't like that you're dating someone. What's Jen's problem? Do you think she's eager for Kent to get his share of your trust fund?"

He hesitated to answer. "I can't be certain what her issue is."

"You didn't expect her to be rude to me, did you?"

"No. But Jen's a complicated person. She'll no doubt feel bad about it later."

Maybe, but neither Hope nor Travis would. Making a conscious effort not to let my irritation show in my expression, I said, "It annoys me that Travis is so intent on having a share of your trust fund."

"He feels that he has more of a right to it than I do because I'm more financially comfortable than he is. But even if I wasn't, he'd still want his share. Really, he doesn't have many scruples—hence why he cheats on Hope so often. But she does the same to him, so …" Dane shrugged.

I shook my head, not understanding why they'd stay together if they were going to disrespect themselves and each other that way. "Do Kent and Jen have a better relationship?"

"Yes, although they're not as close as they once were. And, going by some of the things Kent has said, they argue so frequently he once considered moving out for a while to give them both some space. I don't think he'd have married so young if the conditions of his trust fund hadn't been what they were. I think he might have waited for someone who's better suited to him to come along."

"Have you held out as long as you have because you had some hope that you'd meet someone you cared for?"

"No. I just wasn't in a rush to get my hands on the money the way my brothers were; I wanted to make my own way in life."

And he had, which I deeply respected. He'd set up o-Verve on his own, and he'd built it up through sheer hard work.

I lowered my voice to a whisper as I asked, "If I'd said no to marrying you, what would you have done? Asked one of your other employees?"

"No. I'd have hounded you until you said yes."

I blinked. "You're not serious."

"When do I ever joke?"

"Never, but—"

"Vienna, I'm a man who gets what he wants. Always. No exceptions. I never stop or back down until I have it."

I didn't want to find that a turn-on, but I did, and I hoped that it wasn't written all over my face.

I didn't realize that I was biting my lip until his eyes dropped to my mouth. They traced its shape, bold and blatant. Without thought, I flicked out my tongue to lathe my lower lip. A muscle in his cheek ticked, and the hand on my back flexed.

His gaze flew back to mine, hot and intent. I swallowed hard. Jesus, someone needed to throw a bucket of water over me.

The music changed then, flowing into a tune that was a little faster than the previous song. "I need to use the restroom," I said.

"I'll walk you there."

"That's not necessary," I assured him, but he did it anyway.

In the surprisingly fancy restroom, I did my business. I almost stumbled when I walked out of the stall to find Owen's wife standing at the sink.

She paused in fixing her lipstick and smiled. "Hello again."

"Hi," I said simply. I quickly washed and dried my hands, eager to get out of there. I turned toward the door and—

"You weren't just Owen's friend," Tiffany blurted out. "Were you?"

Shit. I slowly spun on my heel and just stared at her, not sure what to say.

"There's more, isn't there?"

I inwardly groaned. "You really should ask Owen."

"I did. He blew me off, which makes me believe there's a lot I don't know. *Please* just tell me. If you were me, you'd want me to be honest with you."

Fuck if she wasn't right. I licked my lips. "He and I dated in high school. We were also engaged for five months, but he broke it off and we went our separate ways."

She swallowed and took a step back. "He must have regretted it. He named our child after you."

"I was his friend for much, much longer than I was his girlfriend. We were better off as friends, and we both knew it. He was just the first to act on it. It was you he married. You he built a life with and had a child with."

"And me he'll soon be divorcing," she said, a bite to her tone that told me she wasn't as good with that as he seemed to think. "I hate that he gave her your name."

"I hate it, too." Because it caused unnecessary pain to people who didn't deserve it. I opened my mouth to apologize, but the fault wasn't mine. The guilt wasn't mine to feel either, but the emotion settled in all the same.

Tiffany turned back to the mirror and took a shaky breath. Knowing I was the last person she'd want comfort from, I walked out of the restroom.

Dane was waiting a few feet away, deep in conversation with a man I didn't recognize. Pasting an easy smile on my face, I crossed to them. "Thanks for waiting for me," I told Dane, sure my needless guilt didn't show in my expression or voice. But his eyes narrowed.

Before he could ask what was wrong, I introduced myself to his conversationalist, who flirted shamelessly with me. For all of five seconds. The moment Dane slid an arm around me and drew me close, his hold nothing short of proprietary, the other man's sentence trailed off.

"It was good seeing you, Richard," said Dane. "We'll talk again soon, I'm sure." He led me away and whispered into my ear, "What's wrong?"

I sighed. "I saw Tiffany in the restroom. She asked me some questions. She'd already guessed there was more between me and Owen than being childhood friends."

"I'm not surprised. He's been staring at you most of the evening."

He had? I'd been so wrapped up in Dane, I hadn't noticed. "She's hurting right now."

"That's his fault. Not yours."

"I know. I still feel bad. In her shoes, I'd be devastated to hear my husband named our child after his ex. It's not like she can change the kid's name. Well, she *could*, but it would be hard to make the little girl understand why it needed to be done. I don't know if he truly sees that what he did was wrong." I let out an exasperated sound. "I wish he hadn't come here tonight."

"I don't. He needed to see us together and get the message that you're taken. And it's better for his wife that she knows the truth. She would have learned it sooner or later anyway."

"Maybe. But I detest that I was the one who put that look on her face."

He slid his hand up my back and squeezed my nape. "Bear in mind that later—when she's no longer hurting—she'll be glad you were straight with her." He paused. "You ready to leave now?"

"More than ready."

Dane pulled his phone out of his pocket and rattled off a text, no doubt summoning Sam. "Now, if you can, wipe the anger off your face or people will think we're fighting."

I drew in a long breath, dug deep for calm, and blanked my expression. "Better?"

"It will be when you smile."

I thought of Freddie, who could always lift my mood, and felt my mouth curve. "Done."

He squeezed my nape again. "Good girl."

Oh, he shouldn't have said that. My body went all tingly again. "What about your paintings?"

"They'll be sent to my home."

We returned to our table, said a quick goodbye to his family, and then made our way downstairs. People stopped us here and there, wanting to speak with Dane, but he artfully dodged their efforts to draw him into deep conversation.

Outside, we slid into Sam's waiting car. Noting that the privacy partition was up, I turned to Dane and said, "Think we accomplished what we came to do?"

"You mean convince people we're a couple? Yes."

"What happens next?"

"Next I put my ring on your finger. But not until we're in Vegas."

And now my belly was rolling again. "Do I get to pick the ring?"

"No."

I frowned. "Why not?"

"You'll pick something understated."

"So?"

"So I don't do 'understated.' People know that."

I huffed. "Fine. Just don't pick something *too* big and expensive—that's all I ask."

"Hmm."

Not liking that noncommittal sound, I shook my head and turned my gaze back to the window. What a freaking night.

CHAPTER SIX

Having written my to-do list for the following day on a virtual sticky note, I switched off my computer, gathered my things, and slipped on my coat. Dane was out of the office, so I didn't need to pop in and say goodbye. I just headed straight for the elevator.

Most of the employees had already left the building, so I didn't pass many people. Since my "serious relationship" with Dane became public a week ago, some of my co-workers had changed a little toward me. Talk would sometimes stop when I entered the break room. Smiles were occasionally too false. I'd hear people whispering nearby, but they'd shut up if I turned to look at them.

Two women in particular were getting on my last nerve. They mostly just did petty stuff like sneer or titter or pointedly ignore me, but I kind of felt betrayed. These were people I'd once chatted with regularly and had drinks with at Christmas office parties. Now, they treated me like I was a pariah. I figured it was jealousy, since both females had tried and failed to seduce Dane years ago.

I supposed that back then they'd comforted themselves with the fact that he made a point of not sleeping with his employees. It was no doubt a kick to their ego that he'd seemingly now made an exception for me. Still, there was no need for them to be so freaking bitchy.

That Dane made an effort to have lunch with me most days—usually in the privacy of his office—seemed to have exacerbated the issue. I was sure others thought we were getting up to some raunchy stuff in there while on our break. I was also sure that Dane was hoping they would assume that.

Uninterested in lowering myself to the level of the other women, I'd so far ignored it. I also hadn't told Dane about it. Nor had I mentioned that some of the other employees were acting *off* with me. I was no tattler, and I could deal with my own problems just fine. It would all blow over eventually if I paid it no mind.

Most of o-Verve were amazingly supportive of our "relationship." They'd gushed over the online pictures of us that were taken by the photographers at the charity fundraiser. Hanna had dissected each of Dane's expressions, swearing he was "crazy" about me. I'd just smiled and said I hoped it was true.

I was walking through o-Verve's private parking garage, my heels clacking on the pitted pavement, when my phone beeped. I pulled my cell out of my purse without breaking stride, careful to dodge an oil stain on the ground. Looking at the screen, I saw that I had two messages. The most recent was from Melinda, informing me that she and Wyatt would be having a barbeque on Sunday and that Simon, Dane and I were invited. The other message had been sent an hour ago, but I hadn't heard my phone beep.

It was from Maggie: *Hey honey. Haven't heard from you in a week, just wanted to check on you. Simon's missing you xx*

Maggie and Freddie often informed me of how my father was doing, since Simon wasn't the type to share how he was feeling. It was never good for his emotions to build up.

Reaching my car, I unlocked it with the key fob. The resulting beep seemed to echo in the large space. I slid into the driver's seat and then called Simon.

After a few rings, he answered, "Hey, my sweet girl. How are you?"

I smiled, my heart squeezing. "Good, you?"

"Fine, fine. How's everything going?"

"Great. Really great." I bit my lip, hesitant to continue but knowing I'd have to. "I, um … There's someone I'd like to introduce to you."

"Oh? Who?"

"My boss, Dane Davenport. He and I have sort of been seeing each other."

"Well, good," he said, sounding genuinely excited. "It's about time you started dating again. I hate thinking of you up there in your apartment all alone."

I knew he did, just as I knew a large part of him would want this for me. But another part of him … I silently sighed.

"When do I get to meet him?" Simon asked.

"How about Sunday? Melinda and Wyatt are throwing a barbeque at their house. They want me to invite you and Dane."

"Sounds good to me," he said, and I heard the smile in his voice. "What time?"

"Around noon-ish."

"I'll be there. Looking forward to seeing you."

A smile tugged at my mouth. "Same here. Take care, Dad."

"You too, my sweet girl. Love you."

"Love you, too." Closing my eyes, I rested my forehead on the steering wheel, hoping to God his enthusiasm didn't dim or fracture. He could initially take things so well. But then, after putting a little more thought into a matter, he could start obsessing over the smallest elements of the situation and then his whole viewpoint could alter.

Lifting my head, I blew out a breath and started the engine. If there was a problem, Maggie or Freddie would contact me. That was a comfort.

After the hour-long commute from o-Verve to my complex, I whipped my car into my assigned parking space in the lot and then headed to the front of the building. I was just approaching the main door when a familiar figure stepped out of the shadows.

I stilled. "What do you want?"

Travis raised his hands. "Just to talk. There are things … Look, I know you don't like me much, but this is important. Can I come in?"

Was he high? "No." I didn't trust him as far as I could throw him, so there was no way I'd invite him into my home. "But we can take a walk."

He gave a slow nod. "All right."

Our steps were slow and steady as we strolled along the sidewalk. I stayed silent, waiting for him to say whatever he'd come to say. It was at least a full minute before he came to a sudden stop and turned to face me.

"I know you like Dane a lot," said Travis. "I could see it clear as day at the gala. But you don't know him. Not really."

I raised a brow. "I don't?"

"No, you don't. I'm an asshole. I know that. But so is Dane—he's just a different kind of asshole. He's not *all* bad, no. But he always puts himself first. Always. Our father was the same. May the bastard rot in hell," he muttered under his breath.

My brows flew up. "Essentially, you're saying Dane's selfish?"

"Among many other things. He wasn't always like that. But Dane … our father messed up each of us, but Dane worst of all. Oliver's death only made it worse. Dane turned cold and self-centered. And either his sense of right and wrong is warped, or it has ceased to matter to him if he goes against it."

Wondering who Oliver was, I made a mental note to ask Dane about him. "He's ruthless when it comes to business, sure—"

"And when it comes to every other aspect of his life. Dane never does anything for anyone unless there's something in it for him. He has so many people in his pocket because he swoops in when they need aid and then makes them indebted to him."

My scalp prickled. When Dane helped with the whole sextortion thing, I hadn't thought he'd done it *specifically* to ensure I owed him a favor. But was it in him to be that cunning? Yes. Yes, it was.

"If he sees something he wants, he takes it, even if others will be hurt," Travis added. "Take Jen, for example."

I felt my brow furrow. "Kent's wife?"

"She's been part of our lives since we were kids. Kent's always adored her. Dane knew that, but he fucked her anyway. It was years ago, before she got married. He fucked her a few times, actually. And then he walked away. He never intended to keep her. She meant nothing to him. And yet, he didn't keep his distance and let her be *only* Kent's. He didn't care what that would do to Kent. Dane wanted a piece of her, so he took it."

My stomach twisted as I recalled what Dane had said to me at the gala …

"Vienna, I'm a man who gets what he wants. Always. No exceptions. I never stop or back down until I have it."

"Why are you telling me all this?" I asked.

"Because Jen looked at him the same way you do," replied Travis. "You know better than anyone that he's a huge user when it comes to women. Maybe it's different for him this time; maybe you truly do mean something to him. But you'll never be *everything* to him—no woman will be. He sees himself as the king of his castle, and others are just lowly people to be used. He doesn't view them as his equals."

Dane *did* use people, and he *did* seem to consider himself superior to most. But I didn't believe he looked on others as pawns in a game or something.

I folded my arms. "And you think I should break up with him?"

"I think you should just be wary. I didn't warn Jen, and I wish I had. Just like I wish I'd warned Senator Whitman's daughter. Like Jen, we'd known her for years—our uncle was friends with her father. Lorraine was a mess after she miscarried Dane's baby."

"Miscarried?" I echoed, my chest tightening.

"Yes. When she told him she was pregnant, he said the baby wasn't his; he wouldn't take responsibility for it. She was devastated. Then she miscarried and … I've never seen a woman so cut up." Sorrow glimmered in Travis's eyes. "She was only *nineteen*, Vienna. Can you imagine going through that at nineteen? At any age? Can you imagine going to the father of your kid, afraid and pregnant, only to have him send you on your way?"

I wasn't sure if the temperature had dropped or if it was simply me, but I felt cold all of a sudden.

Travis let out a weary sigh. "If I'd warned her that he wasn't the good man she thought he was, maybe she'd have turned him down, and then maybe she'd never have had to lose a baby. But I didn't warn her. That was a mistake. And so I'm warning you. Do what you will with that warning."

The following afternoon, I sat across from Dane in the seating area of his office while we had our weekly half-hour meeting to review his calendar and broach any issues. I still hadn't told him about Travis's visit the previous evening. I'd decided to take the night to think everything over and work through it in my head; to dissect his story and try to separate fact from fiction.

There was *no way* that he'd care if Dane hurt me. But there was just enough truth in his story to make the whole thing sound utterly believable. I was far too suspicious of Travis and his intentions to buy his account as pure truth, though. He'd had an ulterior motive in coming to "warn" me about Dane; he wanted me to break up with his brother.

Of course, I could be wrong in thinking that Travis had tossed the occasional lie into his tale. Just because he had an ulterior motive didn't mean he was lying. But I didn't trust him even a little, so I didn't trust his word.

I'd decided to wait until I got Dane alone before I brought up the matter, but he'd been out of his office all morning. Now that our meeting was almost over, I could finally bring it up.

"Did you take care of the travel and logistics for our trip to Vegas?" he asked.

My stomach rolled, just as it did every time I thought of our upcoming wedding—which would be happening next Wednesday. I cleared my throat. "Yes, I emailed you a copy of your travel itinerary an hour ago."

"Good. I'll read through it once I get a spare moment. Did you remember to book us in for an extra night?"

I nodded. "Yes." It meant that instead of flying home on our wedding day, we'd return the following day. Which made sense, really, because it would have looked odd if we'd been in such a rush to get married but then hadn't cared about enjoying the day.

"How many rooms did you book at the hotel?"

"Two, as usual."

"You'll need to cancel your room; you'll be staying in my suite. We're allegedly a couple now, remember? Don't worry, there's more than one bedroom."

Well, I knew that. He'd stayed in that suite before. It was huge.

"On another note, you said you'd arrange for me to meet your family," he said. "Did you do it?"

I clicked the top of my pen. "My foster parents have invited you to the barbecue they're having at their house on Sunday. My dad will be there." And so I'd need to explain a few things to Dane about Simon, which would *not* be easy. It was often difficult for people to truly understand.

Dane set his notepad on the coffee table between us. "What's wrong? Don't tell me nothing."

I straightened in my seat. "Travis was waiting for me outside my apartment building last night."

Dane's expression went hard. "What did he want?"

"To warn me that you might hurt me."

Exasperation flashed in Dane's dark eyes. "I should have guessed he might try to convince you to break up with me. I'm sure he came across as very concerned about you."

"Oh, he did. He said you're not all bad, but that you're selfish. Selfish enough to sleep with the woman your other brother has always loved." I waited for him to look shocked by the statement and quickly deny it, but he didn't say a word. "It's true?"

"That I slept with Jen? Yes. Once. It was a long time ago."

Once? Travis had claimed it happened a few times. But it didn't really matter *how* many times Dane had slept with her. The issue was that it had allegedly hurt Kent.

I crossed one leg over the other, and Dane's eyes dropped to my legs. "It didn't bother you that Kent cared for her?" I asked, a slight edge in my voice.

Dane's eyes flew back to mine. "Kent was engaged to someone else at the time. Travis didn't tell you that?"

I shook my head.

"Unsurprising. What else did he say?"

"He told me about the Senator's daughter. He told me she miscarried your baby."

"She didn't miscarry. She had an abortion."

My lips parted. "An abortion?"

"Yes. She was pissed when I insisted it wasn't my baby. She thought I'd marry her. She was wrong. I don't know who fathered that baby, but it was not me."

I narrowed my eyes. "You're sure?"

"I'm very sure."

"No type of contraception is guaranteed to work every time."

"True. But I'd had a vasectomy two years before that. I caught a woman using a syringe to extract my come out of a condom."

My mouth dropped open. "You are joking."

"I never joke," he reminded me. "But, out of respect for Lorraine's father, I said I'd have a DNA test done on the child after it was born; that if it was mine, I'd be a part of its life. The next thing I knew, she was gatecrashing Hope's mother's birthday party, drunk off her ass, where she then announced that she'd aborted my unborn child."

I stared at him for a long moment. Dane could lie with utter ease, but my gut told me he was telling the truth.

"I'm not convinced there really was a baby. Lorraine wasn't content that I'd have a DNA test. She wanted me to slide a ring on her finger. So I had to wonder if the whole thing was a scam."

It was possible, I supposed.

"My family—knowing I couldn't possibly have fathered anyone's baby—was furious with her, even Travis. But I see he enjoyed twisting the whole thing to make you turn against me."

"Yes, he did. He also made it sound like you and Jen had a fling."

"Well we didn't. It was a one-night stand—nothing more. She's now happily married to Kent."

"Yet, she was weird to me at the gala. Why?"

"She told me she had a moment of petty jealousy."

I stilled. "She 'told' you that? When?"

Dane idly drummed his fingers on the arm of the sofa. "She called me the morning after the gala and apologized. Apparently, it stung her ego to see me happy with you the way I never was with her. She said she'd apologize to you the next time she saw you."

Huh. Well I'd accept it gracefully, but I wouldn't particularly care to hear it. Snobs weren't my kind of people.

I tilted my head. "Back to what you said before … someone *really* tried to extract your come out of a condom? Seriously?"

He nodded.

I could only shake my head in wonder. "I didn't know people did stuff like that. I mean, I know there are women who'll deliberately get pregnant in the hope of using the kid as a meal ticket." Hell, Heather was one of them. "But not go *that* far to get pregnant. What did the woman say when you caught her?"

"That I wasn't supposed to walk into a bathroom without knocking."

"That's … wow. Just wow." Hearing he'd had a vasectomy wasn't as much of a shock, though. I'd once overheard Dane say that he had no interest in having children.

"Next time Travis bothers you, call me straight away," said Dane. "I wish I could tell you he'll leave you alone after we're married, but I can't guarantee that. If you and I were to divorce before the year was up, I'd be denied access to my trust fund—he knows that."

"Are you going to confront him about this?"

"Yes. He'll no doubt lie that you put words into his mouth."

Probably. Because, as Hanna often claimed, the guy was a weasel. "He said something else."

"What?"

"He said your father messed all of you up, and that the death of someone called Oliver made it worse."

Dane's gaze seemed to ice over; it honestly chilled me just a little. "Travis will no doubt say a lot of things to you," he said, his tone neutral.

"Truths or lies?"

"Probably a little of both."

"And you're not going to tell me more about your father or who Oliver is?"

"You don't need to know."

I almost flinched. Not at his words, but at the way he'd said them. His tone had been sharp. Hard. So cold I was surprised the air hadn't frosted.

Making it clear I'd crossed a line.

Well, that put me in my place, didn't it?

To be fair to him, this wasn't a relationship. He didn't owe me explanations. And there were plenty of things I hadn't told him. Things I'd prefer to never tell him. So, yeah, I'd be a complete hypocrite if I pushed him on this.

I was more annoyed by the fact that I *cared* that he wouldn't tell me. It shouldn't hurt. There was no reason for it to do so. And yet, my chest felt tight.

Had I somehow let myself get pulled into the fantasy that our relationship was real? I hadn't thought so. I'd thought I was doing fine at keeping it straight in my head that it was all fake. But maybe I was wrong, because I'd slipped here. Before the fake-dating began, I never would have asked him personal questions, and I definitely wouldn't have felt hurt if he hadn't wanted to share something personal.

Shit, this wasn't good. Not at all. I couldn't afford to let it all get blurred in my head.

We weren't dating. We weren't bed-buddies. Hell, we weren't even friends. He was my boss, and I was his PA—that was the extent of our relationship. I couldn't let myself forget that. Not even for a moment.

Wrapping my PA-cloak tight around me, I stood. "You have a conference call in fifteen minutes, so I'll head back to my desk. Buzz me if you need anything." I turned and made my way to the door.

"Vienna?" he said when I reached for the doorknob.

I glanced at him over my shoulder. "Yes?"

He watched me closely, those dark, far-too-perceptive eyes roaming over my face. He opened his mouth to speak, but then his cell phone began to chime. He reached for it, just as I'd known he would—work always came first to Dane. "We'll talk later," he said to me.

I nodded, though I wasn't whatsoever looking forward to it.

Fortunately, he got called out of the office and didn't return to the building before the end of the workday. That meant I could leave and spend the evening shoring up my defenses against this man who'd sneakily found his way around them without even trying or knowing.

I was almost home when Ashley called and asked if I'd meet her at the local ice cream parlor—apparently, Tucker had pissed her off again and so she'd stormed out of their apartment.

Inside the parlor, we sat at one of the metal tables. A few other customers sat around, filling the space with the sounds of chatter, laughter, and the crunch of ice cream cones.

I licked at my caramel ice cream, scooping up some of the chopped nuts and crumbled cookies that had been sprinkled over the top. Smooth and cold, the ice cream went down nicely. "Well, what did Tucker do?"

Ashley's lips thinned. "We sat down to catch up on a TV series we've been following. He started 'guessing' what was going to happen. The first time he was right, I was impressed. The second time, I was suspicious. The third time, I was out and out pissed, because I knew it meant that the asshole had watched the episodes without me."

I winced. "Oh."

"He denied it at first. Said he'd never do that to me. But when I threatened to shred his football jersey with a blade if he didn't tell me the truth, he admitted he'd watched the rest of the series while I went to church with my mother on Sunday. What kind of sick person does that?"

Actually, I'd done it to Melinda a time or two, but I didn't say that. "Did he apologize?"

"No. He said I was overreacting. Overreacting would have been to ream his ass with my hair straighteners—don't think I didn't consider it." Ashley licked at her chocolate ice-cream. "You still so sure he loves me?"

"Yes, I am. He did an unfair thing. He's no doubt feeling shitty about it now."

"And so he should," sassed Ashley. "So, how are things going with you and your spectacularly hot boss?"

Ignoring the way my stomach dropped, I took another lick of my ice-cream. "Good."

"You fucked him yet?"

"What do you think?" I asked with a wicked smile that made her laugh.

"I'm betting he's well-endowed. He gives off that big cock vibe."

I frowned. "Big cock vibe?"

"He walks like a man who's fully secure in himself about that department." She narrowed her eyes. "What's with the look on your face?"

I blinked. "What look?"

"The one that says something's bugging you. You weren't wearing it until I brought up Dane. What happened? You two had a falling out?"

"No. Everything's fine."

"Girl, just tell me what's wrong."

"Nothing." I licked at the drips of ice cream that were running down my waffle cone, hoping she'd drop the subject.

"Are you worrying that you'll never come first to him, what with him being a workaholic? Because I would."

I almost laughed. Dane's work would always come first—I knew that for a fact. Still, I vaguely answered, "Most workaholics struggle to balance work with other aspects of their lives."

"True, but he's already put you before his work. I mean, you told me long ago that he doesn't get involved with his employees. He broke that rule for you. I don't think he'd do that if he didn't care for you." She used a napkin to wipe at the ice cream that had dripped down her chin. "I'll find out if I'm right when I see you two at the barbecue. I bumped into Melinda and managed to wangle myself an invite."

My lips twitched. Ashley did that shit all the time. She seemed to know everybody.

"I'll watch him with you, and I'll tell you what I see," Ashley went on. "I do hope Hanna's wrong and he's not a psychopath. You don't want one of those in your bed."

"You've been talking to Hanna about this?" I'd introduced them a few years ago, and they got along like a house on fire.

"She's excited about you and Dane, but she's also worried that he'll hurt you due to him not having a conscience and all."

"I think I'll be fine. And I don't believe he's a psychopath."

"She said you'd say that. She also said to remind you that you thought that Raymond was 'sweet.' You know, the same Raymond who stole your wallet and maxed out your credit card when you dumped him."

"You two are never going to let me forget about that, are you?"

"Nope. What true friend would?"

I snorted.

Once we were finally done with our ice cream, we drove back to our complex in our respective vehicles. Entering the parking lot, I noticed a familiar car parked outside the building. *Hell.* This was not what I needed right now.

Ashley didn't notice Dane until she and I walked toward the main door. He'd obviously noticed my arrival because he'd exited his vehicle and was now leaning against it.

Ashley put her mouth to my ear and quietly said, "I don't know what you two have been squabbling over—purely because you won't tell me—but go sort it out."

"Are you going to take your own advice and make up with Tucker?" I asked.

She sniffed. "Maybe."

Instead of following her into the building, I took a preparatory breath and walked over to Dane. "What are you doing here?" I asked, though not unkindly.

He pushed away from the car. "I told you we'd talk later."

I scratched my forehead. "Can't it wait until tomorrow?" Because I figured the best way to not blur any lines between us in my head would be to only see him at work or when we were on our fake dates. I was on *my* time now, and there was no need for him to be inside my apartment.

He stepped into my personal space and stared down at me. "You're pulling away. Are you planning to go back on your word?"

I lifted my chin. "No, I wouldn't do that. I've told you that before."

My cell beeped. Glad for the distraction, I dug my phone out of my purse.

It was a text message from Freddie: *Code red.*

My whole body seized up. *Shit.* I raced to my car, jabbing the button on the key fob to unlock it, ignoring Dane's shouts. I hopped into the driver's seat and, without another look his way, sped out of the parking lot.

As I drove en route to my father's house, my heart thudded hard in my chest. A code red situation could be anything from Simon having an anxiety attack to him cutting himself again. The latter occurrences didn't happen often. But when they did, they could be bad.

Before long, I was speeding down my father's street. The tires screeched as I brought the car to a sharp stop outside his house. I jumped out of the vehicle and rushed for the door, cursing when I dropped my keys halfway up the driveway. I bent and snatched them—

A hand grabbed my arm and spun me. *Dane.* "What's happening?" he asked.

I blinked, surprised to see him. "You need to go." I tried pulling my arm free, but he held tight.

"What's going on? You're white as a fucking sheet, and you've just been driving around the streets like the hounds of hell were on your tail."

I shook my head. I didn't have time for this. "I can't do this right now. Just go. We'll talk tomorrow."

"I'm not leaving until you tell me—"

"*Fucking go, Dane.*" I tore my arm out of his grip. "This is not your business." I raced up the steps, unlocked Simon's front door and then hurried inside.

Closing the door behind me, I called out, "Dad?" No response. I peeked into the living room. It was empty, but the TV was on. "Dad?" I again shouted. Still nothing.

I stalked into the kitchen and skidded to a halt. He was sitting on the tiled floor, his eyes squeezed shut, his hands fisting his thick dark hair.

I crouched in front of him. "Dad, what's wrong?"

He awkwardly lifted his head and blinked. I realized he hadn't acknowledged my arrival until right then. He'd been deep in his thoughts. In his memories. That was never good.

"Dad, what happened? And why is one side of your face pink?"

He touched his cheek. "I fell asleep at the table and …" He trailed off and squeezed his eyes shut.

I took in the dark smudges under his eyes. "You haven't been sleeping well. Did you have a nightmare just now?" I asked carefully, knowing how badly they could mess with his head.

He shuddered. "I can't stop seeing it, seeing *her.*"

There was only one woman he spoke of with such vehemence—his mother. "Dad, open your eyes, look at me." I gently tugged his hands away from his hair. "Please look at me."

His eyes fluttered open, and they looked so sad my chest ached.

"You've been working on your memories in therapy again?"

He only nodded.

I inwardly cursed. I knew it was important for him to unearth certain memories and face the abuse he suffered at the hands of his mother, but I *hated* the toll it took on him. Especially since it often led to him having vivid, horrific nightmares. Then he'd be so afraid to go to sleep that he'd lay awake for hours most nights.

There were times when he'd recover a memory so sickening, he simply couldn't take it. Then the anxiety attacks would come back, or he'd start cutting himself again.

I didn't say how much I hated what the therapy sessions did to him, though. The therapy was important, and I needed to be supportive of it.

I rubbed his arm. "How about I make us some tea?"

"No tea. I just want to be alone."

"No, you don't." I tugged on his arm as I stood, and he finally pushed to his feet. "You just don't want to talk about your nightmare. That's fine. We don't have to talk. We can just sit together at the table, and you can watch me drink tea. You know how riveting that is."

He took a seat at the scarred wooden table. "I'm fine now."

"Of course you are. But now that I'm here, I might as well stay a while." I grabbed the kettle, filled it with water from the tap, set it down on the—

There was a bang behind me, like the chair had hit the wall.

"Who the hell are you?" demanded Simon.

I whirled. Dane stood in the kitchen doorway. *Shit.* How had he gotten inside the house?

I slipped between them. "It's okay, Dad. This is Dane. My boss. I told you about him on the phone, remember?" He didn't look at me. He kept staring at Dane, his eyes wide, his breaths coming fast. "Dad?"

"You must be Simon," said Dane, all politeness. "I've heard much about you from Vienna."

Ha, *lie.*

Simon's eyes flickered, pain flashed across his face, and his head twitched slightly. Then the alarm slid from his expression and was replaced by pure arrogance. His posture changed in an instant. He held himself taller, steadier, like the world and everything in it was beneath him. He looked down at me, and my stomach sank.

I swallowed. "Hello, Deacon."

CHAPTER SEVEN

"Hello, princess," said Deacon, his mouth curling ever so slightly. His smile often held a mocking tint, but fortunately not when he looked at me.

As a child, I'd automatically accepted the presence of my father's other personalities—or alters, as they were referred to. I'd played games with young Freddie. I'd baked cookies with the very maternal Maggie. I'd hidden behind Deacon while he yelled at whoever had upset Simon or me, which was often my mother. And I hadn't thought anything of it—it had been the norm to me. Until I went to live with Melinda and Wyatt.

They'd educated me on Dissociative Identity Disorder—or DID—so I knew enough about it to understand that I had no need to be afraid. Simon's alters weren't varying degrees of Mr. Hyde. They were his protectors, in a sense. They'd developed to help him deal with the horrific abuse he'd suffered as a child when he'd tried dissociating from it, and they'd made it possible for him to survive it.

There were three "people" inside Simon's system—Freddie, who was eight, Maggie, who was forty, and Deacon, who was thirty-five. Unlike with some cases of DID, they internally interacted with each other. They even had a sort of co-consciousness, which meant that although only one alter would be dominant at a time, the others would be aware of what was going on. It seemed to make things less confusing for them.

Deacon tipped his chin toward Dane. "So this is the guy you talked about, huh?"

I nodded. "This is the guy."

Deacon studied his face. "She didn't tell you about me," he correctly guessed. He sliced his gaze back to me. "What about Freddie? Maggie? You kept us all a secret?" He tutted. "That's not nice."

"Yeah, well, neither are you a lot of the time."

He snickered. "I'm *never* nice, princess."

Deacon wasn't cruel or evil, but he had a "don't fuck with me" attitude and was aggressively protective. He could be violent to those he considered a threat—I'd witnessed it firsthand.

I turned to Dane. "You should go." Deacon could be weird if he felt he had to compete for my attention. Perhaps because he didn't surface often, and I was the only person he *liked* to interact with.

A mocking smile curved Deacon's mouth as he stared at my boss, who hadn't moved an inch. "Aw, he doesn't want to go. He's worried I'll hurt you. How sweet." Deacon sank into the dining chair and stretched out his legs, utterly relaxed.

"I'll be fine," I told Dane.

"I believe you." He leaned against the doorjamb, making it clear he wasn't going anywhere.

For fuck's sake. "You really should go." But he didn't.

Deacon laughed. "Looks like you won't be able to push this one around."

Annoyance fluttered through me. The thing was … I had to veil that annoyance, otherwise Deacon would jump to my defense and toss Dane out. Oh, sure, he found Dane amusing *for now*. That could change in an instant. Deacon was a mercurial character.

The best I could do was ignore Dane altogether in the hope that Deacon—satisfied that he had my total attention—would ignore him, too.

Deacon looked at me as I took the seat opposite him. "Freddie texted you?" It wasn't really a question.

"He thought Simon would need me," I said.

"He did. He was a wreck." Deacon's upper lip curled. "I don't know why he lets the memories of that bitch get to him so much. She was nothing but a worthless fucking skank."

"Agreed."

"Corrine was the same," he said, referring to my mother. "The only thing she was ever good at was fucking with his head. I'd say she eventually learned her lesson."

Oh, Deacon had taught her a lesson all right.

His brows drew together as he glanced around the room. "I need a smoke. Fucking Maggie always throws away my stash. Smoking's bad for you, apparently."

"I thought that was just a rumor," I quipped.

His mouth canted up into a small smile. He looked at my boss again. "You smoke?"

"No, I don't," replied Dane, his voice even.

Deacon shrugged. "I guess nobody's perfect." He turned back to me and gestured at Dane. "What about this guy? He good to you?"

"I wouldn't be dating him if he wasn't," I carefully answered.

"True." Deacon's gaze cut to him again. "If you hurt her, you deal with me."

"Understood," said Dane.

Deacon squinted. "No, I don't think you do really understand. But you will if you ever harm her." His eyes met mine again. "Simon wants to talk to you now."

I held back a sigh of relief. "Okay."

"It was good talking to you, princess. You come to me if Mr. Boss Man here upsets you. Got me?"

"I got you."

He nodded, satisfied. His gaze went out of focus as his head flicked to the side. His brow creased with a brief lash of pain. He blinked a few times, almost as if he had something stuck in his eyes. Then my dad was looking at me. He straightened in his seat and pulled his arms tight to his body.

"Hi, Dad," I said softly.

He cleared his throat and gave me a faint smile. His eyes flew to Dane. "You startled me earlier." He rose to his feet and held out his hand. "I'm Simon, Vienna's father."

Dane reached out and shook his hand, as cool and calm as always. "Dane Davenport, her boyfriend and her boss. My apologies for walking in uninvited. I saw Vienna run in here in a panic, and she didn't close the door properly. I wanted to check that she was fine."

"Understandable. I'm glad you care enough to check on her. She's special, you know."

"Yeah, I do know."

Rubbing at his nape, Simon said, "Um, sit down."

I thought Dane would make his excuses and leave, but he took a seat at the table while I made everyone drinks. They fell into a conversation that quickly turned to sports, of all things. It was as if both of them were determined to lighten the atmosphere, make the moment *normal.*

After handing out drinks, I returned to my seat. It was a little surreal to watch them interact so well. I hadn't expected Dane to take my father's disorder in stride—it wasn't every day you watched someone switch from one personality to another. But Dane didn't refer to it or ask any questions. He behaved as if Deacon had been a separate person who'd now vacated the room. Which, in some respects, was kind of how it worked.

"You're coming to the barbecue on Sunday?" Simon asked him once we'd all drained our cups.

Dane nodded. "I am."

"Good. We can talk more then." They stood and shook hands again.

"I'll walk you out," I said to Dane. I wasn't ready to leave yet. Not until I was confident that Simon was okay.

Dane nodded and followed me to the door. Outside, he turned to me.

"Your father has DID?"

"Yes. You've heard of it?"

"A little. How long has he had it?"

"For as long as I've known him." Simon had once told me he believed he'd started dissociating when he was around four or five, but I didn't say that. Dane would only ask *why* he began to dissociate like that, and it didn't seem right to relay the story without Simon's permission.

"Who is Corrine?" asked Dane.

It took effort not to tense. "One of his triggers." That was as much as I was willing to say on that subject for now. "I know you wanted us to talk, but it can wait, right?"

Dane stared hard at me for a long moment, almost as if he was really *seeing* me for the first time or something—it was hard to explain. "It can wait."

"I'll see you tomorrow."

I kept my eyes mostly on my tablet as I made notes while conversation flowed around me in the conference room. Dane had back-to-back meetings all day, and he'd wanted me to be present for most of them. It could be exhausting, but I was used to it.

I could feel his eyes on me, but I didn't look his way. He'd been watching me all day. Watching me like … It was hard to describe. But it was like I'd become some sort of puzzle he wanted to piece together. Or something. I really didn't know. I just knew the whole staring thing was bugging me.

Well, at least it had stopped me from spacing out a few times with worry for my father. Simon had been fine when I finally left him last night, but the nightmares would continue to come while his brain worked through everything he pulled out of his mental vault.

Once the meeting was finally over, Dane quietly informed me that he wanted to speak to me in his office. Oh, grand. Holding back a sigh, I followed him into the spacious room and closed the door. I held my tablet against my chest and crossed my arms.

Dane leaned back against his desk. "I confronted Travis yesterday about the little tale he told you. As I'd expected, he claimed you lied. He tried twisting the situation to make it sound like you were attempting to cause a divide between me and him."

Like there wasn't already a huge divide between them. "How very predictable."

"Indeed. He talked of confronting you. I made it clear that the consequences he'd face would be … dire if he dared to do so. But he may ignore that warning, which is why I went to see you last night; I want you to be prepared in case he does something stupid."

I thought about pointing out that he could have simply relayed the information via phone, but he continued speaking.

"If Travis does confront you, call me immediately."

I nodded. "Okay." It wasn't like I *wanted* to talk to the little prick.

Dane tipped his head to the side. "Had you ever intended to tell me about your father's condition?"

I felt my mouth tighten. He hadn't spoken a word about Simon or what happened last night until now. He hadn't spoken of anything that wasn't work-related, actually. I was glad. It helped me maintain the distance I needed. But I'd known he'd bring it up sooner or later.

"I was going to tell you before the barbecue so that you wouldn't have been confused if one of his alters surfaced," I said.

"Can you tell me about his other alters just in case they decide to say hello?"

It was a reasonable request. "Um, okay. Freddie is eight. It's unlikely that he'll talk to you. He's shy, and he doesn't trust easily." He'd had it the hardest of all the alters, because he'd been the one to suffer the abuse. "Maggie is forty. She's strong and caring and maternal, so she mothers and spoils me. She'll probably say hi to you, and she'll be nice unless you swear. She doesn't like anyone cursing around her."

"Noted. Are there any subjects I should avoid when speaking to them? I don't want to push any buttons for them."

Surprised and grateful that he'd be considerate enough to enquire—which seemed completely out of character for him, really—I replied, "Don't ask about Simon's family or past, and don't mention Corrine."

"All right." Dane pursed his lips. "Who is Corrine?"

I flexed my fingers. The guy was unbelievably tenacious. "My mother."

"Why is she such a trigger for him?"

"They didn't have a good relationship, and it didn't end well," I replied vaguely.

"Deacon said she'd learned her lesson. What did he mean by that?"

And I was done. "That's not important."

"I think it is. What did he mean?"

"You don't need to know," I said, throwing his own words back at him. I didn't say it to be a bitch. I said it because it was true, and I was subtly reminding him that he was just as tight-lipped about *his* personal life.

Dane's eyes narrowed. "You're upset that I didn't elaborate on the things that Travis told you."

"No, I'm not."

He pushed away from the desk and slowly stalked toward me. My pulse quickened, but I didn't let my nerves show. I wouldn't give him the satisfaction.

He stopped mere inches away from me. Those dark, all-knowing eyes flitted over my face. "You've been different. Reserved. You're always the consummate professional at work, but you've been *distantly* professional since I refused to answer your question yesterday."

Okay, it would be fair to say I'd been using my position as a sort of emotional shield to remind myself that our relationship was purely professional. I hadn't really expected Dane to care, let alone mention it.

"I'm not upset," I repeated. "I was annoyed with myself, not you. I should never have asked you to elaborate on what he said. It wasn't my place *to* ask. I just … forgot that for a second. It won't happen again."

"Hmm." Moments of silence ticked by. "I didn't realize until last night just how much I don't know about you, Vienna. You give people just enough information for them to assume they get the general picture." He tilted his head. "You hold a lot inside, don't you?"

"So do you."

"Yes, we're more similar than I ever would have thought."

Um, I wouldn't have described us as "similar," given that—

Knuckles rapped on the door as someone sang, "Knock, knock." It instantly swung open and Jen swanned inside, wearing a beaming smile that faltered when she caught sight of me. "Oh. I'm sorry. When I saw you weren't at your desk, I thought you might be on your break or something," she said to me. "I should have guessed you'd be in here."

I didn't realize I'd tensed until I felt the warm weight of Dane's hand settle on my hip. That warmth seemed to seep into me and melt a little of my unease. She hadn't come to o-Verve in the entire time that I'd worked there, so it was a surprise to see her.

She had his cell number, so what reason did she have to traipse all the way up here? It had to be important.

"I didn't realize you were coming," he said.

Jen looked at him. "I would have called you, but I figured that if I came here, I could kill two birds with one stone." Her eyes slid back to me. "I want to apologize for my rudeness at the gala. It wasn't me. I'm not that bitchy person. I just had an off-night."

"Yeah, Dane told me you claimed it was petty jealousy," I said.

Her lips parted in surprise. Apparently, she hadn't expected him to tell me. She cleared her throat. "Yes. It was silly and immature and I'm sorry. It will *not* happen again."

No, it wouldn't, because I wouldn't stand for it a second time. "Good to know. Apology accepted." Sort of.

"What was the other reason you came?" asked Dane.

"Ah, well, I'm thinking of throwing a surprise birthday party for Kent this year, since it falls on a Saturday," she replied. "Would you be able to make it?"

"It's a few months away, so I'm not sure what my schedule looks like for that weekend. But Vienna could shuffle some things around for me if need be. She and I will be there."

Her smile was somewhat brittle. "Excellent. I could use your help with the planning. You could spare me a few hours here and there, right?"

I almost gaped. She'd obviously never gotten a peek at his calendar. Or she expected him to happily cancel all kinds of meetings just for her.

"I don't have enough free hours to give you," he said. "Vienna's planned events for me in the past. She can help you, if you really need it. But she's as busy as I am, so she doesn't have a lot of spare time either."

Her smile dimmed, and she flicked a hand. "It's fine. I can ask Hope to help. Thank you, though." She shrugged. "Well, bye." With that, she left.

Dane let his hand slip from my hip. "If she does go through with the party—and she probably won't; Jen comes up with ideas all the time but rarely follows them through—she won't manage to keep it a surprise from Kent. He's a hard man to fool."

Then the guy was much like Dane himself. Nothing got past him. I wondered if Kent handled shocks with the same ease as his brother. It still awed me how well Dane rolled with Simon's switch of personality last night. He hadn't even seemed spooked.

I wasn't looking forward to the other Davenports meeting Simon. If one of his alters took the wheel, I doubted they'd all handle it with the same ease and sensitivity—especially Travis. If they made any taunting comment toward my father, I wouldn't need to step in and deal with them. Deacon would do that, and fists would fly for fucking sure.

CHAPTER EIGHT

Sunday afternoon, I blew out a breath when Sam pulled up in front of my foster parents' house. He and Dane had picked me up on the way to the barbecue. A few cars were parked nearby, including Simon's, Ashley's, and—*ugh*—Heather's.

I'd offered to give my dad a ride to the barbecue, but he'd wanted to get there early to help Wyatt set everything up. The two men got along seriously well, and I loved that. Loved that neither felt threatened by my relationship with the other.

I looked at Dane, whose thumbs were tapping away on his phone. I'd never seen him in jeans before. He didn't look any less appealing. Or any less smart, for that matter. That was mainly due to his crisp, white shirt that was open at the collar and flashing a patch of lick-able golden skin. No one should possess that much natural raw masculinity. No one.

He seemed utterly relaxed. But then, of course he was. He wouldn't be feeling the standard "meeting the parents" pressure. It wouldn't matter to him if my family liked him or not. He didn't need it to matter. He only needed them to buy that we were a happy couple.

"We're here," I told him.

He briefly looked up, but his thumbs didn't still. "So I see." A few moments later, he finally pocketed his phone. "You ready?"

"Yes. Are you? Because they're going to quiz you and study you and watch every move you make. And considering you plan to marry me in a few days"—cue stomach roll— "you're going to need to convince these people that you care for me so that the elopement isn't too much of a shock for them."

"You're not telling me anything I don't already know. Now come on, let's go."

"Wait, one more thing. You should know that Melinda and Wyatt's daughter, Heather, is going to flirt with you. Like *a lot*."

He frowned. "Why, when she believes I'm with you?"

"Being a bitch is kind of her thing. She loves to provoke me; gets off on it. No one's going to tell her to stop flirting, because they'll want to see how you react, so just be aware that your response to her will be watched *closely*. If you show the slightest bit of interest in her, they'll write you off as no good for me."

"Understood."

We both exited the car. By the time he'd joined me on my side of the vehicle, his demeanor had changed. Gone was the cool, curt, indifferent male I worked for. In his place was a guy who looked open and easygoing, and I was confident that he'd fool every person waiting to meet him. And that made me feel like utter shit.

I was going to let him play these people—most of whom I cared for. Hell, *I* would be playing them as well. Although I didn't regret that I'd let him take care of the sextortion extravaganza, I often wished he'd called in a different kind of favor.

"Did you ever take acting classes?" I asked him quietly.

He threw me a slight frown. "No."

Slipping into another person's skin apparently just came naturally to him, then.

Having used the front door key that Melinda had long ago given me, I led Dane through the house and out into the backyard. Music played, but it wasn't too loud to override the sounds of chatter, laughter, and the grill spluttering. The warm air was laced with the scents of smoke, beer, charred meat, and the various foods on the patio table.

Simon, Wyatt, and Tucker stood near the grill, deep in conversation. Junior was playing tug of war with Ranger—both were gripping an old frisbee tight. Soaking up a drink spill on the table with a clump of napkins, Melinda talked with her elderly neighbor, Nancy—who often invited herself to her neighbor's get-togethers. Ashley lounged on a chair, sipping soda, nodding along to whatever Melinda was saying. Heather stood off to one side with her friend, Jana, who was just as much of a bitch as Heather. Well, like often called to like.

Melinda spotted us first. Beaming, she dropped the soggy napkins on the table. "There you two are." She crossed to us, pulled me into a hug, and then eyed Dane with a smile. "You're taller than I expected. And just as hot as Ashley told me you were."

I sighed. "Dane, this is Melinda. She'll remember her manners in a few minutes."

Dane's mouth curved. "I'd like to say Vienna talks about you all the time, but it's more like I have to sneakily coax stories out of her."

Melinda nodded. "Our Vienna's not one to entertain people with life stories, but I have plenty about her that I think you'll find *fascinating*."

I groaned. "You promised me you wouldn't do this."

Melinda's brow puckered. "I did?"

"Yes, you did."

"Damn." She looked at Dane. "Well, that's okay. My husband, Wyatt, didn't make that promise, so I'll just tell him to spill it all."

Wonderful.

Wyatt and Simon appeared then. After giving me a hug, my father greeted Dane warmly, more upbeat than he'd been a few nights ago. Wyatt probably would have been a little more reserved if Dane wasn't carrying a large crate of beers—he'd insisted on bringing them along.

Taking the crate, Wyatt smiled at me. "I'm going to like this guy, Vienna, I can tell."

So easily bought. I almost snorted.

Ranger came over and sniffed at Dane hesitantly.

"This is Ranger," I said as Dane held out his hand for the dog to smell him. "Don't be bothered by his size. He's a big softie."

Dane scratched him behind his ear, making Ranger's eyelids droop in pleasure. Well, he'd won over the dog fast enough.

Once we each had a beer bottle in hand, I introduced Dane to Nancy, who declared him a pretty thing and wanted to know if he'd be open to running off with her.

Ashley pushed out of her chair and gave me an air kiss before then greeting Dane. Tucker joined us to say his hellos, his usual polite self. Then goddamn Heather and Jana strolled over, their hips swaying. I had to grit my teeth.

Heather pushed her sunglasses up to her head and flashed him a smile that was *all* sex. "I'm Heather, Melinda and Wyatt's daughter."

Dane only inclined his head, though he didn't come across as rude.

I was kind of impressed that he'd kept his eyes from dropping, considering she'd dressed in a top that was at least two sizes too small, so her boobs were practically spilling out of it. Her skirt was indecently short and super tight.

I wished I could say she looked skanky. She didn't. She pulled the look off well. Which was annoying, because she'd only dressed that way to get Dane's attention. God, the woman was a boil on my ass.

"And I'm Jana," added her sidekick. "Heather's friend."

Again, Dane inclined his head. He also slid closer to me and draped his arm over my shoulders, keeping the side of my body flush to his. It felt both possessive and protective. It also made a silent statement that he wasn't interested in anyone but me. Not that that would stop Heather from throwing herself at him just to wind me up.

His eyes darted to Junior, who was hiding behind Melinda. "And who might you be?"

"Oh, this is my son, Junior." Heather hauled him to her side as if hugging him, but the move was a little too rough. "Say hi to the nice man, Junior."

"Hello," the kid said shyly.

"Ah, Vienna mentioned you," Dane told him. "She said you're her favorite nephew."

Junior's mouth twitched. "I'm her only nephew."

"It still counts."

I didn't fail to notice the way Heather frowned at Junior when he referred to himself as my nephew. She often made a point of stating that we weren't truly related.

She looked at Dane and seemed about to say more, but he turned to Simon, effectively dismissing her. I had to bite back a grin. She'd soon realize that Dane wasn't the easy mark she'd thought he'd be. My boss was used to having women throw themselves at him—he knew how to handle it.

Conversation picked up, and it honestly lightened my heart to see him and Simon get along so well. Wyatt, Simon, and Melinda quizzed Dane under the guise of polite conversation. They asked about o-Verve, his academic background, and where he lived. He expertly dodged some questions but answered others.

I could see they were surprised to hear that he didn't reside in a swanky apartment like many unmarried businessmen his age. Hell, I'd been equally surprised when I first learned he owned a huge house and a large plot of land. My foster parents exchanged a look, both no doubt assuming he'd bought such a home because he had plans to marry and have children. Not exactly, but I wouldn't disabuse them of that theory.

"You're leaving for another business trip tomorrow, right?" Simon asked me.

I nodded. "Yup."

Dane gently fisted the top of my ponytail. "You all packed?"

"Yes, all done. You?"

"Mostly," he replied, lowering his hand and letting my hair slide out of his fist.

Ashley sipped her drink. "Where are you both going?"

"Las Vegas," I told her, smiling when Junior ran around my legs chasing Ranger.

"Vegas, huh?" Her eyes twinkling, Melinda looked from me to Dane. "How long has this trip been in the works?"

Whoa, did she think it was actually a secret elopement rather than a business trip? If so, she was half-right. I pursed my lips. "About six months."

She gave a slow nod. "Ah. Well, try to have some fun while you're there. Don't be all work, work, work. And bring me back a magnet."

"Will do." She was just as bad as me for collecting them. The breeze fluttered over my arms and ruffled my bangs, and I almost shivered.

Dane settled my bangs back into place and asked, "You hungry?"

"Famished," I said.

"Good, because the hot dogs are ready," declared Tucker.

People pretty much descended on the grill before then crossing to the table where the condiments lay.

When I finally bit into the soft bun, tasting the hot dog, onions, and ketchup I'd tucked inside it, I groaned. *Heaven.*

Dane's mouth hitched up. "Good?"

I gestured at his own hot dog. "Find out for yourself."

He took a bite and nodded. "Yeah, it is." He thumbed a drop of ketchup away from the corner of my mouth. "Having fun?"

Heather let out a little squeal as Ed Sheeran's *The Shape of You* began to play. "God, I love this song." And so she started to dance. And I mean *dance.* She put her whole body into it.

She also watched Dane pretty much the entire time.

The only reason I didn't ream her up first one side and then the other was that he wasn't paying her a blind bit of attention. As such, all she was doing was embarrassing herself. I saw no need to put a stop to that.

While we ate, Wyatt decided to tell some of my embarrassing childhood tales—all were light and funny, and none hinted at the fact that my life in this house hadn't always gone swimmingly well. That was good. Because Dane was too sharp not to pick up on any such hints.

My dad chipped in, the traitor, and relayed a few tales of his own about me. No matter how much humor twinkled in Dane's eyes, he never once chuckled. It was almost as though laughter simply wasn't in him, which was far too sad.

Needing to pee, I tugged on his sleeve and leaned into him. "I'm just nipping to the bathroom."

He let his arm slip away from my back. "All right. Want me to get you another beer?"

"Nah, I'm good, thanks." I looked at my father. "Perhaps you could stop with the cringe-worthy stories now."

"I *could*," said Simon, smiling.

I just sighed and headed into the house. When I exited the bathroom after doing my business, Ashley was waiting for me.

She glanced around to make sure we were alone. "I've decided that Hanna could be right about Dane being a psychopath."

I rolled my eyes. "You can't be serious."

"Just hear me out. I've been watching him work this crowd and *wow* he's good. He just slotted in there like a space was already made for him. Psychopaths are good at that. Blending, I mean. They're social chameleons."

I rubbed at my forehead. "Uh-huh."

"He's got this knack for making people talk about themselves—it's impressive. And, my God, the *charm*. It's not a salesman-type charm. He's not talking non-stop, he's *listening*. He focuses so intensely on whoever's talking to him. Makes them feel so interesting."

He did in fact do that.

"And didn't you once tell me that he always seems to pick up on what you're thinking? Well, psychopaths are *masters* at noticing micro-expressions. You know, the lightning-fast changes in our facial muscles?"

I folded my arms across my chest. "How is it you know so much about psychopaths?"

"I looked them up so I could study him for you. He ticks a lot of the boxes."

I let out a heavy breath. "Ashley, he's not a psychopath."

"Why be in denial about it? It doesn't have to be a bad thing. Not all psychopaths kill. Some are very productive members of society."

"Heather's not a productive member."

"She's not a psychopath. She's just a fucking nutjob. I tell ya, I'm surprised her skin hasn't turned a deep shade of green. She's bitter with envy. This makes me very happy."

Just then, my father sidled up to us. "What makes you very happy?" he asked, his voice light and lilting. As I took in the warmth and softness in his expression and the effeminate air he now carried, I knew I wasn't looking at my father.

I smiled. "Hi, Maggie. Enjoying yourself?"

"Oh, I'm enjoying watching you and your new man," said Maggie. "I was hoping that my saying hello would throw him for a loop, but he didn't bat an eyelid. He was very polite and respectful. I like that. And I like how he is with you. He looks at you like you're the only thing worth his attention."

Ashley nodded. "He is totally into you, Vienna. It's the only reason I'm not panicking for you."

Maggie's brow creased. "Why would you panic for her? Oh, you mean because he's a psychopath?"

I felt a growl bubble up my throat. "*Come on,* seriously?" They *had* to have gotten together beforehand and decided to tease me with this crap for their own entertainment.

Maggie shrugged. "What? You don't think we're right? Deacon is convinced of it. But he still likes Dane; likes that you have someone who can protect you. We all do. Even Freddie. He's not ready to meet Dane yet, though. He needs a little time."

"He can have as much time as he needs—there's no rush," I said.

"That's what I told him. Now you go on back to Dane, Vienna. You can't invite someone to a get-together and then leave them on their own for too long—it's rude."

Trust Maggie to care about that sort of thing. I headed out to the backyard … just in time to watch Heather try to pinch Dane's ass.

Nancy swatted her hand. "Have a little pride, Heather. It's so sad when a young lady shows no self-respect."

Anger flickered to life in the pit of my stomach. It was one thing for Heather to flirt like an idiot. It was another for her to try to *touch* him. But I knew why she'd stepped up her game—she hadn't gotten the reaction from me that she'd hoped for. She wanted to piss me off, ruin the day, and force me to make a spectacle of myself in front of my boyfriend by getting into an argument with her.

Not willing to give her what she wanted, I ignored her as I swiped a bowl of chips from the table and crossed to Dane and Wyatt.

Dane's lips kicked up. "You're back. And you're bearing gifts." He took a chip, stuffed it in his mouth, and then splayed his hand on my lower back; it felt like a claim. "I thought you'd gotten lost."

"Ashley and Maggie were feeling chatty." I tossed a chip into my mouth. "What are we talking about?"

"Fishing," replied Wyatt.

Well, then I would not have much to contribute to the conversation. I mostly stayed silent as the two men talked, happy to simply listen and munch on the chips. At one point, Dane loosely curved his arm around my neck and gently tugged me closer. I leaned into him, hoping I looked as content and at ease as I needed to.

When Wyatt walked away to take a call, Dane and I found ourselves alone. Which was nice, because it gave me a short rest from acting. So I almost snarled when Heather came over.

"You'll never guess who I saw a few days ago," she said to me. "Owen. He was coming out of his aunt's house. I would have gone over to say hi, but he left in a bit of a hurry."

Owen wouldn't have given her a second of his time. He loathed Heather with a passion.

"I spoke with his aunt a little," Heather went on. "She said he's getting divorced. Apparently, it was amicable at first, but then his soon-to-be-ex-wife turned all bitter. She and their daughter have gone to stay with her parents in Washington for a while. I'll bet all this makes you feel better about him breaking off your engagement to go marry someone else. It didn't work out so well for him, did it?" She gasped. "Oh, shit, you *have* already told Dane about Owen, haven't you?"

I sensed she thought the answer was a resounding "no." It wasn't surprising that Heather had assumed I wouldn't be forthcoming about my past. She judged people by her own standards, and she wasn't exactly the most honest person when it came to relationships; she wouldn't hesitate to hold back any detail that wouldn't give her the advantage. "Yes, I have," I told her, almost smiling when her act faltered for just a moment.

She faked a sigh of relief. "Oh, good—I was worried I might have said too much." She looked at Dane. "It was such a terrible time for her. And to think he dumped her *over the phone*."

"Yes, I heard." Dane turned to fully face me and pulled me flush against him, drawing us into our own private cocoon to make her feel shut out. "But I'm glad he was dumb enough to let you go, or you wouldn't now be mine." He lifted one of my salt-covered fingers and sucked it into his mouth, licking away the salt; warmth bloomed low in my stomach. "Actually, that's not entirely true," he added. "I would have lured you away from him somehow."

"I'm not so easily lured," I said.

"But I would have managed it," he assured me, pitching his voice low. "Because what do I always get?"

"What you want."

"Exactly, baby girl." He gently tapped the tip of my nose. "Never forget it," he whispered.

Later on, when the temperature cooled and the sun began to set, people started making moves to leave. Nancy left first, swiftly followed by Ashley and Tucker. Simon left soon after.

Not wanting Melinda to have to tackle the clean-up job alone, I crossed to the patio table. "I'll help you trash the left-over food and—" Something crashed into my back, sending me stumbling into the table. The wrought-iron edge dug painfully into my waist.

Worse, my weight made the table sharply tip up like a goddamn seesaw. Bowls and plates flipped and tipped over, and I found my front splattered with sauces, pasta, casserole, potato salad, spicy dips, and chocolate frosting.

For a moment, I just stood there, my lips parted in stunned surprise. Then I heard snickering behind me. I slowly turned to see Heather and Jana giggling like a pair of schoolgirls.

"Oops, I'm *so* sorry," said Heather, her eyes sparkling with devilish delight. "I didn't mean to bump into you like that. Really, are you okay?"

My cheeks burned. Not with embarrassment. With anger. God, I wanted to punch the piss out of her. Wanted to slap that damn smirk off her face, and maybe even stab her with a fork like she'd once done to me.

There's a child a few feet away, there's a child a few feet away, I chanted to myself. Junior was currently napping in his little tent, but it wouldn't be hard to wake him. I wouldn't frighten him by brawling with his mother.

Dane and Melinda stood on either side of me, checking that I was fine and trying to flick away the food that had stuck to my blouse. I only had eyes for Heather, who was still fucking giggling.

There was once a time I'd been afraid of her. Bitterly afraid. But that time had passed. Because when you looked beyond the surface of a bully, you saw them for what they were—a goddamn twisted coward who needed to slap down others just to feel good, and that was plain pathetic.

I lifted my chin a notch and gave her an indulgent smile. "Feel better now?"

Heather's giggle died off. "Excuse me?"

"Well, you've put some major effort into annoying me over the past few hours. Clearly this makes you happy or is good therapy for you or something."

She let out a little huff. "Just because you're embarrassed doesn't mean you need to take it out on me."

"Why? You take your shit out on me. Like *all* the time. Especially if, God forbid, I'm happy. I guess old habits really do die hard, because I can always count on you to make a fool out of yourself."

Her spine snapped straight. "*I'm* the fool? I'm not the one who crashed into a table and got food all over me."

"And I'm not the one who spent the afternoon flirting with a guy in a way that was plainly cringe-worthy. I honestly felt embarrassed for you."

"You little bi—"

"Heather, no," Melinda cut in. "Now, girls, we've all had a really nice day; let's leave this here."

I didn't blame her for not jumping in to defend me—taking sides would only cause things to escalate. I knew that from past experience. And then Heather would punish Melinda by not letting her see Junior for a little while.

Wyatt nodded, but his eyes were hard on his daughter. "Heather, you should take Jana home."

Heather, her face blazing, ignored her parents. "Think you're so much better than me, don't you, Vienna?"

"You make it hard for me not to." More like impossible, actually.

Her nostrils flaring, she tipped her chin at Dane and scoffed. "You think you'll keep him? That he'll seriously stay with *you* when he has actresses and models and heiresses throwing themselves at him all the time? He'll drop you like a bad habit when he's done with you, just like Owen did."

"No, I won't," clipped Dane, his voice cold and sharp as a scalpel. "And if you thought your behavior here today was going to achieve anything other than make you look immature and pathetic, you were wrong."

"Heather, take Jana home," Wyatt ordered. "*Now.*"

"Fine," she snapped. "I'll be back in ten minutes for Junior." She shot me one last glower and then stormed out.

Dane squeezed one of my shoulders. "Wyatt, Melinda—thank you both for having me. I hope to see you again soon. Right now, Vienna and I need to leave."

Yes, we really did.

Distraught, Melinda gave me one of her tees to change into and insisted on keeping hold of my blouse so she could wash out the stains. Wyatt apologized to both me and Dane on behalf of Heather. I assured him, just like I had a gazillion times before, that he didn't need to apologize for her. He'd no doubt always do it, though.

Stepping out of the house, I wasn't surprised to see Sam waiting. Dane had probably summoned him by text or something.

When we were finally in the car heading to my complex, I closed my eyes and let my head tip back. I really need a hot, relaxing bath.

"Does Heather do that often?" asked Dane.

I didn't open my eyes. "Cause scenes? Yep. She's fun, right?"

"She's jealous of you. She resents that Melinda and Wyatt are proud of you. Did you two ever get along?"

It took an effort not to snort. "No."

"Not even when you two were kids?"

Especially not when we were kids, but I didn't want to get into all that. The memories weren't worth revisiting, so I only said, "Not even then."

Silence fell between us, which suited me fine. I was too exhausted to hold a conversation. I let myself drift, listening to the sounds of the car engine purring and the tapping of Dane's thumbs on what was no doubt the screen of his cell phone.

A gentle touch to my arm woke me a short time later.

"You're home," said Dane.

Lifting my head, I sighed. "Well, I'd say we accomplished what we needed to. My father, foster parents, and friends all think you're serious about me." It was a shame that Heather had felt the need to spoil what had otherwise been a perfectly good day. "They also like you."

"Good. I like them. But I don't like that your foster parents don't have a better handle on their daughter. She has the emotional maturity of a fourteen-year-old."

Her pettiness was going to get her into serious trouble one day—especially if she continued pursuing married men. I reached for the door handle, thinking that she'd sooner or later target a man who, like Dane, dealt with his enemies fast and effectively. Someone who wouldn't let her bullshit go unpunished. Someone who …

My thoughts trailed off as something occurred to me. I released the door handle and looked at him. "Dane, you're not going to do anything to Heather, are you?"

He just stared at me, unblinking.

"Tell me you'll let it go."

His brow creased. "I've told you before, I'd never tolerate a verbal attack on someone who belonged to me. It would be seen as out of character for me to *let it go,* as you put it."

My stomach sank. "She's Melinda and Wyatt's daughter."

"I'm aware of that." And he clearly didn't give a hot shit.

"Anything that hurt her would hurt them. What she did today … it wasn't that big of a deal."

His dark eyes flared. "She insulted you. She provoked you. She tried to humiliate you."

She'd done worse in the past. "And all she did was humiliate herself. Dane, you have to let it go. If you do something to punish her in some way, she won't be upset, she'll be *thrilled.* Because it means she can run straight to her parents with news that will turn them against you, hoping it will also turn them against me."

"They'd never turn on you."

"Probably not. But they'd be pissed if I didn't care that my boyfriend had retaliated against their daughter, and she'd *love* that they were pissed at me. All she's ever wanted is to get me out of the picture. Please don't give her the ammunition to do it."

I held my breath as he stared at me, his gaze inscrutable.

Long moments later, he said, "I'll let it go. This one time. If she does anything else, I *will* deal with it. Nothing you say will sway me from that."

Swallowing, I nodded, knowing it was the best deal I'd get. "I'll see you tomorrow."

"Tomorrow."

And then we'd go to Vegas and get married. Wasn't that ultra-special.

CHAPTER NINE

Placing my small suitcase on the floor beside the front door, I slipped on my shoes. Dane had texted me to let me know that he was outside. When it came to business trips, I usually met him at the airport. We were apparently deviating from our normal routine. Maybe he didn't trust that I wouldn't back out of the trip or something.

God, I was gonna hurl at some point. My stomach was all queasy and fluttery, and the sensations worsened each time I thought about the wedding. I'd gone from dreading it to wishing the time would fly by faster. The sooner it was over and done with, the sooner things would get back to … well, as normal as they were going to be when I was fake married to my boss. The marriage certificate was the only thing about it that would be real.

Grabbing my purse and suitcase, I left the apartment, took the elevator down to the first floor, and then headed outside to where the car waited. Sam took my suitcase and put it in the trunk while I slipped into the rear of the car.

I flashed a smile at the man sitting a few feet away from me. "Hi."

Dane looked up from his phone, and his gaze flitted over my face. His brow creased. "You're tired." He said it like it offended him.

"I didn't have a great night's sleep." I would have made a joke about pre-wedding jitters if the privacy screen had been up.

Before long, we arrived at the airport and boarded his jet. He spent most of the flight working. I did a little work myself followed by some reading, intent on distracting myself from the upcoming wedding.

Soon enough, the jet touched down in Vegas. A luxury, chauffeured car picked us up from the airport and drove us to the opulent hotel that was a favorite of Dane's. After checking into his suite, we ordered room service and then ate dinner while going over some business matters.

In the past, I'd occasionally sat with Dane in his hotel suite while we discussed work, but I'd always returned to my own room to sleep. This time, however, my room wasn't on another floor. It was in his suite, which was big enough that we both had our privacy and wouldn't get in each other's way.

The bed proved to be comfy as hell, but I woke early after yet another annoyingly restless sleep. Fortunately, I didn't look as haggard as I felt.

I could never eat first thing in the morning as my stomach always felt unsettled so, as usual, I first showered, dressed, slapped on some makeup, and styled my hair.

Walking into the dining area a short while later, I found an array of foods spread out on the table. Dane was already there—clean, dressed, alert, and delicious—reading something on his tablet, a plate in front of him on which only a few crumbs lay. He greeted me with a mere raise of his eyebrows before going back to whatever he was reading.

Once I'd eaten a light breakfast during which I scanned both my emails and his, I made my way to the tall window. I felt a smile curve my mouth. I'd gotten a load of the Las Vegas strip before, but the view never got old. It honestly took my breath away every time.

Hopefully we'd get to explore the place a little while here. It wouldn't happen today, though. No, this day would be an eventful one that consisted of two conferences, a business lunch, an industry dinner where he'd make a speech, and then an after-reception during which we'd eat, talk, smile for photographers, and fake the fuck out of our relationship.

"Vienna?"

It really was not fair that that deep, rumbly voice could twist my insides. I turned to see him fluidly stalking toward me, all dark and broody and sinful.

"Put your hand out," he said.

I did so, and he placed a sleek platinum ring on my palm that boasted a sparkling princess cut diamond. I sucked in a breath. "Wow. It's …" Gorgeous. Stunning. Elegant. "Not as subtle as I'd hoped," I finished, not wanting to make a fuss in case he thought I'd gotten swept away in the moment and forgotten that this wasn't real. I never let myself forget that anymore.

"I told you, I don't do subtle."

"I didn't think you were giving this to me until tomorrow."

"The story will be that I proposed this morning, so you need to start wearing it now. But don't mention to anyone that we're getting married tomorrow—you're not supposed to know yet; it's supposed to be something I spring on you."

I nodded. "Gotcha." I slipped it on my finger, surprised my hands weren't trembling. "It fits."

"Of course it fits," he said, seeming offended that I'd assume he'd struggle to correctly guess my ring size. "From now on, you wear this wherever you go."

Well, shit just got serious. "Can I make the story of your proposal all romantic?"

"Only if you don't want it to sound realistic."

I snickered. "Okay, let's just keep it simple and say you slipped it on my finger while I was half asleep, informed me that we're getting married, and then told me I wasn't ever allowed to take the ring off?"

He pursed his lips. "People would buy that."

Admiring the platinum band once again, I found myself recalling the last time I'd worn a ring on this finger. The one Owen bought me had been cheap and cheerful—all he was able to afford back then. But I hadn't cared, because it hadn't been about the ring; it had been about what it represented—that he loved me and wanted to forever be with me. Or so I'd thought.

Now here I was wearing another ring. It was pristine. Sparkly. Breathtaking.

And meaningless.

I felt a momentary pang of sadness. The ring didn't really belong on my finger. It didn't signify that there was someone who loved and was committed to me. It was just a prop.

"What's wrong?"

Wiping all emotion from my face, I lifted my head. "Not a thing. I'm just bowled over by the level of bling."

That steady, unblinking stare narrowed on me. "Hmm."

Hoping to distract him, I was about to ask how much the ring cost, but then he spoke again.

"I want you to move in with me this weekend. No later than Sunday."

My lungs seemed on the verge of seizing up. I coughed. "I don't think I can make it happen that soon, Dane. I'll need time to pack everything. I won't get home until Thursday, and I'll be at work on Friday. There's no real rush, is there?"

"Travis is going to go into a blind panic when he hears we're married. He'll step up his game in an effort to make you divorce me. He already showed up at your building once. The security around my home is tight, so he can't pester you there. Plus, I'm possessive of what belongs to me, and I have enough control issues that I'd want my wife close—my family knows that about me."

Well, at least he was honest. "You don't lack in self-insight, do you?"

"A person should always be self-aware if they wish to succeed in life. Knowing your strengths and blind spots is important."

True. "Back to the whole me-moving-into-your-house thing, what about all my stuff?"

He sank into the nearby sofa and draped his arms over the back of it, claiming the space in that dominant-male way of his. "I have storage space you can use to store anything you don't wish to place in the room I've allocated you. It has all the furnishings it needs. But if you'd rather put your own things in there, it's not a problem."

I shrugged. "I'm not fussed about furniture."

"Then yours can be stored in my outhouse with anything else you don't want to keep close at hand."

I nodded, biting my lip. Although it made sense for me to move into his house, I wasn't looking forward to it. For one thing, I liked to have my own territory. A space where I could relax and unwind and just … be. It wouldn't be so easy to do that in a place where I was pretty much a lodger.

Also, I'd miss my apartment. As I'd told him, it wasn't anything special, but it was my home. And it sucked balls that I wouldn't be able to go back there after the divorce. If I continued paying the rent, the landlord *might* agree to hold it for me, but it was highly unlikely. Even if he did agree to it, I couldn't really do such a thing. It would look odd to my family and friends that I was reluctant to give up the apartment.

"You knew this would happen at some point, Vienna. I made it clear in the beginning that you'd need to move in with me eventually."

"I know. I was just thinking that there's no way I'll be able to keep my apartment on hold. I really like that building. I like being close to my friends."

"If you keep the apartment, people might think you're not 100 percent sure of me, in which case it would look strange that you'd so readily agreed to marry me this soon. Or they'd wonder if this relationship is truly real. It's the sort of thing Travis and Hope will look into, because they'll want to believe that this is all a lie and they'll be desperate to find proof. She's as greedy and money-centered as he is."

"Travis wouldn't have warned me away from you if he didn't believe the relationship was real."

"But he'll be suspicious when he hears how quickly we got married, especially because it will suit him to think this isn't the real deal." Dane tapped his fingers on the top of the sofa. "I'll hire a crew to help you pack your things so that you'll be ready to move in this weekend. Then the pressure is off you. All right?"

I gave him a stiff nod and rolled back my shoulders. Shit, everything seemed to be suddenly moving at hyper-speed, and I was struggling to emotionally keep up.

"Wishing you hadn't gotten yourself into this situation, Vienna?"

I narrowed my eyes at the amusement in his tone. "How did you handle the situation with my ex?"

"The one who tried to blackmail you?"

"Yes. You were delightfully vague when I originally asked."

He twisted his mouth. "You really want to know?"

"Yes, I do."

His gaze intense on mine, he stood and crossed to me, stopping on the boundary of my personal space. "I gave him the beating of his fucking life, and I didn't stop until he told me the location of every copy of that video he made. I erased them all, and I ensured he understood that if he were to bother you ever again in any capacity, the beating he'd just received would be nothing compared to what I'd then do to him."

I felt my lips part. "You … really?"

His brow lifted. "You're shocked?"

Well, yeah. I wasn't surprised that he was capable of such violence, just that he'd been bothered enough by what happened to actually *want* to hand my ex his ass. Plus … "I wouldn't have thought you'd chance that he'd try to have you arrested."

"He wouldn't have done that for fear that he'd be reported for making the video and trying to blackmail you. And if he had called the police, it wouldn't have gotten him anywhere—I'd have had an airtight alibi."

Oh, I didn't doubt it. The ruthless shit always had his bases covered.

He checked his watch. "We'll need to leave for the conference soon."

"First, I'll need to tell my family that you proposed."

His brows knitted together. "It can't wait until later?"

"I wouldn't have waited if this were real. I would have wanted to share my excitement with them."

"All right. Get it done."

"They're going to ask if we've set a date for the wedding. So will anyone who sees this ring."

"We'll just say we haven't finalized anything yet."

I nabbed my phone from my purse, intending to tell Simon first. I bit my lip, a little nervous of how he'd take the news. He liked Dane, so it would probably be fine. The alters would warn me if there was a problem.

I snapped a picture of the ring and texted it to Simon, adding the comment: *Look what Dane slipped on my finger while I was sleeping—he won't let me take it off.*

Simon called me mere seconds later, excited and full of questions. I put him on speakerphone so that he could pass on his congratulations to Dane, who thanked him and assured him that, yes, he did in fact know he was a lucky man. It took everything I had not to snort.

After I sent the same message to Melinda, Dane and I then had pretty much the same phone conversation with her and Wyatt. The process was then repeated with Ashley, who was at work so kept it short. I also passed the news on to Hanna, who squealed over the phone.

I then posted the picture on both mine and Dane's personal social media accounts—it was part of my job to manage his. I didn't wait to read people's comments. I simply returned my phone to my purse. "There. Done. It won't be long before your family starts calling to either complain or pass on their congratulations."

Blowing out a long breath, I rubbed my chest. My heart felt heavy. My family and friends were so happy for me, so supportive and excited … and I was lying through my wisdom teeth. They didn't deserve the deception. It made me feel like one sorry piece of shit, but I kept the guilt from showing on my face, not wanting to—

"You've no reason to feel guilty, Vienna."

But I did need to be concerned that I was in the presence of a fucking warlock.

"If your family knew all the details, if they understood why you owed me a favor and why you had to lie to them, they'd get it. But they can't know. No one can."

"I know. And they probably would understand. That doesn't make me feel any better about deceiving them." But I didn't expect him to get that. It was abundantly clear that he felt no such guilt for fooling his own family.

I thought about asking if it would have bothered him to lie to Hugh, but I bit back the question. It was too personal. It wasn't my business.

"Come on, we have a busy day ahead. Tomorrow will be even busier."

It would indeed. God, to think I'd be married tomorrow. *Married.* Yet not. Because it was only paperwork.

I took a deep breath, telling myself it was no big deal. Actors got married onscreen all the time. This was really no different. Except that the officiant who married us would be a *real* officiant. And that I'd have to *lie* to him, just as I was lying to everyone else.

I groaned. "I'm going to hell." At least I had an "in" with its supreme ruler, having worked for him for four years. Still … "I should have said no to all this."

"It wouldn't have mattered if you had. I told you once before, I would have pressed you until you agreed. Now let's get moving. It's going to be a long day."

He hadn't been wrong. The hours *dragged* on. I couldn't count the number of times I heard the word "congratulations." People gave me hugs, slapped Dane lightly on the back, asked when the big day was, and shamelessly tried to get themselves an invitation to the wedding.

A few commented on how quickly he'd proposed, and I could see they assumed I was pregnant. Each time, Dane shrugged and said, "*I always move fast when going after what I want.*" I merely claimed it didn't feel fast to me because we'd known each other so long and had secretly been dating for a while.

When photographers snapped pictures of us at the after-reception, I said to Dane, "Those photos will probably be posted online."

Standing close to me with his arm curled around my waist, he put his mouth to my ear, making the tiny hairs there stand on end. "I know. And they'll be posted very quickly, due to that ring on your finger."

He was often featured in online magazines for one reason or another. And now I probably would be, too. How lovely.

The urge to chug down my champagne hit me hard, but I sipped at it instead. Honestly, I was a little tipsy. Breathing in Dane's dark cologne didn't help—it seemed to give off seriously potent pheromones. Or maybe that was just the man himself.

Each time he touched me, whispered in my ear, or played his fingers through my loose hair, I came that much closer to melting into him. My body practically throbbed with need. The air around me felt electrically charged, but it was more than obvious that he wasn't similarly affected. If I hadn't had four years-worth of practice at standing strong against the one-sided chemistry, I'd be close to trembling with the power of it. Sometimes, it almost felt like the sensual ever-present hunger had settled so deep into every cell of my body that I'd never escape it.

I needed to put a little space between us and give myself a reprieve, but he didn't seem inclined to let me move. He never let me out of his sight. He had the role of possessive fiancé down to a tee.

"Has any of your family members called you yet?" I asked.

"My brothers did. Travis claimed to be thrilled for me, but he's not as good a liar as he believes he is."

"What did Kent say?"

"He's pleased for me, but he's concerned that I'm moving too fast."

"Well, you are."

"I'm moving at *my* speed. It's not my issue if other people like to hem and haw over things."

I sensed it truly didn't bother him that his brothers weren't 100 percent behind him. On the one hand, I was pleased he wasn't upset. On the other hand, it was kind of sad that he could be so aloof about it.

It was past 1 a.m. when we returned to our suite. He was already back in work-mode, his attention fixed on his phone, so I bid him a quick goodnight and headed to my room. I was just kicking off my shoes when my cell phone rang. I cursed, because the only people who'd call me at such a late hour were my dad or one of his alters.

Hoping to God there was nothing wrong, I quickly grabbed my cell. Frowning at the sight of an unfamiliar number, I nonetheless swiped my thumb over the screen and answered, "Hello?"

"What the fuck, Vee? You're engaged to Davenport? Seriously?"

I stilled. "How did you get this number?"

"Tell me it's a fucking joke," clipped Owen. "Tell me you don't intend to marry him."

"Why would it be a joke?"

"Vee, you've worked for him for years. You know that man's dead inside. He feels nothing. *Nothing.* You'd marry someone who doesn't, and never will, care for you?"

"You've met him twice. You don't know him."

"I don't need to know him to be sure that he's cold right down to his soul. Anyone can see it. I don't understand how you could possibly miss it. You're one of the most observant people I know."

"Then maybe you should consider that you're wrong about him."

"No, Vee, I'm not wrong. He's never going to be or give you what you need."

I bristled. "You don't know what I need. You knew me well once. Not now. Not anymore."

"Wrong, Vee. I know that being Simon's emotional caretaker hasn't been easy on you. I know that having your mother abuse and abandon you fucked with your ability to trust. I know that you blame yourself for what Deacon did all those years ago. And I know that you didn't really find stability with Melinda and Wyatt because Heather kept shitting all over it. You've never felt that the ground was solid beneath you."

I closed my eyes and swallowed hard, hating that he was right.

"If you think you're going to get that from Davenport, you're wrong, Vee. You'll get financial stability from him, but not emotional stability, because he's never going to make you feel loved. Ever."

My gut twisted. Which wasn't good, because I shouldn't care that Owen was right about that.

"Work will always come first to him, and you deserve someone who'll put you first. Why else do you think I broke up with you? It wasn't just because I was selfishly set on pursuing my own goals. I knew I wasn't giving you what you needed. The long-distance relationship wasn't working for you. You hated it."

He was right, I had. Not just because being away from him was hard and I'd missed him, but because he'd called less and less, and those calls had become shorter and shorter. I'd felt him slipping away, and I'd felt helpless to stop it happening.

"But you never would have said anything, because you wanted me to succeed; you wouldn't risk that I'd drop out of college to stay with you. So *I* ended us. I had to do it over the phone because I knew I'd never be able to make you believe it if I'd done it face-to-face; you'd have known I was lying."

The sincerity in his voice was impossible to ignore. He meant it. Meant every word. Once upon a time, that would have mattered. But it was too late. "None of this is relevant now."

"Wrong again, Vee. I couldn't give you what you needed back then. I can now."

The cell was snatched from my hand. I whirled, my heart jumping. Dane stood there, his jaw hard, his shoulders tense.

He put the phone to his ear. "Who is this?"

It was quiet enough in the suite that I heard Owen's sharp intake of breath. "*Put Vienna back on the phone,*" he finally said.

"Who is this?" repeated Dane, though I suspected he knew. "If you're going to have the balls to call my fiancée in the middle of the fucking night, you can at least tell me who you are."

There was a long moment of silence. "*Owen Redford.*"

"Ah, yes, I remember you. Vienna's childhood friend."

"*We were more than that.*"

"Yes, *were* being the key word. You're nothing to her now."

"*What, because you proposed to her? You can't erase the kind of history me and Vienna have. We've known each other since—*"

"I said, you're nothing to her now," Dane calmly repeated. "You had her. You lost her. Now I have her, and I intend to keep her."

Owen barked a laugh. "*You'll never manage to hold Vienna. You might have her fooled into thinking you care for her, but it won't last long. She's not stupid. To you, that ring is just a corporate brand that states she belongs to you. She'll realize that soon enough. When she does, she'll leave you.*"

"Are you finished?" asked Dane.

"*Actually—*"

"You're finished. Believe what you want about me—I don't give a fuck. Just stay away from my fiancée. You don't want to cross me on this, Redford. I can make your life uncomfortable in ways you can't imagine. It's not something I'd enjoy doing for the simple reason that you aren't important enough to matter. But I'll do it in a heartbeat if you don't do the smart thing and keep your distance from Vienna. So be smart." With that, Dane hung up. He looked at me, his dark eyes blazing. "How did he get your number?"

"Not from me. His boss's PA has it. Owen could have gotten it from her."

Dane handed me back my cell. "Block his number. If he tries to contact you again, I want to know about it." His brow furrowed. "What did he say that put that expression on your face?"

"What expression?"

"You look like someone ran over your puppy."

"It's just sad that someone I once considered a close friend has no issue with trying to end what he believes is my current relationship. I would never have done that to him." And because I *really* didn't like that it had hurt to be reminded that Dane didn't truly care for me. That wasn't supposed to matter.

"He's not doing it to hurt you. He's doing it because he's jealous and bitter. He wants you to doubt me so that you'll return my ring and walk away."

"Yeah, I get that. But it's still sad."

"What did you do with the ring he gave you?"

"I put it in an envelope and slipped it through his aunt's mail slot. She doesn't live very far from me." I forced a smile. "Don't worry, I'll give this one back to you in person."

"I don't expect you to give it back to me. It's yours."

I almost jerked back. "It's a prop. An expensive prop."

"That I'll have no use for, so you might as well have it."

"And do what with it?"

He shrugged and walked toward the door as he replied, "Keep it. Sell it. Gift it to someone. Whatever. Your ring, your choice."

"How much did it cost?" Because something told me I could probably feed a small country with it.

"Not much."

Oh, I doubted that. Just as he went to leave the room, I called out, "Dane?"

Sighing, he threw me an annoyed glance over his shoulder. "I have things to do, Vienna."

What a snippy little shit. He did that sometimes if he had work on his mind—went from civil to frustrated in an instant, wishing to be alone.

I *was* going to thank him for letting me keep the ring, but now the idea of pricking at his patience seemed far more appealing. "I just wanted to say … if you hear any noises in here, there'll be no need to investigate."

He frowned. "What kind of noises?"

Hiding a smile, I answered, "Oh, vibrating. Gasping. Moaning. Whimpering. That sort of thing."

He flexed his fingers, snaring me with that relentless stare. Then he shook his head and sighed as he walked out. "Only you, Vienna. Only you."

Snickering to myself, I began to get undressed.

CHAPTER TEN

I'd never really given much thought into what kind of wedding I might one day have. I hadn't envisioned a certain style of dress or a particular kind of venue. But in ordinary circumstances, I doubted I'd have chosen to pledge my vows in front of an ordained Elvis impersonator. These circumstances, however, were far from ordinary. The bride and groom were far from loved-up. And the setting of the ceremony therefore seemed far from important.

Standing before Elvis in the very pretty chapel, I wasn't nervous anymore. On the drive here, I'd felt on the verge of jumping out of my skin and I hadn't been able to stop plucking at my pretty sundress. But now that the ceremony was actually happening, I had the insane urge to laugh.

I mean, I was marrying my boss … in front of Elvis … who kept belching … so Dane kept sighing … and my nose was filled with the smell of onions because Elvis's loud burps *reeked* of them. Each belch echoed throughout the chapel. Sometimes he paused to mutter "excuse me" beneath his breath while other times he managed to talk *through* the burps and didn't miss a beat. It was all just surreal.

I was *so* glad that Dane had insisted on having the ceremony recorded, because this was too precious not to share.

I snuck a quick look at him. His jaw was hard as he stared at poor Elvis, evidently pissed. Dane wasn't the type to appreciate the funny side of such a situation, especially considering it was a wedding ceremony—one he'd paid to make happen. This had to be the only time I'd ever witnessed him bite back his words. He was not a man who held his tongue, and he genuinely looked as if it pained him to do it.

I might not have felt so desperate to chortle if I wasn't aware that I absolutely could *not* laugh right now. The pressure of holding it in only made things worse, as did the way Dane kept giving me the stink eye, warning me not to dare crack up. I'd always had a nervous laugh; it had gotten me into trouble in the classroom more times than I could count.

I tightened my hold on the platinum masculine wedding band in my palm, as if it could give me the strength that I needed to keep my composure. He'd given the ring to me before we left the hotel, and I'd been terrified that I'd drop it somewhere. "*Showtime*," he'd then said.

Yes, it was a show. And I was one of the main stars. Now I needed to play my part. And I was trying really, *really* hard to do it well and keep from laughing, but I wasn't sure I'd be successful at it for much longer.

Elvis belched again.

Dane sighed again.

A snicker popped out of me before I could stop it. I quickly clamped my lips together. Dane shot me another cautioning look, and I almost choked on the laugh that was now stuck in my throat. I held it in, but my shoulders shook, and my body quaked.

Elvis didn't once acknowledge my struggle. I supposed he'd long ago mastered the ability to keep on going, no matter what was happening. Either that or he was simply so embarrassed he'd rather pretend everything was fine.

Feeling my eyes tear up, I slowly lifted my bouquet and hid behind the flowers. God, my stomach hurt, and it felt like my sides were splitting.

The more I told myself it wasn't *that* funny, the harder I wanted to laugh. I practically wheezed out my vows. Tears were pooling in my eyes again when it came time for us to exchange rings. Dane took that moment to cast me a droll "you cannot be believed" look that made a snort bubble up inside me.

I slid the masculine wedding band on his third finger, and he slid a more feminine version onto mine. It was beautiful and shiny and fit perfectly … but it sadly did not help me pull myself together.

Finally, I sensed the ceremony coming to an end. I didn't think I'd ever felt so relieved about anything in a long, long time.

"I now pronounce you man and wife," said Elvis, gurgling the last word since it came out on yet another smelly belch … to which Dane shot him a hard, pained look.

And that was it. I lost it. The laugh shook my shoulders as I bent over, my eyes tearing up again, and practically shoved my face in the bouquet.

Dane sighed. "Finished?"

Not even close. I was worried I might actually pee. But I forced myself to stand upright and knuckled away a fresh tear. "Sorry," I croaked.

He hauled me close and lowered his mouth to mine. I was entirely unprepared for the hum of electricity that swept over me, or for the soft growl that rattled his throat. His tongue sank inside and licked at mine, bold and demanding.

Amusement gave way to need—*so much need.* It was raw and carnal and took away my willpower. I clung to him, wanting more.

A throat cleared, and we pulled back. So much for a chaste kiss. Well, if he'd been aiming to cut off my laugh he'd succeeded.

A little dazed, I blinked and forced my hands to release his shirt.

A woman appeared with a camera. "Congratulations, Mr. and Mrs. Davenport."

Mrs. Davenport. I'd be Vienna Davenport for twelve freaking months. God, it felt weird.

The photographer snapped a picture of us, and then that was it. We were done. Married. *Married.*

Once we'd collected a few copies of the photo and the thumb drive on which the video of our ceremony had been downloaded, we headed outside.

"That was not how I envisioned the wedding would go," I said, trying to stifle a smile.

Dane gave me the side-eye. "You mean the fact that you laughed almost all the way through it?"

"Come on, you have to admit it was funny. Wait, I forgot, you don't have a sense of humor." I paused. "So, what now?"

"Well, we can either go back to our hotel suite or hit a few casinos?"

I pursed my lips. "Casinos? I'm game. But we should probably call my family first."

"We might as well do it here in front of the chapel. They'll feel better that you called them straight away with the news."

I called my father first, surprised at how well he took it. He congratulated us, and I could sense he wholeheartedly meant it. I heard a note of disappointment in his voice that told me he was sad to have not been present, but he didn't come out and say it.

Wyatt, on the other hand, had no problem voicing his disappointment when I called him and Melinda. She wasn't so annoyed. In fact, she claimed that both she and Ashley had suspected Dane and I would marry while in Vegas. Wyatt, slightly appeased on hearing that we had a recording of the ceremony, eventually joined Melinda in passing on his congratulations.

Dane and I then had a group call with Ashley and Hanna, who proclaimed their delight, but I detected in her voice that Ashley seemed a little uneasy—probably at how fast things were moving.

Ending the call, I asked Dane, "Are you going to call your family?"

"No," he replied. "But I'll send my brothers a picture of us standing here outside the chapel. Make sure your rings are visible." He snapped a picture of us and then sent it to them.

Kent called him immediately and seemed genuinely pleased for us. Travis sent Dane a congratulatory text that was no doubt fake as hell.

Dane splayed a hand on my back. "Now that that's out of the way, let's go amuse ourselves."

We were back in San Francisco by 2 p.m. the next day. Sam and Dane dropped me off at my complex. As I wheeled my suitcase toward my apartment, I cricked my neck. I'd fallen asleep during the flight home in an awkward position, and my neck was now stiff as hell.

Reaching my front door, I fished my keys out of my purse and went to insert my key in the lock. It was only then I noticed it had been busted. My heart slammed in my chest. I pushed at the door without thinking, and it slowly swung open. I caught a glimpse of an unholy mess, and my pulse went crazy.

Backing away, I fumbled in my purse, pulled out my phone, and quickly called the police.

"9-1-1, what's your emergency?" a female voice answered.

I licked my lips, feeling my breathing speed up. "I just came home and … I think someone broke into my apartment. I don't know if they're still in there."

Oh, shit, what if they hadn't left yet? What if they were armed?

"Ma'am?" a voice said. "*Ma'am?*"

I snapped back to attention, realizing I hadn't absorbed a single word she'd said. I rattled off my address. "Tell whoever you send that I'll be in my neighbor's apartment. 5D."

After she assured me an officer would be with me shortly, I hung up and knocked on Ashley and Tucker's door.

Ashley answered, a dishtowel slung over her shoulder. She grinned. "Well, hey Mrs. Davenport …" Her face fell. "What is it, Vienna?"

"Someone broke into my apartment."

She grabbed my arm and drew me inside, closing her front door behind us. "Did you call the police?"

I nodded. "They're sending someone."

"Good." She led me to her sofa. "Sit down here, honey. Tucker!" she shouted at the direction of the bedroom before sitting beside me. "Everything's going to be fine," she soothed, rubbing my arm.

Tucker came striding into the room, his hair wet. "What are you yelling for, woman?"

"Someone broke into Vienna's apartment," she replied.

"*What?* Have you called the police?"

"Yes, she has; someone's on their way." Ashley turned back to me. "Did you call Dane?"

I blinked. "No."

"You need to, Vienna. Do it now," she urged.

Still in a bit of a daze, I brought up his number and tapped "Call."

He answered after only a few rings. "Yes?"

I swallowed around a dry throat. "Dane." That was all that came out.

"What's wrong?" he asked, a sharp edge to his voice.

"I think someone burgled my apartment." It all felt a little surreal.

He cursed under his breath. "Do *not* go in there." He ordered Sam to turn the car around.

"I'm okay, I'm with Ashley and Tucker."

"Which apartment?"

"5D. It's next to mine."

"Stay with them, I'll be right there." He rang off.

I looked at Ashley. "He's on his way. Did you hear any noises coming from my apartment today or last night?"

"I didn't hear anything at all today," she replied. "We were at my sister's house last night. She threw a party and offered for us to use the spare bedroom. Tucker, stay with Vienna while I make us all a drink."

The gentle giant sat at my side, asking me questions about my trip and the wedding—trying to keep me distracted, I knew. And I appreciated the effort, but it didn't work well. It didn't exactly slip a person's mind that they'd had a break-in.

A break-in.

Yeah, this kind of shit happened to people every day. I was well-aware of that. But you never expected it to happen to you. Or at least I hadn't.

My complex had decent security measures, but no building was truly impenetrable. Plus, people exiting the complex often held open the door for anyone waiting outside to enter, even if they weren't *positive* said person was a resident.

Ashley set hot drinks on the coffee table. "I'm surprised you didn't go home with your new husband."

"I need to start packing my stuff. He wants me to move in this weekend." I rubbed at my temple. "I'll need to call our landlord. He's on vacation right now in—" I cut off as the intercom buzzed.

"That'll probably be Dane," said Tucker, who then strode to the panel on the wall. "I doubt the police got here this fast."

It turned out Tucker was right.

Soon enough, Dane was prowling into the apartment, looking as dark and dominant and dangerous as always. Crouching in front of me, he settled one hand on my thigh and curved the other around my nape. "You okay, baby girl?"

I nodded numbly.

"What happened?" he asked, massaging the back of my neck.

I took a shaky breath. "I went to unlock the door and realized the lock was busted. I pushed the door open, saw the mess inside, and backed away."

A muscle in Dane's cheek flexed. "Where the fuck are the police?"

"On their way," I replied.

"Takeout food usually gets here quicker than the police do," muttered

Tucker. "I'd say the intruder's long gone. These walls are thin, but we didn't hear anyone moving around in there today. The burglary probably happened last night while we were at Ashley's sister's place."

"You should talk to the neighbor on your other side," Dane advised me.

"She's a little old lady whose hearing went to shit years ago," I informed him. "But we can still ask if she heard or saw anything."

"The police will do that." Ashley puffed out a breath. "Thank God you weren't home last night, Vienna. I know you're probably feeling angry and sick to your stomach, but whatever they took can be replaced. *You* can't be."

As she left to make Dane coffee, he settled on the sofa beside me and slid his arm around my shoulders. He didn't say anything to comfort me. Didn't need to. I felt better just having him, all solid and strong and steady, right there with me. Which was dangerous. Worrying. Annoying.

Soon, Ashley returned and went into a full-blown rant about how many "thieving little bastards" roamed the streets these days. It was during that that the police finally arrived.

The officer who took my statement was sharp, respectful, and thorough. He also seemed a little intimidated by Dane, who stayed beside me while I was questioned, watching the officer with that unblinking stare.

"What happens now?" asked Dane.

Officer Griffin straightened in his seat. "We'll look for fingerprints and footprints, conduct some door to door enquiries, and check the footage from the building's security cameras. If we're lucky, we might be able to ID the culprit. But I can't say I'm hopeful. We've had a string of burglaries in the area recently—the thieves have been careful not to leave evidence of themselves behind." He looked at me. "I'd like it if you could walk through your apartment with me and tell me what you think is missing."

"I'm coming with her," Dane declared.

Griffin nodded. "That's fine."

Still feeling somewhat dazed, I followed Griffin into my apartment. As I got my first look at the mess that the burglar had left behind, I wanted to cry. There wasn't a lot of damage, mostly just pure chaos. But the things littering the floor were *my* things. They might simply be books, cosmetics, clothes, and cushions, but they had value to me.

"Looks like they were going to take the TV but then struggled to carry it," mused Griffin.

I had to agree. The widescreen TV had been taken off the wall but then dumped a few feet away with wires still attached to it. It was possible that it had been accidentally dropped, because there was a long crack running through the screen.

"Do you have any other electronics that might have been taken?" Griffin asked me. "Laptops? Tablets? Phones? Video consoles?"

"I had my laptop, tablet, and phone with me during my trip," I replied. "I don't own a video console."

With Dane close behind me, I continued walking through my apartment, checking every room, almost choking on anger.

"All the obvious places that someone might hide money have been searched," said Dane, peering into my open sock drawer, which had quite clearly been rummaged through.

"I don't hide clumps of cash in my apartment."

Griffin settled his hands on his belt. "What about credit cards? Your passport? Any other forms of ID?"

"I took my passport, driver's license, and credit cards with me to Vegas." I yanked open my closet door, and my heart sank. "Looks like whoever broke in thought they could sell my clothes." Bundles of it were missing, including the gown I wore to the gala. Several pairs of my shoes were gone, along with some bags and purses. I hissed out a breath.

"What about firearms?" asked Griffin. "Do you own any that could have been taken?"

"No. My large suitcase is missing. It was probably used to carry most of what had been stolen." Glancing at the pretty porcelain bowl on my vanity desk, I sighed. "My cheap jewelry is gone." None of the pieces had been real gold or silver—just accessories for me to wear while clubbing so I didn't have to worry about losing them.

I took my keys from my purse, pushed aside my nightstand, and bent down to the plug socket there.

"What are you doing?" asked Dane.

I didn't answer. I inserted a key into the top right earth hole of the socket and twisted it sharply. There was a brief *snick*, and then I pulled open the white cover, which was actually a door to a hidden safe.

"Clever," said Griffin.

"My foster father bought it for me online and installed it." I carefully checked the contents. "Everything's in there, including my real jewelry and spare set of car keys."

A look in the bathroom cabinet confirmed that all the prescription drugs had been stolen. It was lucky that I'd taken my migraine medication with me on my trip. I didn't have migraines often, but when I did … well, they were horrible.

Finally done searching the apartment, I rubbed at my arms. "So what now?" I asked Griffin.

"As I told your husband, we'll search for evidence and make some enquiries. You'll be kept updated. My contact details are on here."

I took the small card he held out. "Thank you."

After a few more minutes of speaking with us, the officer walked away.

Dane stepped into my personal space. "You're coming home with me." He raised his hand when I went to speak. "Don't argue. Don't offer to stay anywhere else. Just grab the suitcase that you took with you on our trip—then you'll have some of your things with you. If I were you, I'd bring the contents of your safe as well."

I thought about protesting, but if I stayed with anyone else, they'd faff over me all night long, which would drive me insane. Dane was not one to faff. Plus, people would wonder why I'd want to stay with anyone other than my husband. And I was due to move in with him in a few days anyway. I might as well get a preview of my new temporary home.

I sighed and said, "All right."

He nodded, satisfied. "You can ride with me and come back for your car tomorrow. Right now, you're too angry and distracted to drive without zoning out. Tell me I'm wrong."

I couldn't, so I didn't argue.

A short while later, we were driving en route to his house. Sinking into the smooth, buttery leather seat, I kept my eyelids shut, hoping it would hold back the angry tears that stung my eyes.

"You didn't hear before now that there was a surge of burglaries in your neighborhood?" asked Dane, his voice low but vibrating with agitation.

"No." I looked at him. "Even if I had heard about them, I wouldn't have been better prepared for the break-in. You never think it'll be your home they target. Fucking assholes."

"Maybe this will be the one time that said assholes left evidence behind."

"Maybe." But I wasn't counting on it.

"Don't forget to call your insurance company to tell them about the break-in. You should also call Simon and your foster parents; tell them what happened and let them know you're all right."

"I will. Soon."

We spent the rest of the journey in silence. When the car slowed as we approached a gated, tree-lined property, I strained to see past the trees but failed. "I take it we're here."

"We're here." Dane tapped the screen of his cell a few times, and then the electronic gates opened.

Sam drove forward. I felt my mouth drop open as I got my first look at Dane's home. It wasn't a house. It was a grand, stately residence that looked more like a hotel. It possessed a timeless elegance yet also a modern twist. Boasting arched windows, stone turrets, and thick white columns, the large property sprawled across three-stories and was situated in the middle of an expansive estate.

Holy shit.

Yeah, I'd known he lived in a huge-ass house, and I hadn't doubted that it would be as impressive and imposing as its owner, but I hadn't expected this level of opulence. It was a concealed slice of paradise.

As Sam drove up the long, circular driveway, I admired the lavish landscape with its pruned trees, flower garden, and manicured hedges. A man-made lake sat in front of the mansion near the courtyard. Yeah, it had a freaking courtyard. With a fountain.

Sam pulled up at the end of the driveway and then grabbed the suitcases from the trunk while I was busy gawking at the house. He said a quick goodbye to us and then left.

Carrying both my small suitcase and his own, Dane headed for the door. Gripping the strap of my purse tight, I followed him. Stepping into the large, bright white foyer with its winding staircase and chandelier, I let out a low whistle. "Wow."

Noticing an electronic pad on the wall, I realized there was some kind of built-in automation system that controlled the temperature, lighting, and alarm system among other things. Fancy. I was guessing Dane had already deactivated the alarm using an app on his phone, because no alarm went off.

"Come on," he said. "I'll give you a tour."

CHAPTER ELEVEN

My heels clicked on the polished, artfully patterned wooden flooring as I trailed after him. I tried not to gawk as we walked from room to room. The high ceilings had intricate rose moldings and pretty lighting. The neutral colors gave the open, airy rooms a welcoming ethos. The large windows flooded the place with natural light, adding to the inviting feel.

The scents of polish, floor wax, and artificial fragrances laced the air. He had to hire cleaners, because there was no dust or clutter to be seen. I doubted Dane went around dusting and mopping.

The den and two living rooms all had plasma screens, feature fireplaces, ample luxury seating, and beautiful artwork. The formal dining room, high-tech media room, and oversized, commercial-grade kitchen were equally impressive.

It wasn't until he showed me the two-floored library with its walls of books and winding staircase that I felt a case of true envy. God, I'd *love* this room. I'd happily sleep in it. Live in it.

As I took a quick walk around, I knew I'd be spending a lot of my free time in here. Not that I had much of it, but still. "Where did you get all these books?"

"Most of them were Hugh's," replied Dane. "Come on, the tour isn't yet over."

He showed me the wine cellar, safe room, indoor pool, home office, well-outfitted gym, and, finally, the bedrooms. There were six, in total.

He didn't show me the inside of his own bedroom, just pointed at the closed door and said, "That's my room. Now I'll show you where you'll be staying." He led me to the opposite end of the wide hall and motioned me through a partially open door.

Stepping inside, I almost gasped. He'd said I'd have a bed, a closet, a set of drawers, and a workstation. He hadn't mentioned the antique dressing table, the cozy fireplace, the private bathroom, the reading nook with the lush recliner, or that the bed was a luxurious queen-sized, French-style antique.

Advancing further into the room, I peeked into the walk-in closet. Shit, it was bigger than my kitchen. The walls were lined with racks, shelves, and mirrors, and it even had a shoe carousel.

Exiting the closet, I realized he hadn't moved from the bedroom doorway. "Has someone been using this room?" Because it didn't feel like a standard guest room, and it didn't look as basic as the others.

"No," he replied simply, setting my suitcase on the floor.

"This stuff is all new?"

"Yes," he said, like it was no big deal. But it was. Because it meant he'd furnished this room with me in mind. He hadn't needed to do that at all. A generic guest room would have suited me fine.

I swallowed. "Thank you." I didn't know what else to say.

He shrugged. "You had to give up your home. The least I could do was make sure you had a decent room."

It was a hell of a lot more than "decent."

"You hungry?"

I shook my head. My stomach was still tied up in knots after the break-in. "No, but thanks."

"I have a few calls I need to make. Get settled and then come find me when you're ready to eat." With that, he was gone.

Alone, I blew out a breath and walked to the large window. It overlooked the rear of the estate. Damn, the man had acreage to burn. There was an outdoor pool, hot tub, cabana, small bar, and stone patio seating area. There were also three small additional buildings. One had to be the outhouse he'd mentioned.

Plopping my ass on the bed, I skimmed my fingers along the cool, gold, satin sheets. It was unbelievable to think that people really lived in places like this.

I lay back on the bed. And almost groaned in delight. It was so damn soft and comfy it would have lured me to sleep if I wasn't so mentally wired.

I still couldn't quite believe he'd gone to all this trouble to make sure I felt comfortable. He wasn't exactly Mr. Considerate. He was so self-focused that he generally didn't bother to even ask himself how another person might be feeling. Whatever his motivation for this, I was grateful. And I was *so* claiming his library.

Forcing myself to sit up, I grabbed my phone from my purse and made calls to Simon and my foster parents to tell them about the break-in. Neither call went well. There was cursing and ranting and fretting from all parties.

They were mollified on hearing I was staying with Dane, who had tip-top security measures. Still, I had to promise to visit them all the following day so they could see for themselves that I was okay. Honestly, you'd think I'd been attacked or something.

Once I'd made calls to the insurance company and my landlord, I plonked my small suitcase on the bed. It was time to unpack. I placed my cosmetics on the vanity dresser, lay my laptop and tablet on the workstation, stuck my e-reader in the drawer of the nightstand, put my travel size toiletries into the spa-like bathroom, and then hid all my valuables—including the ones I'd brought from my home safe—beneath the bottom drawer of the dresser.

Most of my clothes needed washing, but I always took extra underwear and a spare suit when we went on business trips in the event of a wardrobe malfunction, so I placed the clean items in the closet.

As for my wedding bouquet … was it weird that I brought it back with me from Vegas? Maybe. But I just hadn't been able to find it in me to toss it in the trash, despite that Dane had no doubt done exactly that with his boutonniere. Keeping the bouquet wrapped in tissue paper, I carefully placed it on an empty shelf.

I was just contemplating whether to stick my balled-up dirty clothes into a spare pillowcase to carry down to the laundry room—something told me that if I dropped a sock somewhere, I'd have a hell of a time tracking it down—when I heard a loud buzzer. Clearly Dane had a visitor.

Leaving my dirty clothes, I exited my bedroom and crossed to the window at the end of the long hallway. A chic red car drove along the driveway and parked near the courtyard. A female slid out of the car, tall and poised. *Jen.*

Ugh.

She made a beeline for the front door. Moments later, I heard voices coming from the foyer. I crept closer to the staircase to shamelessly eavesdrop.

"You haven't been answering my calls," Jen clipped.

Standing in front of her, Dane shrugged. "You said your piece earlier over the phone."

I frowned, having no idea what he was talking about.

"I doubted you had anything new to add." Dane turned and walked away.

Jen followed him further into the house, disappearing from my view. "Well, you're wrong," she said, her voice echoing in the large space. "Look, I shouldn't have yelled at you, I know that. It was just a shock when I saw the picture you sent to Kent."

"Hmm," was his only response.

"You did this to get your hands on your trust fund, didn't you?"

She was obviously referring to him marrying me. Holding onto the smooth banister, I began to creep down the marble stairs, thankful that I'd kicked off my shoes.

"Does she know that's why you married her? It's not fair to her if she doesn't. She has a right to know, Dane."

"I didn't say that was why I married Vienna. *You* did," he pointed out.

"Because it's the only thing that makes sense. For as long as I've known you, you've never wanted to get married. You were always adamant about it."

"And I meant it. *Then*. Now I don't feel that way anymore."

"I don't believe you."

"It's irrelevant to me what you do or don't believe," he said with such nonchalance I could imagine him giving her that indifferent shrug of his.

Reaching the bottom of the stairs, I silently crossed the foyer and stepped into the wide hallway. From there, I could see that Dane and Jen were standing in the middle of the large den.

She huffed at him, all haughty. "Okay then, if this really isn't about your trust fund, why *did* you marry her? Don't say it's because you *love* her. You don't love anyone, not even yourself. Come on, I want to hear your reason."

Dane's eyes turned as cold as a glacial lake. "Let me be very clear on something. You do not get to question my decisions. You do not get to demand answers from me. I don't owe you explanations. I don't have to justify *shit* to you, so don't walk into my fucking home and come at me like this."

She licked her lips. "Dane." It was an entreaty, an attempt to soothe.

"You don't have to like that I married Vienna—I couldn't care less either way. I don't need approval from you or anyone else." He sank onto the leather sofa and draped his arms over the back of it.

Jen looked down at him. "I just don't get what it is about her that's apparently so special," she said, quiet and subdued. "I might not know her, but I know plenty about her. I did my homework."

He tensed. "You did, what?"

"I wanted to know more about this person you brought into our family. Did you know she grew up in *foster care*?"

I almost snorted in derision. She said it like I'd been raised by inbred cannibals.

"She was taken away from her family because her father beat the shit out of her mother right in front of her and then got himself arrested—the mother wasn't interested in her child."

The fuck? She really had done her freaking homework, hadn't she? Nosy little bitch.

"Did you know she was once engaged?" Jen huffed. "I'll bet she never told you that, did she? Well, I know *all* about it."

"So do I," said Dane. "It's a boring story, so don't bother repeating it. You can leave now."

She didn't, sadly. I leaned against the doorjamb and folded my arms.

Jen put her hands on her hips. "Doesn't it concern you that she's probably just after your money?"

"You would never have even considered that if you knew her," he said.

"And just how does she feel about marrying a man who'd never sleep in the same room as her?"

I blinked. Wait, what?

His face darkened. "What did you just say?" he asked, a lethal note to his voice.

Jen went as still as prey, and her mouth bopped open and closed. "I just … I mean …"

"What? What did you mean?"

"I once heard Hugh say something to Kent about how he hoped you'd one day get over your aversion to sleeping in the same space as others; he said no wife would want to sleep in her marital bed alone. I worried you might have been molested as a child or something, but Kent said it wasn't like that. He wouldn't explain further, though."

"Because it's not your fucking business. My marriage isn't your fucking business. My wife is *definitely* not your fucking business."

"Does she know about us?"

His brows snapped together. "There was never an 'us.' We fucked. Once. That's it. And you probably only wanted it because you were trying to get Kent's attention."

Her head jerked back. "Is that honestly what you think?"

He shrugged one shoulder. "I don't see that it matters either way."

"I would never have used you like that, Dane. Never. I cared about you. *Now* I care for you as a sister, and it always saddened me that you were intent on being alone. I understand what made you this way, but I don't want you to spend your life alone. I want you to have someone who cares for you. If I thought that this thing you have with your PA was real, I'd be delighted for you. But I don't believe it is."

"So you've already said. Now if you're done …"

"I'm not done. I haven't finished telling you what I learned about your PA. Her father has Dissociative Identity Disorder, you know. That's probably hereditary. If you had any children with her, they'd probably get it."

A snicker popped out of me before I could stop it. Both Dane and Jen looked at me. He didn't seem surprised to see me there, so I wondered if he'd already sensed my presence. Jen, however, looked shocked as all shit.

"Oh no, please, *do* continue," I urged, smiling at her.

She licked her front teeth. "Dane didn't tell me you were here."

"I kind of live here now."

Jen's jaw dropped. She looked from me to him, her eyes wide. "You asked her to move in with you?"

Dane frowned. "Where else would I want my wife to be?"

I pushed away from the doorjamb and slowly crossed to her. "You sure do seem very interested in me, what with you doing all that 'homework.'"

She jutted out her chin. "I'm just looking out for my brother-in-law, that's all."

"No, you were being judgy and intrusive and feeling he needed to justify himself to you. Which I just don't get. I mean, do you shove your nose in Travis's business? I doubt it. Yet, you think you should have some say in what Dane does. Maybe that makes sense in *your* head, but it doesn't in mine."

"Dane is my family."

"And now I'm your family, too. How cool is that?" I took another step closer to her. "Here's my problem, Jenny—"

"It's Jen."

"Families should support each other. Should be there for one another. Should want to see their loved ones happy. You, well, you're not being supportive of Dane, are you? And that bugs me, because he deserves to have the support of his family. If you can't give him that, if you can't get off your high fucking horse and quite simply accept his choice of wife, there'll only be one result: You won't come between *me* and him. You'll come between *you* and him."

She shook her head. "That wouldn't happen."

"Don't take my word for it. Ask him."

Jen's gaze sliced to him, blazing with indignation. "You'd choose her over me and your brothers?"

He looked her square in the eye. "In a fucking heartbeat."

Jen sucked in a breath.

I smiled. "Well, now that *that's* out of the way, I'm going to scrounge up some dinner. Anyone hungry?"

Without waiting for a response, I headed to the kitchen. It wasn't a straightforward journey, since I didn't yet know my way around, but I found the room eventually. I was looking through the dark cherry wooden cupboards when I heard footsteps behind me.

"She's gone."

I glanced over my shoulder at Dane, who stood near the kitchen island. "And here I was thinking she'd want to get to know me better. Is she always so judgmental?"

"No, not usually. But if she's determined to dislike someone, she'll find all sorts of reasons to disapprove of them."

"Like that they grew up in foster care, as if it's a major deal. Whatever. I'm done talking about her. She bores me. Your home, however? Far from boring. I had no idea it was this big. Isn't it odd having all this empty space around you?"

"Where you see empty space, I see private space. Plus, I wanted somewhere that had lots of land, no nosy neighbors."

"Where you could be the emperor of your domain." He'd done what his uncle had done. He'd bought himself a huge home. But where Hugh had found himself hating that he lived alone, Dane wasn't bothered by it. Or, at least, he wasn't *yet* bothered by it. That might one day change, but I wouldn't bet money on it. "Are there any rooms that are off-limits?"

"My office isn't off-limits as such. But when I'm not there, it's always locked. If I am in there, feel free to enter. My bedroom is out of bounds to anyone but me," he added with such seriousness that I blinked.

"You have some kinky stuff in there or something?"

"No. It's just off-limits."

"A Dane-only zone."

"Yes."

"You don't like anyone being in your private sanctum, huh?" I suspected it also had something to do with his aversion to sleeping around others. "Do you have a housekeeper?"

"I have two. They only come in when I'm working. They know I like to be alone. You'll probably meet them at some point." He leaned back against the kitchen island. "I've hired a moving crew to help you pack and transport your belongings. They'll start tomorrow after the police are done with your apartment. We'll get everything moved here on Sunday like we originally planned. You should stay with me until then."

Considering it made sense to do so, I didn't argue. "It's fine if you don't want to answer, but what did Jen mean when she said she knows what 'drives' you to spend your life alone? Is it something that, as your 'wife,' I should know?"

"Jen could never understand why I didn't want to get married and have a family, so she felt the need to try to explain it. There is no 'drive,' there's only my preference to be alone."

I wasn't sure if I believed that nothing drove him to live this way, but it did seem that *he* believed it.

"Did Simon really beat up your mother?"

Tension tightened my muscles. Fucking Jen just *had* to go and dig up that shit, didn't she? "It was Deacon."

"Why did he do it?"

"She … she hurt me, and he lost his temper. I know it's wrong for a man to hit a woman—"

"It's just as wrong for an adult—man or woman—to harm a child." A muscle in Dane's cheek ticked. "She was abusive toward you?"

"Sometimes," I replied softly.

"What had she done that made Deacon lose his temper like that?"

I rubbed at my throat. "I didn't want to go … somewhere with her, so she slapped me hard enough to split my lip. Simon walked in just as she was trying to drag me out of the apartment. He realized what was going on and, well, Deacon surfaced and lost it."

Dane slowly crossed to me. "Where was she trying to take you?" he asked, pitching his voice low.

I swallowed. "To see her dealer. He never touched me, but he wanted to. He liked little kids. Mostly little girls. And so he found female addicts who had kids, and he suggested they pay for their drugs by letting him make use of their children. She told me that I was to do whatever he told me to do, even if it hurt."

Dane's jaw looked hard as granite. "Then she's as twisted as he is."

"Was, not is. He was killed in prison."

"Good."

Yeah, it was. "Not a lot of things scare me. But someone who could molest a child, who could find enjoyment in that? They terrify me. Because that's a kind of darkness that should not exist in this world or any other."

"Anyone who preys on those who are weaker than themselves aren't frightening; they're spineless. Worthless. Pathetic. Sick in the head. And they know it, which is why they never target anyone whose strength matches or surpasses their own."

"You sound like you're speaking from experience."

"I wasn't sexually abused, if that's what you're wondering."

I noticed he only specified he wasn't *sexually* abused.

He folded his arms. "Did your father go to prison for assaulting your mother?"

"No. The police realized he had mental health issues. They called in an expert. He was eventually diagnosed with DID. That was when he started getting the help he needed."

"What kind of help?"

"Mostly medication and psychotherapy. They work. He used to have eight alters, but he was able to integrate five of them into his personality with the help of his doctors. But Simon believes the other alters won't be going anywhere. Honestly, I don't think he wants them to." I drew in a steadying breath. "Are you done quizzing me now? I'm going to note it's a little hypocritical of you to launch questions at me when you rarely answer mine."

He closed the small distance between us, edging into my personal space. "Ask me a question. Any question. Just be sure you want the answer."

There were a lot of questions I wanted to ask this man. There were so many things I wanted to know about him. I opened my mouth to speak, but then I snapped it shut.

Dane slanted his head. "What?"

"I don't want to pry out of you something that you don't want to share."

Those pools of dark ink seemed to warm slightly. He very slowly bent his head and pressed a kiss to the corner of my mouth that made me all tingly and shocked me into silence because, hello, this was very un-Dane behavior. "You're a far better person than I am, Vienna." He sighed. "You once asked who Oliver was. He was my twin."

I almost rocked back on my heels in surprise. "What happened to him?"

"He died when we were eight. Anaphylactic shock. He was severely allergic to bee stings. One stung him while he was playing in the backyard."

Oh, God. How awful would it feel to lose your twin, someone who felt part of you? Maybe that was the source of the empty spot inside him.

The back of my throat began to ache. "Were you with him at the time?" I asked, my tone soft.

"No. I would have been, but …" He drew in a breath through his nose. "That's another story."

I worried my lower lip. "Thank you for telling me."

He inclined his head. "Hungry yet?"

Rolling with the change of subject, I replied, "A little, but I'm not sure I can eat much."

"What's your go-to-feel-better meal?"

I pursed my lips. "Grilled cheese sandwiches."

"Then sit. I'll make you one."

CHAPTER TWELVE

I sank my head deeper into the pillow, so damn snug that I didn't want to open my eyes. I'd long ago developed a habit of waking up ten minutes before my alarm went off. Which was annoying, really, because it felt like I'd been robbed of a further ten minute's sleep. But I couldn't shake the habit off, no matter how hard I tried.

I didn't usually sleep well in a strange place—I found it difficult to settle. But I'd slept like a log last night. My new bed wasn't just pretty, it was comfy as hell. And the pillows … God, the pillows were divine. Not too flat, not too soft, not too plump, just perfect.

I wondered if Dane would let me take the bed with me after the divorce. It wasn't like he'd have any use for it.

Yawning, I forced my eyes open. I'd lowered the electronic shades, so the room was still dark. Fuck, I had *electronic shades.* And a walk-in closet. And antique furniture.

Not one thing in my life had prepared me for the eventuality that I'd be living with Dane Davenport—especially as his temporary wife. Just the same, nothing had prepared me for the realization that he'd furnished the room specifically to suit me.

I wasn't reading anything into it. I didn't think it meant he cared or something. I wasn't delusional. I was just stunned. And grateful. Even a little touched, because—if nothing else—it meant he recognized how hard all this was for me, and he wasn't ambivalent toward how I was feeling. For Dane, that was noteworthy. And almost enough to cheer me up after the break-in.

When my cell phone alarm finally went off, I hit the "snooze" option. Purely because I didn't want to leave the bed. But, intent on not being late for work, I jumped up when the alarm went off a second time. Well, I didn't quite "jump" up. It was more like I reluctantly edged out of bed with a petty moan.

In the gleaming private bathroom, I did my business and then made use of the walk-in-shower with its head-to-toe power jets. I also made a mental note to soak in the huge, claw-footed bathtub at some point.

Once I'd dried and styled my hair, I applied some makeup, pulled on my clothes, and headed downstairs. The place was so eerily quiet I might have shivered. I expected to find Dane in the kitchen or dining room, but he was nowhere to be seen. The coffee machine had been recently used, though, so he was obviously awake. He'd probably already had breakfast.

While eating my toast and chugging down my morning intake of caffeine, I sifted through some of the emails that he and I had received overnight, just as I always did each morning—it helped me get a head-start on my workday.

Coming across a particular email, I froze. *No. Freaking. Way.* This had to be a fucking joke.

I'd known Heather would do something stupid out of sheer vindictiveness. I just hadn't thought she'd send Dane an email in which she tried convincing him that he'd made a mistake in marrying me. Basically, she'd pulled a Travis. She'd given a friendly warning to Dane that I wasn't someone he should be with, claiming "my conscience just wouldn't let me stay quiet." Like the woman even *had* a conscience.

Damn Heather. Another person might have thought, "Oh, Dane and Vienna are married now; it's too late to split them up." But Heather didn't believe in the sanctity of marriage. She separated couples all the time. And she was good at it.

Either she had no idea that I screened Dane's emails, or she *wanted* me to be the one to first read it. Whatever the case, I was pissed.

My fingers itched to type a rude response, but I didn't for the same reason that I didn't call her and demand to know what the hell she'd been thinking. I'd deal with her face-to-face. But not until I'd let her sweat for a while—she'd hate that her antics hadn't garnered her an immediate response, so I was all for that plan.

I blew out a breath. I'd have to delete the email. If Dane read it, if he knew she'd made yet another shitty move, he'd retaliate for sure. I couldn't have that. It would lead to a clusterfuck.

Wanting to keep Heather's email as evidence in case I needed it, I forwarded it to my own inbox and archived it. Only then did I delete it from Dane's account.

He would not be a happy bunny if he later found out I'd kept this from him, but he also wouldn't be surprised. If he had a huge problem with it, well, he'd just have to deal with it. If we were true partners, I'd have told him. But we weren't, and so I was entitled to my secrets just as he was to his.

By the time I'd scoffed down my breakfast, he was striding into the kitchen. He looked the epitome of well-groomed with his clean-shaven jaw, white shirt, charcoal tailored suit, black tie, and gleaming back shoes.

That easily, heat coursed through my blood. For the billionth time, I found myself wishing I could feel him moving inside me just once. Because I was *that* stupid.

His dark eyes locked with mine, and he frowned. "You look tired again."

I wasn't so much tired as weary. Weary of Heather's antics, to be precise. "Good morning to you, too. Is Sam outside?"

"Not yet. We're not going to work until this afternoon."

"What? Why?"

"My personal shopper is coming to see you."

I gave my head a little shake, struggling to keep up. "Um, personal shopper? Why?"

He looked at me like I was dim. "Because most of your clothes were robbed yesterday—especially the suits you wear for work."

"I can just head to the mall at some point."

"You're wearing the only suit you currently own. With everything else that's going on, do you have time for a shopping trip?"

I shifted a little on my seat. "Well, not really."

"Then personal shopper it is." He planted his hands on the island. "After work, we'll visit Simon and your foster parents—all of whom have texted me, asking me to keep an eye on you; they're worried and need to see you. Then we'll pick up your car. And if there's anything you desperately need from your apartment, you can grab it tonight, since the police are done searching it for evidence. The moving crew will pack and transport everything else."

"How do you know the police are done?"

"I called the officer who took your statement last night."

I bristled. "I was going to do that myself."

"Now you don't have to. Griffin said the security cameras show a hooded figure slip into the main door just as a woman exited; that same figure later left with your suitcase. But Griffin couldn't tell whether the figure was male or female—they were careful not to look at the cameras. The police found no fingerprints, footprints, or blood samples."

"Hell." I drained the last of my mug, staring at him. "I don't like that you made that call for me."

"I can see that. But why wouldn't I have done it? You are my wife."

"Your fake wife. And even if I'd been your *real* wife, I'd still be unhappy with you taking over."

"And I'd still have done it. You know me well enough to know that." His gaze dropped to my hand. His brow knitted. "Where are your rings?"

I glanced at my finger. "Oh shit, I left them upstairs."

"Why did you take them off?" he asked, like I'd committed a capital crime.

"I don't like to wear jewelry while I shower." I hurried back to my room, slipped on the rings, and returned to the kitchen.

Dane glared at me. "Don't forget them again."

"Stop being snippy."

"I'm never snippy."

I snorted. "Whatever."

"I can't believe you've moved out," said a pouting Ashley on Sunday evening. "I almost cried when the moving van drove off with your stuff. Who am I going to talk to when I argue with Tucker?"

Lounging on a chair in the library while on a video call to both Ashley and Hanna, I smiled. "You can still talk to me. We'll just need to do it over the phone."

"It won't be the same," Ashley complained. "I won't be able to come see you to talk it out. I *so* wished I could have last night."

"What did you and Tucker argue over this time?" asked Hanna, sipping wine.

"The cat's name," replied Ashley.

Hanna's nose wrinkled. "Huh?"

"He stupidly proclaimed that our cat likes him better than me. I said, 'No, she's all about her momma.' He said, 'Nah, I'm Snuggles' favorite.' I was like, 'Her name is not Snuggles, it's Brandy.' He wouldn't accept it. He insisted we'd called her Snuggles. What dumb fucker would forget their cat's name?"

I felt my mouth twitch. Honestly, I sometimes wondered if Tucker annoyed her on purpose just so that she'd storm out and give him a little alone time.

Hanna leaned forward. "How long have you had the cat?"

"*Three years*," Ashley bit out. "He has no excuse for this shit."

"Wow." Hanna chuckled and shook her head. "I adore Tucker but … wow."

"I know."

"Well, at least you have a guy of your own. I'm still painfully single." Hanna looked at me. "It wasn't so bad when *you* were single, too, but now … Damn, I'm still processing that you're married to Dane. No, I haven't finished processing that you're even a couple."

I was still processing it all myself.

"Of course, I suspected he was into you," Hanna went on. "You're one of the only employees at o-Verve whose ass he hasn't chewed a verbal chunk out of, even though you're in his company almost every day. And when that guy from marketing came onto you a little too strong—complete with groping—Dane was *furious*."

Ashley's brows arched. "Yeah? I didn't hear about that."

"Ooh, he reamed the sleazy fucker so hard I was pretty sure the guy would cry," said Hanna. "Dane doesn't yell or blow a fuse when he's mad at you.

He talks quiet and stays in complete control, but he turns ice freaking cold and systemically rips your character apart like a twisted psychiatrist. That's why quite a few people have quit their jobs in tears."

Dane *had* been super harsh with him. Really, though, he would have been furious no matter which employee was groped.

Hanna drank more of her wine. "He's been a lot less eager to jump down people's throats since you became his PA. You do seem to have a way of … I don't know … soothing him, I guess you could say."

"I know what you mean," said Ashley. "I noticed at the barbecue that he's at ease no matter who he's talking to, but he relaxed a fraction more when Vienna was by his side. Like, yeah, she soothed him in some way."

No, he was just *that* good an actor.

"I'm not even sure if he's conscious of it," Ashley added.

"Oh, he'll be conscious of it," said Hanna. "Dane knows himself inside and out. Knows every strength and every fault. And he can live just fine with those faults, because his psychopathy—"

"No, we're not doing this," I cut in, slashing my hand through the air.

Ashley rolled her eyes. "Fine. He's a very well-adjusted, emotionally stable man." She paused. "Are you sure you made the right decision in marrying him so soon?"

I lifted my shoulders. "Why wouldn't I be?"

"He might be a person who moves fast, but *you* aren't. I've never known you to throw caution to the wind. Yet here you are, moving in with a guy you married after only a month or so of dating him."

"Yeah, well, I love him."

"Do you? Because sometimes I worry that you don't really *see* him. And I don't get why you two had to rush into anything. That usually doesn't end well for couples."

Hanna let out a dreamy sigh. "I think it's romantic the way he decided that, hey, he was done fighting what he felt for her and then he just set out to make her his in every way." She gave me the stink eye. "I also think it's unfair that you won't give us details about what he's like in bed."

"You'll just have to use your imagination," I said.

"Oh, I do. Lots. I'll try to stop it now that you're married to him, but it won't be easy. Not gonna lie, I'm jealous."

"Speaking of jealousy … How's Heather taking all this?" Ashley asked me.

I shrugged. "I haven't seen anything of her since the barbecue." I still hadn't dealt with her shitty email, but I figured it could wait. Compared to everything else that was happening, it wasn't important.

"She's going to shit a brick when she sees that iceberg on your finger," said Ashley. "You *know* how much she likes her bling."

Hanna swirled her glass. "It's a shame she has to be that way."

It was. Mostly because the situation hurt my foster parents so much. "The people who matter are happy for me. That's what's important to me."

When I'd visited my father to assure him that I was okay after the burglary, I'd also been careful to monitor how he reacted to my being married. I wanted to be sure he was truly good with it. It appeared that I'd been worrying for nothing. He seemed incredibly content about the whole thing. He loved the copy of the wedding photo we'd brought him, and he'd almost died with laughter on watching the recording of the ceremony.

I'd also visited Melinda and Wyatt, who eventually settled when they saw I wasn't an anxious mess about the break-in. Like Simon, they were thrilled to have a copy of the wedding photo, claiming they loved how "happy" I looked. They'd also laughed their asses off watching the recording of the ceremony.

With tears in her eyes, Melinda had proclaimed, "*It was just perfect. So much smiling and laughing.*"

She'd somehow managed to talk Dane into throwing a post-wedding party sometime in the next few months. I'd insisted it wasn't necessary, but then Wyatt had jumped on board, they'd all started exchanging ideas, and the idea of a celebration took on a life of its own.

I'd later told Dane that I could talk my family out of it, but he'd said a party would help make the marriage look more real. He'd also announced that he'd hire wedding planners to take care of the details.

"Why was Dane in such a rush to get married?" asked Ashley. "Are you pregnant?"

"No, of course not," I said. "He just doesn't see a need to wait. Look, I get that this sounds fast to you. But to us, it's been years in the making. As Melinda once pointed out, he and I were like a platonic couple. But now we're annoyed with ourselves for taking so long to make the jump; we didn't want to waste any more time."

It was a rehearsed response, and it appeared to have mollified Ashley a little. That didn't please me, though, because I hated that I was deceiving her.

"All right, I get it," said Ashley. "I still think it wouldn't have been so bad for you two to wait a little longer, but I won't mention it again."

I let out a long breath. "Thank you." Hearing the buzzer, I said, "Ooh, my stuff must be here." I said my goodbyes, promised to call them again soon, and then left the video call.

When I made my way to the foyer, Dane was already there. "I'll tell the movers where to unload your things," he said. "Are there any boxes you want brought to your room?"

"Yes. When I talked with the packing team over the phone, I told them what stuff I wouldn't be putting in storage. They said they'd clearly mark each of those boxes as 'non-storage.'"

He nodded. "I'll order the crew to move the marked boxes upstairs and leave them on the landing."

Because he couldn't very well tell them to put them in a separate bedroom from his, considering we were married.

It didn't take long for everything to be unloaded. The process of unpacking didn't take long either. Even with the help of Dane's personal shopper, I didn't have enough clothing to fill the walk-in closet, so there was ample space to put my miscellaneous items.

The shopper was a freaking clothes genius. She'd noted my size, asked a few questions, wrote down my budget, and then came back later that same day with all kinds of clothes. Personally, I wasn't convinced she'd stuck to my allotted budget, and I suspected that Dane might have given her extra money to spend, but they'd both sworn he hadn't.

By the time I was done unpacking, the room officially had my stamp all over it, especially with the photos I'd placed on the mantel, the sunrise alarm clock on my nightstand, the blanket I'd slung on the recliner, and the perfumes I'd added to the vanity desk.

A short while later, there was a knock at the bedroom door. Knowing it could only be Dane, I called out, "Come in."

Walking inside, he glanced around and settled his gaze on the empty boxes. "I was going to ask if you needed help unpacking."

"Nah, I'm good. What should I do with all the boxes?"

"I'll take them downstairs. The cleaning staff will get rid of them tomorrow." He twisted his mouth. "I have a few things to do and a conference call coming up, so I won't be having dinner until late. You'll be eating alone."

"Oh. Okay." I flapped my arms slightly, strangely feeling a little lost all of a sudden. "I'll see you tomorrow morning, I guess."

He inclined his head, nabbed the boxes, and then disappeared, leaving me alone. I had the distinct feeling he was going to leave me alone a lot.

CHAPTER THIRTEEN

"Thank you," said Miley, as I rested the tray of drinks on the coffee table in the formal sitting room.

Smiling, I sank onto the sofa beside Dane, opposite her and her colleague, Chris, who were wedding planners. "Is that your portfolio?"

She handed it to me. "It is. Feel free to read through it."

"Thank you."

A week had gone by since Dane had promised Melinda that we'd throw a post-wedding celebration. He hadn't spoken of it once in the past seven days, so I'd thought he'd either forgotten about it or changed his mind. It was only an hour ago, when he informed me that the planners would soon be arriving, that I realized I was wrong.

Well, we didn't really communicate much over non-work stuff. I'd been right in thinking he'd leave me alone a lot. Oh, sure, I saw him every day, but that was mostly at o-Verve.

We rarely shared meals. He usually woke much earlier than I did—he didn't seem to sleep well—so I was often in the kitchen alone of a morning. There had been occasions where we'd eaten dinner together, but that was mostly when we stayed late at o-Verve.

Dane often went straight to his home office after work, no matter how late it was. Other times, he hit the gym upstairs or one of the pools. I never sought him out, respecting that he preferred to be alone. I just did my own thing. I mostly spent time in my room or in the library. Although I did love those little sanctuaries, I missed my family.

I'd invited Simon, Melinda, and Wyatt to come for dinner one evening, since they constantly hinted at it. They'd *loved* the estate, and seeing it seemed to make them like Dane a little more. Not because he had deep pockets, but because he'd never looked down on their homes, despite being used to this level of luxury. Ashley also came to visit me one evening. Being a hedonist, she fell in love with Dane's home.

While he laid out our situation for the wedding planners, I skimmed through their portfolio and read the impressive and confidence-inspiring testimonials. I was surprised to learn they were brother and sister. The resemblance was there, but it was so slight, I doubted that I'd have picked it up on my own.

Chris was tall and stylish and camp as Christmas, and I suspected I was going to *love* him. Miley was warm and friendly and just *oozed* professionalism. Feminine appreciation had briefly glinted in her eyes when she first greeted Dane, but she'd boxed it away instantly—she didn't batt her eyelashes at him, didn't make any subtle attempts at flirting, nothing. So, yeah, I liked her.

Miley clasped her hands together. "What kind of post-wedding celebration are you hoping for? Something small and informal for family and close friends? Like a barbecue or house party? Or would you prefer something grander that has that special wedding feeling?"

"The latter," replied Dane, his fingers threaded through mine. "But my wife and I are busy people. We need to be able to trust that you can see to as many details as possible. We'll collaborate with you on several points, but we'll expect you to take on most of the leg work. Will that be a problem?"

"Not at all," Miley assured him. "Do you have a particular date in mind?"

"Sometime in late autumn that doesn't clash with the holidays."

"We can make that work. Before we get started on the plans, we need to know your budget."

Dane tossed out a number that made my mouth drop open and my heart begin to pound. I supposed it was pocket change to him, but still.

I licked my lips and placed the portfolio on the coffee table. "Dane, that's a lot of money."

He gave me an amused look. "I'm well-aware of that."

"We don't need to spend *that* much. I mean, we're already married."

"And this will, essentially, be the wedding reception we didn't have. Do you really think I'd skimp on something so important?"

No. Which meant he needed to act as if it *was* in fact important to him. Fine. Whatever.

"We also need to know your dream venue and how many people you plan to invite," said Miley.

"I'd imagine there'll be approximately one-hundred and fifty guests in total," said Dane.

Really? I didn't even *know* one-hundred and fifty people.

"As for the venue, we're open to suggestions," Dane added.

"Well, I had an idea when I caught sight of all your lush landscaping," Chris told us. "There's a grand hotel about an hour's drive from here. It has a beautiful, large indoor botanical garden. Would you consider holding the celebration there, if we can secure the date?"

"I like the idea." Dane looked at me. "What about you?"

"Yeah, I'd really like that." I originally wouldn't have thought of such a setting.

Chris grinned. "I was hoping you'd say that. Here, you can take an online tour of it." He brought up the hotel's website on his phone and played the video tour for us. The indoor garden was absolutely stunning for sure.

"Make the necessary calls," Dane said to him.

Chris nodded. "We'll try our best to book the venue for you. If it proves to be impossible, we can find somewhere similar."

"Now, we'd like to ask you a few more questions," said Miley. "If we better know you, we can better determine what type of flowers, food, and décor you might prefer. Then we can provide you with some ideas."

The planners asked us dozens upon dozens of questions, and Miley jotted down notes on her tablet.

Chris looked at me. "Do you plan to wear the dress you wore for your wedding ceremony?"

I poked the inside of my cheek with my tongue. "I think I'd look pretty underdressed if I did, considering Dane has all these grand plans for the party. But I'd also feel overdressed if I wore an extravagant white wedding gown."

"What if it were a different color and the bridal tone was dialed down?" Chris suggested. "There are so many alternatives to traditional wedding gowns nowadays."

I pursed my lips. "Yeah, I'd be happier with something like that."

"Great. We could probably find a designer to custom-make your dress in such a short space of time, but there would be a lot of coming and going for various consultations and fittings. That might not be ideal for you, since your work schedule is busy. You might find it less stressful to select and purchase one from a bridal boutique and then have it altered to fit you—there's a particular one we deal with regularly; our clients all loved it."

I shrugged. "Works for me."

"Excellent." He smiled. "You know, there are so many reasons I love fall celebrations. You have all the pretty foliage, and you can often center your décor around the season—something I think would fit the reception well if it takes place in the botanical garden. I can jazz up the bouquet and boutonniere you wore at your ceremony and make it fit with the theme of the reception."

"Um … will I need a bouquet?" I didn't really want to admit that I'd kept it. "I mean, I'm not having another ceremony."

"But it'll add to the overall wedding-y feel of the party, and it will compliment your gown on the photos."

Hell. I swallowed. "Um, okay," I all but croaked, ignoring the feel of

Dane's eyes on me. "Sadly, Dane lost his boutonniere," I added, saving him from having to explain that he trashed it.

"I *thought* I did," Dane cut in. "But I found it buried at the bottom of my suitcase."

I looked at him, my lips parted. "You … found it?"

Dane's brow creased. "I didn't tell you? I could have sworn I did." He turned to Chris. "Try not to give it too much 'jazz,' I like it the way it is."

Chris gave him a solemn nod, his eyes smiling. "I'll just give it a little something that makes it match with the bouquet and the theme of the reception. We need to pick an autumn color palette and go from there, I think."

Considering the marriage was a sham, I'd figured Dane would leave the plans for the party to me and just throw in an idea here and there. I should have known better. I should have remembered he was a man with very definite opinions. In the end, he tossed out more suggestions than I did.

Once the meeting was over, we shook hands with the planners and showed them to the door. Chris winked and said, "Trust us, we will go above and beyond to ensure this all goes seamlessly. You won't need to worry about a thing."

For the price Dane was paying them, the guy better be right.

Alone again, Dane and I dropped the happy couple act.

I turned to him and tilted my head. "Do I need to find a replacement boutonniere that's identical to the one you wore at the ceremony?"

"No." With that, he turned and headed toward the staircase, no doubt intending to go to his office.

"No?" I echoed.

"It's not necessary. I have the boutonniere upstairs."

I blinked. "You kept it? Why?"

Pausing on the staircase, he glanced at me over his shoulder and shrugged. "I felt like it."

Such a Dane-like answer.

"Why did you keep the bouquet?"

I mimicked his aloof shrug. "I felt like it."

His dark inscrutable gaze searched mine for a moment. "Hmm."

I frowned after him as he climbed the stairs and then disappeared out of view. He'd kept it. He'd kept the boutonniere. If he was anyone else, I might have read something into that. But in this case, I knew better. Because even if the ceremony had meant something to him, he wasn't a sentimental person. He didn't have keepsakes. He did, however, do things simply because he felt like it at the time. Yes, that was very, very Dane.

I sighed and rolled back my shoulders. I now needed to occupy myself for a while. Deciding to switch things up a little, I didn't go to the library. I made some use of the indoor pool. Yeah, I was living life on the edge.

CHAPTER FOURTEEN

Settled on one of the comfy leather seats in the media room, I used the remote control to flick through the movie options on the large TV screen. Over the past three weeks, I'd tried to make use of every room in the oversized house—even the gym, though I had a genuine allergy to exercise.

I grew to love my new temporary home. I really did. But there was something about being mostly alone in such a massive building that sometimes made the quiet feel *eerie* rather than peaceful.

I wasn't a person who craved company. I'd lived on my own since I was eighteen. Now I lived with a man who had such an overwhelmingly forceful personality that he seemed to suck the air out of whatever room he walked into. And yet, I'd never felt more alone. But alone was okay. Until you started to feel lone*ly*. Something which crept up on me now and then, just as it had today. So, honestly, I was in a bit of a funk.

I would have visited one of my friends or relatives, but my doing so had apparently become too much of a habit, because they'd started to question if everything was "okay at home," especially since Dane never accompanied me on the visits.

They bought my assurances that all was fine. Well, Ashley wasn't so easily convinced, but she didn't push me on it. Still, I figured I had to do a better job of playing the part of happy wife, and that meant not leaving my husband at home alone all the time—even though he'd no doubt prefer that.

Not once in the times I went to visit my foster parents did Heather turn up. I wasn't sure if she was simply busy seducing her new boyfriend into leaving his wife or if she was actively avoiding me. If it was the latter, it wouldn't be that she worried I'd confront her over the email—she *loved* to be confronted—it would be that she thought I was gloating over my new financial situation.

Heather seemed to view me as some sort of threat to her self-image. She was driven to have more than me; to have better. As she had money, designer clothes, and an expensive car, she seemed to feel that she'd outdone me. But now that I was married to Dane, she'd probably feel that I'd one-upped her. As she tended to judge me by her own standards, she'd also believe I wanted to rub it all in her face.

Well, I didn't.

She was probably also annoyed that her sly little email hadn't been important enough to warrant an instant response. She'd hate that more than anything. It made her feel insignificant when her efforts to get a reaction failed.

I doubted she'd miss the upcoming reception, though. She'd want the chance to cause a scene. She'd get her wish, since I couldn't *not* invite her without offending her parents.

Chris and Miley had managed to secure the botanical garden as the party venue—they hadn't wasted any time in getting started on the preparations. They'd even created a website that had everything on it for the guests—dates, venue details, maps, dress code, etc. I hadn't known people did that sort of thing. But then, I hadn't attended a lot of weddings.

Initially, I hadn't been all that interested in the reception, but the planners had sucked me right in with their excitement and enthusiasm. Plus, I figured that there was a chance this might be the only wedding reception I ever had, so I might as well make it a good one. I *wanted* to one day marry and have kids, but lots of people wanted that future. They didn't always get it.

Eager to see in person the venue we'd selected, Dane and I had ambled through the botanical garden and wandered around the hotel itself one Saturday afternoon. Both places were an utter delight, and I loved Chris' "vision" of what he'd do to the garden for the reception.

The only time Dane and I really spent together outside of work was when we were coordinating with the planners over flowers, the food menu, and all that jazz—he never missed a meeting, to his credit. We'd also attended a brief tasting session with the caterer he'd chosen.

Chris and Miley also booked me in to see "a bridal couture queen." I took Maggie, Melinda, Ashley, and Hanna along—they'd insisted on coming. The boutique offered a selection of truly breathtaking intricate gowns and, as Chris had promised, some beautiful alternatives to wedding dresses. All were designer, though, so they were also super expensive.

It hadn't seemed right to spend so much money on a dress for a fake wedding reception, but I'd agreed to try on a few, since we'd gone all that way. When I'd modeled a particular one, the girls had started crying and declared "that's the one!" I had to admit, I'd loved it. So I'd agreed. I'd also offered to reimburse Dane, but he wouldn't hear of it.

Hanna had moaned when I vetoed having a post-wedding-bachelorette party, but I'd allowed her to talk me into having a simple girls' night in nearer the date of the reception. As the date fell in late autumn, Chris had suggested adding décor such as pumpkins … which made me think of Halloween, and how I'd probably be spending it alone.

I loved Halloween. Loved driving past the houses in my neighborhood and seeing all the pumpkins, spider webs, and other aesthetics. Loved answering the door to trick-or-treaters and seeing all the creative costumes. Loved hanging up spooky decorations of my own, even if only to get into the Halloween-spirit.

Every year, Ashley and I would dress up for fun and have a scary-movie marathon while drinking punch and munching on junk food. We'd also hand out candy to trick-or-treaters and tease Tucker for jumping and flinching during the horror movies.

Dane was uninterested in most holidays, so he'd probably hole up in either his home office or the one at o-Verve. No trick-or-treaters would come all the way out here, so there'd be no costumes to admire. I had no decorations to hang, since mine were in storage and Dane was unlikely to have any of his own. It would probably just feel like any other day.

I narrowed my eyes and twisted my mouth. Maybe I could still spend it with Ashley and Tucker. Would it look weird if Dane and I didn't spend our first Halloween together? Maybe.

It was thinking of Halloween that had inspired me to grab some candy and go watch a scary movie in the media room. So far, none of the selections had jumped out at me.

Hearing hinges creak, I twisted and watched as Dane strolled into the room.

Stopping near my seat on the front row, he looked from the TV screen to the glass of wine in the cupholder to the bowl of candy on my lap. "What are you doing?"

"Searching for a movie."

"You look like you're sulking."

"That, too." I shoved a piece of candy in my mouth.

"What's wrong?"

"I love Halloween."

He frowned. "And that bothers you?"

"No, it bothers me that I probably won't celebrate it this year. I'm in a funk, ignore me. Did you need something?" Because it wasn't like him to seek me out.

"I came to bring you this." He held up my cell phone. "You left it in the kitchen. I doubted you'd done it on purpose."

I shot him a grateful smile and took it from him. "Thanks. That's the one thing about your house that drives me crazy."

"What?"

"If I lose something, I know there's an endless number of places it could be. Tracking the object down can sometimes take a while."

"You'll get used to it." His gaze moved to the TV screen. "What are you watching?"

"I don't know yet. Something scary. I'd invite you to join me, but you'll say no, and I'm too emotionally fragile right now to handle the rejection."

One corner of his mouth quirked just a little. "Right." He left the room.

I shoved yet another piece of candy in my mouth and turned my attention back to the media screen. After scrolling through yet more options, I finally settled on *Insidious* and sank deeper into my seat. I'd watched the movie dozens of times, but I loved it.

It had only been playing for a minute or so when the door swung open and Dane reentered. I frowned when he sat two seats away and positioned his laptop on, well, his lap. "What are you doing?" I asked.

"Working," he said, his fingers flying over the keyboard.

"In here?"

"Yes. Then you won't be on your own, which seems to be what's truly bothering you."

I swallowed. "Okay. Well. Thank you."

Without looking away from his laptop screen, he inclined his head.

"Have you never thought of unplugging from technology for a few hours when you get home? You're always on the clock, you never seem to wind down. It's not good for you."

He frowned at his laptop screen. "I don't have time to wind down."

Nor did he seem to have any inclination to do it. "Okay."

"I was talking to Chris over the phone earlier. He mentioned that the dress you bought for the reception is perfect. Then he asked me if I liked the color brown. The dress isn't brown, is it?"

I smiled. "No, he's just messing with you. He's got a weird sense of humor." I tossed another piece of candy in my mouth. "And, just so you know, I'm keeping the dress after this is over."

"What do you intend to do with it?"

"Splash fake blood all over it and use it as a Halloween costume next year. It'll be *epic*."

"Hmm."

"You're supposed to tell me I can't stain a designer gown with fake blood and use it as a costume."

He shrugged. "It'll be your gown, not mine."

I sipped my wine. "I'd keep it for my real wedding, whenever that might happen, but I figure that would be in poor taste. And probably bring me bad luck."

His gaze met mine, broody and unreadable. "Your real wedding?" he echoed, his tone utterly flat.

"Uh-huh. Unlike you, I don't want to be all by my lonesome for the rest of my days on Earth."

"What do you want?"

Someone who could give me the things that Dane would never be able to give, just as Owen had pointed out. "A family," I replied. "And a cat."

His mouth twitched. "A family and a cat."

"Maybe I'll call it Dane. That's a cat-like name, right?"

He just shook his head and turned back to his laptop.

My mood surprisingly lighter, I settled in to watch the movie. Just as one of my favorite parts approached, I got the weirdest, most indefinable "feeling" and my vision began to blur. My stomach bottomed out, because I knew what that meant.

I straightened, nearly knocking the bowl off my lap. "No, not now."

"What?"

My pulse quickening, I shuffled forward on my seat and put the bowl on the floor, knowing I wouldn't have long before I was out of commission. "I've got to get to my room."

"Why?" Dane appeared in front of me. "Vienna, what's wrong?"

Seeing double of him—hell, of everything—I blinked hard. "It's just a migraine, but they can get bad." Already, the world was beginning to spin around me, and my head felt so freakishly heavy it was hard to hold it up. "Double vision. Vertigo. Muscle weakness. Sometimes nausea and head pain, too." The symptoms tended to creep up on me one at a time but in fast succession.

I pushed to my feet, and my knees wobbled. "Shit."

Dane scooped me up. "I got you. Come on."

I weakly fisted his shirt as he carried me out of the room. "Listen, I won't be able to move much, and my speech will get all slurry. It's normal. Just leave me on the bed. It'll all wear off."

He didn't say anything. He just carried me through the house and into my room, where he pulled back the satin coverlet and then very carefully lay me on the bed. "You have pills for these migraines?" he asked.

"Nightstand drawer." The words came out low and garbled. Feeling like someone had sucked every bit of energy out of my system, I closed my eyes and lay there like a heavy weight. Despite being mentally alert and not in the least bit sleepy, I couldn't fight the physical lethargy.

Worse, the whole world-spinning-around-me sensation didn't cease when I lay down. No, it left me with the most godawful feeling. Like I was lying on a rocking boat.

"Sit up. Take these." Dane helped me rise just enough to take two pills with a glass of water he must have gotten from the bathroom. "Good girl."

He eased me back down on the bed and then sat beside me, leaning against the headboard.

I would have again told him that he didn't have to stay with me, but I knew the words would have come out all slurry and faint. I hated the migraines. Hated how they left me feeling *so drained* that everything felt like an effort—even the simple process of breathing in and out. Like there was a freaking truck sitting on my chest, crushing it.

There was a whirring sound that I recognized as the electronic shades lowering. Although my eyes were closed, I felt the difference in the lighting.

I curled into a ball—a move that was much harder than it should have been. Not only had my muscle control gone to shit, my entire body felt like it weighed of lead.

When minutes went by and no head pain or nausea came along, I silently thanked the universe. Especially since I really didn't want to hurl in front of Dane. I had my pride.

The familiar sound of his thumbs tapping on a cell phone screen told me he was probably working in some capacity. Typical.

I kept thinking he would get up and leave at some point, but he stayed. And although it really wasn't necessary for him to be there, it … well, it was touching that he'd chosen to stay. He'd no doubt leave when he was satisfied that I was sleeping. Now that the pills had *really* started to kick in, it wouldn't be long before I dozed off.

Fingers slid through my hair and gently glided along my scalp, but not even the pleasure of Dane's touch was enough to hold off the tug of sleep. It soon swept me under.

When I next opened my eyes, the room was light*ish*, courtesy of my sunrise alarm clock. I snuggled beneath the bedcovers and inwardly groaned. I felt groggy as all shit. *Migraine pills,* I thought as the fog of sleep began to dissipate. They always had this effect on me. Well, at least the unnatural fatigue and boat-rocking sensation had faded.

I rolled over … and stilled. Because I wasn't alone. *He's still here.* He hadn't left me.

He was also asleep.

I doubted he'd *meant* to stay the whole night, or he'd surely have laid down. Instead, he'd placed his pillows behind him so that he could lounge more comfortably in a half-sitting position. His phone was still in his hand, as if he'd dozed off while … doing whatever he was doing.

My heart squeezed. See, he wasn't a stone-cold, selfish bastard. If he was as bad as many believed, he'd have simply helped me to bed and then left without giving it a second thought. Hell, he wouldn't have joined me in the media room.

It was no doubt creepy that I just lay there watching him sleep, but whatever. The line between his brows didn't surprise me. I couldn't imagine

Dane ever looking peaceful, not even in sleep. My fingertips tingled with the temptation to smooth away his frown … or maybe to trace the strong line of his jaw. But I kept my hands where they were.

He allegedly had an issue with sleeping in the same room as others, and yet here he was. I didn't really know what to make of that. Maybe, he just didn't like having other people in his bed with him. Maybe he was fine sharing a bed if said bed wasn't his own. Maybe he simply had bad nightmares and didn't want anyone to witness them.

My alarm soon went off. His eyelids flipped open. Didn't flutter, didn't weakly lift. They shot open like he'd been whacked across the head.

I licked my lips. "Morning." The word came out husky with sleep. "Any chance you could switch that alarm off?"

Dane did as I asked and then studied me with slumberous dark eyes. "How're you feeling?" he asked, his voice thick.

"Better."

"Migraine's gone?"

"Yes." I bit my lip. "Thanks for staying with me. If it happens again, though, you really can just leave me here. I'll be okay."

"Hmm."

I yawned. "I'm guessing you didn't mean to fall asleep."

"I was going to leave after a few hours, but then your muscles started spasming. It mostly happened in your hands and feet, but I was worried you were going to have a seizure."

I winced. "Forgot to warn you about the spasms, sorry."

"I didn't know you had migraines. You've never had any at work."

"They usually happen in the evenings. I only have them, like, every six months or so." Anyone who suffered them on a daily basis had my total admiration, because I'd never cope.

"Have you had them since you were a child?"

"No." Feeling a little stiff, I forced myself to sit up. "I had my first when I was nineteen." Melinda had shit herself when my speech went slurry. She'd thought I was having a stroke.

"I've never had a migraine."

"Never? Really? Not even a teeny, tiny one?"

He shook his head.

"The devil's luck," I mumbled.

He slid off the bed and pocketed his phone. "You going to be okay to go to work?"

"Of course. But it's sweet that you'd ask." I flicked back the covers. "As is the way you softly snore."

"I don't snore."

Probably not, but it was fun to poke at him. "I heard you with my own ears."

"You heard wrong." He turned and strode toward the door. "Now get ready and meet me downstairs. We've got a hectic day ahead of us."

"Don't I know it," I grumbled. It was the story of my life.

CHAPTER FIFTEEN

Slotting a book back into its place on the sturdy bookshelf the next day, I did a long stretch. I'd been holed up in the library for hours, unwinding in my favorite way ever. I'd mentally jotted down several of the books here that I intended to read before my inevitable divorce. I was determined to get through them all.

I'd miss this little haven when I left. No matter how hectic my day was, all my tension fell away whenever I walked into the library. Partly because I just loved the woody, earthy scents of old books and leather. I honestly didn't get why Dane never made any use of the space. What a weirdo.

Said weirdo was currently in his home office. Big surprise there. He'd earlier popped his head through the door to inform me that he was back from his dinner meeting with colleagues, but he'd disappeared before I could say anything more than "hi."

I'd almost laughed when Melinda once commented on how "social" Dane was. *Social my ass.* He could certainly feign the fuck out of it when it suited him, though. Just as he feigned the fuck out of being head over heels for me.

Grabbing another book I'd mentally marked as to-be-read, I crossed to what had become my favorite plush chair within the library. I was just about to sit when Dane strolled inside, his eyes hard, his mouth tight.

I lifted my brows. "Something wrong?"

He halted a few feet away and casually slipped his hands into his pockets, but he looked far from at ease. "I just received an email from Heather."

Uh-oh. I should have figured she'd send him another. Or maybe she'd just re-sent the first. "Heather?" I echoed. "What did she want?"

"Firstly, to apologize for that scene she caused at the barbecue. She claims to be ashamed of her behavior and is mortified that she let her family down so badly. She went on to tell me how it saddens her that you two have never been close, and that she regrets never forming a sisterly bond with you."

She'd typed all that in the other email.

"She also apparently feels the need to warn me that you've never gotten over Owen, and she worries that you might just be using me to get his attention, now that he's divorcing his wife. She's quite sure you'd leave me for him if he gave you the slightest indication that he'd be willing to give things with you another try, and apparently her conscience wouldn't let her keep quiet about it."

Yep, she'd said that lump of shit in the original email, too, so it was looking like she had indeed simply re-sent it. The woman didn't know when to stop, did she? "I can see you're pissed, but just ignore her. I'll deal with it, Dane."

He slowly stalked toward me. "Will you? Funny. Because she prefaced the email with how she was sorry to bother me 'again,' but she worried her first email went astray."

Hell.

"I checked my email account, but there was nothing else from Heather—not even among the spam or the deleted emails. Which means either there was no other email, or you erased it so thoroughly you even wiped it from the deleted folder. The look on your face is making me lean toward the latter theory."

I shrugged. "Getting rid of your shit-mail is part of my job."

Impatience flickered across his face. "This is something I would have wanted to know about, which you're well aware of. But you deleted it without telling me about it. Why?"

"You can't guess?"

His nostrils flared. "She's not getting away with this."

My stomach sank. "Dane—"

"No, I made it clear to you that if she made another move, I wouldn't let it go. It's not just about the emails, Vienna. Simon hinted that she'd made life hard for you when you were a child. A *traumatized* child. She should have been dealt with a long time ago."

"She *was* handled. Melinda and Wyatt put a stop to it."

"A stop to what exactly?"

I pressed my lips tight together. It wasn't just that I didn't want to talk about it, it was that I knew hearing the details would only piss him off more.

"She's going to pay, Vienna."

Panic fluttered through me as he turned and headed for the door. "She's quite capable of fucking up her own life, Dane—she doesn't need help with that. Just leave it."

"Not a chance."

"Seriously, it would bother her more if you just ignored her."

"I intend to do a lot more than 'bother' her."

Fuck, fuck, fuck. "Dane, I'm asking you to leave it. *Please.*"

"Not happening, Vienna."

I took a panicked step toward him. "You retaliate, Dane, and I'll walk."

He halted, and his body went rigid. Absolutely rigid. Then, finally, he very slowly turned to face me. His gaze was darker than I'd ever seen it. His eyebrow flicked up. "You'll walk?" he echoed, his tone *daring* me to repeat it.

Refusing to be intimidated, I lifted my chin. "I owe you. I know that. And I don't want to go back on my word. But I can't lose Melinda and Wyatt."

"That's not a reason to let Heather walk all over you. She does these things because you let her get away with it. People will only treat you how you allow them to treat you."

"I don't care if she feels the need to act like a bitch toward me."

"*I* care."

"No, you care that she dared to cross you. That's different. Heather has been a bitch to me since the day I met her. She's never going to change. Nothing you do or I do will make a damn bit of difference. If you acted on this, it would only hurt Melinda and Wyatt. She'd *use* it to hurt them; to make them choose her over me. And they *would.* I know that. I get it. I wouldn't hate them for it—she's their daughter. I'd hate *you* for it."

His brows snapped together. "Me?"

"Yes. Because you know what Heather's trying to do; you know what her game is. If you play into her hands, you'll have done it *knowing* I could lose two of the people who matter most to me. You'll have put your need for vengeance over what I feel and want. And for what? It's not as if you care for me. We'll be divorcing in under a year—that's your plan. What does it really matter to you if your fake wife has to deal with some family bullshit?"

A muscle in his cheek flexed. "It matters."

I inwardly snorted. "I won't lose Melinda and Wyatt just because you don't like people crossing you. They're important to me. I didn't talk for four whole months after Deacon beat my mother, because I didn't want to tell anyone what he'd done; I wanted to protect him. No matter how good Melinda and Wyatt were to me, I didn't trust them. I didn't trust that they wouldn't send me away. So I didn't speak to them, didn't let them touch me. I barely ate. Barely slept. Had nightmares all the fucking time."

Pausing, I crossed to him. "They were so patient with me. So good to me. Never raised their voices, never raised a hand to me, never got annoyed with me for not talking. They just let me be. Even when I started talking, they didn't pepper me with questions. They were … they were what I needed. And they made sure I had Simon in my life and that I properly understood his disorder. If putting up with their daughter's bullshit is the way to repay them for all that, so be it. And I didn't grit my teeth through years of Heather's crap just for you to go and ruin everything now."

He exhaled heavily, a little of the menace in his eyes receding.

"Dane, tell me you'll leave it."

"If I do, she'll step up her game. Ignoring it isn't going to make her stop."

"Neither will threatening her. She'd lap up the drama and cry fake tears to her parents."

He twisted his mouth. "Then we deal with it another way."

"I'm not telling tales to Melinda and Wyatt."

"Not asking you to."

"Then what?"

His eyes narrowed. "Where does she work?"

"She doesn't."

His brow knitted. "She wears designer clothes and drives a Mercedes."

"Using the child support payments she gets from Junior's dad."

"She's single?"

"No. She's dating some guy named Thad Drummond. He's probably married—her boyfriends are always spoken for. She ruins their relationships, milks them for what she can get, and then she moves on."

"So if I were to hire someone to take some photos of her and Thad and then send said photos to his wife, Heather wouldn't be too happy about it, would she? It would be a message: If she stays out of our business, we'll stay out of hers, but if not …"

Actually, that wasn't a bad idea. "You're sure she'll know we're behind it?"

"I'll ensure she suspects it somehow. We'll confirm it when she confronts us, which she will do for sure—she won't be able to help herself."

I gave a slow nod. "All right."

"All right," he repeated. "But …" He closed the short distance between us. "I want to know what she did to you."

I felt my insides seize. "It was a long time ago—" I cut off as he put his face closer to mine, his expression hard, his breath lightly fanning my mouth.

"That woman *is* going to be handled, Vienna. I'd much rather do it my way, which will involve putting the fear of God in her. If you want me to deal with her another way, this is the price."

I should have remembered he rarely did anything for nothing.

"Tell me what she did."

I ground my teeth. "Lots of little things."

"Such as?"

I shrugged. "She'd break my toys. Rip my clothes. Try forcing me to eat dog food. Pinch and twist my skin. Spit in my dinner when her parents weren't looking."

"What else? I'm sensing it escalated."

"She'd bite me hard enough to mark. Slap my face and yank my hair. Pull knives on me. Sneak into my room while I was sleeping and cut my hair or pee on my bed so that I'd get the blame. That sort of thing."

"You never told anyone?"

"At first, I wasn't talking at all. Then when I was, well, she said I'd be sent away if I told anyone what was happening." Sent to a children's home where I'd be beaten, starved, and disallowed to have clothes.

"What made it all stop?"

I hesitated, flexing my fingers. "She and two of her friends …"

"What?" he pushed.

"They locked me in the trunk of Wyatt's car. With her pet rat." The latter might not have mattered so much if it hadn't brought back memories of my life with my mother.

I swallowed hard, remembering how I'd begged them to let me out. They'd only laughed. "Melinda and Wyatt were at a party. Heather and her friends waited for the babysitter to fall asleep and then smuggled me out of the backdoor. They carried me to the driveway at the front of the house, shoved me in the trunk, and then left me there. I screamed and kicked, but no one heard me. Not until Melinda and Wyatt stumbled out of a cab at two in the morning, drunk."

Dane spat a vicious curse. "Then what?"

"They sat me down and demanded to know what had happened. I told them … and everything else that had gone on just tumbled out of me. They were devastated. Shocked. Furious. They asked me if I wanted to leave, but I said no. They came down on Heather hard, and she never touched me again. They were never the same with her after that. They'd sometimes look at her like they didn't know her." I sighed. "So now you know."

He kept watching me with those piercing eyes, holding himself unnaturally still. "Right now, the thing I want most is to make a few phone calls that will shatter her life until she has nothing," he said, his voice low and loaded with anger. "But I made you a deal, and I'll stick to it." He went nose to nose with me. "Don't threaten to walk out on me again, Vienna. Ever." Before I could say another word, he stalked out of the room.

I let out a shaky breath, feeling as though I'd dodged a bullet. For a minute there, I hadn't thought I'd be able to talk him down. But he'd relented when I made him a deal—I'd have to remember that. I might need to utilize such a tactic if we ever again found ourselves clashing over something. Which we would, because he was a pain in my ass.

Returning to the plush chair, I plopped into it. The man was going to drive me to drink at some point—I was sure of it.

Standing at my office desk a few days later, I flashed a falsely apologetic smile at Hope and Travis. "Sorry, Dane's not here; he's making his rounds to other departments."

He liked to catch up with the teams, be visible, and keep his finger on the pulse of whatever was happening within the company. I just hoped he wasn't firing people left, right, and center. He'd been in a major funk since our little argument in the library. Today, however, he was in a *seriously* foul mood, and his level of tolerance was currently paper-thin.

I'd asked if he wanted to talk about whatever was bothering him but, of course, he'd blown me off—and rather rudely, at which point I'd flipped him off and told him to go jump up his ass. "He'll probably be another half hour or so," I added.

"That's okay," said Travis, scratching his chin. "We really wanted to speak to you, actually."

Lord, deliver me. "You've come to apologize for calling me a liar?" I doubted it.

His brow furrowed. "A liar?"

"Yup."

"When did I accuse you of being a liar?"

"When Dane confronted you about cornering me outside my old apartment," I said, sounding as bored as I felt. "You told him I lied about what got said and then you accused me of trying to drive a wedge between the two of you."

Travis shook his head fast. "That's bullshit. He and I argued, sure. He didn't like that I'd told you certain things—Dane likes his secrets. But at no point did I call you a liar."

"Whatever. If you're not here to offer any apologies, why are you here?"

He exchanged a look with his wife and then said, "Last time you and I spoke, I warned you what Dane was like, Vienna. You obviously decided to give him the benefit of the doubt. I would have respected that and let it alone. But then you married him and …" Travis sighed. "It's going to be hard for you to hear this, but we're all in agreement that you deserve to know."

"All?" I echoed. "Who's all?"

Hope lifted her chin. "Me, Travis, and Jen. We talked about it, and we all decided that you needed to hear this."

Oh, this was going to be good. I folded my arms across my chest. "Okay. What is it that I so badly need to hear?"

"Dane … he's using you, Vienna," said Travis.

I raised a brow. "Using me?"

"Our uncle set up a trust fund for each of us. We have to be married before we can access it, and we have to do that before we turn thirty-eight. Otherwise, no trust fund."

I let out a low whistle. "Apparently Hugh was a man who was a big believer in marriage."

Travis snickered. "Not quite. He hadn't experienced it for himself, but he wanted to ensure that we all did. He meant well, really. But Dane's never seen it that way. He's always been adamant that he'd never get married; that he'd never be 'brought to heel by a dead man.' You know yourself that he's a huge commitment-phobe. Funny how that's abruptly changed, isn't it?"

I pursed my lips. "I wouldn't say he was ever a commitment-phobe. He just didn't seem interested in a relationship."

"Until now," said Hope. "All of a sudden, after four years of knowing you, he's eloping with you. And it just so happens that he's doing so at the age of thirty-seven."

I cocked my head. "You think he married me purely so he can access his trust fund?"

She nodded. "I'm sorry, Vienna, but yes, I do. You don't think it's strange how he so abruptly came around to the idea of marriage? Look at how everything moved so quickly between you. I'm not saying he feels nothing for you, just that he didn't marry you for the right reason."

"He obviously didn't mention the trust fund to you," said Travis. "Don't you wonder why?"

I sighed. "Look—"

"He needs to be married to you for an entire year before he can touch it." Travis planted his hands on my desk. "That's all you'll have with him. A year. After that, you'll have nothing. I mean, if you two divorce, there's no way you'll keep working here, is there? No. That means you'll be out of a job. You'll also lose your home. And where are you going to go? You've already given up your apartment for him."

Hope nodded. "Oh, sure, you've probably signed a prenup that states you'll get a nice cushy settlement in the event of a divorce. But I'll bet he put a 'wife gets nothing if she cheats' clause in there. He'll manufacture some 'evidence' that you had an affair, ensuring you don't get a single cent of his money when you divorce."

"Don't think he wouldn't, Vienna," Travis advised. "The man is ruthless through and through. His own interests come first."

Actually, I had signed a prenup. There was in fact such a clause in the contract but, according to my attorney, it was a standard thing. I hadn't really cared about any of the clauses. I didn't want money or anything else from him. Except maybe the bed. "So what are you suggesting I do?"

"Stop letting him use you," said Travis. "He's done plenty of that already. You can walk away now, which will mean his little plot won't have paid off and he'll lose access to his trust fund. Then at least you'll have your pride. If you stay with him, you'll be left with nothing at all. I hope you make the right choice." With that, he and his wife left.

Shit, Dane was going to *flip* when he heard that they'd come here to spout that "advice." Currently, he just wasn't in the mood to deal with this calmly. I could delay telling him until later, right? No, it was probably best that I told him straight away in case someone else mentioned that they saw Hope and Travis in the building. Dane wouldn't like hearing about it secondhand.

My resolve to tell him about it melted when he stalked out of the elevator a short while later looking ready to draw blood. I had no idea what had crawled up his ass and died a terrible death, but he showed no signs of calming any time soon.

He didn't even greet me with a simple eyebrow raise. He marched past me, stormed into the office, and slammed the door shut. Huh.

Knowing from past experience that it was best to leave him alone when such moods had a tight grip on him, I went back to transcribing notes I'd taken from an earlier meeting. The whole time, my mind kept drifting back to something Travis had said …

If you two divorce, there's no way you'll keep working here, is there? No. That means you'll be out of a job.

Stupid as it made me, I hadn't even thought about that. But he was right. There was no way I could continue to work here afterward. Not only because it would look weird to others if I did, but because I didn't think we could go back to being simply "boss" and "PA."

Our dynamics had sort of shifted slightly. The marriage might be a sham, but we'd kissed, touched, shared secrets, and even lived together. He wasn't my husband, no, but he also wasn't simply my boss. I didn't think I could go back to booking dinner reservations for him and his lady friends.

I'd always felt a twinge of jealousy whenever I'd thought of him with other women. But I'd been able to box that away and keep professional walls erected between us. Those walls weren't so steady anymore. And it would be hard to move on because my simple crush no longer felt like a simple crush. It had grown. Shifted. Lost its harmless air.

Plus, how the hell was I supposed to explain to any potential boyfriends that I still worked for my ex-husband? They'd consider that a red flag for sure.

Putting it all out of my mind for now, I went back to work. The rest of the day passed rather quickly. We were soon sitting in the car on our way back to his estate. Dane's black mood hadn't whatsoever improved, and the atmosphere was so thick it was palpable.

He didn't speak a word. Nor did he work on his phone. He just stared out of the window, his expression as hard as stone.

I gave him the space and silence he seemed to need, knowing better than to try to appease him. He'd harshly rebuff those attempts for certain, and then I'd have to flip him off again.

No sooner had the car pulled up in the courtyard than Dane was slipping out of it. Without a word of goodbye to Sam, he prowled up the path and disappeared into the house.

Skirting the hood of the car, I smiled at the driver. "I'll, um, see you tomorrow."

"Tomorrow, Mrs. Davenport," said Sam, giving me a pitying look. He probably thought that me and Dane had had some kind of lover's quarrel.

A little stiff around my neck and shoulders, I decided to go take a bath before I ate dinner. Soaking in the hot water did wonders for my aching muscles, so I was feeling a lot more relaxed when, clad in my pjs, I later went down to the kitchen.

I was rooting through the cupboards, looking for inspiration as to what to have for dinner, when Dane came striding into the room, seeming no less moody.

"I'm making beef stir fry," I told him. "Want some?"

"Sure," he clipped, not even sparing me a glance.

I blinked, surprised. He rarely ate dinner with me these days, so I'd expected him to say no.

As I began to line what ingredients I needed on the countertop, I snuck a quick glance at Dane. He was staring hard at the island, his gaze inward.

I badly wanted to ask what was bugging him so much, but I'd already tried that. He wasn't going to answer. So I just idly talked while I prepped our meal, not once saying anything that required a response. I half-expected him to tell me to shut up or something, but he didn't. He was probably blocking me out.

I continued to talk a little as we ate at the island, and then again when we stacked our dirty plates in the dishwasher, still not expecting a response from him. I often did the same when my dad's mind was elsewhere. Like Dane, he tended to ignore me, but Simon usually relaxed eventually.

Closing the dishwasher, Dane sighed. "Why do you keep telling me how good Ryan's PA is? You've circled back to her three times."

I was secretly pleased he'd finally spoken, even if he was being snippy. "I was hoping to get an idea of what your personal feelings about Patience are."

He shrugged. "She's good at her job."

"Excellent."

"Why is it excellent?"

"Because I was thinking she'd be a good replacement for me when I leave o-Verve."

Dane went very still. "Replacement?"

"Well obviously I can't keep working there after the divorce."

"And why not?" he clipped, frowning.

"It would be weird."

"Why?"

Unable to decide if he was being deliberately obtuse, I tipped my head to one side. "You don't think it would look seriously strange if we divorced but kept working together?"

"No, I don't. There's no reason for you to leave. You can stay where you are."

"Um, no, I can't."

His eyes flared. "Yes, you can. You will."

"It would be too weird. And people would think I'd stayed to be near you; it'd look like I was clinging to what scraps you would give me. No, I have my pride. I can't stay at o-Verve. Patience is a *really* good PA."

"I don't want her. I want you."

God, how I wished he meant something *wholly* different by that. "Dane, just—"

"You're staying. End of discussion."

I felt my lips thin. "Why are you being difficult about this? Look, I know you had trouble finding a PA who 'fit' you and who can overlook the fact that you're an asshole at times. That's *why* I'm looking at a potential replacement now. I can give Patience a little extra training, and then she'll just be able to slot right into my position when I'm gone."

He ate up the small space between us, standing so agonizingly close I could feel the heat of his body; could feel the dark, sheer intensity he gave off like pheromones that made my body pulse with an electric awareness.

"You don't need to give her any extra training," he stated. "She's not going to need it, because she's not going to be working for me. I already have a PA, and she suits me just fine. I don't intend to let her go anywhere."

"You can't *force* me to keep the job."

His brow hiked up. "What do I always get, Vienna?"

I folded my arms. "Okay, tell me how you intend to ensure I stay in a job I'll no longer want. I'm genuinely curious how you think you'll achieve this."

He tilted his head. "Did you ever think you'd marry me, Vienna—sham marriage or not?"

"No."

"And yet, you did. Never think I'm a man who ever settles for anything less than exactly what he wants. I never have, I never will. I know how to get what I want, and I know how to keep it."

"I wonder if you'll be saying that same thing when I'm boxing up the stuff from my office desk after the divorce."

"It won't come to that. You're staying at o-Verve."

God, give me strength. "Dane—"

"You're staying."

"You're being unreason—"

"You're. Staying."

"Oh. My. God. Stop being a brat."

His nostrils flared. "A brat?"

"Yes," I snapped, out of patience. "You're all about what *you* want. For just a few moments, step out of Dane's world and remind yourself that one of the things I really want is to get married for real at some point. Remember we talked about that? I want a partner. And kids. And, yeah, a cat. I want to find someone who does actually care for me; who wants to build a life with me. That's never going to happen while you're in the picture, because no guy is going to be interested in me if I'm working for my fucking ex-husband. That's what you'll be. My. Ex—"

He took my mouth with a low growl, sinking his tongue inside. Hands bunched my hair as he herded me backwards until I hit the counter. It knocked the breath right out of me, but his mouth kept on eating at mine with *so much* greed and urgency. Stunned by the absolute ferocity of his kiss, I could only cling to him, digging my fingers into his upper arms.

Logic, reason, rationality, control—all of it was burned away by the carnal demands of his mouth. I strained to be closer, kissing him back for all I was worth. He growled in approval, punching his hips forward, grinding his cock against my clit. *Oh, God, yes.*

The burn of his hot mouth felt like a brand. The erotic flicks of his tongue demanded more. The sure, confident hands that roamed over me screamed possession. The feel of his dick rubbing my clit felt like a promise.

I really needed him to follow through with that sexual promise, because the molten lust pumping through my veins had whipped my body into a damn frenzy. My nipples were hard. My pussy was damp. My nerve-endings were crying out for more.

He shoved his hand into my panties and thrust a finger inside me—no preamble, no hesitation, only the sheer intention to *take* what he wanted. His finger curved just right, and I gasped. He put his mouth to my ear and pressed on my g-spot. "There?" It was a snarl in my ear. He knew damn well he'd found the right spot.

"Yes," I hissed, arching into his hand.

His finger, so skilled and warm, worked me hard. His free hand yanked up my top, and he latched onto my nipple. I moaned as he sucked, bit, and flattened the taut bud against the roof of his mouth until it tingled and throbbed.

Releasing my nipple, he bit my earlobe. "I'm going to fuck you. Possess you. Tell me you want it," he said through his teeth.

"I want it."

He fucked me harder with his finger, growling as my tight inner muscles contracted around it.

I moaned. Groaned. Demanded more. And then I came. My release hit me out of nowhere and totally swept me under. I sagged against him, breathing hard, my heart pounding in my chest.

Dane withdrew his hand, propped me on the counter, and ragged off my pants and panties. He snapped open his fly, freeing his cock. Fuck, it was *thick*. And long. And it looked almost painfully hard.

He whipped a condom out of his back pocket, donned it fast, and then angled my hips just right. "Going to make you come so fucking hard for me." He rammed his cock balls-deep into my swollen pussy, taking full, instant possession of me in one brutal thrust.

My breath caught in my throat. Jesus, he felt bigger than he looked. He didn't give me a moment to adjust to his size. He pounded into me like it was the only thought in his mind.

I locked my arms and legs tight around him, groaning as his fat cock dragged over long-unused, super-sensitized muscles. It had been at least ten months since I'd last had sex. And, well, this was sure making up for it.

He was all masculine domination as he took and used and fucked me with sheer sexual aggression. I loved every damn second of it. And it wasn't long before another orgasm began to build inside me, making my pussy flutter and tighten.

"Not yet," he bit out. "Hold it."

"Can't," I rasped.

He snarled. "Fucking hold it. You come when I say, not before."

Bastard. I clung to him tighter, as if it would keep the orgasm at bay. There was something primal and almost animalistic about the way he grunted and growled and breathed hard against my neck while he fucked me. And that flipped my switch in a way I wouldn't have expected, which did *not* help me stave off my release.

"Dane." It was close to a sob.

"That's it, baby girl," he praised. "Keep holding it for me."

I felt his cock thicken inside me as he upped his pace, slamming so hard it hurt in a way that only amplified the pleasure. Each savage thrust wound me tighter and tighter, until I was so close to coming, I could practically taste it. And that was it. I couldn't hold it any longer. "*Dane.*"

"Come," he growled. "Want to hear you scream."

Pure pleasure whipped through me like a bolt of lightning. My eyes went blind, my head fell back, my back bowed, and—sure enough—a raspy scream tore out of my throat.

His fingertips bit into my thighs as he rammed harder once, twice, three times. His spine stiffened and he growled a harsh curse, burying his face in my neck as he exploded inside me.

I slumped against him, my lungs burning for air. It took at least a few minutes for my post-orgasm buzz to fade enough for reality to filter into my brain. When it did, I inwardly cursed.

Shit, this had been a bad idea. A really bad idea.

Well, not so much an "idea." I hadn't been thinking. Only feeling. All sensible thought had vanished from my mind the moment Dane's mouth crushed mine. I couldn't even blame him, though. *Both* of us lost control, and I doubted he was any more comfortable with that loss of control than I was.

I straightened as he withdrew his cock. He stepped back, still panting, and stared at me—his gaze utterly unreadable. I stared back, not knowing what to say. Apparently, he had no words either, because he didn't speak.

I righted my top and slipped off the counter. I sensed more than saw him remove the condom and fasten his fly as I pulled on my underwear and pants.

Meeting his eyes, I forced a smile. "Goodnight." Lame, sure, but I really didn't need to listen to a "that was a mistake" speech.

Keeping my chin up, I casually padded out of the kitchen and headed up the stairs, my inner muscles still pulsing. In my room, I sank down on the bed and closed my eyes. Had I really just had sex with Dane?

Yes, I had. Raw, rough, epic sex.

I'd never come that hard in my life. Probably because I'd never once been fucked like that—with such want and need and aggression.

It was like four years' worth of sexual tension exploded between us—because, yeah, it was clear that I'd been wrong; I wasn't the only one who felt it. He'd done an amazing job of fooling me all this time. But then, he was a freaking expert at deception.

Not that I thought he might have some sort of "thing" for me. Nor was I under the mistaken impression that he'd want a repeat of tonight. I wasn't so dumb that I didn't understand one very important thing: I could have been *anyone* to him.

He hadn't been desperate to have me. He'd been angry and needed an outlet for all that pent-up emotion. If I hadn't pushed him tonight, if I'd just walked away when he reacted so badly to my saying I'd leave o-Verve, his control would never have snapped like that, and the sex would never have happened.

Yeah, it stung to know it had meant absolutely nothing to him. But I wasn't going to whine about it. I was a big girl.

The ghostly sensations of his fingers biting into my thighs and his cock moving inside me lingered. And I couldn't find it in myself to regret what had happened. It had been stupid for certain. But life was all about making memories, right? That was what Nancy always said.

Of course, the old woman also said that Charles Manson was just misunderstood.

I sat up straight, determined not to give myself a hard time about sleeping with Dane. After all, what was done was done. It had been a nice way to break my dry spell. This didn't have to be a bad thing. It just needed to be a one-off.

CHAPTER SIXTEEN

Setting my empty coffee cup on the drainer the next morning, I heard footsteps approaching. Determined not to exhibit any awkwardness, I pasted my default smile on my face and turned. *Damn.* Suited-up and oozing authority, Dane looked impossibly gorgeous and totally in charge.

As casual and aloof as always, he arched a brow. "Ready to go?"

Apparently, he was on-board with the "pretending last night never happened" plan. Good. That made things easier.

I nodded and gathered my things. "Ready."

In the car, I turned my gaze to the window and watched his lush landscaping go by as we descended the long driveway. The estate really was beautiful. A lonely place to be at times, but still beautiful.

"It can't happen again, Vienna."

I forced myself not to tense. Without looking away from the window, I said, "I know." Because I'd never mastered the art of separating emotion from sex. Thanks to the developing crush, I was already close to crossing the emotional line with Dane. He just didn't know it. If we made sleeping together a regular thing, I'd struggle to not go past that line.

At least he hadn't branded last night a mistake. He wouldn't have been wrong, but it still would have stung to hear him say it.

Eager to change the subject, I looked at him and said, "Hope and Travis came to see me yesterday while you were talking with the teams."

His dark eyes narrowed slightly. "And you're only telling me this now?"

"You were in a shitty mood yesterday. I figured it could wait."

He raised the privacy screen and asked, "What did they say?"

"They told me about the trust fund—allegedly, Jen agreed with them that I should know. Hope and Travis tried convincing me that you only married me to gain access to it; they think I should leave you now so that you can't use me any more than you already have."

Dane's jaw hardened. "You should have told me *immediately*."

"Like I said, you were in a foul mood. I planned to tell you when we got back to your house, but I didn't have much success at calming you, and then …" *Then you fucked me in your kitchen.*

"Hope should have known better. I warned Travis to leave you alone. Clearly being barred from his favorite casino hasn't inspired him to change his ways."

I frowned. "You had him barred from a casino?"

"After he fed you the last 'Dane is evil' speech, yes. He was trying to cause trouble between us; trying to make my life difficult—I was just demonstrating that I can return the favor. Travis used to play a weekly card game at the casino with a bunch of wealthy assholes who'll gamble everything from money to animals. Now he can't anymore, and he hates that. But he hasn't yet backed down."

"He can no doubt feel his share of your trust fund slipping away from him—he was never going to take that lying down." I really would love to throttle the weasel for being so greedily determined to attain money and assets that weren't rightfully his that he'd actually fuck with his brother's life this way. "They were probably lying that Jen banded with them over this."

"She thinks the same as they do when it comes to you and me, so there's every chance she was involved."

"At least Kent had nothing to do with it."

We arrived at o-Verve a short while later. Inside the building, I'd no sooner fired up my computer than Hanna appeared at my desk. I smiled and pulled a card out of my purse. "Happy birthday. Your usual gift card is inside."

She took it with a huge grin. "Thank you. Like my badge?"

I eyed the round, "It's my birthday and I'll curse if I want to" badge she'd pinned to her shirt. "It screams 'class.'"

"I know." Leaning forward, she whispered, "I'm guessing you fucked Dane's brains out last night."

I tensed. "What?"

"Well I saw him walk into the building a few minutes ago. He's no longer snarling and glowering and generally scaring people."

Oh, right. "Sex is a good outlet for stress."

"Here, here. So, are you still coming out for drinks after work tomorrow?"

"Yes, of course." A bunch of people from o-Verve went to a local bar every year on the Friday closest to her birthday.

"Ace! I'll see you later."

"Later." Turning back to my computer, I got to work.

I'd worried that just maybe things between Dane and I would get a little weird as the day went on, but they didn't. There was no awkwardness, no tension, no cracks in our work dynamics. It was honestly as if nothing had happened last night. But then, for Dane, it really *had* been nothing. Just emotionless, stress-relieving sex. I told myself that that didn't bother me, but it was a damn lie.

The day seemed to go by superfast. Before long, I was slipping on my coat, ready to leave. It was only then that Dane announced he wouldn't be coming home yet—he'd accepted an invitation to a last-minute dinner meeting.

It occurred to me that he'd attended a few of those recently. There had also been evenings where he'd returned to o-Verve alone and hadn't come back home until late. If I didn't know any better, I'd think he was trying to avoid me.

Well, whatever.

No, not *whatever.* He'd asked me to move into his unnecessarily large house, and then he'd developed a habit of leaving me there alone a lot of the time. When he *was* at home, he might as well have been elsewhere.

Yeah, okay, it wasn't his fault that he didn't like company. And no, there was nothing wrong with that. But there was something dull about just the thought of going back to such a large, empty house, even if it was beautiful.

As I hopped into the sleek car outside, I smiled at Sam. "Could you take me to my father's house, please?"

The driver returned my smile. "Of course."

"Thanks."

When he finally pulled up outside Simon's home, I said my goodbyes to Sam, assured him I'd catch a cab home later, and then crossed to my father's front door. I used my key to let myself inside, calling out, "Dad?"

Simon popped his head out of the kitchen and beamed at me. "Vienna, I didn't know you were coming."

"I thought I'd surprise you."

"Well, you did." He gave me a tight hug as I entered the kitchen. "Missed you, sweetheart. No Dane?"

I shook my head. "Not this time. He's at a meeting."

"Story of his life, I suppose."

"You're not wrong."

"Well, what brings you here?"

Following Simon further into the kitchen, I inhaled the delicious scents of meat, bolognaise sauce, and onions. My stomach rumbled. "I wanted to see you," I told him. "I've missed you."

"Glad to hear it. I'm just about to dish out some dinner. I can share. Meatballs sound good to you?"

"Sounds perfect." I set the table while he plated the food.

Twirling some spaghetti around his spoon, he asked, "How are the plans for the wedding reception going?"

"Great. The planners, Chris and Miley, are completely on top of it."

Simon chewed his food and then lifted his glass. "To think my darling girl is now married …" He sipped his water. "Considering everything moved at warp-speed, you must sometimes feel like your head is spinning."

"Yes, it's become a familiar state of mind."

"But you have no doubts about Dane, do you?"

"None at all. I just struggle to keep up with the speed at which he moves. He's like this in every area of his life. So, how's your job going?"

"Fine, fine." He went on to tell me about his new manager.

I'd just finished my last forkful of food when I noticed that he'd pulled his legs up onto his chair and had rested his chin on his knees. Grimacing, he pushed aside his plate. "How do you eat this stuff?" he asked, his voice lighter and childlike. "Meatballs are yucky." He stuck out his tongue, as if the air would clean it.

I felt my mouth curve. "How do you eat bags upon bags of beef-flavored chips in one setting?"

Freddie gave me an imperious look. "They're made from potatoes. That means they're good for you."

I snorted. "If you say so. How are you doing, Freddie?"

"Okay." He watched me from under his eyelashes. "Will you still come see us lots even now that you're married?"

"Of course," I replied.

"You won't let Dane keep you from us?"

"Definitely not. Why would you think he'd want to do that?" I tilted my head, waiting for him to explain.

Freddie picked at the leg of his pants. "He looks at you like … I don't know. Like he'd keep you all to himself if he could."

No, Dane was just *real* good at acting. "I'm sorry you've been worrying about that, but you have no need to. He'd never try to keep me away from the people I love. I'd sock him in the mouth if he did."

Freddie flashed me a boyish smile. But that smile faded. "Do you think he'd hit you back?"

It didn't surprise me that he'd ask that. Freddie had taken the brunt of Simon's childhood abuse; he knew that the people closest to you could often also be the ones that hurt you. "No, never. Do you worry that he would? Does he scare you?"

Freddie looked at the table, his expression pensive. "Yes and no. I think he's like Deacon. Hard. Super serious. Unhappy deep inside." His eyes met mine again. "Deacon doesn't like it if you give other people attention when he's around."

"And so you think Dane won't like it either." I shook my head. "He's not going to try to keep me away from you or anyone else I care for. And if he did try it, I wouldn't want him anymore. You're stuck with me, Freddie, whether you like it or not. Got it?"

His smile was shy. "Got it." He wrinkled his nose. "Can I braid your hair again?"

"Sure. If you help me wash the dishes."

He made a sulky sound. "That is *so* not a fair deal."

Later, I took a cab back to Dane's estate. The driver whistled at the sight of the large electronic gates and asked if I truly lived there. Apparently, I didn't fit his idea of the kind of person who'd afford a place like this.

Hopping out of the taxi, I punched the security code into the intercom's keypad, and waited for the gates to open. It took me a good minute to walk the length of the driveway. I was just thankful it was well-lit—the sounds of wildlife coming from outside the grounds might have otherwise made me a little paranoid that something was stalking me.

Strolling into the foyer, I rolled back my shoulders, tired and ready to collapse into bed. I'd only taken two steps toward the staircase when Dane breezed out of the hallway holding a crystal tumbler filled with amber liquid. "Hey," I said simply.

Swirling his glass, he watched me. "Sam said he took you to Simon's house. You didn't say you intended to visit him." His tone was neutral, but I got the feeling he wasn't too happy that he'd heard about it secondhand.

I shrugged. "It wasn't planned. He says hi, by the way."

"Your hair is loose."

Was that a note of suspicion in his voice? What did he think I'd been doing exactly? "Freddie likes to play with it."

His shoulders lowered just a little. He sipped his drink. "I spoke to Travis and Hope. They both said they mentioned the trust fund to you but never tried to insinuate that I married you to access it. Travis was also again adamant that you're simply trying to cause trouble between us."

"And what did you say?"

"That I believe they're full of shit."

"Do I want to know how you'll retaliate?"

"I've already done it. He's barred from three more casinos, and she's barred from her favorite clothing store."

I gaped. "You can really arrange to have a shop *refuse* to serve a person?"

"If you have enough money and power, yes. Hopefully that will be enough to keep them from playing more mind games."

Honestly, I doubted it would. They stood to gain a whole lot of financial goodness if they succeeded in separating Dane and me.

Fighting a yawn, I gave him a brief wave. "Well, goodnight."

I walked up the staircase, conscious of Dane's eyes on me the entire time. Or maybe I was just imagining it. Maybe I was just being dumb.

Reaching the landing, I glanced down at him. No, I hadn't been imagining it. He was staring at me hard, his body still, his free hand a tight fist at his side. Like he was internally wrestling with something. And suddenly, I felt far too hot.

He took another swig from his glass and then turned away. "Night, Vienna."

I headed to my room and puffed out a breath. I'd just reached my door when the buzzer rang once, twice, three times. I turned and headed to the hallway window. No cars were yet driving up the path, and I couldn't see whoever was behind the gates. Again, the buzzer went off several times, like someone was jabbing it with their finger.

I went back down the stairs just as Dane re-entered the foyer. "Who is it?" I asked.

"Heather, *demanding* to see us," he replied. "And I've just opened the gates for her." He drank another gulp of the amber liquid. "My guess is she believes that we're behind the recent photos Thad's wife received of him and Heather together."

"You had that done *this* quickly?"

"I'm not one to procrastinate. Especially when I need to make a point."

We stepped outside just as Heather hopped out of her Mercedes in the courtyard. Her mouth tight, she slammed the car door closed and marched toward us. "Are you fucking kidding me?"

I felt my brows rise. "Excuse me?"

She curled her upper lip. "Don't pretend you don't know why I'm here. Thad called me. His damn wife knows about us, because *someone* sent her photos of me and him together. Someone who wrote on the back of one of the pictures, 'My conscience just wouldn't let me keep quiet.'"

"Ah, your own words coming right back at you," I said.

"So, what, you got a kick out of coming between me and my man?"

"Isn't that kind of what you tried to do to me?"

"You should have known there'd be consequences to that shit you pulled." Dane sipped more of his drink. "You could have stopped at just flirting with me, but you didn't. You could have stopped at sending just one email, but you didn't. You were determined to have my attention. Well, you got it."

"This is the thanks I get for warning you that the woman you married is still hung up on her ex?" She leaned toward him. "I did you a solid."

"You did what you seem to do best: you fucked up." Dane swirled his glass. "If you'd stayed out of our business, we'd have stayed out of yours. You didn't. If you have any sense, you won't repeat that mistake."

Heather curled her fingers like they were claws. "You're telling me I lost my boyfriend because you didn't like an email I sent you?"

"If you lost him, it's because he chose his wife over you," said Dane. "And that's just *eating* at you, isn't it? Breaking up relationships isn't simply a power trip for you. No, you need—maybe even crave—that feeling you get when someone chooses you over a person they love. Why is that? Because you needed your parents to choose you over Vienna? You needed them to throw her away, like those men threw their wives away?"

Her eyes flickering, she took two unsteady steps backward. "You don't know a damn thing about me," she said to him, a tremor in her voice. "Not one thing."

I stared at her, my mouth agape. He called it. He totally called it. I hadn't seen it before, but he was right—she needed to feel that she'd been chosen over someone else. As if it was the only time that she felt she *meant* anything. But the feeling obviously faded all too quickly, because she'd gotten caught up in a cycle where she kept doing it again and again.

I couldn't believe I hadn't seen it before. Hell, it seemed as if *she* hadn't realized it until now. Her face had gone white, and she looked like she'd had the breath punched right out of her lungs.

"You'll pay for this," Heather hissed at him.

Dane took a step closer to her. "You think this is bad? There are so many ways I could fuck with your life. You think I don't know the truth about the child support payments you receive from Junior's father? You think I don't know it's actually hush money? Rowan doesn't want his wife to know the boy exists, and you've capitalized on that. You're blackmailing the man, pure and simple."

"That's a lie!"

"Imagine if his wife discovered Junior's existence. There'd be no need for secrecy anymore, would there? You'd continue to get money from Rowan, yes, but true child support payments wouldn't amount to anything close to the hush money you're used to. That's assuming Rowan and his wife wouldn't file for custody of Junior—even if only to spite you. In their situation, I'd resent giving you my well-earned money."

Heather shook her head. "You wouldn't contact his wife. No, you're bluffing."

"I never bluff. I made sure Thad's wife knew about her cheating husband. Why would you think I wouldn't do the same for Rowan's wife?"

Heather's lips trembled. "Bastard," she spat.

"There's a lesson to be learned here. You leave me and Vienna be, and we'll leave you be. But if you dare fuck with either of us again, I *will* turn your world upside fucking down."

Breathing hard and fast, she looked from me to him. "You both deserve each other." With that, she spun on her heel and stalked off. Moments later, her car sped out of the gates.

Feeling a little dazed, I turned to Dane. "How did you find out she was blackmailing Junior's father?" I asked, struggling to get my head around it.

"I have my ways," he replied.

"Why didn't you tell me about any of this?"

"I didn't want you wasting emotional energy on her. Every time you think of, speak of, or talk to Heather, you get this tired look on your face. Like she drains you and brings you down. You're wearing it right now. I don't like it. I wasn't going to put that look on your face unless I had to, so I decided to put a pin in this. It wasn't something you urgently needed to know."

I bristled. "I'm not as fragile as you seem to think I am, Dane."

He closed the space between us. "I don't think you're fragile. You're far from it. In fact, you're stronger than I originally gave you credit for. It's a quiet strength. One Heather sees and resents, because she doesn't possess it. That's why she tries to crush it. I think she'll heed our warning, though. It'll kill her to swallow her pride and back down, but she'll want to keep her cashflow nice and steady."

"*And* she won't want us to tell Melinda and Wyatt she's been blackmailing Junior's father. I still can't quite believe she stooped so low. I knew she purposely got pregnant to milk the father for money—she proudly admitted it; thought it made her clever." I raked a hand through my hair. "She's got fewer ethics than I thought. I don't get it. I don't get why she's like this. She's had a good life, Dane. Parents who love and support her. Shelter and food and stability. And yet …"

"Some people can only appreciate the good in their lives when they've had a taste of what it's like to suffer," Dane pointed out. "You had a shit start to life, so when Melinda and Wyatt entered it, you recognized how fortunate you were to have them and the safety that they gave you. Heather's had it good since day one, but she isn't a person who's learned to appreciate it. She doesn't see what she has; she only sees what she doesn't have."

"I almost feel sorry for her. I'd hate to never be able to feel content." I cocked my head. "Is it hard to live a life where you never feel fully satisfied? You're nothing like Heather, I know. But you have that drive to keep seeking more and better. You keep moving the marker. You never seem to feel that you have enough."

"You think I'm unhappy?"

"Not unhappy. Just … not completely fulfilled."

"Neither are you."

"I know. I haven't yet gotten the things I really want from life."

"Ah, yes, the family and the cat."

I gave him a stony glare. "Is there something wrong with that?"

"No. You want to create the very thing you wish you'd had—a strong family unit. You want people who'll love you unconditionally, and people who you can love freely without others hating you for it; people who make you feel safe and secure and accepted. It's not wrong to seek the solid, normal family you never had."

"You've gone the opposite way from me, haven't you? You've decided you don't need the solid family you never had; you've decided that you don't need anyone and that you're better off alone. That's not wrong either. We just want different things." But I couldn't try to make my plans a reality until I was no longer Mrs. Davenport. "At what point next July are you going to want me to sign divorce papers? The day after our anniversary might seem odd, but I guess it won't matter at that point—you'll have access to your trust fund, which is all you want."

He hiked up a brow. "So eager to go through with the divorce, Vienna?"

"No, I was just asking."

The corner of his mouth curved into a mocking smile. "One day, you'll no doubt have the devoted husband you want."

I narrowed my eyes at his sardonic tone.

"But for now," he added, pitching his voice lower, "you're here with me, wearing my rings, living in my home, using my surname." The note of possession in his tone made my nape prickle. "Essentially, you're mine for the time being, Vienna. And I'll let you go when I'm good and ready."

CHAPTER SEVENTEEN

I lifted my highball glass and sipped at my drink; the fruity taste burst on my tongue. "I'm wondering at the wisdom of the multi-colored striped carpet. I mean, this is a bar—drinks must get spilled *all* the time. It would make more sense to have wooden flooring."

Hanna's nose wrinkled. "You think about the weirdest stuff when you're drinking."

"No, I don't."

"No? Just minutes ago, you 'pondered' whether people would be better adjusted adults if they didn't watch Disney movies as kids."

"Come on, those movies are full of tragedy and sorrow. Bambi's mom died. Simba watched his father be murdered. Old Yeller was shot. An entire village was decimated in *Mulan*. Dumbo's mom was locked up for trying to protect her son. Tod's adopted mom abandoned him *in the woods*—okay, he was a fox, but there were hunters."

"That scene *was* sad. But it was *My Girl* that destroyed my childhood. I mean, Vada's best friend died after being stung by bees! I was terrified of them for *months* after that."

"God, that movie was traumatic. The part where little Thomas is in the coffin and Vada loses it and starts balling her eyes out … it all left a scar on me for sure."

Mouthing the lyrics to the song playing, I glanced around the upscale bar. It was trendy with its red, gold, and black color scheme. It wasn't crowded, but it was busy. Patrons drank, talked, laughed, and even sang along to the music.

As I'd arranged the previous day, I'd come here straight from work with Hanna and some of our coworkers. Since I'd forgotten to tell Sam and Dane about it, I'd earlier rattled off a quick text message to the driver, informing him that I'd be taking a cab home tonight. I'd also texted Dane—who was attending another late dinner meeting—to say that I wouldn't be back at his house until late. He hadn't replied until half an hour ago, and that had only been to ask what bar I was at—no "have a good time" or anything like that.

Hanna took my hand and admired my rings. "I just love these. I don't know why you won't let me try them on. I'll give them straight back."

"You don't think Dane would freak?"

"He'd never know."

"We're surrounded by coworkers who'd *totally* tell him."

Her shoulders lowered. "Yeah, you're right." She leaned closer and said, "Sorry that some of them are being weird toward you—I didn't expect that. They don't act that way at work."

They did; Hanna just hadn't been around to see it. "But now they're not at o-Verve and there's no Dane around to fire them, so they feel comfortable being rude."

The two women who usually gave me attitude at work, Rachel and Lianne, were now leaning into each other and whispering while staring at me. They also let out the occasional snicker. Ugh. Whatever.

The guys were worse. A few of them kept making passive-aggressive remarks and jokey comments that weren't actually funny. They seemed to find themselves hilarious, though. Well, at least *someone* was laughing. The worst offenders had gone to the bar to flirt with some random strangers, and I sure hoped they stayed there.

Hanna adjusted her cleavage. "I don't think it's a coincidence that the ones being rude are either guys *you* turned down or women that *Dane* turned down. They're just bitter. And jealous. And having an ego-related crisis because they were rejected in favor of someone else."

"Hmm-mmm." I shifted slightly, making the red leather cushion beneath me squeak a little. The sofa was long and stylish, much like many of the others that lined the walls of the bar. Not comfier than the furniture at Dane's place, though. Speaking of which … "When are you *finally* going to get over your aversion to my house? Every time Ashley and I try and plan for the three of us to have a girls' night there, you put us off."

"I don't have an aversion to your house. I've told you, it would just feel weird to hang out in my boss's home."

"It's *my* home, too." I placed my glass on the square napkin beside the lemon wedge I'd fished out of the drink. "And it's not like you'll have to hang *with him.* He'll make himself scarce to give us privacy."

"I know, but … I would just find it super hard to relax there. It's Dane's haven. He doesn't even like having people in his office much. I'd feel out of place. Like I shouldn't be there. Also, I'm not really in a rush to step into the home of a psych—"

"And we're done."

Hanna gave a little huff. "Look, if you don't want to see the dark side of him, that's fine. But blinding yourself to it won't change that it's there."

"People can have a dark side without also having asocial personality disorder. Now stop trying to change the subject and tell me you're going to get over your issues to enjoy a night in with me and Ashley."

Just then, the two obnoxious o-Verve guys who'd disappeared to the bar returned to our group. One of them, Jeff, stumbled backwards, almost knocking into a server who held a tray of colorful drinks above her head.

Laughing at himself, Jeff slumped into the chair opposite me. His eyes hardened when they met mine. "Ah, Vienna, Vienna, Vienna. You know, I really didn't take you for a gold-digger."

Wow, he'd really gone there. I mean, he'd been hinting at it all evening in a jokey way, but I hadn't thought he'd actually come right out and say it.

Hanna flapped her hand in his direction. "Go away, Jeff. You're an ugly drunk."

He frowned. "I'm not drunk. I'm just being blunt." He pointed his beer bottle at me. "I remember I asked you out years ago. You told me you never mix business with pleasure. I should have known you'd break that rule for a guy if he had a big enough bank balance."

I cocked my head. "Is that what you tell yourself? Does it make you feel better to think I broke my rule for Dane purely because he's rich, not because I thought he was *worth* breaking it but didn't believe the same of you?"

Jeff's face reddened. "I'm only saying what everyone else in the company is thinking."

Hanna sat up straight. "I'm not thinking it."

"Neither am I," said one of the other guys.

"Nor me," another man piped up.

Smirking, Jeff dragged his chair closer to the table and leaned toward me. "Don't listen to them, Vienna. They talk smack about you when you're not there. All the teams do."

"If that was the case, it would say everything about them and absolutely nothing about me," I said.

The guy beside Jeff—who'd made just as many sly remarks as him—put a hand on Jeff's shoulder and said, "Pipe down. This isn't worth losing your job over."

Jeff shrugged off his friend's hand and snorted. "Dane's not going to fire me. He was talking about promoting me."

"And a few words from her could make you miss out on that promotion," his friend persisted.

Jeff made a dismissive sound. "Like she has any sway over him." He sliced his gaze back to me. "How'd you get him to propose anyway? Pretend to be pregnant?"

I sighed. "Seriously, if being an asshole burned calories, you'd be fucking anorexic. Now maybe we could talk about something other than me and Dane. Like how Hanna's birthday went yesterday."

"*Or* maybe we could get you to admit that you only want Davenport for his money," said Jeff.

I drained the last of my drink. "You know, your parents should have tossed you over a cliff and just kept the stork."

"Here, fucking here," muttered Hanna.

Jeff flashed me an ugly smirk. "You haven't once denied you want him for his money."

"What would be the point?" I asked, idly twirling my glass. "You'll believe whatever your itty, bitty ego—which, let's face it, is the equivalent of a fragile, sensitive, hormonal teenager—needs you to believe. Who am I to mess with that?"

"Who indeed," said Hanna, all haughty. "She just wasn't into you, Jeff. Deal with it and stop being a dick."

"Women are such bitches," he sniped.

Every female at the table bristled at the generalization. Jeff did not realize it, but he'd united us all that easily.

Hanna lifted her hand. "Hang on a sec. *You're* the one acting like an ass, but *women* are in the wrong purely because they called you on it?"

I sighed. "Ever notice how women always get the blame for men being dicks? Their mom didn't hug them enough, the girls at school made fun of them, their adult ex-girlfriends jilted them, their ex-wives used to nag at them. And if you reject a guy, it can't possibly mean you simply don't like him—no, it means you're stuck up or a frigid bitch or something."

Rachel nodded. "I've noticed that. It's pretty ridiculous."

"I know," agreed Hanna. "You fear turning a guy down because it's possible he'll get ugly and make a scene."

"I get that it's hard for men to make a move," began Lianne, "they have to suck in their insecurities and put themselves out there; that can't be easy. But it doesn't make us bitches if we politely say no."

"Yup," I agreed. "Don't get me wrong, not all men do it. Some will take it with grace. But those that don't? They ruin the dating scene for everyone else."

Jeff thumped his bottle of beer down on the table. "How did we go from discussing Vienna whoring herself to men being assholes?"

I clenched my fists. "Jeff, stop."

"Stop what? Speaking the truth?"

"Seriously, Jeff, just shut the fuck up."

"Why? You can't handle being called out for what you are?"

"You *really* need to stop talking."

"And you need to stop being a gold-digger, sweetheart. But life doesn't always work out the way it should."

Everyone in our group fell quiet. Which should have been a dead giveaway that something was wrong. But Jeff just kept smirking at me, either too drunk or too stupid to pick up on anything else.

I'd warned him to shut up for a very good reason—I'd noticed a certain someone heading to our table. And now that certain someone stood behind Jeff.

Totally done with this evening, I smiled at the newcomer. "Hey, Dane."

Jeff froze. I thought he'd laugh and accuse me of trying to call his bluff, but as his gaze swept over the people sitting either side of me—all of whom were no doubt staring at their boss—the color drained from his face.

He twisted in his seat and blinked up at Dane. That easily, the idiot's level of machoism bottomed out in a rush. Understandable. Dane stood unnaturally still, tension coiled in every muscle … making me think of a viper poised to strike. His bold, unblinking stare was wholly focused on Jeff, who was hopefully coming to the self-realization that he was one seriously stupid prick.

"Dane. I, um …" Jeff rose and offered him the chair. "Sit down. I didn't know you were coming. Can I buy you a drink?"

Taller by at least a foot and a half, Dane stared him down. There was a lethal glint in the depths of those dark eyes that made my scalp prickle. "I couldn't help but hear you brand my wife a gold-digger," he said, his voice steady and dripping with caution. "Why would you go and do a thing like that, Jeff?"

Jeff's mouth bopped open and closed. "It was just banter. I was … you know … just joking."

"Yeah? I didn't find it funny. More importantly, neither did she."

Jeff forced an easy smile. "I was fooling around, Dane. Really. It was just supposed to be a bit of harmless banter. Right, Vienna?"

"Don't look at her," Dane said to him. "Look at me."

Jeff's gaze flew back to his. "Dane, man, it was just—"

"A joke, banter—yeah, I heard you. The thing is … I know you're lying to me. But I don't think you *truly* believe my Vienna's a gold-digger. You just wanted to hurt her. Why would that be, Jeff? Were you one of the ones who singled her out when she first came to work for me? One of the ones who crashed and burned?"

"I wasn't trying to hurt her—"

"You're still lying to me." Dane tipped his chin toward the exit. "Why don't you come outside with me, Jeff?"

Uh-oh. I gripped the table, ready to push to my feet if necessary. "Dane."

Jeff shook his head. "I'm not going to fight with my boss."

"I'm not your boss anymore," Dane told him. "As of two minutes ago, you no longer work for me. Now get outside."

I stood. "Dane, he's not worth it."

"No, he's not. But you are."

Jeff stood his ground, the dumb bastard. "Why go outside? Why not just take care of this in here?" He cast a quick glance at our group, and I realized he expected one of them to intervene and stop the fight before it could start. But no one said a word or made a single move, as if striving to remain off Dane's radar.

"Because if we do it in here, I'll have to make sure it's over with quickly—the management will overlook a sucker-punch, but it doesn't like brawls." Dane took a fluid step toward him, so tightly controlled yet so alive with menace. "*Outside*."

"Nah," said Jeff. "I say we just—"

Dane slammed his fist into the prick's jaw like a fucking pro. Jeff's head snapped to the side with the force of the blow, and his eyes went out of focus. *Lights out*. Jeff dropped to the carpet, almost knocking down his chair. It all happened so damn fast … and I wasn't as progressive as I'd like to believe, apparently, because all that strength and power affected me on a very primal, viciously sexual level.

God, I needed help.

I rounded the table and touched Dane's arm. "We should go." The spectacle hadn't gone unnoticed, and I didn't fancy watching my fake husband get arrested. "Hanna, thanks for inviting me." I promised to call her soon and then exited the bar with Dane.

Outside, I took a long breath. I didn't know who I was angrier with—Jeff for being a sack of shit, Dane for coming here to pick me up like it was past my curfew, or myself for finding that little display of violence something of a turn-on.

"Well that was fucking fun." I sighed. "Why did you come here?"

"It would have looked rather strange if I hadn't, since I'm a man who wouldn't like even the thought of my wife sitting in a bar without me right beside her. You should have called me the second things got ugly in there."

"I was handling it."

"You shouldn't have to. Did anyone else in there try some 'banter' with you?"

Knowing a bunch of people would lose their jobs if I told him what happened, I instead replied, "No."

Dane put his face close to mine. "I want their names."

"Nobody said—"

"Don't lie to me, Vienna. I want every name, and I want to know everything they said. You can tell me about it in the car." Dane took my hand and began to lead me across the wide road. "Is this going to become a thing now?"

I frowned. "What?"

"You not coming straight home from work."

"No more than you returning to o-Verve or attending late dinner meetings has become a thing, I'm sure," I said primly. As we reached the center of the road, I dropped my purse. "Shit." I bent down and grabbed it.

Hearing an engine rev up and tires screeching, I looked to see a pair of blinding headlights speeding through a red light while swaying almost drunkenly. The jeep collided with another car, sending it skidding along the road … toward us.

I froze for what felt like endless seconds as an old memory hit me hard. But I snapped out of it when Dane began yanking me toward the curb.

I could hear the car still skidding toward us. I could smell the burn of rubber chafing the ground. It slowed to a halt just as we reached the sidewalk. It was right then that my heel caught on something and I tripped.

Only Dane's grip on my hand stopped me from falling flat on my face on the sidewalk. Stumbling, I reflexively threw out my free hand to help brace myself, hissing as my palm scraped along the ground.

Dane helped me stand upright and looked me over, his face hard. "You okay?"

My heart pounding, I blinked at him. "I'm fine. You?"

He gave a curt nod.

I looked at the two cars and took in the crumpled metal and ghost-white faces of the passengers that were jerkily sliding out of both vehicles. None looked badly hurt, but one had a vicious cut above their eye.

Dane slid an arm around my waist. "Come on, let's get you out of here. You sure you're okay? You're pale."

I licked my lips. "Yeah, I'm good. I … I was hit by a car when I was nine and, yeah, the past and present kind of fused for a second, but I'm okay."

He led me to the car, assured Sam we were both fine, and ushered me onto the rear passenger seat. Sliding in beside me, he took my hand in his, and I flinched. Frowning, he looked at my palm.

"It's just a graze from where I tried to steady myself when I almost fell." It stung like a bitch.

I wrapped my arms around my middle, feeling slightly chilled. It was only then I realized I was shaking a little.

Dane's arm came around me, warm and strong. He gently drew me to him and tucked me into his side. "Settle," he said, smoothing his hand up and down my arm. "You're shaking like a leaf."

"I'm not doing it on purpose."

"I know, it's just the adrenaline. You'll be all right."

I shamelessly burrowed into him. "At least all the passengers were okay."

"Hmm. You were hit by a car when you were nine?"

I nodded.

"How badly were you hurt?"

"I had a broken leg, a skull fracture, and some bruises. I didn't really feel the pain until I got to the hospital. I was in shock." I could still remember how numb and disconnected I'd felt. Could remember how everything around me had seemed so distant. The driver and bystanders had talked to me gently, but I hadn't really been able to absorb their words.

"I kept telling the driver—man, the guy was a mess—that I was okay to walk home," I added. "What's weird is that it all happened *so* fast I didn't get the chance to *feel* scared. And yet, I had nightmares for months after."

His arm tightened around me. "I'm pretty sure anyone would have."

Silence fell between us. I stayed snuggled into Dane, letting his body heat chase away the chill in my bones. At one point, he dug out his cell phone. I rolled my eyes. We'd almost been hit by a car and he was casually answering work emails. Typical.

We soon arrived at the estate. By then, my heartbeat had steadied, and the full-on body shakes had faded to a faint tremor in my hands.

Inside the house, Dane gently guided me into the kitchen and lifted me onto a stool at the island. "Be still." He examined the smarting graze on my palm. "It's not deep, and there's no gravel in it."

"It doesn't hurt badly."

"It might when the adrenaline fully bleeds out of your system."

"You should ice those knuckles." They were red and a little swollen from the punch he'd delivered to Jeff's jaw.

"I'll do it later. Stay there."

And then, well, one of the most surreal moments of my life occurred. Dane very gently cleaned, patted dry, and applied a sterile adhesive dressing to the graze. He was careful, thorough, and precise—as professional as any nurse. He also refused to let me help; just instructed me to sit still.

Done, he said, "Antiseptic creams can damage the skin and slow healing, so I didn't bother putting any on you."

"How do you know that? How do you know how to treat grazes so well?"

He shrugged. "I Googled it when we were in the car."

I stared at him. "You … you Googled it?" My heart melted. I thought he'd been working to keep himself occupied. No, he'd been looking up how to treat grazes. "Thank you," I said, my voice soft and a little raspy.

He inclined his head. "Want a drink?"

In truth, what I wanted was to have him inside me again. This whole night—the knockout punch, the adrenaline rush, the heart-melting—had my body all fired up even as an odd sense of exhaustion began to settle in. But even if he would have been game for that, I knew better than to let anything happen between us again.

"I want you to ice your knuckles. Then I want to sleep." But, not trusting that he wouldn't go to bed without first seeing to his hand, I didn't move until he'd iced it enough to make the swelling go down.

"You sure you don't want a drink?" he asked, flexing his hand.

"I'm good, but thanks." I slipped off the stool. "And thanks for hauling me out of the way of the car." He only inclined his head again, so I gave him a faint smile and padded out of the room. As nights went, this one had been damn bizarre.

CHAPTER EIGHTEEN

"Shh, you're all right."

I snapped awake with a loud gasp. The room was dark, but I didn't panic at the sight of a figure sliding into my bed; I knew it was Dane; knew that voice and scent.

I was breathing hard, my pulse was racing, and I felt a lingering echo of anxiety. "I was dreaming," I remembered. Dreaming about screeching tires and bright headlights. There'd been a jumble of images—some from when I was nine; some from tonight. More, it was Dane who'd been knocked over … and Travis had been the driver. It didn't take a psychologist to work out what had prompted that part of the dream.

"I know, I heard you," he said.

I winced. "Sorry if I woke you."

"You didn't. I was getting undressed when I thought I heard you call out something. I came to check on you and quickly realized you were having a nightmare."

Keeping my arms folded, I shuffled closer to him, feeling cold. It was only then I realized his chest was bare, but I still didn't move, needing the warmth that radiated from him.

Dane snatched the covers, which I'd apparently kicked off in my sleep, and dragged them over us both. He slid his hand under my tee to splay on my back. "Now settle."

Settle? How could I do that when he was lying so close, smelling so damn good, with his palm pressed against my bare skin? The memories of the last time we'd been so close, of him pounding into me like a man possessed, flipped to the forefront of my mind. *Hell.*

It was a good thing I'd folded my arms before I'd shifted nearer to him. It not only meant my hands couldn't wander, it meant he wouldn't know my nipples had tightened.

I really did despise how effortlessly he affected me. It had been bad enough *before* we slept together. But now that I knew what it felt like to have him moving inside me, it was so much harder to ignore his pull.

A low growl sawed at the back of Dane's throat. "Stop thinking and sleep."

"I'm trying."

"Try harder."

Sighing, I closed my eyes and tried blanking my thoughts, figuring it would be useless. But I must have managed to doze off at some point, because the next time my eyelids fluttered open, sunlight was creeping around the edges of the electronic shades.

I licked my lips. And froze. Oh, shit, I was *half-sprawled* on top of Dane.

My head was pillowed on his chest, my arm was slung around his waist, and one of my legs was curled over his. Moreover, one of his hands was loosely curved around the calf of the leg I'd hooked over his; the other hand had dipped into my panties and shorts to palm my ass.

I tensed. Well this wasn't good. Not wanting to wake him, I carefully tugged my leg free of his hold and straightened it. Just as slowly, I pulled back my arm and tucked it between us. I shuffled backwards, hoping the arm he'd curved around me would slip away and that his hand would then slide out of my panties. But that arm stayed where it was … as did his hand.

Giving up on moving him, I stared at his frowning face. He was such a remote, troubled, relatively remorseless man who struggled with empathy and seemed largely indifferent to the feelings and sensitivities of others. But he'd punched Jeff for calling me a gold-digger. He'd dragged me away from the skidding car. He'd treated my graze with utter gentleness. He'd come to me when I had a nightmare. And he'd stayed with me the rest of the night, even though he allegedly didn't like sleeping in the same room as others.

Fuck, how was I supposed to keep an emotional distance from him when he was chiseling at my defenses?

Desperate to remain on solid ground, I reminded myself that none of it actually meant anything. I mean, he'd *had* to punch Jeff—it would have looked weird if he hadn't defended me. People all over the world had pulled perfect strangers out of the way of cars; put in that light, his behavior wasn't such a huge deal. He wouldn't have treated my graze if my hands hadn't been trembling too much for me to do it myself. And *of course* he'd wake me when I was having a nightmare—who wanted to listen to someone make all kinds of noise in their sleep? It also had made sense for him to stay with me, since it would have made it easy for him to snap me out of any further nightmares.

Yep, everything he'd done had been motivated by pure common sense, nothing more.

I flexed my sore hand. Damn, my palm stung. At least I'd have the weekend to help it heal before going back to work.

Maybe it made me a little shameless, but I was truly considering flipping back the covers so I could get a better look at his bare chest. What I could see of it was certainly impressive—he looked deliciously toned. Downright lick-able, in fact.

My nose tingled and twitched as a sneeze built up out of nowhere. I covered my nose and mouth as the sneeze burst out of me. His eyes flipped open. I seriously had no idea how anyone could snap awake so easily. It concerned me, really. It made me wonder if there'd once been a time when he'd needed to be on his guard during the night; if he'd needed to wake at the slightest sound in order to protect himself. The very thought made my chest tighten.

His head turned toward me, and those lazy, slumberous eyes met mine. Just like that, my stomach clenched.

"Morning," I said.

His eyes flitted over my face, searching. "You okay?"

I nodded. "I slept pretty well, all things considered. You?"

"Not so bad," he replied, smoothly and casually sliding his hand from my ass to my hip. "Don't know what it is about this bed, but I always sleep longer when I'm in it."

A faint smile tugged at my mouth. "It's an awesome bed." And it was a lot more pleasant to lie in when I had Dane bare-chested beside me, but I kept that little nugget to myself. "Thank you for staying with me. Again."

He shrugged, releasing my hip and letting his arm flop to the mattress. "You don't snore, wriggle around, hog the covers, or take up too much space."

I almost barked a short laugh. If he'd woken a little earlier, he wouldn't have said the latter.

Since I desperately needed to pee, I edged out of bed. "Nature calls." I padded to the bathroom, hearing him rise behind me. It took all of my self-control not to glance over my shoulder and get a better look at that chest. In the bathroom, I gave myself a mental pat on the back in reward and then went about my business.

Dane leaned against the counter while I poured coffee into two mugs. "I want to know who else at o-Verve thinks like Jeff."

I sighed. I should have known he'd circle back to that eventually. "Dane, can't you just let it go?"

"You know me better than that." He picked up his cup. "Was it confined to last night, or have things also been going on at the company?"

I set down the coffee canter. "Nothing's been going on … per se."

"Elaborate on 'per se.'"

I explained how people had changed toward me, though I downplayed it slightly. "It was nothing, really."

"It wasn't 'nothing.' And don't think I'm not aware you're downplaying it."

See, total warlock. "I knew there'd be people who'd accuse me of marrying the boss to get my hands on his money. No one actually said anything to my face until last night. And that was mostly just Jeff."

"Mostly," Dane echoed. "Who else?"

Knowing the graze on my palm would burn like a bitch if I grabbed my cup, I carefully lifted it by the handle and then sipped my coffee. "It's not worth the bother."

"If I let this go, if I don't come down hard on it now, it will not only continue, it will get worse. So tell me who they are. I won't drop this until I have their names. You're already well-aware of that. Save yourself any further aggravation and just tell me what I want to know. Consider it an order from your boss."

I reluctantly gave him the names. "I think two of them are actually on our reception guest list."

"They won't be after I tell Chris and Miley to cross them off it." Sipping at his coffee, he stared at my rings—something he'd begun to do often. I wondered if he'd decided to keep the engagement ring after the divorce.

"Jeff, the two-faced fucker, shook my hand and congratulated me after hearing you and I got married," Dane went on. "He said we made a great couple and that he'd always thought there was a 'spark' there. He'd been 'rooting' for us, apparently."

"You believed him?"

"Not for even a millisecond. He's not half as good an actor as he believes he is, and I've caught him mooning over you often enough to know he'd be far from happy for us. But I didn't think he'd pull the kind of shit he did last night."

I set down my cup. "I think he felt emboldened by you hinting at promoting him. I don't know if the alcohol had muddied his thoughts, but he seemed to believe it meant he was too valuable to o-Verve for you to fire."

Dane frowned. "There's only one person in my company who's an irreplaceable employee. That's you. Which is why you're not leaving."

Explicit memories crawled all over me. "I'm not even touching that subject again."

His eyes shimmered with something that made my stomach flip, and I wondered if he too was drowning in some very delicious memories.

I didn't realize I'd fisted my hand until my nails pricked the pad-covered graze on my palm. I uncurled my fingers and gently stroked over the pad.

"Does it hurt much?"

"It itches and stings sometimes, but it's not so bad." I leaned against the island. "I called Officer Griffin before I came down here. None of the enquiries into the burglary amounted to anything."

"That's not all that surprising, since—"

The buzzer sounded.

I frowned. "Are you expecting anyone?"

"No." His thumbs tapped on the screen of his phone, and then his brow furrowed. "It's Kent and Jen."

Oh, wonderful. Hey, I had nothing against Kent, but his wife was a moron. "You let them in. I'm going to make some cereal. Want anything?"

He shook his head and left the room.

I poured some fruit loops into a bowl, added some milk, and then settled on the stool at the island. I expected Dane to escort his visitors into the den or something, but he brought them to the kitchen. Chewing cereal, I gave them a little wave.

Kent's smile faded. "What happened to your hand?"

"I was performing a random gravity test but ended up almost giving the sidewalk a hug," I replied.

Dane came to stand at my side. "A jeep crashed into a car as we were crossing the road," he told our visitors as they slid onto the stools opposite mine. "The car skidded toward us, so we had to hurry to reach the sidewalk." He looked down at me. "Thankfully, you reached it *before* you tripped."

"I might not have made it if you hadn't hauled me out of the way." I put a hand to my chest and sighed up at him. "My hero." I snickered at the droll look he sent me.

"Thank God neither of you were hit," said Kent. "What about the passengers? Did they survive?"

"None died or appeared badly injured," replied Dane.

Jen braced her elbows on the island. "They were lucky, then. As were the two of you."

I shook my head. "It wasn't luck for us. It was Dane's super-human speed and reaction time. Seriously, I wouldn't have been surprised if he'd done an Edward Cullen and stopped the moving car with his hand." I looked up at him. "You're not a vamp, are you? Because it would explain your predatory nature, aversion to garlic, why you never seem to get sick, how you seem to be able to read my mind, and why you keep biting me during sex. Not that I'm complaining about the latter. It's hot."

Dane sighed, but his eyes lit with a faint glimmer of amusement. He gently flicked the diamond on my engagement ring. "You have a drop of milk on your chin."

I frowned. "You usually don't complain when I don't swallow properly. I don't know where I am with you."

He fisted my hair and tugged my head back. "Behave." He pressed a soft kiss to my mouth. "You're going to pay for that later." He released my hair.

"Eat your cereal."

"Fine. But don't think I didn't notice that you avoided my question."

Dane shot me a look of impatience and then turned back to our visitors. Kent had sucked in his lips to hide a smile. Jen was gazing out of the kitchen window, pointedly ignoring our back and forth.

"What brings you both here?" Dane asked them.

Kent hesitated. "I didn't want to do this, it feels too much like tattling, but …" He exchanged a distressed look with his wife. "I wanted to warn you that I think Travis might try to cause trouble for you and Vienna, Dane. He came to our home drunk last night. He's really not happy that you married Vienna. He kept bouncing from insisting the marriage was fake to snickering about how she's tricked you into a whirlwind wedding, like he didn't know what to believe."

"Hmm." Dane twisted his mouth. "I appreciate the warning, but it's redundant. He's already tried to cause trouble. He told Vienna *twice* that he thinks she should leave me. He and Hope even tried to convince her that I only married her to access my trust fund."

Kent softly swore under his breath.

"According to them, Jen was in on it."

Jen's eyes widened. "What? That's a load of crap."

"Is it?" Dane asked airily.

She gaped at him. "You really think I'd do that?"

"You made it clear to me once before that you thought it was all about my trust fund, didn't you?"

Wincing, the woman dropped her gaze to the hands she'd rested on the island.

Kent's brow furrowed in confusion. "Jen, what is he talking about?"

She slouched and looked up at Dane, her expression pained. "I owe you an apology, I know. You just went *so* fast from being against marriage to being determined to bind her to you. I couldn't wrap my head around it. But it wasn't my right to question it or you. And although you might be utterly ruthless, I don't think you'd manipulate a woman into believing you wanted to marry her unless it was true. Especially a woman you respect enough to have hired as your PA." She looked at me, then. "I'm sorry for the things I said, Vienna."

I wasn't so sure I believed her. Or maybe I just wasn't feeling particularly charitable toward her after she'd spoken of DID like it was a virus.

Kent twisted in his seat to face her. "Wait, you accused him of *using* Vienna that way? You said the same things Travis has been saying? When?"

She closed her eyes and ducked her head. "I came to see Dane the day he got back from Vegas. And yes, I said those things. I was just … there's no excuse."

Kent's face twisted in anguish. "*Jen.*"

She raked a hand through her hair. "I know, I feel terrible about it now." She looked from me to Dane. "I'm determined to put it right by supporting you both from here on out. So if there's any help you need with the reception preparations or anything else, please let me know."

Um, yeah, I'd pass on that until I was satisfied that she'd meant what she said here today. I didn't trust her not to try and fuck the plans up.

Kent stared at her, shaking his head. "I can't believe you went behind my back like that. You didn't think I at least deserved to know about it after the fact?"

"I didn't tell you because I was ashamed of myself," she began, "and I knew how disappointed you'd be that I'd let you down this way. It won't happen again."

"No, it won't," said Dane—it was a warning, pure and simple.

She blanched and nodded.

Kent stiffly stood. "Dane, Vienna—I'm sorry to you both for what Jen did. As you can imagine, she and I need to talk, so we'll be on our way."

Jen slowly stood to leave and, avoiding anyone's eyes, followed her husband to the front door.

Before leaving, Kent turned to Dane. "Hugh would be thrilled for you."

I inwardly winced. If the comment made Dane feel in any way bad, there was no sign of it on his face.

Once the couple was gone, I blew out a breath. "Hopefully we won't have any more surprise visitors." I wasn't feeling in a particularly social mood.

"Yes, hopefully." Dane drained his coffee mug. "Let me know when you're ready to have lunch. I've got calls to make."

"And I've got books to read so, yeah, see you in a few hours."

CHAPTER NINETEEN

Returning to my desk after a quick trip to the restroom, I saw that a pile of mail had been delivered. I suspected that, as per usual, most would be addressed to Dane. He was currently out of the building, but he'd been clear that he would pick me up from o-Verve at the end of the workday.

In the week that had gone by since the incident with Jeff at the bar, Dane had … well, I couldn't say he spent time with me, but he avoided me less than usual. He hadn't attended so many late external meetings, so we'd eaten dinner together on his free evenings—sometimes at the office, sometimes at home. He'd also accompanied me on my visits to Simon, Melinda and Wyatt, and even to Ashley and Tucker.

It had been a calm week. I hadn't had any further contact from Travis or Hope. There hadn't been a peep out of Heather either. It had just been … normal. But I wasn't confident that it would last.

Now, standing at my desk, I screened Dane's mail, separating the letters he'd need to respond to personally. Only once that was done did I flick through my own mail.

Tearing open a brown bubble envelope, I slipped my hand inside and pulled out a small jewelry box. I double-blinked. A gift from Dane? I doubted it. Since he was out of the building, I couldn't even ask him.

It had better not be a damn gift from Owen. I'd thought he'd given up trying to stupidly "win" me back.

I opened the box, expecting to see earrings or something. I felt my face scrunch up as, instead, I found a USB flash drive. *The fuck?*

I glanced inside the envelope. There was no note, just as there was nothing written on the envelope itself that would indicate who sent the package.

Picking up the flash drive, I pursed my lips and glanced at my computer.

I should put my "gift" back in the box and deal with it later. I was working right now, and I highly doubted that whatever was on the flash drive was anything to do with work. But curiosity won out, and I soon found myself inserting the flash drive into my computer.

A few clicks on my keyboard later, I discovered there was only a single folder saved to the memory stick. It had been named: "Just thought you should know." I frowned. What the hell was this?

My scalp prickled. Part of me wanted to eject the damn thing from my computer and put it back in its box. But, again, curiosity overrode my wariness.

Using the mouse, I double-clicked on the folder to open it. I felt my frown deepen. Nine photographs had been saved into the folder, all titled from "Pic1" to "Pic9."

My heart began to pick up speed, because I had the distinct feeling that I wouldn't like what I was about to see. I clicked on the first small thumbnail to enlarge it. I found myself looking at a side-on view of Dane standing on the doorstep of a house. A slim brunette stood in the doorway, clad in only a tank top and shorts. My stomach did a slow roll.

God, please don't let this be what I think it is.

Licking my lips, I enlarged the second photograph. The camera lens had zoomed in so that I could see Dane *inside* the house. He stood in the living room facing the brunette, who was a mere foot away. I flipped to the next photo. Now they were standing closer, and his hand was cupping her chin. My chest went tight, and I swallowed hard.

In the next picture … oh God, she was in the process of peeling off her tank top. I hissed out a breath and shut my eyes. I didn't want to look at the other photos. Hadn't I seen enough?

No. No, I *had* to know what else there was to see.

I took a deep breath and continued down the list of pictures. The next two were also taken at her house, but they were clearly taken on a different day from the first three—hers and Dane's clothes were different. They weren't in her living room this time.

They were in her goddamn bedroom.

I gripped the mouse so tight I was surprised it didn't crack. In one image, she and Dane were standing near her bed, facing each other, and he was holding a pink sweater … as if he'd just stripped it right off her. In the following picture, she was on her knees in front of him, her head bowed in a somewhat submissive pose, her hair shielding her face.

So, what, was he into BDSM or something? Was she a sub? *His* sub?

I didn't realize my hands were shaking until I struggled to focus the cursor on the seventh thumbnail. I finally brought up the picture, blinking in surprise to see that the setting had changed. It showed Dane walking toward a large, black building. His suit was once again different.

My nose wrinkled. I didn't recognize the place, and it wasn't surrounded by other buildings, so I couldn't even guess at the area.

I clicked on the eighth photograph, hoping it would give me some clues, but it only showed him disappearing into the same building. Biting my lip, I enlarged the final picture; it was an image of him exiting the place, his tie dangling from his hand, and his shirt open at the collar.

Not whatsoever understanding why anyone would think to send me the latter three photos, I took a better look at the building. There was a sign above the door on which something was written in red and gold lettering. I zoomed in on the image. *Club Euphoria.*

I'd never heard of it.

I brought up an online search engine on my cell and typed in the name of the club. I scanned the list of results that then came up, finding a club of that name based in Redwater City. A sex club. It was a fucking sex club.

The urge to send the computer crashing to the floor was so strong I had to back away from the desk. Breathing hard, I rubbed at my aching chest. Really, I could be getting wound up over nothing, couldn't I? These could easily be old photos.

Grasping that thought hard, I checked the meta data of each picture. Allegedly, they were taken in the last month. But that info could be faked, right? Maybe. I didn't know enough about meta data to be sure.

When would he have a chance to sneak around with other women anyway? He was busy all the time, going to meeting after meeting.

And, up until a week ago, spending many of his evenings alone at o-Verve. And then there were those external dinner meetings that had run late.

My blood ran cold. What if he hadn't truly spent so many evenings at o-Verve, and what if those meetings hadn't *truly* run so late? What if he'd been going to see *her*? The brunette. Or what if he'd been indulging himself at the club?

Grabbing the planner, I checked the dates on the photos alongside the dates on his schedule. My stomach sank. He had indeed had external dinner meetings on the evenings he'd—if the photos were to be believed—been visiting the brunette.

There'd been no scheduled meeting on the evening he was supposedly at the sex club, though. Closing my eyes, I thought back to that day; remembered how Dane had curtly turned down my offer to share a pizza with him; remembered how he'd claimed he needed to return to o-Verve and would eat there. And if the photos were dated correctly, he'd fucking *lied.*

Even as it hurt to do it, I flipped through the pictures again, as if I might somehow see something that would convince me I was being played by whoever was holding the camera. They might have put the flash drive in a jewelry box as if the info was a gift to me, but they'd done it with the intent of hurting me enough to make me walk away from Dane.

I took a closer look at each of the images, trying to read the expressions on his face. No matter how close he stood to the brunette, he never looked turned-on or like a man who was anticipating sex. *But he was touching her.*

It *was* possible that these pictures were taken before I began "dating" Dane; that the meta data had somehow been tampered with.

My instincts were pricking at me, telling me I was missing something. Something small and obvious—

The tie. The tie he was wearing on the first three photos was new. The personal shopper brought it to his house on the very same day she brought me a bunch of new clothes to replace the ones that had been stolen. Which meant that the first three pictures couldn't be old, and so the others probably weren't either.

God, I was going to be sick.

The bastard. The lying, deceitful, *horrible* bastard.

We weren't a true couple, so he hadn't exactly cheated on me. But it *felt* like a betrayal. Emotional betrayal, more than anything else, because he'd lied to me … and I'd believed him. He'd said we'd *both* need to take a vow of celibacy until after the divorce. Either he'd only ever intended for that to apply to me, or he'd been unable to last and so he'd sought pleasure elsewhere—like from his sub.

Jealousy speared me so hard it hurt. More, it pierced right through the lies I'd told myself. I wasn't close to crossing an emotional line with him. I'd already done it. I'd grown to care for this man who'd never feel the same way for me. And he'd played me like a cheap harmonica.

Did he really have so little respect for me? Apparently so. Because he had no qualms with repaying my loyalty to him—a loyalty I didn't actually owe him, given that the marriage wasn't real—by sneaking around with other women and making a fool of me.

It was really a good thing he wasn't in his office or I'd have stormed in there and fucked his shit up. I didn't want to do this at o-Verve. Others might overhear, and I didn't fancy sharing with everyone else just how stupid I'd been. It was goddamn embarrassing to think that he'd had me *so fooled.*

I should have known better than to buy into his bullshit. I'd known he was a master at deception. I'd known he played people well. I'd been dumb to assume he wouldn't deceive me in such a way. The devil always lied, didn't he?

I took a few moments to get my shit together, knowing I couldn't afford to let my anger loose here. I was glad that he wouldn't be returning to the building until the end of the workday—it meant I had plenty of time to find *some* semblance of calm.

Ejecting the flash drive, I slipped it into the side pocket of my purse. But the images didn't leave my thoughts as easily as they left the screen of my computer. They remained at the forefront of my mind all day long as I worked, distracting and taunting me.

Dammit, it shouldn't pain me this much. But it did. Which was why I held onto my anger so tight I thought it would choke me. It staved off the emotional crash I knew I'd experience later, when I finally let myself really *feel* the full impact of his betrayal.

There were several times throughout the day when, as weak as it made me, I found myself questioning whether the photos were truly what they seemed. There was no denying that they looked bad or that they were as incriminating as hell, but they didn't show him fucking the brunette.

Surely if Dane had screwed her, the cameraman would have sent photographic proof of it, because he clearly *wanted* me to believe Dane was cheating on me. Why only send pictures that hinted at it? Maybe he just liked the idea of me being confused and only able to guess.

Who was the bitch anyway? Dane sure seemed to know her well, and he was comfortable enough in her home to venture up to her bedroom.

If there was anything innocent about his association with her, he wouldn't have lied that his dinner meetings had ran late on those particular evenings. He would have just said he'd visited a friend—or whatever the hell she was to him. So, no, I wasn't going to let myself hope that he could explain all this away.

At the end of the workday, my phone beeped just as I switched off my computer. I picked up my cell and swiped my thumb over the screen.

It was a message from Dane: *Sam and I are waiting for you outside the main entrance.*

I ground my teeth and harshly dumped my cell in my purse. Shit, I needed to keep it together. I didn't want to have a full-on blowout with him in front of Sam. The conversation needed to be had, but not until we were alone. The thing was, Dane didn't like to wait. He'd easily sense I was pissed. He read me too well. He'd want answers straight away.

What I really needed was to avoid talking with him throughout the journey. That meant I needed to have something else that required my attention; something that would also distract me and keep me preoccupied.

I paused as an idea came to me. Ashley *loved* to talk on the phone. She could do it for hours. I could call her as I was leaving o-Verve and keep the conversation going until I arrived at Dane's house. He wouldn't think anything of it, and he'd probably occupy himself by doing work-related stuff on his phone anyway.

As I made my way to the first floor, I called Ashley. Just as I'd hoped, she was more than happy to talk. Outside, I slipped into the car and gave Dane a too-quick smile without even pausing in my conversation with her. A conversation that turned out to be very easy to keep going.

It wasn't until we pulled into the courtyard that I said, "I've got to go now, Ash."

"Sure thing, girl," she said. "See you soon. Tell Mr. Hottie I said hi."

I ended the call, gave Sam a wave, and followed Dane into the house. He often went straight to his home office, but today he headed to the den and slipped behind the small bar.

He flicked me a look as he poured brandy into a crystal tumbler. "Are you going to tell me what's wrong?"

I folded my arms. "When you made it a habit to retreat to o-Verve of an evening and started attending those dinner meetings that always seemed to run late, I thought you might be avoiding me. Avoiding being here alone with me for some reason, like you worried I'd get caught up in all this and forget it was fake. Did you really go to o-Verve on those evenings, Dane? Did those meetings really run so late? Or were you spending some time elsewhere?"

Frowning, he set down the brandy bottle. "What is this, Vienna?"

"You didn't answer my question."

"Because I'm wondering why you'd even ask it."

"You stipulated that neither of us would sleep with anyone while we were faking being a couple."

One brow arched. "Are you accusing me of not following that stipulation?"

"Just answer my question, Dane."

His eyes narrowed. "Have Travis and Hope been whispering shit into your ear again? Is that what this is?"

"You're *still* dodging my question." I took one step closer to the bar. "Either you be straight with me about this or I walk."

A dark emotion flickered across his face. "Didn't I tell you not to threaten me with that ever again?"

"I let you keep your secrets, Dane. I respect your right to have them—it's not like we're a real couple who needs to be open with each other. But *this* is different, so I want to know the truth."

"You think I've been sneaking around with other women? That's what you think?"

My heart sank. He was avoiding the question because he didn't want to admit the truth. Anger rose up sharp again before the pain could swallow me. "Fuck this." I spun on my heel and stalked across the room.

"Vienna—"

I whirled and jabbed a finger in his direction. "No, if you don't respect me enough to give me a straight answer then I'm *done* here. I don't expect you to care for me, confide in me, or bare your soul, but you could at least be straight with me when it counts." I dipped my hand into my purse. "Oh, I think this will appease your curiosity." I tossed him the flash drive, which he caught easily. "Have fun," I spat.

Breathing hard, I hurried upstairs and marched into my room. Closing the door behind me, I flipped the lock just in case he thought to follow me. I wasn't interested in anything he might have to say. I needed to pack my shit and *go*.

I stilled, remembering that I only had my small suitcase. Shit, I'd have to leave most of my things and just pack some clothes and essentials. Then I could go to … well, I wasn't sure yet. Anywhere but here.

Storming into the walk-in closet, I grabbed the small case from a shelf and began to fill it with the clothing I'd need. The back of my throat ached, and it felt as though a massive pressure sat on my chest.

Tears stung my eyes—not just tears borne of hurt, but of anger. I would *not* cry. No. I refused to shed any tears over him.

I used the tricks I'd learned as a child to fight back tears—pinched the skin between my thumb and forefinger and pushed my tongue to the roof of my mouth. It was Freddie who'd taught them to me. They worked now, just as they always had in the past.

Marching out of the closet, I tossed the other items I'd need into the case and then yanked the zipper closed. Taking a moment to compose myself, I scrubbed a hand down my face and closed my eyes. Instantly, images of him with the brunette popped into my head.

My chest squeezing, I snapped open my eyes. Fuck, it shouldn't make me feel so sick and cold to think of him with another woman.

Hooking the strap of my purse over my shoulder, I picked up the suitcase and left the room. My insides seized as I began to descend the winding staircase. He stood at the bottom, barring my path.

"We're going to talk," he said, his tone non-negotiable.

Refusing to let him see the hurt churning inside me, I gave him a blank look. "Another time."

"Who sent you the flash drive?"

"I haven't a clue. There was no note. It was posted to o-Verve and addressed to me. Now, if you'll excuse me, I'd like to go."

His brow raised. "You don't want to know who the woman is? You don't want to know why I was at that club? I know how those pictures must look to you. Collectively, they paint a very ugly image of me—one that clearly had the desired effect, because you want to walk. But none of it is what it seems."

Yeah. Right. "Like I said, we'll talk another time."

"No, we're going to do it now. We can have the conversation right here, if you like. Makes no difference to me."

I ground my teeth. "Dane, I'm not in the mood to—"

"She was Hugh's favorite call girl."

I felt my lips part. "Excuse me?"

"Even when he was in his later years, plenty of women—young and old—were eager to share his bed because he had money and power. But Hugh wasn't interested in having a pretty ornament who'd lyingly profess to love him; he said it would be no different than him paying for sex, only he'd have to deal with the aggravation that came with a shallow relationship. So he stuck to high-end call girls, because then at least everyone knew where they stood.

"He developed a fondness for Lacey—she had a shit childhood and got into prostitution because there was nothing that she wouldn't do to provide for her eight-year-old son. She became his regular. Before he died, he told me he'd be leaving her fifty grand in his will and one of his apartments, but that she could only have those things if she gave up her job as a call girl and went back to school, just as she dreamed of doing.

"He was sure she'd do it, and she did. He made me promise to keep an eye on her, because he didn't trust that her pimp—who scares the everloving shit out of her—wouldn't harass her or bully her into going back to that life. The guy liked having control over her, and he hates that he lost it. Whenever things are going to shit, he seeks out his favorite whipping girl. Lacey knows to call me if he makes an appearance."

I narrowed my eyes, searching his face. He looked and sounded so very sincere. But then, he always did—even when lying his ass off to my family.

"Those photos of me in her living room … I was there because she called to say he'd broken into her home and smacked her around," he went on. "I was holding her chin while I got a good look at the bruised side of her face—you can't see it from the angle on the picture. She was lifting her tank top to show me the bruises on her ribs from where he'd kicked the shit out of her. Again, you can't see those marks from the angle the picture was taken.

"I went to the club the next night because he owns it, and I knew he'd be there. As I've done many times before, I beat the shit out of him—I even wrapped my tie around his throat and choked him until he almost passed out. When I called Lacey the following day to tell her I'd dealt with him, she didn't answer. Thinking he might have gotten to her again, I went to her house and I found that she was packing to leave.

"I snatched a sweater from her hand before she could toss it in the case; I talked her into not running. She knelt on the floor because that's where she'd set the suitcase—something you can't see in the picture—and she'd agreed to unpack it. If you want, I can take you to meet Lacey right now; she'll tell you everything I just told you."

"If it's all so innocent, why didn't you tell me about her?"

"Probably for the same reason you haven't told me everything about Simon's past and what made him develop DID: because it doesn't affect me; it's not something I need to know. That you haven't told me isn't personal, is it?"

No, it wasn't personal. As our relationship was a sham, I saw no need to tell him things about people who didn't affect him. And that worked both ways, didn't it? I was okay with that. The problem here was that he'd lied to me. "The night you went to the club, you told me you were going to o-Verve."

"And I did. Before coming home, I paid her pimp a visit."

"You knew I'd assumed that the meetings simply ran late. You let me believe that."

"Not out of some wish to deceive you. I've lived alone for a long time, Vienna. There was no one to care where I'd been or when I'd be home; no one who'd want a rundown of my movements. If you'd outright asked me why I was home late, I'd have told you because it was no big secret. But you didn't ask, so I thought you didn't care. I'm not a man who'll automatically explain where he's been—I've never had to."

Okay, yeah, I could understand that. But would he have *really* told me the truth if I had asked questions? I just wasn't sure. My emotions were all over the place, and I couldn't seem to reason everything through. "I don't know if I believe you."

"It's understandable that you're not so quick to trust what I'm telling you. I lie, I scheme, I manipulate. I'm not a good person. But my word is gold—I never break it. Which was why Hugh made me vow to watch over Lacey," he added in a put-out tone.

He tilted his head. "Why do you want out of our agreement, Vienna? You didn't just demand answers from me, you threatened to walk. It's the second time you've done it. As if your first instinct is to run from me, which tells me you want out. Why?"

Truthfully, I wanted "out" because I was swimming in emotional waters with Dane—that could only lead to me drowning, given that he could never give me what I needed even if he wanted to.

"Why, Vienna?" he pushed. "And don't say it's because you're tired of Travis and Hope's antics—you're too strong for them to break you." His gaze flitted over my face. "Is it because your last engagement didn't end so well? Owen might not have cheated on you, but he did betray your trust by hurting you the way he did."

"This has nothing to do with Owen." But I wasn't going to tell Dane the truth of why I wanted out, so I gave him another truth. "I'm sick of lying to the people I care about, Dane. Sick of living a lie. I didn't anticipate just how hard this was going to be, and that's on me."

He narrowed his eyes. "There's more to it than that."

Motherfucking warlock.

"You clearly don't feel ready to let go of your anger yet, but ask yourself honestly—do you think I lied to you about the pictures? Do you think that was one big bullshit story I just told you?"

I wanted to say yes. I wanted to say that his story didn't add up or something. But I'd have been lying, and he'd have known that. I licked my lips and took a long breath. "No."

"But you still want to walk out, don't you?"

I gave a slow nod.

"Why, Vienna? Tell me."

He was such a tenacious bastard. Knowing he wasn't going to drop it, I decided to give him an understated version of the truth. "It bothered me a lot more than I thought it would."

"What?"

"The thought of you with another woman."

He frowned. "You think the thought of you with another man doesn't bother me?"

"I don't know, Dane. I just know that this whole situation is a lot more complicated than I'd expected it would be. I'm not a runner. I face things head-on, but … Look, I don't think I'm the best person to play the part of your wife."

"You're the only person who I'd want to play it. We've come this far. No matter what shit went on around us, we forged ahead. We have to do that again now, Vienna, because I can't let you walk out. You knew I wouldn't."

I'd known he wouldn't let me go without a fight, because I was really his last hope of getting his hands on his trust fund. He didn't have enough time to do the whole fake relationship thing with someone else—not if he wanted to make it seem realistic. Especially since he'd be expected to take a break between our "divorce" and the beginning of another relationship. He'd be forced to elope again and, yes, it would definitely look fake.

He reached out and cupped the side of my neck. "I need you, Vienna. I need you to trust me when I say I didn't break my word. I need you to stay on board. You said you were in this until the end," he reminded me.

I had, and I'd meant it. But now … now, well, nothing had really changed, had it? Because I *did* believe he hadn't broken his word. Which meant he hadn't really done anything to deserve my anger. I was directing it at the wrong person.

I was also being a little unfair. Whoever sent those pictures wanted to break us up. They could have as easily followed *me* around and took photos of me that would seem incriminating. If they had, I would have wanted Dane to hear me out. No, I'd have expected that he'd have had the common decency to hear me out. And if I'd properly explained the truth of the photographs but he'd *still* doubted my word or wanted to walk out on me, I'd have been pissed. Not to mention hurt that he'd think so little of me.

Dane wasn't angry with me, though. He wasn't telling me to be rational or to cut him a break. He was being uncharacteristically patient and understanding. And me? I was playing right into the hands of the person who sent the flash drive. They'd wanted to hurt me, and I'd let them have that power. Which was utterly stupid.

But wouldn't it be just as stupid to stick around when I was clearly in far too deep with him? Wouldn't it make much more sense to leave now? Or would that just be cowardly?

I'd never thought of myself as a coward. But as I stood there weighing whether or not to walk out on him, which would mean not only breaking my word but leaving the guy in the lurch, I felt somewhat gutless. My mother was the one who ran; who always put her own needs first and didn't give a shit how her actions affected others.

Dane gently brushed my bangs aside. "When I can prove it was her, I *will* make Heather pay for this."

I blinked. "Heather?"

His brows hiked up. "You think it's a coincidence that I sent incriminating pictures to Thad's wife—ruining Heather's relationship with him in the process—and then you're sent a flash drive on which there are photos of me that appear at first glance to be equally incriminating?"

Actually, I hadn't made the connection. It would indeed seem like one massive unlikely coincidence. Still … "I can see why you'd think it was her, but this is not Heather's style. She doesn't do 'low-key.' She'd come to o-Verve and toss printouts of the pictures on my desk. She'd want us both to know how clever she was in finding you out. She'd want to see the hurt on my face; want others in the building to hear that you were screwing around on me."

"Not if she feared dealing with blowback from me. This way, she got to hurt you without suffering the consequences—she'd prefer that over backing down completely. I'll bet she's at her parents' house right now, expecting you to turn up any second in tears carrying a suitcase full of your things. She wouldn't want to miss the show. Heather can't stand the thought of you being happy. She wants to ruin this for you. She tried to convince me to leave you, but it didn't work, so she decided to try to make *you* leave *me*."

It made sense, and yet I wasn't sure I agreed Heather was the mastermind. It could have as easily been one of the other people so intent on coming between me and Dane.

I sighed and dropped my head, so fucking tired of people trying to play me in one way or another. And, of course, they were no doubt counting on that, the bastards.

Dane stepped closer and palmed my nape. "I swear to you, Vienna, if you'd asked me where I'd been those nights, I'd have told you. I just didn't think you cared."

That made my throat ache all over again. I doubted he thought *anyone* would care much about what went on in his life, not even his relatives. The Davenports weren't a family in the truest sense of the word. *I'd* have cared where he'd been, but I'd given him no reason to assume that, so he wasn't at fault for thinking differently.

He also wasn't at fault for someone having sent me that flash drive, and it was time I stopped making Dane pay for their actions. I was better than that. And I wasn't going to give them what they wanted and walk out on him.

As if sensing my capitulation, he slowly and carefully took the suitcase from my hand. "Let's take this back up to your room. Yes?"

My shoulders drooping, I lifted my head and nodded. "Okay," I whispered.

He squeezed my nape and pressed a kiss to my temple. "That's my girl."

No, I wasn't his girl. Which was part of my problem, but that wasn't his fault either.

Dane shepherded me up the stairs and into my room. He helped me unpack my case, and I wondered if he wanted to ensure that I couldn't dash out with it the moment his back was turned.

Although I wasn't feeling all that hungry, I let him talk me into joining him downstairs after I'd changed into my sweats. We mostly ate our dinner in silence, but it wasn't an awkward silence; wasn't filled with things left unsaid.

Afterward, he took my hand and said, "Come on."

I frowned. "Where are we going?"

He didn't answer. He simply led me outside, past the patio and pool, and over to the wooded area behind it. He tugged me through a slim, easy-to-miss opening in the tall hedges. I felt my mouth drop open as we stepped into a water woodland garden. There was a Japanese-style bridge, pretty waterfall, artfully weathered sculptures, decorative stones, flowering trees, and vividly colorful flowers.

Tucked within the grove of trees, it was cut off from the rest of the lavish landscape, making it feel like a secret pixie garden. It was so cozy and restful and Zen-like. A place where someone even as stoic as Dane could unwind and just shut off for a while.

"This is amazing," I said.

"Yes, it is." He tugged me over to a bench that was positioned within a vine-covered arch. He sat down and patted the spot beside him in invitation.

I lowered myself to the bench, finding it surprisingly comfy. I glanced around once more, only then noticing the gnarled, moss-covered tree and the elegant water fountain. "I could sit out here for hours and just … be. Or read."

"Feel free to come out here whenever you like." He curled his arm around me and drew me closer, so I rested my head on his shoulder. It wasn't wise to be close to him like this, but I'd lecture myself about it tomorrow.

He didn't talk or even pull out his cell phone. He just sat there, silent but so solid. Again, there was nothing awkward about the silence. It was more like we were both just absorbing the peaceful atmosphere around us.

Lulled by the floral, earthy scents and the relaxing tinkle of the small waterfall, it wasn't long before tiredness settled over me—that emotional rollercoaster ride had taken a lot out of me. Closing my eyelids, I leaned a little more into Dane, knowing and not caring that I'd fall asleep right there.

Fingertips danced up and down my arm, surprisingly relaxing, and I soon drifted off.

The fog of sleep thinned slightly when I sensed myself be lifted. My eyelids briefly fluttered open, and I saw that dusk had almost fallen. I was cradled against Dane's chest, and he was walking. Drained and relaxed, I didn't move a muscle; just let him carry me, my mind so hazy the whole thing felt very dreamlike.

I barely stirred when I felt myself be lowered to the bed. I was too tired to even open my eyes. The weight of the soft coverlet came over me, and I almost let out a contented sigh.

Fingers brushed my hair out of my face, and a warm mouth grazed my temple. "You should have known better than to think I'd so easily let you go," he whispered, the words so low and soft I barely caught them.

I felt something flick my engagement ring, adjusting its position, and then footsteps padded out of the room. Sleep tightened its grip on me and swept me under yet again.

CHAPTER TWENTY

Well, this was different.

Feeling somewhat befuddled, I stood in the doorway of the kitchen the next morning and just stared at my fake husband. Not once in the entire time I'd lived here had I come downstairs to find him cooking breakfast for us. There were occasions when we'd sort of "crossed paths" in the kitchen and so we'd eaten toast or cereal or Danish pastries *at the same time*. But neither of us had ever prepared food for the other in the morning. Until now.

I wasn't complaining. It smelled so good, and I was famished. But, yeah, it made me a little suspicious. Perhaps that just meant I was cynical. I supposed I'd soon find out.

As if sensing me, Dane glanced over his shoulder. "Morning."

"Morning."

He tipped his chin at the island. "Sit," he invited and then went back to plating the food.

I crossed to the island and slid onto a stool. There was a mug of steaming coffee waiting for me, along with cutlery. How solicitous. And very un-Dane-like.

He set two plates down on the island that were topped with eggs, bacon, sausages, toast, and breakfast potatoes. My brows lifted. He'd gone *all* out.

"Thank you," I said, picking up my cutlery.

He sat on the stool opposite me. "Sleep well?"

"I did, thanks. You?"

He shrugged and dug into his food.

I did the same and, damn, it was good. One thing I'd learned about Dane was that he knew his way around the kitchen. He was competent at so many things; it made me feel a little inadequate. I'd have been able to better enjoy the meal if it weren't for the nagging feeling in my gut that this apparent good deed wouldn't be "free."

Halfway through my meal, I asked, "Okay, what is it that you want from me? I'd rather just know now."

He lifted his mug. "I must have an ulterior motive if I cooked us breakfast?"

"You generally don't do things out of the goodness of your heart," I pointed out. "Don't get me wrong, I appreciate that you cooked, no matter why you did it. I'd just prefer to know now what it is that you're after."

"All I want is for you to finish your breakfast." He took a sip of his coffee and then went back to his meal.

Still uneasy, I nonetheless turned my attention back to my food. No matter what the dude said, I was quite sure this wasn't merely a kind or courteous gesture. Maybe he'd done this to soften me up. It was possible he worried I might still be too upset to stay; that he thought trying his hand at being "nice" would make me less likely to walk. Dane's motivations sometimes only made sense to him.

Feeling his eyes on me, I looked up to see him studying me over the rim of his mug. I frowned and swallowed the last of my eggs. "What?"

"You should invite your family to come here for dinner one night."

He … he *wanted* people to come to his house? This was new. "Why?"

"Because you miss them." He put down his mug. "You went from visiting them often to barely seeing them. Why?"

"They kept asking if something was 'wrong at home' because I visited them so frequently; they thought you and me might be having problems, especially since you didn't go with me to see them."

His brow furrowed. "I was with you when you last saw your foster parents, and the last two occasions you visited Simon."

"Yes, and they watched us like hawks the whole time, looking for clues that our marriage might be on the rocks already."

"That's all the more reason to invite them here. They need to see that everything is fine."

But things didn't *feel* fine. Not when I was now aware of just how easily this man could hurt me. The crush had allowed for a degree of emotional separation. I didn't have that anymore; he'd penetrated my defenses, and the strong sense of possessiveness I felt shook me up.

In general, I struggled to lower my guard around people. I was too wary, too distrustful. It didn't matter how nice a guy was, I always seemed to be waiting for him to mess up. I hated that about myself; hated that I expected people to hurt me. It wasn't fair to them.

Dane wasn't sweet or cuddly or kind, and I suspected that that was *why* he'd been able to slip around my defenses. I hadn't expected him to be a real threat to them, so I hadn't been fully on my guard. I'd pretty much handed him the power to hurt me on a silver fucking platter, and it sucked *large.*

"I don't know how good I'd be at convincing my family that all is 'fine.'" It wasn't just that I was so emotionally off-balance; it was that I was somewhat pettily pissed that I was the only one having this emotional crisis. If he'd been sent incriminating pictures of me, he'd have been angry that I might have broken my word, but he wouldn't have felt any of the black jealousy that had slithered through me last night.

"Why is that?"

"Having people play games all the time is starting to get to me," I fudged. "I think it would affect my … performance, shall we say?"

"Performance?" he echoed, a dark note in his tone.

I pushed my empty plate aside and shrugged one shoulder. "Isn't that what we do? Perform?"

"Hmm." He pinned me with that hunter stare, raising the hairs on the back of my neck. He edged off the stool and crossed to me, never once moving his eyes from mine. "Tell me."

I felt my brows draw together. "What?"

"Tell me what's on your mind. Don't say nothing. You were fine until you received the flash drive—and once I can prove Heather was behind it, I will make her pay. Now you look like you're carrying a heavy weight on your shoulders."

There were times when I really despised how perceptive he was. Like *seriously* despised it.

"You said you believed my explanation of those photographs," he went on. "Was that the truth?"

"Yes. I believe you."

"Then what is it that's bothering you?"

"Like I said, having people play games with us is getting to me. I'm tired of it."

"That's all?"

"That's all."

Dane put his face closer to mine. "I don't believe you," he whispered. "Something's wrong, and it's connected to that flash drive. We're doing enough lying to the outside world, Vienna. We can't bullshit each other as well; we need to be on the same page. Last night, you said you need me to be straight with you when it counts. I will be. You have my word on that. I told you everything you wanted to know. Now, I need you to be straight with me."

Did he have to be so rational and fair? "I already told you last night."

"You mentioned that the lying is getting to you. But I know that you'd rather be lying to your family than be asking them to partake in the deception, so that can't be what's weighing on you." His gaze turned inward, as if he was deep in thought. Then those dark eyes snapped back to the present. "You don't like how much the photos got to you," he remembered.

"No, I don't."

He carefully shackled my left wrist and lifted my hand. He looked at the rings, his eyes glinting with something I couldn't quite name. "You see these as props. They might not have the same meaning to us that they have to other married couples, but they're not meaning*less*. In a sense, they represent the agreement we made that night in your old apartment. If I'd thought you'd betrayed my trust like you thought I'd betrayed yours, I'd have been just as pissed as you were—if not more."

His eyes darkened as he tightened his grip on my wrist. "And if I'd thought you'd let another man fuck you, I wouldn't have been anywhere near as calm as you were last night," he said, his voice pitched low and deep. "I wouldn't have been in the mood to talk and ask questions. All I'd have wanted to do is hunt the bastard down and beat the living shit out of him. He'd have been pissing blood for a fucking week. For as long as you wear these rings, you're mine; no other man has the right to touch you. I'd never fucking allow it."

I swallowed, downright blown away by the possession blazing in his eyes. "And the ring on your finger?"

"Says I'm off-limits just the same. There's no gray area here—no other man touches you; no other woman touches me. So bear all this in mind if someday soon you think you've met the man who'll make the perfect husband. I wouldn't let you wriggle out of our deal. I wouldn't let him have you. And I wouldn't feel in the least bit remorseful about holding you to me. Does that make me a selfish asshole? Yes, without a doubt. But you already knew that about me." He nipped the heel of my palm and then released my hand.

I stared at him, somewhat appeased to realize I wasn't the only one feeling a little territorial. It was nice that I wasn't going through the struggle all by myself; it made me feel not quite so pathetic.

"Call Simon and your foster parents at some point today. Invite them to come here for dinner one night." He lifted a brow. "Okay?"

I gave a slow nod. "Okay."

He squeezed the side of my neck. "Finish your coffee. Sam will be here soon."

Melinda adjusted the cushion behind her. "How are the plans coming along for the reception?"

"Great," I said, snuggled into Dane on the other sofa. I was bloated after the three-course meal we'd had, courtesy of him. I'd helped him prep the meal here and there, but he did the bulk of the cooking. "Chris and Miley are totally on the ball, and they keep us up to date on every little thing."

"They are very efficient, aren't they? And so nice. Have you picked up your dress yet?"

I shook my head. "I have my final fitting next month."

"I'm looking forward to finally seeing this dress," said Dane, his arm loosely curved around my neck, his fingers threaded through mine so that our joined hands hung near my collarbone. "Chris is constantly telling me that I'm going to love it."

Chris was constantly telling me that Dane was going to want to rip it off me. "You're not getting a sneak preview. You'll have to wait until the reception."

"I don't like to wait."

"You're kidding," I said dryly.

Simon chuckled. "Yeah, we noticed that about you when you proposed to her *and* married her all in the space of two days. I really can't wait for the reception." He leaned forward in the armchair to set his empty mug on the coffee table. His gaze drifted to the wedding photo that we'd framed and hung on the wall. "I do love that picture."

"Me, too," said Melinda, her eyes bright. "I show my copy to *everyone* who visits."

"She's not exaggerating," Wyatt told me, sitting beside her. "Every person who walks through the door is guided right over to it."

Melinda lifted her chin. "You do the same thing, Wyatt, and you know it. Oh by the way, Vienna, my sisters promised they'd come to the reception. They're looking forward to seeing you again and meeting Dane." She looked at him and explained, "My sisters live in Oregon with their families. I was born there, too, but I moved here with Wyatt when we were in our early twenties. We originally planned to move to Australia with his brother and parents, but I couldn't handle the snakes and spiders."

A nostalgic smile curved Wyatt's mouth. "The first time we went to visit my family in Australia, my brother warned us to always tip our shoes upside down before putting them on, just to be sure there were no spiders in them. He said he'd never found anything in his own shoes, but it was best to check. I was in the bathroom one morning when I heard Melinda scream. There'd been a spider in her shoe. She was so convinced it might have laid eggs in there that she threw it in the trash."

"You can never be too careful," said Melinda.

"After that, she wrapped her shoes in clingfilm every night before getting into bed, just to be sure nothing could crawl in them."

"The spider was as big as my fist, Dane."

Shaking his head, Wyatt put his thumb and forefinger an inch or so apart. "Tiny," he mouthed.

Melinda, oblivious, added, "*And* it was hairy and had big fat legs."

Again, Wyatt shook his head. "Lies," he mouthed.

Simon chuckled. "I caught Vienna playing with spiders a few times when she was little; she liked them. But she hated beetles."

"Still do. Have you ever stood on one? That horrible crunching sound it makes …" I shuddered. "Can't stand the things." I looked at my dauntless boss. "I don't suppose you're creeped out by insects, are you?"

He shrugged. "They're just creatures, same as us."

"What about snakes?" asked Melinda.

He shook his head. "I've never been bothered by them."

Well, of course not. They were agents of the devil.

"You must have at least one fear," Melinda insisted. "Everybody fears something."

He pursed his lips. "I do get uneasy whenever Vienna attempts to bake something."

I gasped, bristling. "Hey!"

"You cook like a pro, baby girl, but the ability to bake somehow eludes you."

Simon, the traitor, nodded. "He's right. I'm sorry, sweetie, but he is."

"Baking is a completely different ball game," I defended, trying to pull away from Dane.

He tugged me closer using the arm he'd curved around my neck. "Don't be mad," he coaxed, all soft and sweet.

I sniffed, haughty. "I'm not mad."

"Then why do you look like you want to scratch my eyes out?"

"I don't need a reason."

Melinda snorted. "While we're on the subject of food, Heather's booked a table at her favorite restaurant for her birthday next week."

I expected Dane to tense at the mention of Heather, given how pissed he was that he hadn't yet been able to prove she'd sent the flash drive, despite having looked into the matter earlier. But his body language remained completely relaxed.

"She hopes you'll both be there," Melinda added.

I highly doubted that Heather had any such hopes. "Her birthday falls on the Friday, right?"

"It does," Melinda confirmed.

I gave her an apologetic look. "I'm afraid we can't make it." I really hoped no one could tell I was doing a happy dance in my head.

Dane nodded. "We leave for New York on Friday afternoon. We won't be back until Sunday evening."

"Is the trip for work or pleasure?" asked Simon.

Dane looked down at me, his eyes smiling. "We can ensure it's a bit of both, can't we?"

"We can," I said.

"Please apologize to Heather for us," he said to Melinda. "If we could cancel the trip, we would."

Ha, pure lies.

"She'll understand," Melinda assured him. "You've been on business trips to New York before, right?"

I nodded. "I love the place. It's hectic but so vibrant."

"Do you ever get tired of traveling so often, Dane?" asked Wyatt. "I know it doesn't bother Vienna."

"I'm used to it," Dane told him. "It's simply part of the job."

"I meant to ask you," Simon cut in, "where did the name o-Verve come from?"

Dane's fingers imperceptibly tightened on mine for the briefest moment. "It was one of many ideas," he said, casual, but I sensed that he was feeling far from it. "My uncle and I tossed lots of them around."

Melinda's brows lifted. "Your uncle?"

"Yes, Hugh. My brothers and I lived with him for many years. He was a good man." Dane looked down at me. "He'd have liked you."

"From everything you've told me about him, I'm sure I'd have liked him," I said.

The buzzer sounded.

Dane pulled out his phone and checked the camera feed through the security app. "It's Kent and Jen."

Again? I inwardly groaned. Which made me feel like shit, because it was good for Dane that his brother paid him regular visits. I just didn't like being around Jen.

"Kent?" echoed Melinda. "That's your brother, isn't it, Dane?" She sat up straighter and adjusted her blouse. "Good, I was hoping to meet him at some point. Vienna said he's very nice."

Yeah, I'd forewarned my family that, with the exception of Kent, the rest of the Davenports weren't terribly pleasant people, but I hadn't gone into any real detail.

Dane dropped a kiss on my head and then left the den. Moments later, he returned with our visitors. Both Jen and Kent were polite and cordial as they introduced themselves to my family. Melinda looked from me to Jen, and I suspected she'd noticed that my greeting to the brunette wasn't quite as welcoming as it was to Kent.

He flashed me a sheepish smile. "I'm sorry. We didn't realize you had company until we saw the cars in the courtyard."

Melinda waved away the apology, even though it hadn't been directed at her. "It's no problem for us. I've been looking forward to meeting Dane's family." Shameless, she began to quiz the guy. How long had he and Jen been married? Did they live far from here? Did they have children? Would they be at the reception?

Kent easily answered her questions, thankfully not looking in the least bit bothered by her sheer nosiness. He was just as friendly toward Wyatt and Simon, talking with the same ease and grace that Dane often showed them. I wondered if the brothers had picked it up from Hugh and channeled their uncle on occasion.

Jen was just as affable, if not a little stiff at times … as if feeling somewhat awkward. I had to wonder if she thought I'd told my family about her bitchy behavior. She also kept watching my father like she expected him to turn into Mr. Hyde at any moment and start doing crazy shit, which pissed me off. I was worried he'd notice, so I was actually relieved when my family announced they needed to leave.

At the front door, I waved them off. Dane then slipped his arm around my waist and led me back into the den.

Kent cast me another sheepish smile. "I was happy to meet your father and foster parents, but I still really am sorry we intruded."

"It's not a problem," I told him. "They were glad to finally meet you."

"What brings you here?" Dane asked him.

"Two reasons," replied Kent. "They're not terribly important, but I didn't want to bother you at work. One, I know you're already married, but I was wondering if you'd be interested in a post-bachelor-party."

I snickered. "Dane? Have a party? Oh, you're funny."

Dane frowned. "Not everyone's a party person."

"Hey, I'm not judging. I have to say, I'm surprised you even agreed to a wedding reception." I turned back to Kent. "It was Melinda's idea. I didn't expect him to roll with it."

Jen nodded. "Ah, it's your way of apologizing to her family for eloping."

"No," said Dane. "I have no regrets about eloping, and I feel no need to apologize for making Vienna mine so fast." He tightened his arm around me as he snared my gaze with his. "I want the reception because I want to celebrate the most important day of our lives."

"We celebrated it plenty, as I recall," I said with a suggestive note in my tone.

His mouth hiked up at the corner. "But I know you would have wanted a reception. Would have wanted the dress and the flowers and to share the day with the people you love. So I'm giving that to you. It's important to me that you're happy."

Oh, he was so smooth and believable *I* almost bought it. "Thank you for being so kind and thoughtful."

"I'm not kind or thoughtful. And you're the only person who has ever implied differently."

"Well, you're nice to me. Don't worry, I won't tell anyone else. I wouldn't dare shoot your badass rep to shit."

"Good. Then I won't tell people you bite your toenails."

I gaped in horror. "I *never* bite my toenails." I didn't even like feet.

"I didn't say you do it. But I *will* say that if you go around telling people I'm kind and thoughtful."

I gasped. "You wouldn't."

"Wouldn't I?"

"Probably," I muttered. "Maybe you're not so kind after all."

"Glad we understand each other." Dane cut his gaze back to his brother. "What's the other reason you came?"

"I have to write a speech for a presentation I'm making next week," replied Kent. "I was hoping you could read over it and give me a second opinion. Something about it is annoying me, but I can't quite figure out what it is. I need a fresh pair of eyes."

"I'll take a look."

"I have it on my phone."

"You can read it to me while I make drinks. Coffee?" he asked me.

I shook my head. "I'm good, thanks."

He lifted a brow at Jen in question.

She smiled. "Coffee would be great. Two sugars, no milk."

Dane dropped a kiss on my mouth. "I'll just be a minute." He left the room with his brother.

I retook my seat on the sofa, which placed me across from Jen, who sat with her back so straight I would bet it ached.

Crossing one leg over the other, she pasted a smile on her face that didn't reach her eyes. "Your family seems very nice."

"They are. I'm lucky."

She cleared her throat. "I asked your wedding planners if there was any way I could help with the preparations for the reception. They said to ask you."

"The planners have it all covered, but it's nice of you to offer."

She squinted, watching me closely. "You don't trust me not to sabotage anything," she guessed.

"No, I don't." I saw no need to deny it. I wasn't being a bitch; I just wasn't going to insult my intelligence or hers by drumming up silly excuses.

"I suppose I can understand that. But I'm asking you to give me a chance. I just want to make up for what I did and said."

"Why bother?" I asked without heat. "Let's be honest here, or we're not going to get past this. You don't like me at all. I can feel it in every interaction we have, so why offer to help with the reception plans?"

"Dane isn't just my brother-in-law, he's my friend—he has been for a long time. He matters to me. He's never been angry with me before. Now that he's giving me the cold shoulder, everything feels … off."

"You can't really blame him for being mad at you."

"I don't blame him at all. This mess is on me, and I want to fix it. I want my friend back."

"I don't see that happening unless you shake off how determined you are to dislike me. It's not really an issue for me, but it is for Dane. Put yourself in his position. I doubt *you'd* want to be around someone who so strongly disapproved of Kent." Then again, maybe she wouldn't care. In all the times I'd seen them together, they never behaved like a couple—there was no handholding or cuddling or even a tiny "spark," but there was esteem there. Like they were close friends.

She frowned. "So I have to like you if I want him to forgive me? That's hardly fair. We can't always help who we do or don't like."

"We can if we're *finding* reasons to dislike someone rather than giving them a chance," I argued. "Look, you and I are never going to be BFFs. But we can at least be civil to each other. For his sake, if nothing else."

"I can do 'civil.' Like I said, I want to fix my mess. But that can't happen if you're standing in the way."

I felt my brow furrow. "How am I standing in the way?"

"I'm asking you to give me a chance to make up for what I did, but you won't."

"There are plenty of ways you could try to fix your fuckup," I pointed out. "I won't get in the way of them, but I also won't trust you with plans for the reception. Find another way."

"And you'll support my friendship with Dane?" she challenged, folding her arms. "You won't feel threatened by how close he and I are?"

Threatened? Was she serious? "I don't think you two are quite as close as you'd like me to believe."

"And why not?"

"Because people share their happy moments with those who are closest to them. He never called you to tell you about our engagement. He never called you when we stood outside the chapel. He didn't even send you text messages. And I heard him tell you more than once that what you believe is irrelevant to him. That kind of says it all." So it was downright insulting that she expected me to think differently.

Color rose in her face. "You just don't like that he and I were once an item."

"An item? Oh, Jenny, this shit's just petty."

"It's *Jen*."

"You and Dane slept together. Once. The end. Why do you want me to think it was more than that? I honestly don't see what you'd get out of that on a personal level. Unless you have none-too-platonic feelings for him."

Her eyes sparkled like chips of ice. "I'm married to his brother."

But maybe she'd wanted to marry a different Davenport. Maybe she'd settled for Kent. Or maybe she just felt some sense of ownership over Dane due to their past one-night stand or long-term friendship.

"I love Kent," she stated.

That didn't necessarily mean she loved him as a wife should love her husband, or that she didn't have feelings for Dane as well.

"I care for Dane, he's family to me," she added.

"Coming into his home and acting this way toward his wife—that's not what family should do to family."

Jen went to speak again, but then she stilled at the sound of footsteps coming down the hall. She plastered a butter-wouldn't-melt-in-my-mouth expression on her face and let the tension leave her posture in a rush.

The brothers entered the den, talking amongst themselves.

She smiled sweetly at Dane when he handed her the cup of coffee. "Thanks, Dane."

His eyes narrowed slightly. It seemed he wasn't buying her act. He sank on the sofa, retaking his earlier spot beside me, and draped his arm over my shoulder. "You all right?"

I pouted and forced my lips to wobble. "No. Hold me."

He gave me a droll look.

Kent's mouth quirked. "I like that you don't take him too seriously. He needs that. Who knows? You might even help him develop a sense of humor."

Unlikely. "Let's not expect miracles."

"I have a sense of humor; I'm just not easily amused," said Dane. "Unlike some people, who'll laugh at the most inappropriate moments. Like during their wedding ceremony."

The memory made my shoulders shake with silent laughter. "It wouldn't have been half as funny if you weren't so annoyed."

"You still haven't showed me the video of the ceremony," Kent said to him.

Dane pulled his cell out of his pocket. "I downloaded it onto my phone."

I blinked. He did? I'd saved it on my laptop, but not my phone. I honestly figured Dane would have stuck the thumb drive in a draw somewhere and shoved the recording from his mind once he'd showed it to the relevant people.

Taking the phone, Kent scooted closer to Jen on the sofa. As they watched the video, he snorted and chuckled and shook his head in disbelief. Jen actually smiled, amused in spite of herself.

Kent handed the cell back to his brother. "God, Dane, your expression was priceless."

Dane pocketed his phone. "Hmm."

"Well, it'll be something to show the grandkids," said Kent.

It was only by sheer force of will that I didn't drop my smile. There'd be no kids, no grandkids. Not for me and Dane. I'd be gone in under twelve months. That was almost as sad as the thought of him living in this big house alone, year after year, growing older and older.

I could only hope that, unlike with Hugh, loneliness never eventually struck Dane. I didn't want him to live with regrets. I didn't want him feeling alone and empty, even if that meant he never once regretted our upcoming divorce.

After Kent and Jen drove through the security gates a short while later, Dane closed the front door and turned to me. "What's wrong? Don't tell me nothing. You were good at hiding it from them, but something's bothering you."

I was still feeling a little down at the thought of our inevitable divorce. I wouldn't only leave this house, I'd leave o-Verve … and I'd probably never see Dane again.

"Did Jen say something to you?" he pushed. "Did she upset you? You didn't look upset when I walked back into the den, but she was wearing her 'I'm so innocent' expression. What did she say?"

"Nothing upsetting. She just wants to fix the 'mess' she made," I answered vaguely, not seeing the sense in making things worse between them by adding what a tool she'd been.

"And?"

"And she was hoping I'd let her do that by involving her in the plans for the reception. I suggested she find another way of making it up to you."

He narrowed his eyes. "What else?"

"Nothing interesting."

He stepped into my personal space, which he did far too often these days, the bold bastard. "Vienna, tell me the rest."

I sighed. "She was just being petty, making out like you guys are super close and were once an 'item.' I suggested that she stop being so insistent on disliking me and try being civil. You never know, she might actually follow my advice."

"So, if it wasn't Jen that upset you, what did? We're being straight with each other from here on out, remember. So tell me."

"You'll just say I'm being stupid."

He frowned. "I would never call you stupid."

I blew out a breath. "Okay. Fine. When Kent made the throwaway comment about how the video would be something to show the grandkids, I got to thinking how there wouldn't be any for you; that you'd forever be here in this massive house all alone. It made me sad to think of you being on your own year after year. Which is silly, I know, because you *want* that for yourself, so go on: tell me I'm being stupid."

His steely, dark eyes began to soften, and his frown slowly smoothed away. "Vienna," he whispered with a sigh, palming the back of my head. His gaze dropped to my mouth and heated. Darkened. Glittered.

I drew in an unsteady breath as the air snapped taut. My stomach twisted, and my nerves went haywire. I felt my pulse quicken. Felt excitement flare low in my stomach.

He stood very still, his nostrils flaring, his muscles tight. It was clear to see he was wrestling with himself. It seemed that common sense prevailed, because he lowered his hand and took a step back. I wasn't sure if I was relieved or disappointed.

I grasped onto an inane subject in an effort to douse the sexual tension. "Anyway, I'd say the meal with my family went well. They didn't seem worried about us when they left."

He tilted his head. "You told them not to ask me about my parents, didn't you?"

Busted. "Only because I knew they would—it's a mundane question that most see as harmless. I just said it was a sensitive subject for you, the same way I asked you not to mention Corrine or his mother to Simon. I didn't want you to feel uncomfortable."

His face went soft and languid, but then all emotion seeped from his eyes, and his expression was once again hard. "You need to be careful, Vienna."

"Careful?"

"I'm a very selfish being. If you keep being so sweet, I'll get used to it, and I might not want to lose it. Then we'll both be in trouble." With that, he walked away, leaving me standing in the middle of the foyer with my mouth open wide.

Yeah, he was definitely going to drive me to drink.

CHAPTER TWENTY-ONE

Strolling into the den Saturday morning, Dane frowned when he caught sight of me slumped on the sofa. "You're sulking again."

I tossed him a miffed look. "Not feeling in the mood to be judged right now."

He came to a stop in front of me. "What's wrong?"

"I want to go to the zoo."

"And, what, you're eight-years-old?"

"Hey, it's not just for kids. Adults go too, you know."

"So what's the problem?"

"There's no one to go with me." I folded my arms across my chest. "Simon is working, Ashley has plans with Tucker, Hanna's spending the weekend with her sister in Long Island, and my foster parents are going to the mall with Heather and Junior."

"Why are you so eager to go to the zoo?"

"There was an article online that said they've just brought in Pallas' cats. I love them; I've never seen any in real life."

"I don't even know what they are."

I brought up the article on my phone to show him the picture. "There. Aren't they adorable?"

"Not even a little."

I felt my lips thin. "You know what? I don't need your negativity right now." I pushed to my feet. "See you later."

"Where are you going?"

"The zoo."

"By yourself?"

I headed for the door. "Yep."

A heavy sigh. "Give me ten minutes to get a few things sorted. I'll come with you."

"Funny."

"I don't joke, remember. Ten minutes."

I came to a halt and turned to stare at him. "Wait, *you'll* go to the zoo?"

A line formed between his brows as he crossed to me. "You think I have something against animals?"

"No. But you don't do good ole regular fun. You do fancy restaurants and galas and wine tasting events."

"Yes, and I suspect I'll be bored out of my mind, but I don't want you going alone."

Was he honestly serious? He couldn't be. "But you're uber busy."

"The company won't crumble if I come away from work for a few hours."

My back straightened. "Okay, now you're starting to freak me out. You're not sick, are you? Because I don't make a good nurse." He didn't *look* ill, but the symptoms weren't always visible.

He shot me a droll look. "Get your things together."

"This is for real? You'll go to the zoo with me?"

"I already said I would. Ten minutes," he reminded me.

Walking toward the zoo entrance, I smoothed a wrinkle out of my long-sleeved tee. "I like that the light breeze is cool. The animals tend to hide inside the buildings or in shady spots when it's too hot, so you don't get to see as many then."

Despite being a grown woman, I couldn't help but feel excitement bubble in my stomach. I loved the zoo. Loved the sights and the smells and the sounds. Loved the relaxed atmosphere and that there were so many things to do, leaving you the option to do as little or as much as you liked. And having Dane with me, wearing jeans that hugged his fabulous ass and a tee that stretched tight around the muscles in his chest, made it even better.

He was not at all keyed up like me, of course. That he expected to find himself bored out of his mind only made his offer to come with me all the sweeter.

"Is this really necessary?" he asked, looking at the disposable cooler bag he was carrying. "Surely they sell food."

"They do, but we're better off taking our own lunch. The queues for the restaurants are often super long. Want me to carry the bag?"

The dark look he gave me was *all* offended alpha. Like I was trying to emasculate him or something.

I raised my hands, fighting a smile. "I was just asking."

My offer to pay for the price of our admission was just as quickly rebuffed. Ignoring my protests, he paid for both our tickets.

Once we'd passed the security checkpoint and were walking toward the turnstiles, Dane threw me a sideways frown. "Why do you keep looking at me funny?"

"I'm still not convinced that you're not sick," I replied. "You sure you don't have a fever or anything?"

He gifted me with another droll look.

Finally inside the zoo itself, we moved aside and consulted a map that he'd swiped from a tiered stand. "Where are those things you want to see?" he asked.

"They're not things, they're wild cats. Pallas' cats, to be precise. They're at the southern side of the zoo." I pointed to the correct spot on the map. "We'll make our way around to them eventually. I also really want to see the bush dogs, leopards, and red pandas."

"I didn't think they'd have bush dogs in zoos."

Something about the way he'd said it made me ask, "Have you ever been to a zoo before?"

He didn't look up from the map. "I went to one on a school field trip when I was about seven, but I don't remember much about it."

I swallowed hard. Compassion welled up inside me. He might have come from a wealthy family who could afford to take him and his brothers to all sorts of places, but I often got the impression that there'd been no "family time" like daytrips.

Knowing any display of sympathy wouldn't be welcome, I asked, "What about you? What animals do you want to see?"

"None."

"Come on, there has to be at least *one* animal you like."

He shrugged. "Rhinos."

"I can see why. They're just *you* all over. Formidable and determined and moody." I turned left. "Come on, this way."

We walked along the sidewalks, passing enclosure after enclosure. It wasn't always easy to get a good look inside them or to snap decent pictures, since so many people gathered near the plastic fences. But Dane had a way of getting crowds to part—people just tended to move out of his way, like they sensed a predator coming or something—and then he'd usher me to the front, which was ace.

Some animals dozed. Some paced or sat eating. Others played and ran and swam.

Dane and I, well, we had an eventful morning. We held our breath while walking through the pungent-smelling monkey house. We shivered in the cold air of the penguin house while watching them get fed. We did a fast tour of the bat cave, which stunk like a rancid ass. And, little by little, Dane began to loosen up.

Instead of just staying at my side like a bodyguard, he pointed things out, read information signs, asked questions, found the difficult-to-spot animals for me. I wouldn't go as far as to say he was having fun, but he was *engaging*. He didn't even complain when I took a few selfies of us here and there.

Although I was saddened to know he'd only ever been to a zoo once and that he barely remembered the experience, I kind of liked that I got to see his expression when he saw some animals properly for the first time. Seeing them on TV wasn't the same.

"Aw, look at the baby meerkats." I snapped a few pictures of them. "Dane, I can't take this level of cuteness. You can't tell me your heart isn't melting right now."

"Can't I?"

"No. Even the adults are cute."

"Hmm." There was something strangely endearing about the way he looked at them as if he didn't really know what to make of them.

"Did you know that a group of meerkats is actually called a mob?"

"A mob?"

"Yep." Noticing that a little toddler with pigtails was looking up at Dane like he was a fairytale prince, I felt my mouth twitch. "A little girl is staring at you all starry-eyed," I whispered.

"And the man behind you keeps looking at your ass." Dane palmed said ass, the bold bastard. "Let's move before I kill him."

"One more pic—"

"You'll have no memory left on your phone before this day is over. Come on." He took me by my wrist and began leading me toward the next enclosure.

I gasped. "Look over there, zebras! They're—oh. *Oh*." I turned away. "I'll take photos of them later."

Dane glanced down at me, his eyes smiling. "When two of them aren't mating, you mean?"

"I'm no prude, okay, but I can't watch animals go at it. It feels weird. I like to pretend the storks deliver the babies. Ooh, I see flamingos. Did you know they're not naturally pink? It's their diet that causes them to turn from white to pink."

"Thanks for clearing that up. The mystery's been bothering me for years."

I blinked. "Did you just make an attempt at humor?"

His brows drew together. "If I wanted to make you laugh, I could make you laugh."

I clamped my lips together as I fought a smile. "Of course you could."

Sighing, he shook his head. "Just keep moving."

My heart did a silly little flutter when the fingers he'd curled around my wrist slid down to thread with mine. We walked around hand in hand, peering at more of the many animals.

I was downright *thrilled* when we finally reached the Pallas' cat enclosure. I'd watched a documentary about them once, and they absolutely fascinated me. They'd been branded the most expressive cats in the world, because they made the oddest faces.

One was curled up on a rock, staring at everything and everyone as if they were completely beneath it. No one could do "disdain" like cats. "I want to take it home."

Behind me, Dane settled a hand on my hip. "You've said that about almost every animal you've laid eyes on."

Someone knocked on the plastic fence, and the feline peeled back its upper lip.

I chuckled. "How amazing are these cats?"

"They're odd."

"That's what *I* was thinking," cut in the woman beside us, eyeing Dane with sexual interest. "Their eyes are so humanlike they freak me out."

I sniffed and started snapping photos of the cat, ignoring how the woman kept talking to Dane like she'd known him for years, even though he completely blanked her.

Was it annoying to have to deal with this crap? Oh, yes. But I had the comfort of knowing he'd never respect anyone who'd flirt with a man who was taken, so I didn't have to worry that she'd snatch his interest.

"I can't see any of the other Pallas' cats," I said. "Can you?"

Shuffling closer to me from behind, he rested his chin on my shoulder. "No. They're probably inside. Are you finished taking pictures of this … are you sure it's a cat?"

"I'm sure. I'll bet it's called Dane."

"What?"

"It's the perfect name for cranky creatures."

He snapped his teeth at my ear. "Ready to eat now?"

"Yep. Then we'll go find the rhinos and the red pandas."

We settled on the grass in the outdoor picnic area and dug into our lunch. It was only sandwiches, potato chips, bottled water, pots of fresh fruit, and mini chocolate muffins, but it all went down well.

Done, I stuffed our rubbish in the disposable lunch bag. "I didn't realize how hungry I was." I looked at my fake husband, who was lying on his side, propped up by his elbow. "You're enjoying yourself. Admit it."

"Watching your reactions to the animals is interesting. You blushed when a chimp flashed you. You shivered from head to toe when a praying mantis moved one leg. You squealed when a bat flew at you in a rage … even though it didn't really fly *at* you, let alone in a rage."

"I felt its hatred."

He shook his head. "Only you, Vienna. Only you."

"Come on, be honest; you're not as bored as you thought you'd be."

"Hmm."

It might be a non-committal sound, but … "I'll take what I can get." I cocked my head. "Did you mean it when you said the New York trip didn't have to be all about work, or did you just say it for Simon's benefit?"

He eyed me suspiciously. "Why? Where do you want to go?"

"The Museum of Natural History. I'm not asking you to go with me—I know you won't want to. I was just hoping you'd agree to free me up a few hours so I can go."

His brows pulled together. "You can't go strolling around New York on your own."

"Why? It's not a warzone, it's a city."

"Where any number of things could happen to you while you're alone. If we can find the time to go, we'll go."

"We?"

"We."

I put a hand to my mouth. "Oh, God, you really are sick, aren't you? How bad is it? Should we be picking out eulogies?"

He tugged on my hair. "Brat."

Once we were ready to continue our walk around the zoo, I threw our bag of rubbish in the trash. "I need to use the bathroom. You?"

"No, I'm good."

"According to the map, the closest restroom's over there," I said, pointing to the nearby restaurant.

He walked me to the entrance. "I'll wait here. Don't be long."

Like I planned to paint my toenails in there or something? I just shook my head and went inside. Just as I'd anticipated, the place was packed with people ordering their lunch and searching for empty tables. Yep, I'd made the right choice by bringing a pre-packed lunch.

I made a beeline for the bathroom, where I quickly did my business, and then walked back into the restaurant. I carefully shouldered my way through the throngs of people, not wanting to crash into someone who might be holding a tray of food or drinks.

"Excuse me," I said to one particular man, who was tall and heavily built. He slid out of my way with an apology, and then my stomach sank. Because Owen stood mere feet away, and he was staring right at me. *Shit.*

"Vee," he said in surprise and swallowed hard.

I gave him a curt, awkward nod. "Owen."

"You … you look good—"

"Daddy, I need the fork."

I twisted to see a little girl sitting at the nearby table with a plate of food in front of her. The same little girl whose picture Owen had once shown me.

"Sorry, honey." Owen handed her the plastic cutlery and then gave me a weak smile. "This is my daughter."

"Hi," I said to her, feeling super uncomfortable.

She used her fork to wave at me, her expression curious.

I forced a bright smile. "Well, you two have a good day."

"Wait, Vee. Who are you here with?"

I sighed. "Owen, just focus on having fun with your little girl. Okay?"

"Have you realized it yet?" he asked when I tried to shrug past him.

"What?"

"That marrying Davenport was a mistake," he said too quietly for his daughter to hear. "Because if you haven't, you will eventually."

"Forget about me and what's going on in my life, Owen. Concentrate on fixing your own."

"Did he tell you that he had me banned from o-Verve? I went there to see you a few weeks ago. I didn't even get past the security checkpoint. He didn't tell you, huh? Well then, he probably also didn't tell you that he called me later that day and said he'd make sure I lost my job if I ever tried to get near *his wife* again. Not 'Vienna.' His wife. Like you're a thing. A possession."

I rubbed my temple. "Owen—"

"He's going to hurt you, Vee. He probably won't mean to. He probably won't even particularly want to. But he'll do it, because that's what people like him do. They hurt. They betray. They don't think past their own wants."

"This again? Seriously?" I shook my head. "I'm going to go now." I pushed past him, but he grabbed my arm.

"Wait, I—" He cut off, his lips thinning as he caught sight of something.

I tracked his gaze to see Dane heading our way, his eyes hard, his expression cold.

Owen dropped my arm and took a step toward the table at which his daughter sat, as if to protect her from the newcomer.

Dane stopped in front of me. "I came to see what was taking you so long," he said to me, but his eyes were on Owen.

I fisted Dane's tee and gave it a little tug to get his full attention. "His kid is sitting right there," I told him, my voice low. "For her sake, can we just walk away?" He hit me with that unblinking hunter stare, saying nothing. Tension thickened the air, winding me tight. "Please, Dane."

Something flickered across his face. He reached up and untangled my fingers from his tee. Instead of dropping my hand, he clasped it tight. "Come on."

Thank fuck for that. Without a backward look at my ex, I let Dane lead me out of the restaurant.

Outside, he turned to me, his expression still cold. "What did he want?"

"To tell me it was a mistake to marry you. Did you really have him banned from o-Verve?"

"Yes. I didn't trust that he wouldn't harass you there. You should be able to do your job without worrying people will turn up and talk shit to you. I want you to feel safe there."

I always had felt safe there. Until recently. Not that I'd thought I was in *physical* danger but, yeah, certainly at risk of being bugged by dumbass people. Thinking of said dumbasses, I asked, "Did you have anyone else banned?"

"Travis, Hope, Heather, and Owen's soon-to-be-ex-wife."

"Why Tiffany?"

"I doubted she'd bother you, but I didn't want to take the chance."

"Have any of them tried to enter since you gave their names to security?"

"Only Hope."

"I'll bet she was furious when they refused her entrance." And probably embarrassed as all hell.

"She was. But I'd told her to stay away from the building. If she'd listened, it wouldn't have happened."

I tilted my head. "You wouldn't really try to get Owen fired, would you?"

Dane put his face closer to mine. "You already know the answer to that." He tugged on my hand. "Come on. You still want to see those red panda things, don't you?"

"They're not things."

"Well they're not pandas."

True, actually, but whatever. I was disappointed when we finally reached their enclosure, because only one of them seemed to be outside, and it was so high up a damn tree I could only see part of its head.

I tried zooming in on the panda with my phone to get a better look, but the effort came to nothing. "I'm bummed I can barely see it."

Dane slid his hand up my back and rested it on the crook of my neck, probably unaware that it sent a pleasant chill dancing along my spine. "Be still."

"Why?"

"Because you have what looks like a mosquito on your nape." He moved my ponytail aside and flicked off whatever insect had landed on me. His thumb brushed over the back of my neck, making the skin tingle. "Doesn't look like it bit you."

I cleared my throat. "Thanks." Plastering a blasé smile on my face, I turned to him. "Let's go find your spirit animals, shall we?"

"My what?"

"The rhinos."

It turned out that there were quite a few of them. Two were awake and walking around—one of which was a baby, and my heart just melted into a pile of goo. I really had no idea baby rhinos could be so freaking cute.

I leaned against the fence, fascinated by it. Apparently, I watched it a little too long, because Dane eventually curled an arm around my waist and bodily moved me away.

After that, we meandered around the reptile house. I wondered if the snakes might react to the presence of their evil master, but no. We paid a brief visit to the petting zoo before then following the themed animal trails and checking out the interactive exhibits. It took some convincing, but I managed to coax Dane into watching a sea lion show in the outdoor amphitheater. He didn't seem particularly entertained, but he did enjoy his ice cream.

Later on, as we walked through the gift shop, I swept my gaze around the large space, checking out the plentiful merchandise. I did a double-take when I noticed a magnet with Pallas' cats on it. I took it from the display and flipped it over to check the price.

Dane sighed. "You want that, don't you?"

"Who wouldn't?"

He all but snatched it from my hand with a put-out sound and crossed to the checkout desk. Having paid for the magnet, he shoved it into my hand. "There."

Not in the least bit bothered by how gruff and rude he was acting, I smiled. "That was kind of you."

He tossed me a frown. "I'm not kind."

"But the *deed* was kind. Come on, your terribly plain fridge is waiting for its new decoration."

In the parking lot, we headed to his Aston Martin and slid inside. I was so used to Sam chauffeuring us around that it was strange to have Dane drive us places, but I liked it. I didn't know what it said about me that I found it hot to watch him drive but … it was just the way he looked so focused, at ease, and in complete control. I dug it.

"Thank you for coming with me," I said as he reversed out of his spot, his arm curved around my headrest.

His eyes met mine. "Maybe I want something."

I tensed. His ideas of "favors" could be extreme. "Like what?"

"I said maybe."

"You like keeping me off-balance, don't you?"

He switched gears and drove forward. "Vienna, I like doing that to everyone."

CHAPTER TWENTY-TWO

I was running late. I rarely ran late. But I hadn't slept well last night. Partly because it was a strange bed—the hotel's mattress was divine, but it hadn't helped me settle—and partly because I'd woken at dumb 'o' clock feeling *wired.* If it was a nightmare that woke me, I didn't remember it.

I'd lain awake for hours. Eventually, I'd given up trying to sleep and simply sat near the window overlooking the New York skyline. And now, tired and groggy, I wasn't quite as speedy as usual as I moved around the bedroom, getting ready for the conference that would soon start.

My hair and makeup were finally done, though, and I'd pulled on my underwear. All I really needed to do was slip into my suit and high heels. I wasn't going to have time to eat breakfast, which was a bummer. Maybe I could munch on an apple during the elevator ride or something.

"Vienna, have you seen the—" Dane came to an abrupt halt in the doorway.

I squeaked. *Squeaked.* But, hell, I was standing there in my damn bra and panties! And there was nothing close that I could grab to cover myself with. "Can't you knock?"

His dark, broody eyes raked over me, focusing on me so intently it made my scalp prickle. I stilled, feeling trapped. Uncomfortable. Exposed. The air charged with an electric tension that made my body tighten.

I didn't move an inch. I couldn't. I felt rooted to the spot by the blatant heat in his gaze. There was something very predatory about him right then. Something that made me feel … not quite threatened, no, but *hunted.* And yet, a dangerously wicked hunger unfurled in my stomach.

It occurred to me that I'd frozen just like prey. That chafed at my pride. I wasn't easily intimidated or unnerved. But, yeah, I was rattled right then.

Nobody had ever looked at me with such open need and bold possession, like it was their right to do so.

Well, it *wasn't* his right. Not at all. But I didn't dare say that, because it would sound like nothing short of a challenge.

His eyes locked with mine, still hot and hungry. "I figured you'd already be dressed. You're usually ready on time."

"I just need a minute," I practically croaked.

"I see that." He flitted his gaze over me once more and then left the room.

A shaky breath stuttered out of me. I quickly snatched my shirt and slipped it on, determined to put that little eye-fuck out of my mind and get on with my day. But with my pulse racing and my blood hot, I wasn't so sure it would be that easy.

When I was finally dressed and ready to go, I headed to the sitting area to find Dane stood there, his expression carefully blank. *Okay.* We left without a word to each other.

The downward trip in the elevator was … interesting. The moment the doors slid closed, the air seemed to hum and thicken. I'd never been more keenly *aware* of him; of his scent, of his body, of every single movement he made. Like my sexual radar was honed on him.

My hormones went crazy, the tension mounted, and everything feminine in me reached for him. Honestly, it was almost like the eye-fuck had primed my body or something.

I sat at his side throughout the conference. My nerve endings were so raw and sensitive that small touches—hell, even the mere brush of his arm against mine—could make my entire body react. A spark of excitement would zip up my spine and cause little bumps to sweep along my flesh.

I'd thought the sexual buzz would fade soon enough, but it remained on "simmer" throughout the day. Each touch of his hand on my back, elbow, or hip only seemed to fuel it.

As such, I was a hot mess by the time we returned to our hotel suite after dinner. I quickly changed in my room for the after-reception, lamenting that I didn't have enough time to get myself off—that would certainly have calmed my libido.

When I exited the room clad in an elegant red dress, a muscle in his cheek ticked, and his jaw hardened. For a moment, I thought he was going to ask me to change. But then he ushered me out of the room, muttering something under his breath.

I frowned. "What?"

"Nothing," he bit out.

Of course, we played the part of the happily married couple during the after-reception. That meant plenty of tasteful PDA, which we'd mastered at this stage. But it turned out that "performing" was a lot more difficult when the chemistry was so electric. There'd been times in the past when I was able to tune it out, to treat it as white noise—well, to a degree anyway. Not tonight, though. I was wound too tight. It took effort not to jump or tense when he touched me.

He didn't seem to be having a similar struggle. He was as cool and composed as ever. Though I noticed he occasionally gritted his teeth or tightened his hand on my hip if I whispered into his ear or touched his chest. His eyes kept dropping to my mouth and tracing its shape—each heated glance made my pulse spike.

"When I first heard you'd gotten married, I wasn't sure I believed it," a man standing nearby said to Dane. "But I have to say, married life suits you."

I barely bit back a snort. Nothing would ever suit Dane *less* than holy freaking matrimony.

The guy's wife smiled at me. "Did you ever imagine when you first started working for Dane that you'd one day become his wife?"

Not even in an alternate universe where unicorns existed, animals could talk, and I'd look good in a tutu. "No, I hadn't seen that coming. Especially since he's my boss—I don't believe in mixing business with pleasure. But, well, some things are just inevitable. Fighting the inevitable is quite simply pointless."

She gave me a dreamy, "it's all so romantic" smile.

Dane squeezed my hip and put his mouth to my ear. "Dance with me."

I couldn't help but tense. I was *all* for walking away and escaping the conversation, but dance with him? That was, like, *the worst* idea. I tried making excuses to avoid it, but he ignored them; ignored my body language and led me to the dance floor.

Usually, I melted into him, but I was too stiff with tension tonight. And what did he do? Tugged me closer and held me flush against him.

"Relax," he coaxed, splaying his hand on my back.

I tried.

I failed.

Never had I felt so uncomfortable being plastered against someone, but my raw nerve-endings simply couldn't handle the contact. I felt edgy and tingly and far too fucking horny. I was sure he could sense it, but he didn't comment on it.

Worse, he didn't give me even a modicum of space throughout the rest of the night. He kept me at his side every minute. The only time I got a reprieve was when I used the bathroom, so I retreated there several times. But as soon as I exited the restrooms, he'd draw me to him, and then the giddy tingles would be back in full force. It was *torture*.

I'd never been more relieved to return to a hotel suite. Standing in the middle of the living area, I swallowed. "Goodnight."

His unreadable gaze met mine. "Night."

With that, we parted ways. After taking a shower during which I made myself come, I slipped on my silk camisole and matching shorts. I pulled the curtain three quarters of the way closed so that the rays of sunlight would gradually brighten the room as it crept into the morning hours. Only then did I slide into bed. My system was so damn tired after a day of being in a constant state of sheer want that I quickly drifted off.

I wasn't sure what woke me. It could have been a sound, a weird dream, or maybe just a simple case of mental restlessness—I wasn't sure. But I instantly felt uncomfortable. Tense. Not alone.

I forced my eyes to open. It was dark, but I noticed the figure sitting in the chair in the corner of the room—the moonlight coming through the window streamed over him, leaving only his face in shadow.

Frowning, I lifted my head. "Dane?" I said, my voice thick.

He didn't respond. He just sat there, taking over the chair in that alpha-male way he had. The arm dangling over the side of the chair held a small glass of liquid.

Had I had a nightmare and woken him? If so, I couldn't recall any of it. He was still dressed in his shirt and pants, so I doubted he'd been to bed yet.

"Why are you in my room? I wasn't talking in my sleep or something, was I?" Still no response. Unease crept up my spine. "What's wrong?"

He took an easy swig of his drink and then let his arm dangle over the side of the chair again. But he didn't say a word.

I sat up and shoved my hair out of my face. "Okay, you're starting to freak me out. What's wrong?"

He leisurely pushed to his feet, his face still in shadow. Seconds ticked by as he simply stood there, tall and still. Just as I was about to question him again, he began to stalk toward the bed. Each step was slow, deliberate, and fluid. My pulse started to quicken.

As he passed through the rays of moonlight that beamed across the room, I got a glimpse of his face. *So cold.* And yet, his eyes were hot and gleaming.

My stomach flipped, and every muscle in my body went tight. That hunted feeling rushed back. My fight-or-flight instinct stirred, telling me to move, to back away, to put some *serious* space between us. But I did as I'd done earlier; I froze.

He stopped beside my bed, looking down at me. My eyes were fast adjusting to the darkness, so I could see him better now; see the greed and lust stamped all over his face. My thighs clenched, and I swallowed hard.

He took a casual swig of his drink, like it was totally the norm to come into my bedroom like this. Keeping his gaze locked with mine, he set the glass on the nightstand. And then he started unbuttoning his shirt.

My heart thudded hard in my chest. Shit, how much had the guy drank? He was obviously smashed. Although … he didn't look drunk. His eyes weren't glassy, and he wasn't weaving. He looked determined. Focused. Hungry.

Need flared inside me and tightened my nipples. Shit, this couldn't happen again. It couldn't. It shouldn't. But *hell* if I didn't still want it to, despite my better judgement.

"Dane," I said, my voice low and calming, like I was talking to someone on the verge of jumping off a bridge. The situation just felt so precarious. "Dane, you *know* this is a bad idea." An attractive idea, but an unwise one all the same.

He didn't speak, didn't react. He also didn't stop unbuttoning that freaking shirt.

I shuffled backwards on the mattress and then got to my knees, ready to edge off the bed to effectively place the piece of furniture between us.

"Don't move." The quiet command rang through my body, reverberating in my very bones, and I couldn't help but freeze. His eyes went heavy-lidded with approval. "Good girl." He slipped off his shirt and let it fall to the floor.

I felt my lips part. Jesus, his chest was packed with muscle. My hands itched to smooth over all that sleek skin; to trace the lines and dips of his abs.

Giving myself a mental slap, I lifted a hand to ward him off. "We agreed this couldn't happen again. Remember?"

His hands lazily dropped to his waistband. Still moving slowly and casually, he snapped open the top button of his fly and then lowered the zipper—holding my gaze the entire time. I sensed more than saw him kick off his shoes.

"Seriously, Dane—" Oh fuck, he'd shoved down his pants and boxer shorts. His fat, long cock was *rock hard.* Damn if the bastard hadn't been blessed with a body that was designed to seduce and pleasure. The broad shoulders, the solid chest, the perfect V of his hips, the seriously impressive cock … I hadn't thought my mouth could get any drier. I'd been wrong.

I closed my eyes, digging deep for some willpower. I heard shuffling sounds and wondered if he was removing his socks or something. I didn't look. "You really should go." Nothing. No response, no movements.

I opened my eyes. He *still* stood there, *still* staring hard at me. And I found my gaze roaming down his body again.

His cock twitched, tapping his belly. I remembered how it felt to have it filling, stretching, and thrusting inside me. Remembered coming harder than I ever had in my life. And damn if I didn't want him in me again. Which made me my own worst enemy, really.

It didn't help that he was so deliciously and blatantly dominant. I wasn't ashamed to admit I got off a little on that. Having all his alpha energy focused on me was *way* more than my self-control could bear.

"Come here."

I jumped at the softly spoken order—and it *was* very much an order. "Are you just going to overlook the fact that you're not thinking clearly? Because I can't, Dane. One of us needs to be the voice of reason."

"Come here," he repeated, his voice low and deep and carrying the punch of authority.

"Don't ignore me. This is serious. You don't get to be blasé about it."

"Not going to tell you again, baby girl. Last chance."

I clenched my fists, feeling a little desperate. Because I knew myself. Knew my resolve would waver if he touched me. No, not waver. Vanish. This need I felt for him ... It was too hot. Too basic. Too powerful. I didn't stand a sliver of a chance against it.

"For fuck's sake, Dane, *listen to me.* I don't know how much you've had to drink—"

He clamped his hands around my upper arms and dragged me to him, keeping me on my knees, so that his hard cock then dug into my abdomen. "Yeah, that's where I want you." His hands bunched my hair, and he slowly lowered his mouth until it hovered a mere inch above mine. Everything seemed to go still and quiet.

I should protest. Push him away. Something. *Anything.* But, stupid or not, I wanted this. Wanted him. Wanted to pretend for a little while that he wanted more than just a roll in the sack.

My breathing picked up. So did his. Anticipation wound me tight, making my nerves ragged.

His unblinking gaze dropped to my mouth and flared. "Everywhere we go," he said, his voice thick with need, "I catch someone staring at your mouth. And I know they're wondering what it'd be like to sink their teeth into this plump lower lip—I did the exact same thing the first time I saw it."

I blinked. He had?

"So soft and bitable." He caught my bottom lip with his teeth and tugged. My lips parted on a gasp, and his tongue boldly swept inside.

He took my mouth in a kiss so hot, wet, and explicit that I felt myself melt into him. Every bit of hesitance drained from my system in a rush, just as I'd known it would. God, the man. Could. *Kiss.*

I splayed my hands on the twin columns of his back, digging my nails into his skin. His cock throbbed against my abdomen, hot and hard and insistent. That untamed quality about him had never been more palpable than it was right now as he ruthlessly ate at my mouth, his grip so tight on my hair it hurt a little. But even as he exuded a dark sexual energy that held an edge of aggressiveness, he was still calmly forceful and totally in control.

Me? I wasn't so cool and composed. I wanted to climb him like a fence post and wrap my legs around his waist. Wanted to impale myself fully on his shaft so that he was balls-deep inside me. Just the thought made damp heat spill from my core.

His blunt nails scraped my scalp. I let out a soft, needy moan and tore my mouth free of his. "Dane—"

"Fucking love your hair," he said, combing his fingers through the soft strands. "I want to see it spread out on the bed while I'm moving inside you. First …" He tugged on the strap of my camisole. "This has to go. Take it off."

Gladly. I shed the garment and tossed it aside.

His gaze locked on my bare breasts, staring at them so intently it felt like a physical touch. His eyes seemed to trace their shape. "Pretty," he breathed, lightly skimming his knuckles over one hard nipple. *Too* lightly. "The perfect handful."

I arched into him as he filled his palms with my breasts. He squeezed just right and thumbed both nipples hard, sending streaks of fire to my clit. He then curved his arm around me and hauled me up his body so that his mouth was level with my breasts. All that casual strength made me shiver a little.

I clung to his shoulders as he lavished attention on my nipples using his mouth and fingers, repeatedly switching from one bud to the other. He was careful at first. He began with gentle tweaks, light tugs, and brief nibbles; teasing me, I knew. Soon he was pinching, twisting, and suckling on my nipples until they throbbed.

I felt every touch in my aching core and, God, I had to be embarrassingly wet. I didn't care. Didn't care about anything other than finding some relief.

Dane gently lowered me to the mattress. "Lay back, baby girl."

I did as he asked, but I kept myself propped up on my elbows and watched as he snaked his hands up my thighs, caught the waistbands of my shorts and panties, and peeled both off.

"Spread your legs wide. Wider, Vienna. That's it." Dane stared at my pussy, his eyes glittering with so much naked greed my inner muscles clenched. He reached for the glass on the nightstand without even looking at it and took a swig of his drink.

I ground my teeth, not a big fan of being made to wait for what I wanted when I was this damn horny. "You just gonna stare at it all night? Because it's not going to come by itself."

His eyes flew to mine, dancing with humor. "Not all night, no," he said, setting down his glass. He leaned over me, forcing me to lie flat. "I was actually thinking of doing this." He swiped the tip of his finger between my folds and then dipped it inside me. He hummed. "So slick already. Yeah, this pussy knows me now, doesn't it? It wants more." He drove his finger deep. "What does it want?"

I licked my lips. "More."

He skimmed his nose along my jawline and around to my ear. "Do you know what I want?"

Sliding my hands over his shoulders, I swallowed. "What?"

His teeth scraped my earlobe. "To know what you taste like." He went to his knees on the carpet, gripped my thighs, and yanked me toward him. His warm hands spread my legs as wide as they could go, giving him better access. "Hands above your head," he said, nuzzling my folds.

"Why?"

"Because I want them there." He licked at the crease of my thigh. "Do it, Vienna."

Gritting my teeth, I followed his directive. Lifting my head, I glared at him. "Happy?" *Asshole*, I barely resisted adding.

He sucked hard on my inner thigh and then gave it a sharp nip. "Stop swearing at me in your head."

See? Warlock. "I'm not—" My breath caught as he rolled the tip of his tongue around my pulsing clit. I let my head fall back, moaning as he fluttered his tongue between my folds.

He hummed deep in his throat and then, well, I discovered that he was a champ at going down on a woman. He used his tongue, lips, and teeth to learn and ruthlessly exploit every sensitive spot I had. Seriously, if it wasn't for the strong hands pinning my hips flat to the mattress, I'd be bucking all over the bed.

Flooded by endorphins, I moaned and squirmed as that skilled tongue licked, swirled, delved, and lapped … until I was a trembling, mindless mess. My system *screamed* with sexual frustration; with a desperation that bordered on feverish.

Only in my wildest dreams had I envisioned Dane eating me out. The reality was a million times better than any fantasy.

My back bowed as he shoved his tongue deep, and I felt my inner muscles spasm around it. "I'm gonna come." My release was barreling toward me fast.

He suckled on my clit and jammed two fingers inside my pussy. My thighs shook, my inner walls clenched, and four pumps of his fingers later I came with a choked cry.

Replete, I sagged against the mattress, breathing hard.

Dane rubbed his face on my belly and gave it a little nip. Rising, he snatched a condom from the pocket of his pants. "I need you to twist around so you're not lying horizontal across the bed," he told me, moving to stand at the foot of it.

My pulse still racing, I returned to my original position with my head on my pillow and let my legs fall apart.

Having rolled on the condom, he knelt between my thighs and draped himself over me. "I'm going to give you my weight. If you can't handle it, tell me." He eased his body over mine, effectively pinning me in place—pushing a major sweet button for me—and then wedged the broad head of his cock inside me.

Gasping, I tried tilting my hips to take more of his shaft, but I was trapped beneath him and couldn't move. I splayed my hands on his back and moaned as he began gently nibbling my neck. "Dane."

He rammed his cock deep with such shocking force that my back would have arched right off the bed if his weight wasn't pinning me down.

I sucked in a breath and dug my nails into his back. "Jesus, Dane." God, the pressure, heat, and thickness of his shaft felt amazing.

He planted his lower arms at either side of my head and flexed his hips. "I've thought about this pussy far too often since I last had it. I thought about how tight it is. How wet it gets for me. How good it feels." He smoothly reared back until only the tip was inside me. "Thought about fucking it again. And again. And again." He slowly sank his cock into me but stopped halfway. Then he drew back.

I felt my brow furrow. I was hoping to get fucked raw. "What are you doing?"

He thrust his whole length inside me. "Indulging myself." He once more pulled back. "I'll give you what you need when I'm done." He fed me a few inches of his cock and then drew back yet again.

It went on like that for what could have been hours. Sometimes he'd bury himself balls-deep, sometimes he'd stop halfway, sometimes he'd give me only a few inches. He constantly switched it up, so I never knew what to expect.

There were times when he'd give me a few slow, hard, full-on thrusts but then go back to teasing me—leaving me hanging on the knife-edge of what I just *knew* would be a mind-blowing orgasm. I was so frantic to find my release I could literally cry.

"If I had a knife, I honestly think I would stab you with it. I'm not even kidding," I said, my voice cracking.

I felt him smile against my neck, the bastard. Right. That was it. I was just going to have to flip him onto his back and ride him.

Only that didn't work out, because he was *way* stronger than I'd anticipated.

He easily held me down—even going as far as to pin my wrists either side of my head. He put his mouth to my ear. "Do you need to be fucked now?"

I'd never needed anything more. "You know I do."

He brushed his mouth over mine. "You don't come until I say, got it?"

"You must be fucking joking."

"I never joke, baby girl." He began pounding me into the mattress, his mouth set into a cruel slash. "No other pussy ever fit my cock this good."

I clung to his hips with my thighs. He drove so deep, so fast, so fucking *hard.* The air rang with soft moans, deep grunts, heavy breaths, and the slap of flesh against flesh.

There was no more teasing. He never once slowed his pace or eased up on the intensity of his thrusts. No, he kept ramming into me like he'd never get enough.

He snarled into my ear. "You love having my dick in you, don't you?"

I did. I absolutely did. Especially right at this moment, when the mother of all orgasms was *so close*. I could feel my pussy begin to quake—

"Hold it, Vienna."

Bastard. I wouldn't manage it for long. I couldn't. Every part of me felt over-sensitized—my skin, my nipples, my clit, my inner walls.

More, I felt buzzed from the feel-good chemicals that were swimming through me. It was hard to think, let alone exercise any damn self-control. Being trapped beneath him while he held my hands down only made me even hotter. "Dane—"

"Hold it just a little longer."

I hissed. "I can't."

"Hold it or I slow down."

Mother*fucker.* I dug my nails into his hands as I tried getting free, but he only tightened his hold and gave me more of his weight.

"You're going nowhere, baby girl, until I'm done." He kept me pinned as he selfishly took what he wanted. And I realized now that I'd never really been *taken* before. I'd had rough sex, and I'd thought it was the same thing.

I was wrong.

I wasn't simply being fucked by Dane. No. Right now, he *ruled* me; exerted a sexual power over me that felt dangerously addictive.

I moaned, gasped, trembled, and squirmed as every unrelenting slam of his cock pushed me closer and closer to exploding. My thighs tightened around his hips just as the walls of my pussy tightened around his dick yet again—a dick I could now feel swelling inside me. *"Dane."*

His eyes smoldered. "Yeah, fucking come."

Pure pleasure surged over and through me in a furious, mind-blowing rush. My eyes went blind and a scream tore out of my throat. Violent tremors racked my body as the pleasure went on and on and on.

I was only vaguely aware of Dane squeezing my hands harder as he forced his cock deep and exploded with a harshly whispered curse. Moments later, we both collapsed.

CHAPTER TWENTY-THREE

So now, what?

Sitting upright in bed the next morning, I nibbled on my thumbnail. I'd woken up alone. I honestly couldn't say whether Dane had slept beside me. For all I knew, he cleaned himself up and then went straight to his own bed. It was the first time in my life that I'd fallen asleep right after sex.

Then again, it was also the first time someone kept my body hanging on the edge of an orgasm for so long that my eventual release drained every bit of energy from me.

Did I regret last night? Not even a little. And I probably wouldn't regret it if it happened again, to be honest. After all, I'd already crossed emotional lines with him. There'd be no reversing that for as long as he was around. So the idea of taking what I could get and making some delicious memories didn't seem so bad.

However, there was a chance that Dane was now regretting last night. It was the "not knowing" that made anxiety curdle in my stomach.

Did I go out there and act like nothing had happened? Did I make a glib comment about it to dispel any awkwardness? Would he even *feel* awkward?

Unlikely.

Nothing seemed to make Dane feel uncomfortable. I just hoped he didn't plan to treat me to a "it was a mistake" talk. It would be no different than a slap across the face.

Deciding to go ahead with my morning ritual, I went straight to the bathroom, did my business, and took a hot shower. A bath would have been better, since I was a little sore from last night, but I didn't have the time. I'd do it later, when I was back at home. Well, *Dane's* home.

I wrapped a plush towel around me, opened the door, and took a step into the bedroom. I stopped dead, tensing. Dane—fully dressed and looking as hot as ever—stood a few feet away.

If this had happened yesterday morning, I'd have ushered him out of my room with a horrified squeak. But after last night, I felt off-balance and unsure of where I stood.

His dark gaze bore into mine, giving away nothing. Literally nothing. There was no heat, no emotion, no gleam of … anything. "The museum opens in an hour," he said.

I blinked. That was pretty much the last thing I'd expected him to say. "I'm sorry?"

"You said you wanted to go to the Natural History Museum while we're here."

"I do." But our day had been so hectic yesterday that I hadn't had time to spare, so I hadn't bothered to bring the subject up.

"If we leave here soon, we can spend a few hours there before we fly home," he said, not sounding in the least bit enthusiastic about it. But he was willing to go with me anyway. I might have read something into it if he hadn't agreed to this prior to our trip.

I cleared my throat, still feeling stupidly awkward. "Okay. Great. Thanks."

Amusement lit his eyes, and one corner of his mouth hiked up.

"What's funny?"

He pursed his lips and shook his head. "Be fast." As he turned toward the door, his eyes flicked to the nightstand. "Don't forget your rings."

Watching him walk out of the room, I took a steadying breath. Well it was safe to say that, as I'd anticipated, he didn't feel awkward. It also seemed that we weren't going to address what happened last night, which suggested that he might well regret it.

Disappointment sat heavy in my stomach. And I realized a tiny part of me had held some pointless hope that last night was the beginning of something. It was the same tiny part of me that had gotten us into this entire freaking situation by making a deal with the devil. So, yeah, that "tiny part" was absolutely fucking stupid—there was no question about it.

He might have been so brazen as to waltz into my room uninvited like it was his right, but there'd been no morning kiss, no eye-fuck, no touching—hell, he hadn't even wished me a good morning. So it was abundantly clear that nothing between us had changed. I had to accept that they never would.

Shaking off my dull thoughts, I quickly got ready to leave and packed my small suitcase. After placing my luggage near the front door beside his own, I headed to the dining area to grab something from the spread of breakfast foods on the table.

Dane was nowhere to be seen. His empty cup and plate told me he'd already eaten.

I poured myself a coffee, nabbed a few Danish pastries, and took a seat at the table. I was halfway through the last Danish when he appeared. And I immediately felt awkward again.

He lifted a brow. "Ready?"

I pushed away from the table. "Yep," I replied, going for casual.

That glint of amusement was back in his eyes, as was the odd little curve to his mouth.

I frowned. "Is something funny?"

He shook his head, but that secret smile didn't dim.

We left our luggage with the concierge on the understanding that we'd collect it in a few hours when we were on our way to the airport.

Walking around the museum with Dane was much like it had been when we strolled around the zoo. At first, he showed little to no interest in his surroundings. But bit by bit, that changed. And, although I suspected he'd rather swallow glass than admit it, he did actually enjoy himself. Well, to an extent anyway.

He didn't once bring up last night—not even to say that there couldn't be a repeat of it. He behaved perfectly normally; didn't touch me any more or less than usual. It was honestly as if nothing had happened between us. I supposed that was because it had been of no significance to him. Damn if that didn't chafe.

He behaved just as normally on the flight home. We didn't talk much, as per usual. He mostly worked, and I mostly read.

Finally back at the estate, I let out a long sigh as I stood in the foyer. Despite my efforts to fight it, I'd began to think of the place as "home." And I'd missed it. It had become my safe zone; somewhere I could fully relax.

"I have a conference call soon," Dane declared. "So I probably won't eat dinner until late. Don't wait for me."

Oh, we were back to that, were we? Ugh. "No problem," I said, aloof.

I headed up the stairs and went straight to my room, somewhat annoyed that he seemed intent on putting space between us *again*. Fine. Whatever. It wasn't as if I cared.

God, I hated it when I tried bullshitting myself.

I quickly unpacked, none-too-gently returning each of my things back to their original place. After bagging up my laundry, I tried calling my father. The call went to voicemail, so I dialed Melinda's number instead.

She answered after a few rings. "Hello?"

"Hi, how are you?"

"Good, thanks, honey. I take it you're back from New York."

I frowned. There was an odd note in her voice that I couldn't quite interpret. "Is everything okay?"

"Of course. Wyatt and I are doing fine. I paid your dad a visit yesterday; he's fine, too. I also spoke with Maggie for a few minutes at one point; she confirmed that all is good with him. Oh, and Heather's birthday meal was a lot of fun. Such a shame you couldn't be there. The food was amazing."

"That's great," I said, conscious that Melinda had quickly taken over the conversation before I could question her further. "But something is wrong. What?"

"Nothing," she replied, the word loaded with a little *too* much innocence. "How was your flight?"

"Melinda, you are the worst liar *ever*. Tell me what's wrong."

She sighed. "I can't talk about it right now," she said, lowering her voice. So, what, she didn't want Wyatt to overhear? Or was it that she had visitors? "I promise you that everyone is fine," she added. "But, well, there's something you should know. I'll come see you at o-Verve tomorrow, okay? Take care, hon." Then she hung up.

I stared at the phone, unease trickling through me. I wanted to call her again and demand answers, but there was no sense in it if she didn't feel comfortable talking about this "something" in front of Wyatt.

What could possibly have happened while I was gone? Could it have something to do with Heather? Had she come clean to Melinda about Junior's father and told her that Dane had threatened to expose Heather's secret? Possibly. I wouldn't put it past the heifer to confess everything to her mother while crying fake tears—feigning regret and self-hatred—and then making Dane out to be a cold, dangerous bastard. Especially since she could claim I was in on it.

I turned to the door, needing to warn Dane. But then I halted. There was no sense in getting him all wound up about Heather again when I might be wrong. For all I knew, this could have nothing to do with her at all. This could be a completely unrelated matter. And I knew the whole thing would play on my mind all evening.

The phone in my hand began to ring. *Simon.* I answered with a smile, "Hey Dad."

"Sorry I missed your call, sweetheart, I was in the shower."

"No worries. How're things with you?"

We chatted for a while and, satisfied that he was indeed fine, I ended the call on a promise to visit him soon. Hungry, I headed downstairs to the kitchen and ate dinner alone—such fun.

I also stuck the magnet I'd brought from the museum onto the refrigerator. A magnet that, like the one from the zoo, Dane had bought me with a put-out look on his face.

Deciding to finally have that bath I'd earlier yearned for, I returned to my room, and went into the attached bathroom. I stripped naked while I waited for the water to reach the right level. That done, I scooped my hair up into a high messy knot and sank into the hot water.

Leaning back in the tub, I let out a long sigh and closed my eyes. The heat together with the scent of the lavender bubble bath was heavenly. It wasn't until now, as the stiffness began to seep from my muscles, that I realized just how tense I'd been.

I lazed there for a while, not asleep but in a sort of hazy state that gave me an escape from the questions that had pricked at me since my conversation with Melinda. A state that was free of thoughts and stress and worries.

A sound snapped me out of it, causing my eyelids to flutter open. I stilled at the sight of Dane striding into the room. *The fuck?*

I hadn't locked the door purely because it hadn't occurred to me that he'd ever so boldly enter. He'd never done it before.

I sank deeper into the bubbles—many of which had melted into the water, so there wasn't much to conceal my body. "What are you doing in here?"

He crouched beside the tub, casual as ever, and braced his arms over the edge. He'd rolled up his sleeves and opened the top few buttons of his shirt, just as he often did in his office. "I came to find you," he replied.

"I'm kind of having a bath right now."

"I noticed." He dipped his fingers into the water and frowned. "It's barely lukewarm, how long have you been in here?"

"A while." I was about to suggest he leave, but then he rested his warm hand on my thigh where it peeked out of the water; his fingertips whispered over the sensitive skin of my inner thigh—it was such a simple touch, and yet I almost shivered.

"Chris called me. He said he tried calling you but didn't get an answer. He wanted to know why we'd decided to cancel the reception."

Huh? I gave my head a little shake. "I'm confused. Who told him that?"

"The hotel employee he's been coordinating with over the reception plans. The employee said you called the hotel claiming you wanted to cancel it."

I knifed up. *"What?"* Feeling cool air dance over my breasts, I realized they were now above the water level. I sank back down into the tub. "*I* didn't call the hotel."

"I know that. The employee thought the whole thing was odd, especially since you'd been communicating through Chris and Miley up until then, so he called Chris to check if maybe you'd made the call while drunk and upset."

"Motherfucker," I muttered. "It had to have been either Hope or Heather."

"Or some random woman that was put up to it by either Travis or Owen."

"Owen?"

"It's possible. It was obvious by his behavior at the zoo that he hasn't given up hope that he can come between us. Forget about it for now. I'll look into it more tomorrow." Dane pulled my thigh toward the edge of the tub and slid his hand further down.

I stilled, and my pussy clenched. "Dane—"

"I need you to tell me something," he said, stroking over the spot on my inner thigh where he bit me last night. "And I need you to be honest."

"What?" I rasped, unsure if I wanted him to stop or keep going.

"Are you sore?"

"Excuse me?"

"I didn't go easy on you last night. I took you hard." He danced his fingertips over the folds of my pussy. "I want to know if you're sore."

I swallowed, resisting the urge to buck into his hand. "A little."

"Hmm." Dane pulled out the plug and stood. "You need to get out of this water before it gets any colder." He grabbed the soft towel I'd placed nearby and held it wide open in invitation.

I kind of just sat there, unsure what to make of his behavior.

"I haven't got all night, baby girl. You suddenly shy?"

No, I was plain confused. Nonetheless, I stood. Ignoring the way his gaze roamed over me, I stepped onto the bathmat. He wrapped the towel around me and began to gently pat me dry. Okay, this was getting weird. Not that I didn't *like* it. This behavior just wasn't very Dane-like.

I eyed him curiously, wishing I knew what thoughts were going through his head right at that moment. Of course, he noticed me watching him. That damn secret smile curved his mouth *again*.

I narrowed my eyes. "What's so amusing? You keep looking at me like you're internally laughing at me. Like you know something I don't."

He dipped his head to kiss my neck. "You smell good." His tongue flicked out and lashed my pulse. "Taste good, too."

I went to speak, but then he took my mouth, greedy and ruthless and dominant—making my thoughts scatter and my body melt into his.

He hummed and broke the kiss. "I'm not going to fuck you tonight. Not when you're sore. But I am going to make you come."

Was I supposed to object? Well, I didn't.

He carried me into the bedroom, ordered me to lay down flat on the bed, and ate my pussy like there was a freaking award for it. As I lay there afterward—sated, shaking, and boneless—he knelt over me and pumped his cock. The first rope of white, hot come that erupted out of him landed on my breasts. He kept pumping, covering my flesh in his come, until he was fully spent.

Masculine possession gleamed in his eyes. "You make a very pretty picture right now." He curved his body over mine and took my mouth in a deep, lazy kiss that made my toes curl. "So sweet." He dipped a finger in his come and then painted my lower lip with it. "It's a shame you can't wear me on your mouth every day. I'd never get any fucking work done if you did."

I licked up the drop of come, inwardly smiling when his pupils dilated.

"Next time, you'll drink it all down. Every last bit of it."

After using a wet cloth to clean me up—he insisted on doing it himself—

he urged me to get under the bedcovers and then slid in beside me.

"You're staying?" I asked in an unintentionally shy whisper.

He shrugged one shoulder and drew me to his side. "I sleep better in this bed. As a bonus, you'll be right there when I want to fuck you in the morning."

Yeah, that was a definite bonus. So I snuggled into him and closed my eyes.

CHAPTER TWENTY-FOUR

Returning from an internal meeting with Dane to find Melinda sat in the reception area near my desk, I smiled. Her answering smile was so shaky and strained it made my own dim. "Hi, Melinda."

"Hi," she said, rising from her seat. Her gaze danced from me to Dane, who she couldn't seem to look in the eye. "I hope you both managed to find time to have fun in New York."

"We did, thank you," said Dane. "What can we do for you?"

"I was hoping to talk to Vienna for a few minutes. About some reception-related things," she hurried to add.

His steely eyes scrutinized her, and I could sense he wasn't buying it. "All right." He cut his gaze to me. "Join me in my office once you're done."

"Will do," I said.

He nodded at her. "Take care, Melinda."

Wearing yet another strained smile, she gave him a little wave. Once he'd disappeared into his office, she bit down on her lip and looked at me. "Is there somewhere we can go to talk in private?"

"You're really starting to worry me now." I glanced around and shrugged. "We can use the bathroom."

We headed inside the restroom. After I'd checked that it was empty of people, I locked the main door and turned to Melinda. "Go on."

She nervously rubbed her hands together. "I'm sorry in advance if any of this hurts you, but you have a right to know."

"Okay."

"Dane's brother, Travis, came to see me. He was very nice, very polite. And very concerned for you."

Oh, Lord. "Melinda—"

"He told me something. Something that has me very worried. He wanted to come to you about it, but he thought it might be less hard on you if you heard it from someone you love. Dane has a trust fund, Vienna. Hugh left it to him. But there are conditions. He has to be married before he can access it, and he has to be married before he's thirty-eight or he can never touch it. Dane's thirty-seven now."

I folded my arms across my chest. "And?"

She looked at me, bewildered. "In light of that, don't you think it's a little suspicious that Dane pushed you to marry him so soon? I'm not saying he doesn't care for you. I believe he does. But I also believe there's a good chance that he only wanted to marry you so fast because he wanted to get his hands on the trust fund."

God, Travis was *such* a bastard. "Have you told my father?" Because Simon might very well lose his shit.

"No. I haven't even told Wyatt yet. I wanted to tell *you* first." She touched my arm. "I'm sorry to be the person who gives you this news. I know that it must hurt."

"I already knew about the trust fund."

She gaped. "You knew?"

I nodded. "I've known about it since before Dane and I started dating. He told me himself."

"And it didn't ring any alarm bells when he proposed so soon? You didn't think to ask him to wait a while just to see what he'd say?"

Ugh, now I was going to have to tell even more freaking lies than I already had. "He didn't push me into marrying him in Vegas, Melinda. He said he'd like me to, but that he'd give me a fairytale wedding back at home if that was really what I wanted."

"Then why didn't you wait?"

"Because it wasn't really the dress and reception and flowers that I wanted. I just wanted him. I've *always* wanted him. Travis isn't the nice man he pretended to be. He neglected to tell you a few things. Like that he's well aware I know about all this. Like that he's been trying to cause trouble between me and Dane for a while. Like that Dane's trust fund would be divided between his brothers if he didn't meet the conditions to access it. Travis just wants his share. He isn't concerned about me. He wants me out of the way, even if it means ruining my and Dane's marriage."

Melinda's expression softened slightly. "Poor Dane. To have his own brother working against him like that ..." She exhaled heavily. "I can't say I'm totally convinced that Dane's rush to marry you wasn't prompted by the conditions of the trust fund. It just seems too ... iffy for me. And I'm shocked that you're so wrapped up in him you don't even care if he proposed so soon for the right reason."

"And if it had been you and Wyatt? Would you have asked him to wait just to prove to you that what he felt was real?"

She hesitated. "I don't know. Maybe."

"I *like* that I can help him access the trust fund. Dane's a man who has pretty much everything. But this is something that I can do for him that he wouldn't have been able to do himself. And if we later divorce at some point, I won't regret that I helped him."

"Vienna …"

"You said you believe he cares for me."

"I do."

"Then can't that be enough?"

She turned away and thrust a hand through her hair. Seconds ticked by as she said nothing. Finally, she faced me again. "It won't be enough for Wyatt. He's a suspicious creature. He's going to want to talk to Dane about this."

And that "talk" would no doubt get heated *fast.* "I'd imagine that's what Travis hoped for."

"What?"

"That you, Wyatt, and Simon would all turn on Dane. Just bear that in mind when you tell Wyatt what Travis told you, and ask Wyatt to bear it in mind, too." I escorted Melinda to the elevator. I waited until it began to descend before heading to Dane's office.

I knocked on the door, and he quickly bid me to enter. I walked in, closed the door behind me, and leaned back against it with a heavy sigh.

His brow quirked. "Problem?"

"Travis has been up to his old tricks again." I pushed away from the door, took the seat opposite him, and brought him up to speed. "Melinda doesn't suspect that the marriage is fake. She believes you 'care' for me; she's just not so sure that you married me so soon *purely* because you care for me."

His expression hard, Dane drummed his fingers on the desk. "I suppose I should have seen this coming."

"At least Travis never went to Simon. We'd have found ourselves facing Deacon for sure. He likes to settle things with his fists."

Leaning back in his chair, Dane rubbed at his jaw … just as he'd rubbed my pussy that morning to get me wet before he took me hard in my bed. I shook off the memory fast, set on keeping work and play completely separate—something which wasn't proving to be easy for me, but Dane seemed to find it simple enough. Then again, he'd never struggled with our attraction. It was a wonder my ego was intact.

"We should tell Simon, though, just in case Travis decides to," he said.

I frowned. "You're serious?"

"We need to do damage control. Invite your father and foster parents to our house tonight. I'll tell them about the trust fund and convince them that it wasn't the motivation behind my proposal. I'll also make it clear that neither Travis nor Hope's word can be trusted."

Ignoring the tingly feeling that the statement "our house" had given me,

I said, "I'm not sure it'll be so easy to convince them. I have plenty of faith in your acting skills, but I know my family. None of them trust easily."

"A little like you."

"Yes," I admitted. "Even if you do manage to convince them you're not the guilty party here, you'll still find yourself being confronted by all three of them at some point."

"Why?"

"Because once we divorce after being married for only a year, they'll take it as an indication that this was about your trust fund all along." Which was why I'd never meant for them to find out about it. "They'll be beyond furious."

Dane twisted his mouth. "Then maybe we should stay married for longer than a year."

Um, say what? "Longer?" I was surprised the word didn't come out on a squeak.

"Yes." He turned to his computer.

Frowning at the blatant dismissal, I shook my head. No. No, that was a bad idea. Walking away from Dane after the year was over would be hard enough. Prolonging the whole thing would only make it more difficult. "That's not necessary."

"So you want it to look obvious to your family that this was a sham?"

"Well, no—"

"Then you might want to consider putting an extension on it. Give it some thought. We'll discuss it again at a later date."

"Just how big of an extension are we talking?"

"That depends on a few things," he answered vaguely, typing away.

I was about to question him further, but then his cell phone rang. He immediately answered it, of course. Shooting him a scowl that he didn't see, I pushed out of the chair and left the office.

Taking my position behind my desk, I got back to work. The entire time, one question kept floating around my brain: If I did agree to an extension, what "things" would its duration depend on?

My family turned up at the house shortly after dinner. All I'd told Simon was that Dane had a little something he wanted to explain, which was no doubt why there was none of the hostility in my father's eyes that could be seen in Wyatt's. Melinda had obviously told her husband everything.

I offered them drinks, but only Simon and Dane took me up on the offer. The two men fell into an easy chat while I made them coffee. They each then grabbed their own cup.

Dane took my free hand in his and urged my family to follow us through the kitchen and out onto the patio. It was incredibly impressive with its lavish stonework, ample seating, outdoor kitchen, stone firepit, and koi pond.

Simon let out a low whistle. "Wow. Looks just like my backyard."

I chuckled, but my foster parents didn't even crack a smile. Annoyance made my nostrils flare. I couldn't blame them for being suspicious—they were right to be. But they'd never *once* been rude to Heather's boyfriends, even though said boyfriends were married. So it didn't seem fair that they'd act this way toward *my husband.*

Dane invited my family to take a seat as he sat me beside him on one of the rattan sofas. For a moment, no one spoke. There were only the sounds of fire snapping in the pit and water lapping at the edges of the pond.

"We wanted you to come here tonight so I could share something with you," Dane told them, curving his arm around me. "You've heard me mention my uncle Hugh before. He took in my brothers and me after our father killed himself."

Melinda gasped with the same shock that slapped me.

"He shot himself in the head to escape the many debts he'd racked up," Dane went on, sounding remarkably unemotional. "He could have sold the large house we lived in and bought something smaller; could have sold his rental properties, shares, or small businesses. But he was too prideful for that. He didn't have it in him to face people, to let them see how he'd failed. So he took his own life."

I slid my arm around Dane's waist, my shock giving way to anger at his father for being so proud and selfish.

"I'm so sorry," Melinda said to him. "That must have been terrible for you."

"Not as much as you might think. He wasn't a good person," said Dane, a dark note in his tone. "A man like that has no business having children. He's the reason my brothers and I aren't close."

I barely stopped myself from frowning, wondering just what exactly he meant by the latter. I couldn't question him; my family would think it weird that I didn't already know.

"My mother had died of cancer years before that, so we had nowhere to go." Dane looked down at me. "We could have easily ended up in foster care as you did, but we had Hugh. He didn't just take us in. He tried to teach us how to make something of ourselves, how to play to our strengths and be mindful of our weaknesses."

Ah, so Hugh had been his mentor.

Dane sipped at his coffee. "The lessons didn't stick with my youngest brother, Travis. He and his wife are people who want the easy way in life. That's why he married early. You see, Hugh left trust funds for each of us, but we weren't allowed to access them until we were married. He didn't want us to make the mistake he made: to never have a family of our own."

Pausing, Dane smoothed his hand up my back and palmed my nape. "I didn't want to build success on the heels of Hugh's. I wanted to build something for myself. Wanted to implement all the lessons he taught me. Wanted the trust fund to be purely a gift from him, not the kickstart to success that Travis perceived it to be.

"But, as Vienna once pointed out, I'm never really satisfied with what I've achieved. I always have that nagging sensation that I need to do more. I guess that comes from feeling like you have to live for two people. I lost my twin when I was eight."

Simon winced, and Wyatt's scowl faltered.

I tightened my arm around Dane in a silent show of support.

"My cousin lost her twin as a child," said Melinda. "She suffered from survivor's guilt all her life; she tried to keep her twin's spirit alive by living for both of them. She also pointedly avoided letting others close."

"It's hard to keep someone at a distance when they're part of your everyday life," said Dane, casting a meaningful look my way. "But I tried. I held out for four years. Four very long years. Then I realized that all I'd really done was waste time. I didn't want to waste anymore. I didn't want to risk that someone would come and steal her from under me. So, yes, I moved fast—as you all noticed."

"Yeah, we noticed," said Simon.

"Travis wasn't happy when I started dating Vienna." Dane took another sip of his coffee. "He tried coming between us right from the start."

Simon's brow furrowed. "Why?"

"Because our trust funds came with an additional stipulation—if we didn't marry by the age of thirty-eight, the fund would be divided between our siblings. Travis and his wife, Hope, want his share of mine. To them, Vienna is in the way of that. They tried making her doubt my feelings for her by telling her about the trust fund. She already knew about it, so that didn't get them anywhere. Travis's attempts to poison her mind about me failed." Dane's gaze cut to Melinda. "Which is no doubt why he went to you."

Simon looked at her. "Travis spoke to you?"

Melinda nodded, but her eyes were on Dane. "He made it sound like you only married Vienna so you could access the trust fund," she said, not sounding convinced that it wasn't the case. "I wouldn't have believed him. But when he mentioned you'd lose access to it if you didn't marry by the time you turned thirty-eight—which is less than a year away …"

Simon's gaze sharpened and then narrowed in suspicion. *Shit.*

Dane pursed his lips. "My guess? Travis hoped that if he could poison all your minds against me, then you'd get between me and Vienna in a way that he wasn't able to do. I'd say he's counting on you to encourage her to leave me. You may in fact intend to, despite what I've told you tonight. If so, he did his job well."

"Dane didn't pressure me to marry him in Vegas," I told my family. "He asked. I said yes."

"You can see why it looks suspicious," said Wyatt, a little belligerent.

"Depending on what angle you look at it from, yes, it does," Dane conceded. "But I don't need my uncle's money. I've never wanted to need or rely on it. If I had, I'd have done as Travis did and married at the age of eighteen just to get my hands on it."

"Why is he so desperate to have a share of yours?" Simon asked, his eyes still narrowed. "He can't have squandered all of his own."

"Probably not all of it," said Dane. "He received it in three separate, age-dependency payments over the years. He received the final one at the age of thirty. I doubt he's spent all of it, but I do think he's banked on having his share of mine."

"He's thought of it as a fourth payout, so he hasn't been careful with his own," guessed Simon.

"What about Kent?" asked Wyatt.

"He always swore he'd give me his share of my fund," said Dane.

Wyatt tilted his head. "But you don't trust that he will."

"The only person I trust is Vienna," Dane told him, sounding so utterly sincere I wanted to believe it was true. "She's never betrayed me. Never let me down. Never asked or expected anything of me. She won't even let me buy her a new car," he grumbled.

"You did it anyway," I pointed out. The brand-new vehicle had appeared in the garage a day ago.

Dane's mouth twitched. "You'll use it eventually. I've seen the way you look at it."

Melinda sighed. "I want to believe that you're *all* about Vienna; that your marrying her so soon isn't whatsoever connected to the stipulations of your trust fund. But the timing just seems too coincidental."

Dane shrugged. "I can't make you believe me. If what I've shared with you here hasn't rid your mind of doubt, there's nothing more I can do."

"I *do* appreciate that you told us all this—I know it couldn't have been whatsoever easy," she went on. "It's just … I have to feel *sure* of you, because Vienna's heart is on the line."

I straightened. "*I'm* sure of him."

"I know that," she said. "But sometimes we can be so emotionally wrapped up in a situation that we don't see it logically. I want to be positive that you've made the right choice," she said, like I was naïve and didn't know my own mind.

Okay, that got my back up. "Really? Heather splits married couples up on a regular basis. Couples like you and Wyatt, only rich. She uses one man after another just because she can. That's not the 'right choice.' You've ignored it. You've pretended it away. You've never once lectured her over it or been rude to her partners, most of whom were still married at the time she introduced you to them. But you'll question *my* ability to make a rational decision, and you'll expect Dane to explain himself to you? Sorry, but that seems just a little bit shitty."

Melinda grimaced. "Vienna—"

Dane cupped my jaw. "Don't, baby girl. Don't let this cause an argument. Travis would just love it if this created so much drama that you felt you had to choose between me and your family. Don't give him that power."

"We'd never ask her to choose us over you," Melinda told him.

"We just worry for Vienna," said Wyatt.

"I understand that," said Dane, sliding his hand from my jaw to my nape. "I'm glad that you care for her as much as you do. I invited you here tonight and shared these things with you because I don't want Travis to come between her and the three of you. I don't want her to lose the people she loves. As I said, I can't make you believe me. But I'd ask that you don't make this difficult for Vienna. Don't make her suffer for whatever doubts you may have. She's never done anything other than believe in me. She doesn't deserve to be punished for that."

"We don't want to punish her for it or cause problems for her." Melinda looked down at her hands. "We made mistakes with Heather. There are things that you may believe we should take her to task over. But if we do that, she might keep Junior from us." She met my eyes. "We couldn't handle that."

"I know," I said. "But if you're going to sit back and let her live her life as she pleases, you can surely do the same for me. That's all I'm asking."

Simon sighed and rubbed at the back of his neck. "I know what it's like to be let down by family, Dane. I know what that does to a person. So I know it couldn't have been at all easy for you to let Vienna in, to let yourself love her." He paused. "You married her solely because you love her? Really?"

Dane nodded once. "She's the only woman I ever have loved."

"I believe that," said Simon. "More, I believe in Vienna. If she says that this isn't about your trust fund, I'll accept that. And I definitely won't give your asshole of a brother the satisfaction of creating a divide between me and my daughter. But, having said that, if it ever turns out that my faith in you is misplaced, we'll be having an *entirely* different conversation, and it won't end pleasantly." His gaze slid to me and softened. "Love you, sweetheart."

I smiled. He was the best. "Love you, too."

"I have to warn you to be careful," Dane told him. "Travis or Hope may get the bright idea to approach you and feed you some tales. Please don't be quick to believe what they tell you."

Wyatt leaned forward. "If Vienna had asked you to wait and marry her at a later date, would you have agreed to that?"

"Yes," replied Dane. "I'd hoped that she wouldn't ask that of me, because I wanted her tied to me as fast as possible. But I would have waited and given her the fairytale wedding if she'd asked for it. She didn't."

Wyatt licked his bottom lip and sat up straight. He slowly nodded. "All right. I believe in giving the benefit of the doubt where it's due. Just … don't hurt our girl."

"I can't promise that," said Dane. "But I can promise that it's something I'd never want to do."

All eyes turned to Melinda, who was biting hard on her lip and staring at the ground.

Finally, she looked up at me and weakly flapped her hands. "If you truly believe he married you for the right reason, I'll trust that."

In other words, she didn't entirely trust *him* anymore, but she'd back down and let the situation lie. Given Melinda's character, that was really the most I could have hoped for.

It was another half an hour before my family announced their intention to leave. The goodbyes between Dane and my foster parents were a little stiff, but Simon made an effort. My father was probably so willing to give him a chance because, having heard Dane claim his own father wasn't a good man, Simon suspected he'd been abused. It was easy for your mind to go there when you'd been through it yourself. You knew it happened; knew what scars it could leave behind.

Dane had told me that he hadn't been sexually abused, but he hadn't said there'd been no abuse at all. I suspected that some awful shit had gone on in his house when he was a child. I just didn't know what. And it wasn't my place to ask.

After my family left, I stacked the empty coffee mugs into the dishwasher. "I'm sorry that you were put in a position where you felt the need to share all that stuff with them," I told Dane, who was leaning against the counter, staring into space.

His gaze snapped to mine. "It's not your fault."

"I know. It's Travis's fault. And don't think I don't want to throttle him." I closed the dishwasher. "You could have given me a heads-up that your father committed suicide—I almost fell off the sofa in shock."

"I only wanted to talk about it once."

I could understand that. "What are you going to do to Travis? Don't tell me nothing, I won't believe that. He's ignored every warning you've given him. There's no way you'll simply issue him another one."

Dane closed the distance between us and settled his hands on my hips. "I won't do anything to him that he isn't attempting to do to me."

I frowned. "You plan to try to wreck his marriage?"

"Not quite." Dane dipped his head and kissed the side of my neck. "Come take a shower with me."

I swear my entire body brightened at the idea. Still, I pushed, "What are you going to do to him?"

"I already told you."

"No, you *replied* to my question, but you didn't actually answer it."

Dane slid his hands down to palm my ass. "He's not important. We've wasted enough minutes of our day talking about him. Let's be done with that." Tightening his grip on my butt, he hauled me up.

I curled my legs around his waist. "Translation: you're not going to tell me?"

"Translation: I want to fuck you, and I don't want him in your head while I do it."

"Oh. All right, then."

CHAPTER TWENTY-FIVE

I was sure he did these things just to keep me on my toes.

With the exception of going to meetings or business-related events, Dane mostly stayed home. I'd originally thought that was purely because, being a workaholic, he preferred to be in his home office when not at o-Verve. But I'd come to realize that, actually, he was a home bird. He seemed at his most relaxed when on his own territory.

He never took off on his own to do "guy stuff" or ever proposed that we go anywhere together. So when he'd picked me up from the bridal boutique after my final fitting to take me straight to a very popular restaurant, it had been something of a surprise.

Other men might take their wives out for meals all the time, but not Dane. It not only meant coming away from work, it meant leaving the house. Plus, he preferred home cooking—he didn't even like takeout much, the weirdo. And considering I wasn't the true definition of a wife, he had no need to romance me or anything, so there was really no need for him to put himself out—something which, as a rule, he rarely ever did.

Yet, he sat opposite me at a table in this large but cozy restaurant. And I didn't know what to make of it.

It sometimes felt like things had once more shifted between us. But although we'd introduced sex into the mix since returning from New York two weeks ago, we'd never once fucked or slept in his bed. That could be his way of making it clear that it was *just* sex; that he hadn't officially moved me into his life.

He hadn't done or said anything to imply that we were an actual couple, and he was still *religious* about using condoms. It seemed unnecessary when not only had he had the snip, but I was on the pill *and* we were both clean. As such, I wondered if the condoms were, for him, also a barrier against emotional intimacy or something. Probably.

Things *had* changed, though. He spent more time with me at home. We almost always ate our meals together now. We often even cooked them together. There'd been the odd occasion when he joined me in the media room, or when we both sat in his magical garden—which I'd begun to think of as my alfresco reading nook—and just talked or simply basked in the peaceful atmosphere.

He also slept in my bed every night. I suspected he had nightmares or was easily yanked out of sleep, because there had been times when I'd woken to find him working on his laptop in my chair. I never commented on it for fear that he'd start going somewhere else to work. Besides, he sometimes came back to bed or woke me in style shortly before the alarm went off.

Although we did spend time together, we still spent the majority of our free time apart even while under the same roof. So, things were different yet not. And now he was, what, taking me on a date? Was that what this was? Did he want something?

Well, whatever his motivation, I was grateful, because this pizza was *the shit.* He seemed to be enjoying his own meal—some kind of pasta dish that I didn't have a prayer of pronouncing. He'd forked a piece of it earlier and offered it to me, so I could attest that it did taste good.

The whole thing reminded me of when we'd gone for a cake-tasting session that Chris and Miley organized. Dane had fed me several small pieces of various party cakes. If I liked it, he'd tried it. If I didn't like it, he'd vetoed it on that basis. We'd eventually settled on one particular cake. It was freaking amazing.

I glanced around the Italian restaurant. It smelled exactly as such a place should: of garlic, grilled meat, tomato sauce, creamy mozzarella, and hot bread. It was a big place yet had a cozy feel. It also possessed a distinct charm with its earthy colors, muted lighting, dark wood flooring, photography prints of Italian villages, and ornamental tables and chairs.

Having finished my meal, I used a wet wipe to clean the grease and crumbs from my fingers. "I can't quite believe the reception is in a month's time. Have you sorted out a tuxedo for it yet?"

"Yes," he replied, lifting his glass of wine. "When will you pick up your dress?"

"It will be ready for collection on the Saturday before the reception. Chris is going to pick it up for me." I'd bought my footwear while I was at the boutique last time, so that was done. I hadn't yet shown Dane the ivory lace knee-high boots. There had been occasions when, at home alone, I'd worn them to go on a wander through the house; breaking them in and getting a feel for what they were like depending on the type of flooring.

I used the soft napkin to dry my clean hands. "Onto a whole other topic, are you *sure* you're okay with spending Thanksgiving with my family?"

His brow creased. "Why wouldn't I be?"

"Because Melinda's still a little off with you. *I* wouldn't like to eat my Thanksgiving dinner at a table where there's tension." The meal was in a few weeks' time, but Melinda had already called the people she wished to invite, including my father.

"You want to go, so we'll go. Just be aware that if Heather cancels the plans she's made with her friends and *does* attend the dinner, I won't be anything close to friendly with her. I can't prove she sent that flash drive, but that doesn't mean she didn't."

"I highly doubt she'll cancel her plans. She's always left Junior at her parents' home on Thanksgiving so she can go spend the day drinking with her friends. To each their own, I guess. You sure the tension won't put you off your meal?"

"Unlike you, I'm not interested in the holidays. It will be just another day to me."

"So I won't be able to convince you to dress up on Halloween?"

His brow furrowed. "Is that a serious question?"

And there went my dream of him dressed in a fireman's outfit. I leaned back in my chair. "I guess I can spend the day with Ashley and Tucker."

His frown deepened. "You'll spend it with me."

"Doing what? You'll hole up in your office."

"We'll go to the city's annual Halloween festival."

My mouth almost dropped open. I sat up straight. "Okay, you're really starting to worry me now. Daytrips, meals, festivals. You're not dying, are you?"

He gave me a droll look. "Do you want to go to the festival or not?"

"Yeah, obviously, but there'll be no tickets left. They sell out fast."

"I'll get some."

I was going to warn him that it wouldn't be so simple, but then his phone began to ring. I waited for him to answer it, but he didn't. "Aren't you going to get that?"

"We're talking."

I almost fell off my chair. "But you … Okay." I wasn't gonna complain that I had his full attention. I really didn't know what to do with it, though. And now he was back to wearing that secret smile. I narrowed my eyes. "You're doing it again."

"What?"

"Looking at me like you know something I don't."

"Vienna, I probably know a lot of things you don't."

I might have bristled if I wasn't so pleased that the oh so serious Dane Davenport was actually teasing me. "Arrogant fucker," I muttered.

A godawful cramp in my stomach yanked me out of sleep. I moaned and pulled my knees up to my chest. Every muscle in my stomach seemed to contract and twist. Then a strong wave of nausea slammed into me.

Oh God, I was gonna be sick.

I felt the vomit begin to rise; knew I'd never be able to hold it back.

I scrambled off the bed and rushed to the bathroom like my ass was on fire. I made it to the toilet just in time. I retched violently as vicious contractions racked my stomach. It was so bad I could barely catch my breath between the flows of vomit that surged up my throat and sprayed the toilet pan.

"Vienna?" A hand settled on my back just as Dane bent over me. "Shit."

Mortified, I tried waving him away, but he wouldn't be budged. He held my ponytail out of the way and rubbed my back as I hurled like a champ. The stench of stomach acid and vomit stung my nostrils.

Finally, the contractions stopped, but the queasy feeling remained, telling me it wasn't over yet. Glad of the reprieve, I flushed the toilet, sank to my knees, and sat on my haunches. Jesus, that was intense. My eyes watered, and my breaths were coming fast.

I grabbed some toilet paper and wiped my mouth. "I think I caught a stomach bug."

"Or food poisoning." Crouched beside me, he put his palm against my forehead. His jaw went hard. "You're running a fever."

"I don't feel hot." If anything, I felt cold.

"You're shaking a little. Do you have the chills?"

I went to answer, but then my stomach turned over. Groaning, I lurched forward and retched again. And again. And again.

"Wait there," said Dane.

Where did he think I was going to fucking go?

I kept on heaving as my stomach lurched, twisted, and cramped. Soon, Dane was at my side again, rubbing my back. How he was able to stay in the room when the stench was so vile, I had no idea.

The contractions eventually eased off again. I flushed the toilet once more and wiped my mouth with the fresh tissue Dane handed me. My shoulders drooping, I sat back on my haunches again. Feeling all hollowed out, I might have slumped to the tiled floor if Dane hadn't steadied me.

"Here." He gave me the bottle of water I'd earlier placed on my nightstand. "Don't guzzle it down; take sips."

Easy for him to say—the back of his throat wasn't burning from bile. Still, I only took small sips of the water.

He rubbed a very gentle circle on my back. "The symptoms of stomach bugs and food poisoning are pretty similar." He held up his phone for a moment, adding, "According to this website, you don't need to go to Urgent Care or the ER unless you've got any of the symptoms listed. So far, the only one you have is the fever."

My eyes fell closed. God, he'd Googled it. There was just something so endearing about it that my heart went all light and warm.

"I still think you should go to the ER."

I shook my head. "I don't need a doctor. I've had a bug before; I'll be fine. But this is gonna be a rough night." I blew out a shaky breath. "You don't have to stay with me."

He gave me a dark look. "You think I'd leave you when you're sick?"

"What I think is that it *reeks* in here. No one would blame you for wanting fresh air or preferring to not watch someone hurl."

"I'm staying."

A cramp twisted my stomach again. I turned back to the toilet and heaved over and over and over. Until my stomach muscles ached.

I blinked my watery eyes and swayed toward the toilet, feeling shaky and depleted. "I forgot how much I hate being sick."

"I really think you should see a doctor," said Dane, concern creasing his brow.

I weakly shook my head. "Don't need one." What I needed was to stick close to this toilet.

His nostrils flared. "All right. But if you start showing *any* more of the food poisoning symptoms, I'm taking you to Urgent Care—I don't give a damn what you say."

"Agreed." Another wave of nausea gripped my insides, and my stomach dry-heaved again. Fuck. "Go. Run. Save yourself."

"I'm staying."

I would have called him a masochist if another dry-heave hadn't seized my insides.

Two days of nausea, vomiting, cramps, muscle aches, and diarrhea went by. And even though—against my wishes—he had a doctor come visit who asserted that I didn't need to be hospitalized, Dane hovered around me like I was on my death bed. I was surprised he didn't invite my family and friends here to "say their goodbyes" or something.

He insisted on working from home, as if leaving me would somehow worsen the stomach bug. In fact, he hardly left my side. I wouldn't say he was sweet or sympathetic. He was gruff and bossy and curt, seeming a little out of his depth.

He kept flicking from one website to another, comparing lists of symptoms to be sure there was nothing he was missing. He felt positive it was food poisoning and was ready to call up the Italian restaurant until he read—again, on a website—that symptoms of food poisoning could take weeks to come on, so I could have caught it from any number of places. The doctor who came to visit had confirmed that.

Melinda, Wyatt, and Simon stopped by to see me, but Dane didn't let them stay long, claiming I *needed my rest.* Which they all seemed to think was beyond cute, but they didn't say as much to him. Nor did they comment on how much he needlessly faffed over me—ensuring I had drinks of water close by, keeping me covered with a blanket, handfeeding me crackers—like I couldn't do anything for myself. It was pretty sweet, really.

Although the symptoms passed after two days, I was still groggy and felt like shit. I worked from home for the next few days. Dane, to my surprise, did the same.

By Sunday morning, I was fully recovered and raring to go back to work the next day. He got all snarly and surly. He thought it would be better if I took it easy for another week or so. I thought it would be better if he shoved that idea up his ass.

Standing in the middle of the den, I sighed. "I was sick, Dane, not terminally ill. I'm fine now. There's no reason why I can't go back to work."

"You're not at one-hundred percent yet," he insisted.

"No? I feel it." I crossed to him, touched by his concern but also a little exasperated. "The doctor told you there was no reason I couldn't go back to work." Which I knew had pissed Dane off. He'd been relying on the doctor to back him up.

"You can keep working from home."

"No, I can't. Nor do I want to. You've put off countless meetings, and many people are eager to reschedule—especially some guy named Blake Mercier, who called three times today. Stop clucking like a mother hen, I'm fine."

"You had *food poisoning,* Vienna. That's not always simple to recover from."

I let out a *pfft* sound. "I had a stomach bug."

"Even the doctor said it could have been food poisoning."

"Yes, *could* have been. But he couldn't be sure without a fecal sample. And I'm quite certain you'll remember that I hadn't been able to provide him with one. I'd been fresh out of shit. Literally. My body had purged itself in a major way."

He sighed and shook his head. "Only you, Vienna. Only you."

"Even if it *was* food poisoning, that wouldn't mean I have to work from home any longer."

A muscle in his cheek ticked. "You have to promise to tell me if you get too tired or need to go home."

I almost rolled my eyes. "I promise."

He sighed. "Then we go back to work tomorrow. You know, a lot of people would find it weird that that makes you smile."

"I consider myself lucky that I have a job I enjoy." But after Dane and I divorced, I'd lose the position for sure. And I'd miss the fuck out of it, just as I'd miss the fuck out of this man who'd been a very attentive—albeit curt and rude—nurse.

I got the feeling he'd never watched over someone who was sick before. He could have asked another person to stay with me. He could even have hired someone to do it. But he hadn't. I wished he had, though, because he just kept sneaking deeper beneath my defenses with every sweet thing he did.

"What's wrong?" he asked, frowning. "You don't feel sick again, do you?" He actually felt my forehead to check my temperature.

I had to fight a smile. Yeah, my defenses stood no chance against this side of him. "I'm fine, Nurse Nancy. Thank you for taking care of me, by the way."

He shrugged, as if it was no big deal. "It was a one-off. If you're ever ill again, you're on your own."

CHAPTER TWENTY-SIX

Something was wrong. Very, very wrong.

I'd seen Dane like this before. Four other times, in fact. And always on November 1st each year.

He was colder than usual. Harder. Apathetic. So incredibly distant that his gaze seemed to skim *over* people, like he'd dissociated from everyone around him—it was hard to explain.

The others in the room had noticed, despite him barely saying a word. The latter wasn't unusual when he met with the development team; he often allowed them to do the talking. He mostly listened, offered input where necessary, and let the team members work through their ideas. But this afternoon, they were too distracted by his icy demeanor to be productive. That wasn't good at all, because he had far less tolerance with indecisiveness and ineptitude when in this state of mind.

A few of them glanced at me for guidance. I just waved my hand, encouraging them to continue. The absolute worst thing they could do would be to ask him if he was all right. He'd bite their fucking head off. He wouldn't yell or rave, but he'd speak in that low voice that dripped with frost and could lash you like a whip.

It didn't take a genius to work out that this particular date was somehow significant to him, so I was usually prepared for the change. But this year, I hadn't seen it coming. We'd had such a blast yesterday at the Halloween festival. Well, *I* had a blast. He'd behaved much as he had at the zoo and the museum—he'd enjoyed himself *in his own way*. So the abrupt change in him earlier today had come as a shock.

He hadn't been there when I woke, which was rare. I'd wondered if he was in the kitchen making breakfast for us or something, so I'd quickly gotten ready for work and headed downstairs … only to discover that he was nowhere to be seen.

I'd gone in search of him and eventually found him in his office. When I'd entered the room and found myself the focus of that vacant stare, I'd remembered the date. Rather than ask if he was okay—I'd learned from past experience that it was best not to draw attention to the change in him—I'd asked if he was coming down for breakfast.

"*I've already eaten,*" he'd said, his tone flat. "*I'll meet you in the foyer when Sam arrives.*" And then he'd turned back to his computer, dismissing me.

Deciding to give him whatever emotional space he seemed to need, I'd left the office and eaten breakfast alone.

He'd barely spoken a word during the drive to o-Verve. Had barely even looked at me, actually. Although there'd been mere inches between us on the leather seat, I might as well have been looking at him through plate glass. It was like he'd erected four huge walls around himself. No one was getting through them, and they'd be a fool to try.

It shouldn't have been possible to calmly snap at someone, but he'd done it several times this morning; one employee had actually teared up as they walked away. Dane had a way of making you feel an inch tall, and he could do it with only a few words.

He'd been terse and abrupt toward me, but I'd so far managed to avoid being barked at. I'd probably feel the sharp edge of his tongue eventually.

When lunch time had arrived, he'd declared that he was heading to his office and didn't want to be disturbed. So I'd eaten alone at my desk, like I had many times in the past before we became a fake couple.

It was the first time in a while that I'd actually *felt* like I was purely his PA. It was a reminder that, in fact, I wasn't more than that to him. A reminder that we weren't in a real relationship.

After our lunch hour was over, we'd headed straight for the meeting with the development team … bringing us to the present moment. Which wasn't going well.

At one point, when one of the guys was verbally fumbling his way through an explanation, Dane raised his hand. The guy immediately quieted, and a boom of silence hit the room.

Dane's eyes took in the whole team as he spoke. "You've had four weeks—*four*—to generate some fresh ideas. And this is the best you've come up with?"

I winced. Okay, so I could admit that the team could have done better, but the scorn dripping from his voice was unnecessary. By the time he'd finished verbally slapping them down, I was surprised they still had the will left to live.

When he returned to his office, he slammed the door shut behind him. If it was any other day of the year, I'd have followed him inside and told him that the asshole-behavior needed to stop. Not that he'd have apologized or admitted to being at fault. But I'd have called him on his shit anyway.

This wasn't a simple case of him being a prick, though. Something was fucking with his head. Something big. And that same "something" continued to bother him throughout the rest of the workday.

He was just as quiet on the journey home as he had been on the way to o-Verve that morning. At least he hadn't snapped at me. Yet.

No sooner had we stepped into the house than he disappeared upstairs without a word. All right then.

I spent a little time reading in the library before heading to the kitchen to make dinner. I sent him a quick text to let him know I was making spaghetti, just in case he was hungry.

He didn't respond to the message. He also didn't come downstairs to eat.

After dinner, I went to my room and caught up on some work. I then watched the new episode of a series I was somewhat addicted to. When 10 p.m. came crawling around and there was still no sign of Dane, I decided to check on him. I wouldn't be able to sleep unless I knew he was at least relatively okay.

I tried calling him, but it went to voicemail. I frowned. It was exceedingly rare that Dane didn't answer his phone. It was like an extension of his freaking hand.

I went to his office, expecting to find him sitting in the dark with only the glow of his computer screen to light the room, but he wasn't there. I checked the kitchen, thinking he might be having a late dinner. He wasn't there either. I checked the gym, since it was possible that he'd decided to work his issues out on the punchbag. No sign of him.

My shoulders dropped. Maybe he'd gone to bed. His *own* bed.

I made my way to his room and knocked on the door. No response. I'd never once stepped inside the room, respecting his boundaries. Peeking through the door didn't count as entering though, did it?

I twisted the knob and pushed the door so that it slowly swung open. I glanced inside, taking in the very masculine space with its geometric lines, neutral tones, and dark woods, but I didn't see him anywhere. The bedcovers hadn't been disturbed.

Sighing, I shoved a hand through my hair, wondering where he could possibly be. Then it came to me. *The garden.* He'd obviously headed to the garden for some peace and quiet.

It was a little chilly out so, since I was clad in only a thin tee and shorts, I hurried to the little oasis among the trees. But he wasn't there either. "For fuck's sake," I muttered. How hard could it be to find *one* man in his own home?

Okay, I'd just have to stand in the foyer and yell his name until he answered.

As I was passing the pool on my way back to the house, a cool breeze came along and rustled the cabana curtain. And there he was. I halted with a relieved sigh. *Finally.*

Even though I knew my presence probably wouldn't be welcome, I slipped inside the cabana. Lounging on the rattan sofa with a glass in his hand, his eyes met mine. His intense stare was so disturbingly blank it made my skin itch.

I eyed the half-empty bottle of whiskey on the table beside him. Unease fluttered through me. Dane was not a big drinker. He'd have a glass of this or that here and there, but I'd never known him to make off with a bottle.

I opened my mouth, about to say that I'd come to check on him, but then I thought better of it. No grown man wanted to be checked on. And given the mood Dane was in, it would only piss him off.

His unwavering gaze didn't shift from mine once—not even when he took another swig of whiskey. I genuinely couldn't get a read on what he was thinking.

I stood there, not knowing what to say or do. Although I felt like an intruder, I didn't want to leave him alone. He probably wouldn't welcome company or comfort, but it felt wrong to just head back into the house.

So I crossed to the sofa and sat beside him, keeping a few inches between us so that he wouldn't feel crowded. I didn't speak. Neither did he. We simply sat there, our gazes on the rippling pool water.

Feeling a little cold, I pulled my legs up to my chest and wrapped my arms around them.

Dane exhaled a heavy, put-out sigh. "Go inside."

Oh, he speaks. It was good that he wasn't slurring. I rested my chin on my knees. "I like it out here."

Silence fell between us again. A tense loaded silence that rubbed at my nerves.

Endless minutes went by as he took idle swigs of his drink, seeming lost in his own thoughts. Maybe it was the whiskey or simply that he was fully dressed, but the cool evening air didn't appear to be bothering him at all. I couldn't claim the same; goosebumps covered my arms and legs.

The breeze rustled the curtain again and swooshed inside. It was like a lash of cold to my bare limbs, and I couldn't help the little shiver that ran through me.

He let out another of those disgruntled sighs. "Go. Inside."

I looked at him, but he didn't meet my gaze. "I'll go if you go."

He took another swig of whiskey. "I'm good here."

"Then so am I." I expected him to snipe at me. Instead, he rubbed at his temple, looking *so tired* all of a sudden. My chest squeezed. Before I thought better of it, I straddled his lap and burrowed into his warmth, resting my head on his chest.

He went rigid. "Vienna."

"I know you're good at being alone, Dane, but you don't always have to be."

He didn't hold me. Didn't touch me. He sat very still, tense as a bow. His body language screamed *get off me and go*, but I didn't. I stayed snuggled into him like a kitten, hoping he wouldn't shove me off his lap.

If he was anyone else, I'd have soothingly rubbed his chest. But my instincts told me that Dane wouldn't respond well to any show of sympathy or comfort right now.

I badly wanted to know what was eating at him, but I didn't dare ask. The question could wait until tomorrow, when he was back to himself. And he *would* be—the swift transformation happened every year like magic.

He let out a long breath and placed his hand on my lower back. Such a small thing, but it made me want to smile.

We stayed there like that for a while, saying nothing. Gradually and slowly, the rigidity seeped out of him, muscle by muscle. I wouldn't go as far as to say he relaxed, but it was no longer like cuddling a rock.

He smoothed his hand up my back and curved it around my nape. "It's late. You need to go inside."

I wasn't about to leave him out here in the cold and the dark. "Only if you're coming with me." I could *swear* I heard his teeth grind.

The hand on my nape delved into my hair, fisted it tight, and snatched my head back. I winced, and his pupils dilated. What's more, his cock twitched and began to swell.

He snarled, his eyes cold and flinty. "If I go upstairs with you now, I'll fuck you. Hard. But it wouldn't be for you, it would be for me. I wouldn't care whether or not you liked it, whether or not you came, whether or not it hurt you. All I'd care about is making my head go quiet for a while. I don't want to use you like that. So no, Vienna, I'm not going with you." He roughly released my hair. "Now go to fucking bed."

My heart just about broke. He'd avoided me all night because he didn't want to use or hurt me. And now here he sat, alone in the dark, lost in thoughts that were obviously wrecking him.

It was sad that his instinct when feeling so desolate was to turn to something sexual. Had he ever been hugged? Cuddled? Consoled? I didn't think so.

If something sexual was the only form of comfort that he'd allow me to give him, I'd go with it. Not by letting him fuck me—he'd be too rough and then he'd regret it tomorrow; he'd be pissed at us both for it. But I could *show* him comfort in a form he'd accept.

I shuffled off his lap, but I didn't stand upright. I sank to my knees between his legs.

He stiffened, and his thigh muscles bunched tight. "Vienna."

I lowered his zipper, fished his cock out of his boxers, and curled my hand around it. Even semi-hard, it was impressive.

I'd licked and sucked it on occasion, but he'd always stopped me at some point, wanting to fuck me.

"Vienna." It was a warning.

I slanted my head and licked the side of his shaft from base to tip. "You don't want me to suck you off?"

His eyes flared. He put his hand on my head, as if to push me away, but then he snarled again. "Don't start this unless you're prepared to finish it." In other words, he'd want to come in my mouth.

I lathed the silky head with my tongue. "Why else would I have started it?" I closed my mouth around the tip and sucked hard.

He drew in a sharp breath through his nose and whispered what could have been a curse, I wasn't sure. I also didn't care. I had him; he wasn't going to push me away. That was all that mattered, because I couldn't leave him alone like this.

Humming, I slid my mouth lower down his shaft and sucked as I retreated. I did it again. And again. And again. His cock hardened, lengthened, and thickened, stretching my lips. I fisted his shaft a little tighter, liking how it pulsed in my grip.

"Other hand, Vienna. I want to see your rings while your fingers are curled around my dick."

My nipples beaded. Um … okay. I switched hands and then closed my lips around the broad tip again.

Dane gathered my hair and bunched it on top of my head. "That's it, baby girl, keep sucking my cock."

I expected him to take over; to guide my movements. But he seemed content to just watch my head bob up and down his long, thick shaft.

I took him into my mouth over and over, keeping the suction tight, gliding the flat of my tongue along the underside of his shaft. He whispered praises and encouragements; they feathered over my skin and sank into my bones.

"I don't like knowing that my wife's had other men's cocks in her mouth." Right then, his dick hit the back of my throat. He groaned and dug his fingertips into my scalp.

I took him a little deeper, but I couldn't swallow all of him. So I added some hand action; jacking him off while sucking as much of him as I could take.

Sometimes I'd work the entire shaft with my mouth and hand. Sometimes I'd simply curl my fingers around the base while concentrating on the head, licking and sucking and blowing cool air over it; teasing the hell out of him.

I occasionally stopped to twirl my tongue around the tip, dip my tongue into the slit to scoop up pearls of pre-come, or flick the sensitive bump beneath the crown. All the while, I'd fist his shaft tight, loving how he was so hot, full, and heavy in my hand. And then I'd swallow him down again.

Feeling his cock throb and thicken in my mouth, I knew he was close. I tightened my lips around him and sucked so hard my cheeks hollowed.

He hissed out a breath. "Fuck." Gripping my hair, he pumped his hips, forcing me to take him deeper. "I'm going to fill that talented little mouth with my come. You're going to swallow it all. I want you to feel it sliding down your throat. I want every drop of it in your belly."

I gave up control without a fight. I sucked harder, faster, took him as deep as I could as he literally fucked my mouth. His hold on my hair tightened until my scalp stung so bad my eyes watered, which made his own eyes flare.

"Swallow," he bit out. Dane lifted his hips and erupted with a low growl, keeping my head still, ensuring I couldn't pull back as thick jets of hot come spurted out of him.

Finally, his orgasm subsided. His eyes closed, he relaxed in his seat, breathing hard. The hand he'd bunched in my hair loosened its death grip but kept my head in place. "I don't want to lose your mouth yet," he said, his voice thick. "Let me keep it a little longer."

I could really do with a drink of water right now, but I didn't struggle. I just stayed still and simply held his softening cock in my mouth, knowing he was probably too sensitive for me to suckle on him.

He glided his fingers along my scalp, kneading and lightly massaging. It felt like a reward. Or maybe even an apology for almost ragging the strands out of my head.

Soon, his eyes opened. They were all soft and languid, like dark velvet. His hand slipped away from my head. "Up, baby girl."

I stood upright, surprised my stiff knees didn't crack. The floor was not comfortable. I made a mental note to use a cushion if there was a "next time."

Sliding forward on the sofa, he settled his hands on my hips and then planted his face in my stomach. He let out a sigh that seemed to come all the way from his soul.

I palmed the back of his head with both hands. Honestly, I was a little fired up, but I didn't want him to return the favor. I wanted this, here and now, to be about him.

"I don't know about you, but I'm dog tired," I said. "Bed?" I held my breath, hoping he wouldn't push me away or insist on staying here alone.

He looked up at me and gave my hips a gentle squeeze. "Bed," he agreed.

My shorts and panties slid over my hips, down my legs, and then were gone. I frowned, shifting slightly. Warm hands spread my legs and smoothed along my inner thighs, reverent and possessive. I mumbled an unintelligible sound and squirmed.

A mouth brushed over my navel. "Shh, let me have my way."

The folds of my pussy were gently parted, and there was a flutter of cool air that made me jump. A tongue licked my slit, acting like a lash of wet heat. I moaned, wanting more. I got more. And more. And more. And more.

Hot and restless, I bucked as that same tongue rubbed at the side of my clit. Oh God, that felt good. Too good.

It felt even better when the tongue rolled around my clit and then licked its way down to where I wanted it most. It didn't enter me, though. It circled the entrance of my pussy—a tease, a promise of things to come. I frowned, writhing with frustration.

"Be still, Vienna."

The cobwebs of sleep cleared from my mind. I opened my eyes to find that it was partially light, thanks to my sunrise clock. Lifting my head, I blinked at Dane, who'd settled between my thighs.

His gaze met mine, hot and determined; not blank as it was yesterday. "Morning, baby girl." He clamped his mouth around my pussy and drove his tongue deep inside.

I arched and gripped the bedsheet. *Jesus.* My eyelids fluttered closed as his tongue did a slow swirl, stroking my inner walls. "Don't tease," I rasped.

Dane didn't respond. He settled in and feasted—licked, nipped, lathed, rubbed, rendered me a quivering mess. Then he was pumping his tongue inside me, making me burn hotter and hotter, luring my orgasm closer and closer.

"Gonna come," I moaned.

He growled and thrust his tongue faster, digging his fingers hard into the globes of my ass to hold me still.

My thighs quaked. My pussy rippled. My back bowed. And I came with a sob.

I slumped to the mattress, shuddering and panting. *Best wake-up alarm ever.*

Dane wiped his face on my stomach and knelt between my thighs. "Pull up your tee so I can see your tits while I fuck you," he ordered, hooking my legs over the crooks of his elbows. "That's it, good girl."

My lips parted as I felt the broad head of his cock push inside me, stretching me open. I'd gotten used to the burn; liked it. He slowly but forcefully sank inch after inch of his dick into my pussy, relentlessly pushing his way past swollen muscles, refusing to be impeded by their resistance. It seemed forever before he finally bottomed out.

I closed my eyes, feeling blissfully full. His cock throbbed inside me, so hot and hard and … My brow puckered as I realized something. "Condom, you forgot—"

"I'll put it on in a minute," he said, curling his hands around my thighs. His eyes flicked to the nightstand, and I saw the condom waiting there. "Just had to know how it'd feel to be bare while deep inside you."

He slowly reared back, watching his cock withdraw from my body, looking almost riveted by the sight of his shaft all wet and shiny. He let out a low growl and surged forward, burying himself balls-deep again.

I fisted the bedsheets as my back arched and my inner walls rippled around him.

He ground his teeth. "So fucking hot and slick."

Again and again, he lazily pulled back, stretching out the moment, and then rammed his cock deep. I moaned, bucked, and whimpered as he stuffed me full over and over.

I'd never been a fan of "slow and hard" until Dane. The lazy rhythm forced my sensitive inner walls to really *feel* every thick, long inch of him; to feel every ridge, vein, and pulse of his cock. I loved it just as much as I loved feeling him hammer into me.

Pulling his hips back once again, he slid his gaze to the condom on the nightstand, a look of resolve etched into his face. I expected him to reach for the foil packet. He didn't. He just stayed very still, his jaw tight, his mouth set into a harsh line.

"Dane?"

His gaze met mine—alive with heat, hunger, and possession—and his look of resolve crumbled. "Fuck it." He rammed his cock home so hard my entire body jolted. Then, gripping my hips for leverage, he furiously pounded into me.

All sexual power and pure male domination, he used me. Possessed me. Ruled me. Took what he wanted how he wanted it. And I absofuckinglutely loved it.

There was something almost … feral about the way he fucked me. Like he was all primal instinct in that moment. It was rough and raw and wild, and all I wanted was more.

Still thrusting hard and fast, he curled over me, shifting his angle, hitting my clit, and going *so fucking deep*.

I groaned. "Fuck." I scratched at his nape and shoulders. "God, don't stop."

"Not stopping until I've pumped my come inside you." He snapped his hand around my throat and squeezed—not enough to affect my breathing, but enough to push my buttons in the best way.

My pussy began to spasm and tighten as my release crept up on me. I thought he'd ask me to hold back the orgasm, but he didn't. He upped the pace of his thrusts and jackhammered into me.

"That's it, come for me." He squeezed my throat again.

I screamed as the orgasm tore through me like a fucking whirlwind, making my body shake violently and my pussy clamp down on his cock.

Dane bit out an expletive as he rammed into me once, twice, and then exploded. I felt his dick swell and pulse, felt jet after jet of hot come splash my inner walls. Then the energy seemed to leave us both in a rush.

Panting and shuddering, he buried his face in the crook of my neck and let my legs slip down to my sides. I weakly stroked his back, lost in my post-orgasm daze. We stayed that way for long moments.

Lifting his head, he dropped a light kiss on my shoulder and pulled out his softening cock. His gaze dropped to my pussy, and his eyes went heavy-lidded in pure male satisfaction. "I like seeing my come leaking out of you."

Hmm, well, I didn't need to ask if he regretted not wearing a condom.

He lay on his back beside me. Rolling onto my side, I used my finger to idly doodle circles on his abs. The room was much lighter now, so I knew the alarm would go off sometime soon.

"It was the anniversary of Oliver's death yesterday," he said, staring at the ceiling.

My heart sank. Losing a sibling would be bad enough. But Dane hadn't simply lost his brother, he'd lost a part of himself. He'd been living with that void ever since, never daring to let anyone fill it. But, having seen what that date did to him, I had the feeling that there was so much more to it than grief.

"I hope you don't blame yourself for what happened, Dane," I said softly. "In your shoes, I'd probably blame myself. But I'd be wrong to do that. You didn't fail him by not being there, by playing in the house instead of outside with him."

"I wasn't playing, Vienna," said Dane, his voice remarkably flat. "I was curled up on the basement floor after my father caned my back, thighs, legs, and the soles of my feet."

My head shot up as anger spiked through me. "He fucking *caned* you?" *Motherfucker.*

"Barron liked to hurt people. He was fond of delivering kidney shots, but he was content to punch you anywhere. He would make us stand in one spot for hours or sit in stress positions until our muscles cramped. I preferred the beatings, even when he used the cane."

What a fucking bastard. "Didn't your mother try to protect you?"

"If we looked to her for help, she'd say, 'take it like a man' and walk away. Sometimes he made her watch while he caned us, or when he tried forcing us to cane each other."

My mouth dropped open in shock. "He tried forcing you all to …" I couldn't finish the sentence; couldn't wrap my head around what he'd said.

"The 'offender' would have to stand on a chair. Barron would instruct one of us to cane the back of the 'offender's' legs. Oliver would go light with the cane; we'd flinch as if it hurt so that Barron wouldn't notice. Kent used to go somewhere else in his head and get it over with. Travis couldn't switch off from what was happening; he'd sob during and after, which Barron thought was amusing."

God, that man was *such* a fucking monster. I slid my arm around Dane's waist and kissed his chest, even knowing it wouldn't really comfort him.

Dane looked at me. "I refused to hurt any of them, but don't think my conscience stopped me. I'm not even sure I had much of one. In some ways,

Oliver was my moral guide. I just hated Barron so much I refused to be under his control. He was set on beating the defiance out of me, so I spent a lot of time on the basement floor. He'd sometimes sneak into my bedroom in the middle of the night and drag me all the way down there to be 'disciplined.'"

Which explained why he could snap awake so quickly and why he hated having anyone in his room. I swallowed. "This is what you meant when you said it's your father's fault that you're not close to your brothers. He tried to make you all hurt each other so that there'd be no trust or loyalty." And he'd made it automatic for them to never bond with the people around them.

"Divide and conquer." Dane licked his front teeth. "People are easier to control when they're not united. The reason Barron forced our mother to watch was that he wanted us to see that she'd never defend us; that we had no one to turn to."

I rested my chin on Dane's chest. "It's a wonder any of you communicate with each other."

"It's our way of flipping Barron the middle finger, I suppose. And maybe the shared experience bonded us in a strange way. But it's not a sibling bond. More like a survivor bond. And our years with Hugh helped. He gave us 'normal.'"

"I used to wonder how Travis could so easily try to ruin your 'marriage.' But he was encouraged from an early age to hurt and betray; shaped to believe it was the norm. I guess that didn't 'stick' with Kent."

"It's as if Kent decided he would be the absolute opposite of Barron. Maybe that was his own personal form of rebellion. Travis never finishes a meal, and I know that's because Barron would force us to either eat every bit or eat the rest for breakfast the next day. But Travis also picked up some of Barron's bad habits—the gambling, the cheating, the knack of getting into debt. He hates me."

I frowned. "Why? You never hurt him."

"Exactly. I held out against Barron. Travis hates that I resisted when he couldn't, even though we were just kids and it doesn't whatsoever make him weak."

"He resents your strength," I realized.

"Just as Heather resents yours."

I kissed his chest again. I understood him so much better now. Understood his need for peace, quiet, and space—he'd quite simply never had those things. He'd spent most of his childhood in a house filled with fear, shouting, crying, pain, and abuse. The silence reminded him that he wasn't there anymore. He only felt safe when alone. It was a wonder he hadn't stuck me in his guesthouse.

I also now understood why he held himself apart and was always seeking *more*. The only person Dane had ever truly bonded with was his twin. After losing Oliver, Dane hadn't ever let anyone close enough to fill the void he'd been left with, and so he moved through life feeling unfulfilled no matter what he achieved or gained. It was all just so … gutting.

The alarm went off, breaking into my thoughts.

Dane reached over and switched it off. "Do you have a problem with me not using condoms from now on?"

I blinked, taken aback by the abrupt change of subject. Then again, maybe I shouldn't be. Dane only ever revealed sneak peeks of himself. Really, I was surprised he'd told me as much as he had. "No," I replied.

Satisfaction flared in his eyes. "Good. I like coming inside you."

Yeah, I'd noticed.

CHAPTER TWENTY-SEVEN

As I unplugged my hairdryer from the wall socket on Saturday morning, I heard my cell phone begin to chime. Clad in only a plush towel, I crossed to the dresser and picked up my cell. Seeing Ashley's name on the screen made me smile. I suspected she meant to double-check that I still intended to go shopping with her and Hanna tomorrow.

I swiped my thumb across the screen and answered, "Morning."

"I'm gonna kill him one day, Vienna," she said, her voice dark. "It's gonna happen. I'm telling you. I've watched enough CSI episodes to know how to get away with it."

I bit my lip. "What happened?"

"I caught him red-handed."

"Doing what?"

"Watching porn. Worse, he was jerking off while he watched it. Oh, he doesn't think there's anything wrong with it. I'm telling you, it's the same as cheating. *He* said it's no different than when I read erotic books. I said that's bullshit, because you don't see me lounging on the sofa with tissues and lube close by while I touch myself. Sorry to put that image in your brain but, you know, I had to make my point."

"No problem," I said even as I grimaced.

Just then, my fake husband strode into the room. He'd headed to his own bedroom after our shower, and now he'd returned fully clothed and looking delicious. His steely eyes drifted over me, bold as brass. I expected him to whip off my towel, but he instead sank into my bulky armchair.

"What would you do in my position?" Ashley asked me.

"Well, I can't say I'd like to walk into a room and find Dane watching porn—" I frowned as I heard three loud bangs. "What was that?"

Ashley huffed. "Oh, Mr. Porn Addict doesn't like that I've locked myself in the bathroom, so he's pounding his fist on the door."

"*I'm not addicted to porn,*" I heard Tucker complain. "*Jesus, Ashley, men and women all over the world watch porn. It's normal.*"

"Men and women all over the world also commit first degree murder," she shot back. "Doesn't make it right."

"*You're comparing what I did to* murder?" he asked, his voice dripping with disbelief.

"Well, you murdered my trust in you. It's in tatters right now. I don't see how we can come back from this."

"*You said that yesterday when you didn't like the way I loaded the dishwasher.*"

"Well it's not fucking rocket science, Tucker! Excuse me, Vienna, I have to go deal with this cheating asshole."

"*Woman, I did* not *cheat on you.*"

"All right, Ash," I said, unable to hide my amusement from my voice. "I'll see you tomorrow."

"Tomorrow." She ended the call.

Tapping his fingers on the arm of the chair, Dane lifted a brow. "You have interesting friends."

"I do," I agreed, putting my phone on the dresser.

"Chris just called me. He and Miley are stuck in traffic, so they'll be a little late getting here."

I was looking forward to their arrival, since they were bringing my dress with them. It was hard to believe that Dane and I would be having our reception in exactly a week's time. The months had *flown* by. It didn't feel like that long ago that he and I stood in front of a burping Elvis in the chapel.

"Well, I'm almost done here," I told him.

"I can see that." He sank deeper into the chair, as if settling in to watch a show.

"You're going to sit here and watch me get ready?"

He just shrugged.

I gave my head a little shake. "All right."

His eyes followed the movements of my hands as I smoothed lotion into my skin. I thought he'd cheekily offer to give me some help with it, but he remained in his seat, seemingly content to just watch.

We hadn't spoken again of the revelations he'd made about his father a few days ago. He'd been a little different since then. Not *bad* different. But ... pensive. Distracted. Quieter than usual.

I'd sometimes catch him staring into space, lost in his thoughts. Other times, I'd catch him staring at me, his expression so blank it made my skin prickle. If I asked what was wrong, he'd merely shrug and blow off my question.

I wondered if he regretted telling me about his childhood. Dane was very self-contained and wouldn't like to feel exposed. Having someone know your darkest, most painful secrets could indeed make a person feel stripped bare.

He didn't even like to have people in his bedroom, let alone inside his head, and fuck if I didn't hate his father for that. Your bedroom should be a place where you felt safe and secure and perfectly at ease.

It was humbling that he felt relaxed enough around me to sleep beside me at night. It demonstrated an element of trust. Although I'd still often wake to find him working in the chair he was now comfortably lounging in, I never commented on it.

Right then, his eyes never left me as I dressed, dabbed on some makeup, and slipped on my earrings. "Don't," he said when I went to tie back my hair. "Wear it down for me."

As we weren't going anywhere, I relented and dropped the hair tie back into the drawer.

He pushed out of the chair, grabbed my rings from the nightstand, and slid them both onto the third finger of my left hand. He'd done it a few times over the last few weeks. I'd never had to return the favor, because I hadn't yet seen him without his wedding band.

He tugged on my hand. "Breakfast."

"Breakfast," I agreed as he guided me out of the room, down the stairs, and into the kitchen.

"Coffee?" he offered.

"As if there was any doubt," I said. "I'm in the mood for French toast this morning. Want some?"

"Sure."

We each ate French toast and drank coffee as we alternated between talking and checking the seemingly endless number of notifications on our cell phones.

It had been a fairly uneventful few days. Thanksgiving dinner at my foster parents' house had gone well. As I feared, there'd been a little tension between them and Dane, but he hadn't seemed whatsoever effected by it. He'd talked mainly with my father, who'd constantly tried to engage him in conversation … as if he'd hoped to distract Dane from the tension.

I hadn't commented on it, because it would be unfair of me to expect them to shove aside all their concerns when—in truth—they were right to be concerned. They hadn't once mentioned Travis or the trust fund, so they seemed to be respecting my wish for them to just let me be.

Heather thankfully hadn't made an appearance on Thanksgiving while we were present. She'd dropped Junior off at her parents' house long before we arrived, and he was still there when we left.

After Dane and I finished our breakfast, I cleaned the counter and island while he stacked the dishwasher. He'd no sooner switched on the machine than the buzzer sounded.

"You make the coffees," said Dane, his half-full cup in hand. "I'll take Miley and Chris into the formal sitting room."

"All right." Remembering how the planners took their coffees, I prepared the drinks and made myself a fresh cup. Once I'd placed all the mugs on a tray, I carried it into the formal sitting room and then set it on the coffee table while saying my hellos.

"We brought your gown," announced Miley.

I smiled. "So I see." You couldn't exactly miss the big, bulging dress bag. "Thank you."

As usual, all four of us settled on the sofas. Dane interlinked our fingers and rested our joined hands on his thigh.

Glancing down at her tablet, Miley said, "We touched base with everyone—the photographer, the florist, the vendor, the band, the cake baker, and the lighting technician. All the details have been confirmed; everyone knows where they're supposed to be and when."

Chris handed us a sheet of paper. "We've finalized the seating arrangement. If you're happy with it, we'll send it to the necessary people. I was impressed that none of the guests missed the RSVP deadlines—there are usually a few we have to chase up. You should be flattered that no one wants to miss it."

I scanned the seating arrangement and nodded, happy with what I saw. The guests were mostly family, o-Verve employees, and Dane's closest associates.

"The arrangement is fine," said Dane, his thumb brushing the top of my hand.

"Excellent." Chris tucked the sheet of paper away. "Don't forget you have your hair and makeup trial on Wednesday, Vienna. Now that you have your gown, you need to try on the full ensemble one more time just to be sure you're fully happy with it. Did you break in your new footwear?"

I nodded and took a sip of my coffee. "But I'll take blister plasters to the reception with me in case I need them."

"Good. Did you pack an overnight bag for your reception so I can have it delivered to the hotel for you?" asked Chris.

"Yes, it's in my room. I also prepped the box you asked for with the cake knife, guest book, and all that stuff so that you can send it to the venue."

Chris grinned and lifted his mug. "I love it when my clients listen to me. This is good for you, too. The more things you've checked off the to-do-list, the less stressed you'll be."

I'd actually felt remarkably unstressed about it up until now, since the planners were taking care of everything for us and the reception had always seemed so far off into the future. Now that I had only a week left to go until the event, my stomach gave the odd flutter whenever I even thought about it.

"The guest packages will arrive at the hotel the day before the reception and they'll be delivered straight to the rooms of your guests," said Miley.

Dane gave a satisfied nod. It had been his idea to secure rooms at the hotel for the guests. Many were traveling to be here, including Melinda's sisters and Wyatt's family. Some of the guests who lived locally had opted to stay overnight at the hotel so that they wouldn't have to get a taxi home in the early hours of the morning.

Miley turned to me. "You've already had your wedding ceremony, so I assume you have your old, new, borrowed, and blue items."

I blinked. "Actually, I didn't have them with me on the day. We didn't go to Vegas planning to get married, so I wasn't prepared." I pursed my lips. "I'll have pretty much all of the items on the day itself, incidentally. Except 'the something blue.' I'll think of something."

"If you need any ideas, let us know," said Chris. "Did you choose someone to collect the gifts, cards, and bits of décor you'd like to have as keepsakes? You don't want to be doing that on the night of your reception."

"Hanna volunteered to do that for us," I replied. "Ashley's preparing the reception emergency kit you said I'd need. So far, it's got everything from tampons to safety pins. She's changed the bag three times because she keeps adding more stuff to the kit and so needs a bigger bag."

Miley smiled. "Trust me, it's best to have those little things and not need them than to not have them at all. I've seen brides break down in tears because they weren't prepared for those minor emergencies. It's best to have a kit with you." She looked at Dane. "Are there any last pieces of attire you need? Shirt? Cravat? Cuff links? Shoes?"

He shook his head. "No, it's all sorted."

Chris's mouth curved. "I do adore how organized you both are."

We talked for at least another half an hour. After they left, I grabbed the dressing bag that concealed my gown. Damn, it was heavier than I remembered.

"Are you going to show it to me?" asked Dane.

"Nope." I gave him a smile that was all mock sympathy. "You'll have to wait until next Saturday."

"I don't like to wait."

"That's not fresh news. The answer is still no."

He went to take the bag from me. "I'll carry it."

"Oh no. I don't trust that you won't accidentally-on-purpose bust the zip or something just so you can have a peek." Conscious that he was trailing behind me, I hauled the bag up to my bedroom closet. Hoping like hell that the rail didn't snap under the weight of the bag, I carefully hung it up. The rail thankfully held.

I was eager to try on the full assemble, but I wasn't going to do it when Dane stood a few feet away from me. I decided to try it on either later or tomorrow while he was preoccupied with other things.

Honestly, I had mixed feelings about the reception. On the one hand, it would be fun to see how Chris and Miley brought their "vision" to life, and it would be great to have the people we liked and cared for gathered together in the same place.

On the other hand, it would be as fake as the ceremony, which put a real downer on it all. Moreover, there would also be people there who wanted nothing more than to be a pain in my ass in whatever ways they could. Especially Heather and whoever she took along …

That was when it hit me.

My brow knitted, I turned to Dane. "It only just occurred to me that Heather didn't have a guest on the seating arrangement."

"I told Chris and Miley that she wasn't allowed to bring one," he explained.

"You did? Why?"

"Because I don't trust that she won't invite someone like her friend from the barbecue and have them aid her in doing something stupid."

"Yeah, she probably would have brought Jana along. I'm really hoping that Heather chooses not to attend the reception. It is possible that she'll pull out at the last second and claim she has the flu or something."

He cocked his head. "You think so?"

"Yes, because she'd have to behave herself. She doesn't want her parents to know she's blackmailing Junior's father, and she knows you'll out her if she pushes you too far."

"Hmm."

"You don't agree?"

"No. Heather knows you'd much prefer that she didn't attend, so she'll come to the reception purely to spite you."

I felt my nose wrinkle. "I never thought of that." I puffed out a breath. "Being without a guest won't stop her from making a scene if it's what she's intent on doing."

"I know that. Which is why I asked Ashley and Hanna to keep an eye on her."

I felt my brow furrow. "You did?"

"I don't want you to have to waste a second of the day worrying about where Heather is or what she's doing. I'd prefer to scratch her off the guest list altogether, but that would offend your foster parents, who might then refuse to come to the reception. You're right that she won't want us to out her blackmail scheme. I doubt she'll attend the reception *planning* to cause drama. But that's not to say she won't do something stupid. You're going to be the center of attention—she'll hate that. She may not handle it well."

True. She'd never handled it well in the past. "If it makes you feel any better, Melinda's sisters will probably do their best to stop Heather from doing anything dumb. They know how she can be. Whenever they came to visit over the years, they always chimed in whenever she said or did anything bitchy to me."

"At least someone did." His eyes darkened. "Be aware that if she steps out of line at the reception, I won't ignore it, Vienna. You've dealt with enough shit from that woman. Those days are over. She doesn't get to do that to you anymore. I won't allow it."

I'd wax my eyebrows clean off before I'd admit it, but his protectiveness woke my libido right up every time.

"The same goes for Travis and Hope," he went on. "They'll be just as closely watched, and they'll be just as swiftly handled if they decide to play games. In other words, don't worry about any of them."

"I'm not worried. I'm just *so* done with their bullshit. In fact, can we not talk about them? They only ever bring my mood down."

His eyes slid to the dressing bag. "We can talk about the gown that's hanging on that rail over there."

Like a dog with a bone. I folded my arms. "I'm not showing it to you."

"You can give me one peek."

I shook my head. "Not happening."

He took a step toward me. "I could persuade you," he said, his eyes raking over me in a way that was nothing short of an eye-fuck.

"Nu-uh," I said, backpedaling, but he matched me step for step. "You'll have to wait."

"But I don't want to."

"Well, you'll just have to. I mean it, Dane, I'm not showing it to you." I halted as the back of my knees hit the futon. "Good things come to those who wait."

"Good things come to those who pursue them." He very gently tipped me backwards, so that my ass landed softly on the futon. "Undo your jeans."

"If you think you can sexually torture me into agreeing to show you the dress, you're wrong. But you're very welcome to try." I snapped open the buttons of my fly. "I'm not one to turn down an orgasm."

A wicked smile curved one side of his mouth. "Who said anything about me making sure you came?"

At dumb 'o' clock in the morning, I dried my wet hands using the small towel in my private bathroom. I'd woken from a bizarre dream and would have gone straight back to sleep if I hadn't desperately needed to pee.

Having done my business, I padded out of the bathroom and softly closed the door behind me. The slight creak of the hinges made me wince. Sure enough, Dane's eyelids flipped open. More, his entire body went rigid, and something that resembled panic flashed across his face. But then his gaze landed on me, and the stiffness leeched out of him.

God, I *hated* his father. Hated him. There were times I wanted to piss on his grave.

Pretending not to notice Dane's reaction to the noise, I climbed back into bed and lay on my front.

He turned on his side to face me. "Are you all right?" he asked, his voice low.

"Yeah," I quietly replied. "I had a weird dream; it woke me up."

"What was it about?"

"Simon and Corrine. They were arguing at an airport. I was trying to play peacemaker, but then I got pissed because she tried to snatch my suitcase." I shrugged. "Like I said, it was weird."

Dane slid his hand under my camisole and stroked the pads of his fingers along my back. "Do you dream about her much?"

"No. Her face isn't always very clear when I do. It was a long time ago that I last saw her." I wouldn't be surprised to hear she was dead, given the lifestyle she'd led.

"Has she ever tried to contact you?"

"Nope."

"Do you wish she had?"

"Not at all. The only good thing she ever did for me was stay out of my life."

"What about Simon?" Dane began to slowly trace each bump of my spine. "Has she ever contacted him?"

"If she has, he and his alters have all kept it a secret from me. I can't envision them doing that. Freddie would definitely tell me if she made contact."

"Why?"

"He's afraid of her. That's why he never surfaced around her. She didn't even know Freddie existed. He made me promise to keep him a secret from her."

Dane slid his hand all the way up my back and rested it between my shoulder blades. "Did the other alters converse with her?"

"Mostly one of Simon's previous alters, Stella. She was eighteen. She hated the world and used to bitch at Corrine." To me, Stella had been like a big sister who was never mean but never loving—she'd tolerated my presence but hadn't wanted my company. "Maggie would sometimes scold Corrine like an imperious aunt. Deacon would deal with her if he caught her hitting me, but he only physically harmed her the one time."

"Simon never dealt with her himself?" There was no judgement in the question, only curiosity.

"No. It was like Simon was too intimidated by Corrine to stand up to her.

I think she reminded him of his mother, in some ways. Although he hated his mother, abusive relationships were all he'd ever known. To him, that was 'love.' I guess we're sometimes most comfortable with what we know. Other times, we set out to find the opposite."

"Did Corrine deal with Simon's DID well?"

"She was too wrapped up in her drug addiction to care much what was going on with others. I learned that her father has schizophrenia, so I suppose being around someone with mental health issues was the norm for her."

"Did any of Simon's alters ever hurt you?"

I frowned. "Oh no, none. That was why Melinda and Wyatt were so supportive of my contact with him. They knew he wasn't a danger to me. There's so much stigma attached to DID that some people judged Melinda and Wyatt for not keeping Simon out of my life."

"I don't think they'd have managed it anyway. He would have found some way to see you. He loves you." Dane dragged his hand down my spine, over my shorts-clad butt, and down to the back of my thigh. "He sings your praises to me constantly, like I don't already know you."

I felt my mouth hitch up into a smile. "I know. I've heard him."

"He's proud of you. And so he should be."

I swallowed. "You don't have to answer … but what wakes you those nights I catch you sitting in my chair?"

He twisted his mouth. "Not dreams or nightmares. I'm a very light sleeper. The slightest noise can wake me, and sometimes I can't get back to sleep. If that happens, I'll do some work to pass the time."

I licked my lower lip. "Thank you for telling me."

Dane smoothed his hand up my bare thigh and under the leg of my shorts.

I gasped as his fingertip slid past the gusset of my panties and swiped at my slit.

"Spread your legs wider," he ordered.

I lifted a defiant brow. "Maybe I'm not in the mood."

He scraped his teeth over my shoulder. "And maybe you're being a brat. Spread them wider."

I sniffed. "You're just cranky because your plan to sexually torture me into showing you my dress didn't work."

"How can I be mad when you asked me so nicely to let you come? There was begging involved, as I recall."

I felt my face heat. It was no surprise that the dominant bastard got off on it. "Which was a one-off. It won't happen again."

A wolfish smile crept onto his face. "Baby girl, you really shouldn't have said that."

CHAPTER TWENTY-EIGHT

Knuckles rapped on my car window the next day as I sat in Dane's garage, trying to make my car start. Grinding my teeth, I eased up on the ignition and looked up to see him sipping from a cup. I rolled down the window and glared at him. Oh, I could *kill* him right now. Or maybe just rearrange his face with a shovel.

"Problem?" he asked, playing clueless when we both knew he was anything *but.*

"The engine won't start."

A line marred his brow. "At all?"

I felt my lips thin. "No. It's as if the battery's dead. Or as if someone's *taken* it."

One brow hiked up. "You think I stole your car battery?"

"I think you did *something* to my car, because it was working just fine up until now." I'd been trying to get it moving for a full two minutes, but nothing was happening. I could lift the hood and check things out, sure, but I wouldn't have a clue what I was looking at.

Dane shrugged. "It's an old model, baby girl. Sometimes they just give out."

"And sometimes people tinker with them when the owner's back is turned."

Really, I should have known he'd do something like this. He hadn't tried pushing me to drive the new Audi he'd bought for me. He'd been so sure I'd eventually give in and accept it that he hadn't once complained about me not using it. But Dane wasn't a man who waited around for people to start dancing to his tune, was he? He made things happen. And he always managed to outmaneuver people.

"Fix it," I insisted.

He frowned. "Do I look like a mechanic to you?"

"Undo whatever you did."

"If you want me to call someone to come take a look at it, I will. I can't promise they'll get here any time soon, though." He glanced at his wristwatch. "I doubt you want to hang around here and wait for a mechanic to arrive or you'll be very late meeting up with your friends."

Yes, I would be. Which was exactly *why* he'd pulled this crap today. He'd known I wouldn't miss out on this trip to the mall; he'd known I'd promised both Ashley and Hanna that I'd meet them there.

He took a sip of his drink, looking infuriatingly casual. "Do you want me to drive you to the mall?"

"No, I don't." What I wanted was to slap him across the face. Hard.

He pursed his lips, thoughtful. "I suppose you could ask Ashley to come pick you up. Of course, she's probably halfway to the mall by now, but she'd turn back for you if you asked. I'm sure Hanna wouldn't mind waiting at the mall by herself for the two of you to arrive."

He *knew* I wouldn't put Ashley out like that, just as he knew I wouldn't want Hanna to be standing outside the entrance of the mall for God-knew-how-long.

I tapped my fingers on the steering wheel. "You think you're clever, don't you?"

His eyes danced. "I have been called that once or twice."

Arrogant prick. "I could just call a taxi."

"You could," he easily agreed. "It's rare that any happen to be driving around these parts, but you might get lucky. If not, you won't have to wait too long for a taxi to arrive. On average, they usually take something between twenty and thirty minutes to get here."

If I hung around that long, *both* Ashley and Hanna would be standing around waiting for me to arrive. Which meant I either needed to accept a ride from Dane, who I'd much rather sucker punch right now, or choose the lesser evil.

I sharply swung open the door, disappointed that he smoothly backed up and evaded it. I slid out of the vehicle and put my hands on my hips. "You really are an asshole, you know."

Taking another sip of his coffee, he held up the car key to the Audi that was parked further along the garage.

I snatched the key out of his hand with a snarl.

He gave a satisfied nod. "Good girl."

"Fuck off. And fix my car while I'm gone."

Ashley pulled me into a hug. "I still haven't gotten used to not seeing you every day."

I hugged her back. "Can I take it that you've forgiven Tucker?"

She drew back. "I don't want to talk about it."

"Fair enough." I turned and greeted Hanna, who hugged me just as tightly, even though I last saw her only two days ago.

"I noticed you drove here in an Audi," said Hanna. "I'm guessing that means Dane wore you down."

"I don't want to talk about it," I mumbled.

She did her best to stifle a smile. "All right."

Ashley fluffed the back of her hair. "Well, girls, let's get moving. I have a dress to buy for the reception."

"So do I," said Hanna.

The cool air conditioning hit us as we walked through the automatic doors. The mall was *huge*. It honestly seemed to go on forever with its many stores, kiosks, and eateries, so there was no shortage of places for us to shop.

Hanna gently nudged me with her elbow. "Is married life still treating you well?"

I smiled. "It is, thanks."

"I'm happy for you," said Ashley. "But I also wish you'd move back into your old apartment. The man who lives there now is a miserable old fart who's always banging on the wall, complaining that me and Tucker are too loud."

I suspected the man was just annoyed by how often his neighbors argued, but I kept that to myself.

"We should have our upcoming girls' night at my place and be extra loud just to make him cry," Ashley added.

Hanna frowned. "Nu-uh, we agreed we'd have it at my place."

"It would make more sense to have it at mine," I cut in. "There's a media room, a small bar, no neighbors who'll complain. Plus, I have guestrooms. You'd be able to stay over instead of getting a taxi home late at night."

Hanna gave me a pained look. "I'm sorry, Vienna, I just can't. It's *my boss's house*."

I rolled my eyes. "Hanna, we've been over this."

"I know, I know. It would just feel weird to go there and …" She trailed off and frowned at something over my shoulder. "Well, it seems like Heather's bagged herself a new man."

Ashley tensed. "What? Where? Oh."

Sure enough, Heather was sitting opposite a guy in the café nearby, oblivious to our presence. As I took in the way they were leaning toward each other, looking somewhat cozy, my stomach twisted.

I drew in a deep breath through my nose. "Fucking unreal," I ground out.

"I don't know who I want to slap more—her or him."

"Wait, you know him?" asked Hanna.

I licked my front teeth. "Oh, I know him. Remember the guy I told you about who I was briefly engaged to?"

Hanna's mouth fell open. "No way."

Ashley's brows flew up. "Wait, *that's* Owen in the café over there?" She'd heard about my ex but never met him.

I swallowed. "That's Owen." I flapped my arm, at a loss. "This doesn't make any sense. He *loathes* her. And she detests him because he never fell for her charms."

"It might not be a date, though they do look *mighty* friendly," said Hanna. "I thought he was married."

"He recently separated from his wife," I told her. "They filed for divorce."

Ashley glared at them, shaking her head. "If he's dating that skank, he's doing it for one reason only—he thinks you still care for him, and he wants to hit you where it hurts."

"I thought Heather didn't date single guys," said Hanna. "I know he's still married on paper, but …"

"She'd date him if she thought there was the slightest chance it would upset Vienna," said Ashley. "God, I want to smack this bitch down *so bad.*"

Hanna looked at me. "I agree with Ash; they're doing this to upset you. Is it working?"

I sighed. "It doesn't feel good to know that they're both so eager to hurt me. Especially Owen. He was important to me once." I narrowed my eyes as Heather reached across the table and linked her fingers with his. Owen smiled at her, though it wasn't a full-on smile.

I turned away from them, grinding my teeth yet again. I wouldn't have thought he'd ever go this far—dating someone who'd treated me like shit for years—in an attempt to hurt me.

Ashley rested a hand on my shoulder. "At least you know about it now. They can't sucker punch you with it at an odd moment and take you off-guard, which is probably what they meant to do, or Heather would be *crowing* about it by now."

I nodded. "Let's just keep moving. The last thing I want to do is bump into them. I'd only lose my shit, which they'd both just *love* to see happen."

Ashley curled her arm around my waist and guided me forward. "They're not worth it, hon."

"Here, fucking, here," clipped Hanna.

Stepping into the foyer of Dane's house later that day, I let out a long sigh and felt my shoulders droop. God, I was tired. Tired of the people around me acting like assholes.

I didn't want to be so pissed by Heather and Owen's sly little move. I didn't want to waste that emotional energy on them. But how could I not be pissed that my ex-fiancé —a man who I'd once trusted not to hurt me—was now, at the very least, co-conspiring with the woman he *knew* hated me as much as I detested her? How could I not be pissed that said woman wouldn't just concentrate on living her own life instead of always setting out to shit all over mine?

I'd tried shoving the whole thing out of my head as I browsed the stores at the mall. I'd told myself not to give the assholes the power to fuck up my day. But, yeah, it hadn't worked.

Although I'd assured my friends that I was fine, neither of them bought it. Still, they'd thankfully let me be—likely well-aware that talking more about the matter would only make me angrier.

Not once in my life had I returned from the mall empty handed, but I just hadn't been interested in shopping; hadn't been in the mood to buy anything or have fun with my friends.

Questions kept pricking at me. Were they dating? Were they conspiring to cause trouble? Were they—

"Vienna?"

Blinking, I looked up to see Dane on the landing, his expression so carefully blank that my nape tingled.

"Come up here," he said, his tone flat.

I didn't move from where I stood. "Why, what's wrong?"

"There's something you need to see."

I frowned. "What does that mean?"

He turned away and walked out of my view, replying, "Like I said, there's something you need to see."

"Define 'something,'" I called out. No response. "Dane, what is it?" Again, nothing. Cursing, I stalked up the stairs, ranting, "Dammit, Dane, just tell me what's wrong. My imagination is going haywire here."

I found him in my bedroom, his face still utterly unreadable. My stomach did a slow roll. "What is it?"

"Follow me." He walked into my closet.

I trailed after him, stopping only when he halted near the shoe carousel. "What is it?"

His gaze briefly slid to one of the shelves. "Look."

I looked. And I did a double-take. My lips parted, and my body went utterly still. I had to be seeing things. I really had to be. Because there was no way that there'd be a—

"It's your 'something blue.'"

I blinked at Dane. "My what?"

"You told the planners you had something old, something new, and something borrowed, but that you needed something blue," Dane reminded me. "Well, now you've got it. In fact, her *name* is Blue. I'm guessing her previous owner named her after the color of her fur. Not very original."

"Her?" I echoed, feeling my mouth dry up. "You found her?"

"At the cat rescue center, yes. Her owner died. There was no one to care for her."

Whoa, back the fuck up. "You … you went to a cat rescue center?"

He nodded. "I went while you were at the mall. I didn't go there looking for a Russian Blue cat. But when I saw her and remembered what you told the planners, I figured she'd do."

I swallowed. He'd gotten me a cat. A cat. And now I was feeling all choked up. With one act, he'd turned a shit day into the best day ever. The backs of my eyes burned with hot tears, and my throat began to ache.

I turned back to the gorgeous feline, who was curled up in a ball on my shelf, looking wary and cautious.

"Well, do you want her or not?" he prodded, impatient.

My eyes widened. "Of course I want her. I'm just shocked. I mean, you don't really like animals."

"But you do. And you wanted a cat. Now you've got one." He crossed to the shelf, eyeing her just as he'd eyed those meerkats at the zoo. "She's not so bad. Just a little unsettled. Which is probably why she's hiding in here."

I swallowed again and nearly choked on the knot of emotion clogging my throat. I hugged him tight. "Thank you," I rasped. "Really, thank you. She's the best gift anyone's ever given me."

His arms came around me, and he rubbed his jaw over the top of my head. "You're welcome."

I closed my eyes. "Why?" I asked, my face in his chest. "Why did you do this for me?"

He squeezed my nape. "You know why," he said, his voice low.

Yes, I did know. He'd gotten me a cat … because it was all he *could* give me. The other things I wanted out of life—children, a real husband—weren't things he would ever want to offer me. Although that thought made my chest ache, it didn't dim my happiness at the gift he'd given me. Because he hadn't *had* to do it. It wasn't like it was my birthday or Christmas or anything. No, he'd done this utterly sweet thing for me … just because.

I didn't need to ask why he'd picked a cat from a rescue center. The animals there were all in the same position we'd once been in—they had no one to care for them and needed a new home.

Blinking my teary eyes, I lifted my head. "She'll need food."

"It's in the kitchen, along with cat litter and a bunch of other stuff that was on the list."

"List?"

He shrugged. "I don't have a clue what cats need. I had to Google it. I bought it all on the way home."

My heart melted. I smiled. "Dude, you're so getting lucky later." I crossed to the shelf and whispered nonsense at the cat while gently scratching the top of her head. She was tense, but she didn't hiss or take a swipe at me.

I petted her, loving the soft, silky feel of her coat. The more I stroked and whispered to her, the more she relaxed. But when I tried scooping her up, she retreated.

My shoulders sagged. "She doesn't want to come down."

Dane sighed at her. "You can't hide up there. It's stupid." He effortlessly lifted her and held her against his chest—the move so natural I would bet my life he'd Googled how to carry and hold a cat.

I smiled at the way she settled in his arms. "She likes you."

"She just recognizes me as the person who got her out of a cage," he said a little gruffly.

I watched as she rubbed against him, scent-marking him. My smile widened. "Yeah, Blue is so *not* my cat."

He frowned. "What?"

"People don't own cats, Dane. Cats own us. And this one has decided you're hers." I shrugged.

He shot me a droll look and thrust her at me. "Here."

I happily took her and cuddled her close. I stared into her beautiful green eyes and fell in love right there. "Hello. Hungry? Hmm? Let's go find out."

Downstairs, I discovered that Dane had in fact bought everything necessary for a cat. We set most of her things up in the sitting room that was barely used—her cat bed, litter tray, scratching post, feeding bowl, and water fountain.

Blue watched us closely from a shelf the entire time. Coaxing her down didn't work, but I wasn't surprised by that, given that these were brand-new surroundings for her. I was just glad she wasn't frightened. She was a little edgy and twitchy and seemed to feel safer when up high, but I figured that was normal.

"The woman at the rescue center said not to let her outside for at least three weeks; said Blue needs to settle into her new environment first," Dane told me.

I turned to him, deciding to let her alone for now. She'd come down when she was ready. "Has she had all her immunizations?"

He nodded. "I left all the paperwork on your workstation before I opened the cat carrier to let her out. I didn't expect her to hide."

"She's just nervous. New place, new people, new scents."

He tilted his head. "I also didn't expect you to come back from the mall empty-handed."

My smile dimmed. "I didn't see anything I liked."

"You looked tired in the foyer. Drained, even." His eyes narrowed as they drifted over my face. "Did something happen?"

"Not exactly."

He took my chin between his thumb and forefinger. "Tell me."

I sighed. "I saw Heather at the mall. She didn't see me. She was in a café with who is quite possibly her new boyfriend." I backed up a few steps and slumped onto the sofa. "I also saw Owen at the mall."

Dane's face hardened. "What did the fucker say?"

"Nothing. He didn't see me either. He was the guy sitting opposite Heather in the café."

Dane's brow pinched. "You said he hated her."

"He does. And she doesn't have warm, fuzzy feelings for him either, because he never succumbed to her advances. But they looked real cozy earlier."

"Hmm."

"I don't know if they're dating or up to something or both. Whatever the case, it pisses me off, because what have I really done to upset them other than live my life in the way I chose? Nothing. So, yeah, I was in a real shitty mood. Then I came here, saw you and Blue, and it all fell away. So thank you." I took in his inscrutable expression and slanted my head. "What are you thinking?"

He sat beside me on the sofa and twisted to face me. "I'm thinking I want to fuck them both over, because they can only be doing this in the hope of hurting you. But if I do that, they'll believe they've succeeded. I don't want either of them to have that satisfaction."

"Neither do I, which is why I didn't confront them at the mall. Although it ruined my shopping trip, I'm glad I saw them. Like Ashley pointed out, they can't sucker punch me with this now." I blinked as Blue leaped onto the back of the sofa. I hadn't even realized she'd left the shelf.

I felt my mouth curve as she rubbed the side of her neck over Dane's head, leaving her scent on him. "She really does like you."

Looking unimpressed, he said, "Only because I got her out of the cage."

"Ah, the power of hero worship."

I slowly reached up and stroked her, smiling when she didn't pull back. "I always wanted a cat."

"Didn't you ask Melinda and Wyatt to get you one?"

I shook my head. "It may sound melodramatic, but I didn't trust that Heather wouldn't have harmed it. She often damaged, broke, or stole my things. Maybe she wouldn't have gone as far as to hurt a living creature, but I didn't want to take the risk."

"It was probably a good call on your part."

"Did you ever have any pets?"

"My grandfather had a dog. A Basset Hound. It was the laziest fucking creature you can imagine."

I stilled in surprise. He'd never spoken of his extended relatives before.

"Did you see much of your grandfather growing up?" I asked, half-expecting him to blow off the question.

"No, he wasn't welcome at the house. Barron hated him because he felt that Hugh was 'the favorite.'" Dane shook his head. "Barron actually smiled all the way through my grandfather's funeral. I was only a child, but I remember it well."

"What about your paternal grandmother?"

"She died before I was born."

"Your maternal grandparents?"

"My mother had nothing to do with her family. They contacted me about five years ago, claiming they wanted to 'connect' with their grandchildren. I told them to fuck off. So did Kent and Travis. Because we knew from Hugh that they tossed our mother out at fifteen after forcing her to have an abortion."

I felt my upper lip quiver. "A person's family should be their safety net."

"But you and I both know it doesn't always work that way."

Blue sprung onto Dane's lap and butted his hand.

"I'd be jealous that she likes you better than me if the whole thing wasn't so adorable," I said.

He shot me a withering look and placed the cat on my lap. "Hungry yet?"

"I am actually."

"Will stir fry noodles work for you?"

"Yeah, I can get behind that."

CHAPTER TWENTY-NINE

Walking up the path toward my foster parents' front door, I blinked my watery eyes. God, I felt like shit. I'd woken with a bitch of a hangover from my girls' night in. Even though I'd taken pain relief pills three times during the day, my head hadn't stopped throbbing until an hour or so ago.

Hanna had thrown the get-together at her house last night and invited both Ashley and Melinda. Wyatt had insisted on coming, saying he felt "left out." As I'd anticipated a simple evening of drinking wine, watching movies, and having fun, I'd said he was welcome to stay.

If I'd known it was a lingerie party, I'd have urged him to stay home. Hanna, the minx, didn't warn him or anyone else. He'd gotten the surprise of his life when a woman entered the house with a rack of sexy lingerie and an array of sex toys. He'd left so fast I was surprised his shoes didn't leave skid marks on the floor.

We'd had a ball—ate, drank, laughed, and sifted through the lingerie and sex toys. Dane had picked me up afterward, refusing to let me get a taxi home. Then he'd fucked me silly in bed. All in all, it had been a good night.

Melinda had texted me earlier, asking me to pop in on my way home from work. She hadn't said why, but she had assured me that nothing was wrong. Hoping that was true, I used my key to open the door and called out her name.

Moments later, she walked into the hallway and beamed at me. "Hi, sweetheart." Her brow creased. "Dane isn't with you?"

"He's at a meeting, but it'll finish soon. Sam's gone to collect him. He'll bring Dane straight here."

Junior came rushing out of the living area with a playful battle cry and hugged my leg. "Did you bring your new cat?"

Smiling, I ruffled his hair. "Can't. She'd probably claw Ranger. My girl has attitude in spades."

He pouted and released my leg. "I want to see her."

"I'll bring her to visit one day. Promise."

"How is Blue?" Melinda asked as we strolled into the living area.

"Oh, fine," I replied. "She's all about Dane, though."

Her mouth quirked. "I noticed that when we visited you Monday evening. He doesn't seem to know what to do with all that feline affection."

"He grumbles about her, but he likes her. I can tell." I'd worked from home Monday and Tuesday so that Blue wouldn't be alone in the house. But she was never completely alone anyway. The cleaning crew came daily, and the women fussed over her.

Blue never sought company, though. Unless it was Dane. She adored him and constantly rubbed herself all over him. She *had* purred for me, though. A little. Once.

Wyatt looked up from the armchair. "Hey, honey. Damn, you look rough."

I gave him a dirty look. "And you no longer look crimson at the sight of all the lingerie," I whispered, conscious of Junior, despite him wearing headphones while playing on his tablet on the sofa.

Wyatt glowered. "Hanna could have warned me."

Melinda snickered and raised her brows at me. "Coffee? Tea?"

I flapped my hand. "I'm good, thanks." Honestly, my stomach still felt a little queasy from the hangover.

Melinda gestured for me to follow her through the arch that led to the dining area and urged me to sit at the table. She crossed to her computer desk and rifled through one of the drawers. She pulled out a small, white box and then turned to me. "So, I called you here because … I was going to give you this on Monday evening, but I thought it would be better if we were alone."

Intrigued, I sat up straighter. "Okay."

She took the seat beside me at the table. "I know you have your old, new, borrowed, and blue covered, but … well, I was hoping you'd maybe still clip this to your bouquet for the reception, or maybe clip it to your clutch."

"What is it?"

"See for yourself."

I took the box from her and carefully pulled off the lid. My lips parted. Inside was a large safety-pin on which four small charms had been hooked—a sixpence, a horseshoe, a blue heart, and a photo frame that featured a picture of Simon holding me when I was a baby.

Feeling my throat thicken, I looked at her. "Melinda … thank you."

"I was inspired by something my friend did for her daughter." She bit her lower lip. "I'm sorry that I've been a little stiff with Dane since Travis told me about the trust fund. I just … I was *so* afraid of you getting hurt, and I made the whole thing about me. I shouldn't have, and I'm sorry. I've been watching you two together and … he loves you, Vienna. It's in everything he says and does for you. That's what's important."

He loves you, Vienna. How I wished that were true. Keeping my smile on my face by sheer force of will, I closed the box and said, "Thank you. I'll most definitely clip it to my bouquet. Did Simon give you the picture of us?"

She nodded. "He thought the safety pin was a great idea. He's really looking forward to the reception. Are the plans for it still going well?"

"Yep. I couldn't have done it without Chris and Miley, though. I'm glad Dane hired them."

"They are very good at—" She cut off when Wyatt yelled at the TV—or, more precisely, at the football players on the screen. "Jesus, Mary, and Joseph," Melinda muttered. "Wyatt, can you keep it down?"

Wyatt leaned around his chair to scowl at her through the arch. "Can't a man watch a game in peace anymore?" he griped.

Melinda rolled her eyes. "It won't kill you to lower the volume and stop yelling."

Just then, the front door opened. And since only one other person had a front door key to their house, it was no surprise when Heather breezed into the living room. But the sight of Owen trailing behind her? Yeah, that was new.

Heather said a brief hello to Junior, who gave her a quick wave and went back to his tablet.

Wyatt, looking kind of puzzled by my ex's presence, flicked a concerned look at me. I hadn't told my foster parents about what an ass the guy had been since I'd first begun "dating" Dane, but they did know how Owen had broken our engagement all those years ago.

Melinda's brow furrowed. "Owen, is that you?"

He smiled. "It's me. How are you?"

"I'm well, thanks," she told him, casting me a brief worried glance.

His gaze cut to me. "Hi, Vee."

Heather puffed out a breath. "I didn't realize you were here, Vienna. Well, this is awkward. Then again, it's probably best that you hear it from us anyway." She briefly glanced at Junior, who still had his headphones on and was tapping the screen of his tablet like crazy. "Um, Owen and I are dating now," she told me.

Melinda stiffened. Wyatt cursed beneath his breath. And I knew they'd both toss him out of the house if I gave them the slightest indication that I wanted him gone. *Pfft.* Like I'd give either Heather or Owen that satisfaction.

I smiled at her. "Good."

She stared at me for a long moment. "Good?"

"Well, I was hoping there'd come a day when you'd date a guy who wasn't taken," I said. "That day has finally arrived."

She blinked. "It … really doesn't bother you?"

I lifted my shoulders. "Why would it?"

"Well, you guys *were* engaged at one time."

"That was a long time ago. He and I have both moved on. I'm mean, I'm kind of married now," I reminded her.

Her mouth opened and closed a few times. "I'm glad to hear it's not a problem for you."

Hmm, I doubted that. I turned to Melinda. "Thank you so much for this," I said, tucking the box into my purse. "I absolutely love it."

"What is it?" asked Heather, frowning.

"A bridal charm," I replied, to which Heather made a weird face. Whatever.

Melinda quickly pulled me into a conversation about idle shit. Wyatt did the same with Heather and Owen in the living area, as if to keep me and the terrible twosome from engaging any further. That suited me just fine. Heather did still try to get my attention a time or two, but Wyatt distracted her fast.

Hearing my phone ring, I fished it out of my purse. *Chris.* He often called when he wanted to run something by me. As I didn't wish to have a conversation about the details of the reception in front of Frick and Frack, I pushed out of my chair and told Melinda, "I've got to take this. I'll just be a minute."

I went into the kitchen as I answered, "Hello?"

"Darling, sorry to bother you, I just wanted to coordinate with you on a few points," said Chris.

"No problem," I told him.

Seeing Ranger scratching at the back door, I let him out and followed him into the yard as I talked with Chris. It was a few minutes before, satisfied with my responses, he rang off. I turned to head back inside the house and saw that Owen stood in the doorway.

His arms folded, he stepped onto the deck. "I always knew you had a good poker face, Vee, but I didn't realize how good an actress you were until just now."

I tipped my head to the side. "Excuse me?"

"You didn't even flinch when Heather told you about me and her. You took that news *far* too well."

"How did you think I'd take it?"

He snapped his mouth shut, as if to bite back words. "You didn't even look shocked."

"Oh, it *was* a surprise, given that you always claimed you hated her, but it's not a bad surprise. If you make each other happy, that can only be a good thing for both of you."

"I'm not buying that you're really so blasé about this. I'm not just some ex. We've known each other a long time. We were friends, lovers, *engaged.* We have a lot of history."

"Yes, *history*. That's all." I narrowed my eyes. "If I didn't know any better, I'd think you wanted me to feel hurt. But that can't be the case, can it? You wouldn't really do that to someone with our 'history,' would you?"

His nostrils flared. "Why him, Vee? Why, of all the people in the fucking world, would you marry Davenport?"

I felt like groaning. "Owen, will you just let it go."

His brows flew up. "Let it go?" he echoed, crossing to me and standing *far* too close. "I could have handled losing you to someone who'd be *good* to you; who'd love and adore you and give you all the things you need and want from life. I could have handled that, because I'd have known that you'd be happy. But Dane Davenport—"

"Is my husband. *My husband.* I love him. And I'm done listening to you badmouth him. You don't have to like him. You don't have to like that I married him. You just have to stop fucking *whining* about it. Butt out of my life and concentrate on this thing you have with Heather."

"Fuck Heather." He lunged and slammed his mouth down on mine.

Anger surged through me in a hot rush. I shoved him back and slapped him hard across the face. "You *prick*. Don't you *ever* touch me again."

"What the hell is going on here?"

At the sound of Wyatt's voice, I looked to see him stood in the doorway, his face like thunder. Melinda stood slightly behind him, her mouth agape. Heather was beside her, smirking—not at me, though. No, the bitch was smirking at the person who stood at Wyatt's side.

"Dane," I said, my voice low.

He didn't look at me. His unblinking gaze was locked on Owen, dark with fury. He slowly and fluidly stalked toward him like a panther—a predator closing in on its prey.

Glaring at him, Owen lifted his chin, belligerent. "If you think I'm going to apologize—"

Dane's fist snapped out and connected with Owen's jaw hard enough to make him stagger backwards. Damn, that was going to leave one *hell* of a bruise.

"Bastard," spat Owen. He balled up his hand and took a clumsy swing at Dane, who easily dodged it and then punched him again. Before Owen could retaliate, Dane dealt him a hard blow to the temple that knocked the shithead right on his ass.

Watching my ex pick himself up off the deck, I winced at the deep cut above his eye. *Ouch.* He'd need a few stitches for sure. But I wasn't feeling very sympathetic right then.

"Maybe you should do something, Vienna," said Melinda, sidling up to me.

I gave my foster mother a helpless shrug. No one with a brain would try to get between Dane Davenport and something he wanted. And right then, what he seemed to want was to pummel my ex-fiancé into the ground.

I would not at all be opposed to that.

Owen had been something of an asshole lately. Today, he'd gone too far. He might not have made himself as problematic as the others who were set on separating Dane and me, but he'd certainly had this coming.

Melinda turned to her husband. "We can't just stand here."

"Why not?" asked Wyatt. "Owen should have known better."

Why yes, yes, he should've.

Dane stared the prick down. "I warned you, didn't I? I warned you time and time again to stay away from her, but you didn't listen," he reprimanded, his tone soft. "Worse, you pulled *this* shit. For someone who claims to care for Vienna, you sure don't show it."

Owen clenched his fists. "I *do* care for her, she's—"

"Not yours," Dane finished. "They're *my* rings on her finger. It's *my* name she's taken. It's *my* bed she shares. She is mine. So whether you care for her or not isn't fucking relevant."

Owen swallowed. "She was mine first."

"And you should have held tight to her. You didn't. You let her go. That was your mistake."

"I did what was best for her."

"No, you did what was best for you. You might have cared for Vienna, but you didn't put her first. She was *never* your priority."

Owen nostrils flared. "I was young back then. A kid."

"A kid who wanted the space to pursue his ambitions. She gave that to you; she didn't curse you for it. And how do you repay that? By trying to break up her marriage. You think she'll thank you for that? That she'll *want* someone who'd do that to her?"

My ex's jaw hardened. "What I think … is that Vienna deserves to be loved. You'll never love her—you don't have that in you."

Those words stabbed me right in the chest … because they were true. Dane didn't love me. Never had. Never would.

I shouldn't care. I wasn't supposed to care. And I definitely didn't like that I did. But I'd gone and fallen for my fake husband. Yeah, I was *that* stupid.

Dane sighed. "So you've said before. I didn't care what you thought then; I still don't care now. You're of no interest to me. And you're of no interest *to her*. You need to man the hell up and accept it, because I won't have you playing these games with her. You're going to leave here, and you're going to stay away from her."

Owen jutted out his chin. "You don't get to dictate what I do."

"When it comes to my wife, I absolutely do."

"You won't keep her in the long-run, you know. She'll see that I'm right about you eventually. Then she'll leave you."

Dane tilted his head, looking at him curiously. "Now why would you think I'd let her do a thing like that?"

Owen's head jerked back. "You can't *force* someone to stay with you."

"Vienna knows I'd never let her go."

Damn, Dane was so good at acting that if he hadn't been so clear to me that he didn't want a real marriage, I might have believed him.

"She's just a possession to you," Owen insisted.

"My most prized possession, as it happens," said Dane. "And I have every intention of keeping her. Deal with it. Accept it. Leave her alone. Get rid of this dream you have of winning her back. It won't happen."

"And if I *don't* stay away from her?"

Dane's mouth curved into a cruel, chilling smile that almost made me shiver. "I'll make you wish you had."

Owen's eyes flickered. "She can do better than you. You don't deserve her."

"And you think you do? You, who just behaved like a complete asshole, think you deserve her?"

Shame flickered across my ex's face. "Maybe neither of us do. But—"

"There are no 'buts.' You're mistaken in thinking that you'd be married to her now if you hadn't messed up. I'd have lured her away from you, even if it took me years. Don't think for one moment she would be yours if A, B, or C hadn't happened. I would have made her mine one way or another. You'd be wrong to think I don't mean that. I'm ruthless in going after what I want. Quit banking on me fucking up and losing her the way you did. I'd never let someone so important to me walk out of my life."

Owen narrowed his eyes, studying Dane hard. "Son of a bitch, I think you might just actually care for her in your own way."

Dane's gaze slid to me, burning with possession, impatience, and something … more. Something that made my pulse quicken and my breath catch. But Owen was wrong. Dane didn't care for me. There was no way he'd want this marriage to be real. He didn't even want a girlfriend, let alone a wife … right?

Right, I asserted. Of course he didn't want more. I knew better than to let myself forget he was simply just playing his part.

"Vienna knows how I feel about her," he told Owen. "That's all that matters to me. I don't give a damn what you think. I just want you to let her be. She's made it clear that she doesn't want you in her life. I definitely don't fucking want you in her life."

A sly smirk curled Owen's mouth. "Well, now that I'm with Heather, I'll be around whether you and Vienna like it or not."

"No, you won't," Wyatt cut in, crossing to us. "If you think I'll let you use Heather to hurt Vienna, you're highly mistaken."

Heather stormed over to her father, her eyes wide. "Wait, you can't tell me who I can or can't date."

Wyatt turned to her, his mouth tight. "You … you're my daughter, and I love you—I always will. I've never agreed with your choices of 'boyfriends' over the years. I made that clear to you many times in the beginning, but nothing I said ever got through to you. So I eventually let you be, figuring you'd one day learn from your mistakes. But I won't let *this* be. You're using Owen just as much as he's using you, because the two of you have a common goal: to hurt Vienna. Nothing more, nothing less. The pair of you should be ashamed of yourselves, but I'm getting the sense that you're not."

Melinda sighed at Owen. "It pains me to see the person you've become. Vienna was a good friend to you for a long time. I never would have thought there'd be a day when you'd set out to hurt her."

"I don't *want* to hurt her," claimed Owen. "I want her to open her eyes and see *him* for what he is."

Wyatt frowned. "Tell me how you thought 'dating' Heather would achieve that?"

Owen opened his mouth, but no words came out.

"You're not fooling anyone," Wyatt added. "You wanted to lash out at Vienna, and you figured that claiming you're with Heather was the best way to do it. Only that didn't work out, so you took it a step further and forced a kiss on her. But it wasn't really a kiss, was it? You did it in anger."

Owen closed his eyes. "I didn't mean to, I just …"

"Maybe in the beginning you wanted to win me back," I cut in. "But I think that changed at some point; that it became more about you wanting to beat Dane. I'm not a prize to be won in some game. I'm a person."

"I know that," said Owen, opening his eyes. "I just want you to be happy. Safe. Loved. You'll never be those things while you're with him."

I shook my head. "No, Owen, you only want me to be happy and safe and loved providing I'm with *you*. That's different. You don't hate that I'm with Dane because you think he isn't good for me. You hate that I'm with him because he *does* make me happy. You resent that. You resent him for it. And you're making me pay for that."

"Vienna made her choice," Wyatt interrupted. "That choice wasn't you, Owen. Just as your choice all those years ago wasn't her. That ship has sailed. If you really do care for her, you'll respect that, cut your losses, and move on. Can you do that?"

Owen's gaze slid to me. "You really love him? He's who you want?"

I nodded. "Yes and yes."

He swallowed, openly sad.

Dane stepped toward him. "You're done here. You've said your piece, she listened, she's made her wishes clear. Now leave. And this time, don't make the mistake of coming near Vienna again."

"*Or* Heather," Wyatt added. "Stay away from both my girls, Owen."

She scowled at her father. "Who I date is *my* business."

"You're not dating him, you're playing games." Melinda slashed a hand through the air. "It stops *now*."

Heather put her hands on her hips, glaring at both her parents. "You can't meddle in my life like this—I'm not fourteen."

"Be assured that I won't go near either of them again, Wyatt," Owen interrupted. He looked at me, the image of defeated. "You probably won't believe me, but I do love you, Vee. All I wanted was to have the chance to prove it. I was determined to win you back. But somewhere along the way, I let bitterness take over. I really didn't mean for things to get like this; didn't mean to go this far." He swallowed. "I won't bother you again." He bowed his head and disappeared into the house.

I let out a long breath and rolled back my shoulders.

Heather began arguing with her parents, pointing her finger and jutting out her chin.

Dane crossed to me, eating up my space. He slid a hand up my back and curved it around my nape. "Are you okay?"

I nodded. "Glad it's over. Can we go?"

He swiped his thumb over my mouth, as if to wipe away any trace of Owen. "Sure. Once I'm done with that bitch over there." He made a beeline for Heather.

Uh-oh.

She paused in ranting at her parents when she saw him coming. Her eyes widened as he stepped right into her space.

"You went too far," he said, his voice low but like a whip. "You knew what would happen if you fucked with my wife again, but you did it anyway."

"Again?" echoed Wyatt.

"Say goodbye to your blackmail money, Heather," said Dane. "Because that money well is going to dry up the moment the man's wife finds out about the kid's existence."

She shook her head, her eyes panicked. "You won't do anything. You won't."

"*Blackmail?*" Wyatt repeated. "Will someone please tell me—" He cut off at a hard nudge from Melinda, who was staring at the house.

Tracking her gaze, I saw Junior standing on the doorstep, his headphones hanging around his neck. He glanced from person to person, taking in the tension and seeming uneasy.

The others then noticed him, but it was Melinda who hurried over to Junior and tried leading him back inside with little success.

"Let's just go, Dane," I coaxed, crossing to him. I put a hand on his back. "I'm hungry and tired and my head's starting to throb again."

His gaze slid to me, dark and hard, but then cut back to Heather. "Don't even think about turning up to the reception on Saturday," he told her. "You've burned every chance that Vienna asked me to give you—you're now officially out of them."

CHAPTER THIRTY

Looking up from my e-reader the next evening, I sighed at the cat sitting in front of me on the bed. She was staring at me, twitching her tail. "He'll be here when he's done in his office," I told her.

Dane had been very insistent the first night he brought her home that Blue didn't sleep in the room with us. But after hearing her meowing and scratching at the door for what felt like hours, he'd given in. She didn't actually sleep near us, though. She made herself comfy on my closet shelf. Understanding she'd claimed the spot as her own, I'd moved her bed in there.

When Dane had earlier headed upstairs to his office after dinner, I brought her to my room. I'd fed, petted, and played with her before she disappeared into the closet for a nap. But, yeah, she was apparently tired of me now. She wanted her hero.

I went back to my e-reader, needing to wind down a little. I felt completely wired. Up until now, I hadn't been nervous about the reception. I mean, it was just a party. But now that it was only two days' away, I felt constantly restless.

I wasn't nervous in a *bad* way. It was the kind of nervousness you felt during the run-up to something important. There was a sprinkle of anticipation and a thread of excitement all mingled in with it.

It only made it better that Heather was officially uninvited. Neither Melinda nor Wyatt had objected or been upset with Dane's decree that she wasn't to attend. Which was a very good thing, because nothing they could have said would have made him change his mind. They'd just stared at their daughter, their eyes sad.

Heather had stormed out of the house, dragging Junior with her. She hadn't been bothered that her invitation was revoked. No, she'd been pissed that her parents didn't put up a protest. And it was then I realized *why* she'd claimed to be dating Owen. It wasn't merely to hurt me. She'd wanted Dane to kick up a fuss so that her parents would intervene. She'd expected them to defend her and toss Dane out of the house, knowing I'd have left with him. And then, bingo, she'd have *finally* caused a divide between me and her parents.

It was a good plan. Her parents had always defended her in the past, so she'd had every reason to be certain that they'd do so again. Hell, even *I* hadn't expected them to speak up last night. Although I was glad that they did, I was sad that they'd been put in a position where they had to do so.

They were hurting now and worried she'd keep Junior from them out of spite. She probably would, but only until she needed a babysitter. Then she'd appear at their door and act like she was doing them a favor by letting them see their grandchild. Really, she'd just want him off her hands for a short while.

When Melinda called me last night to apologize for Heather's behavior—to which I, as usual, told her it wasn't necessary—she also asked about the whole blackmail thing. I advised her to ask Heather, figuring the annoying woman had the right to tell her parents herself, but then Melinda's voice cracked, and she got all emotional and … well, I told her the truth. It didn't go down well, and I suspected Wyatt would be equally upset.

Hearing my phone chime, I nabbed it from the nightstand and glanced at the screen. I smiled on seeing it was a text message from Dane.

I swiped my thumb over the screen and opened up the message: *No, if I start going out at night, Vienna will ask questions. She'll think about those pictures again and wonder if I was lying. I warned you we wouldn't see each other as much until I divorced her. You said you could deal with it, so deal with it. I'll come to you when I can. You've got no reason to feel jealous, you know you're the only one I want.*

I stilled, and my thoughts scattered … like my mind just went blank and couldn't compute the words—or as if it didn't want to.

I shook my head and blinked hard. That text was … it didn't make any … was it some kind of joke?

No, Dane didn't joke.

I re-read the message. My hand clenched tight around the phone. I genuinely couldn't wrap my head around the content. One thing was clear. He hadn't meant to send this message to me. He was responding to a text from someone else. Someone who was "the only one" he wanted.

Pain stabbed my chest, and the phone slipped from my hand. I began to shake, and my breaths started coming sharp and fast. No. *No*, he couldn't have been fooling me all this time. There was no way. There couldn't be anyone else. He slept in *my* bed with *me*. He wouldn't do that if he had another woman in his life.

Unless … Oh God, what if he'd only started fucking me to throw me off the scent? My stomach twisted painfully.

Questions suddenly crowded my mind. Was the woman Lacey? Had they grown close after Hugh died? Had she ever really *been* a call girl? Was her name even Lacey? Or could this be someone completely different? Had he pictured the bitch when he fucked me?

I squeezed my eyes shut for a moment. This could *not* be happening. It made no sense. None.

Maybe he hadn't sent the text. Maybe someone had taken his phone. Maybe they'd cloned it.

Or maybe I was just desperate to believe I hadn't let him play me all this time.

I wanted to think he'd never do that to me. I wanted to think—no, trust—that, if nothing else, he'd have more respect for me than to do something like this. I'd begun to believe that I mattered to him in *some* way. Now? Now it seemed I'd been fooling myself. And he'd been fooling me too.

Hot tears burned the backs of my eyes. My throat felt so tight I was surprised it hadn't closed over. I quickly pinched the spot between my thumb and forefinger to fight back the tears. I was *not* going to cry. Nor would I shout or rave or yell at him. No, if he'd really been playing me all this time, he wasn't worth the emotional energy. And I'd be *damned* if I'd let him see just how much he'd wrecked me.

Not intending to wait for him to appear, I grabbed my cell and slipped out of the room, leaving Blue behind.

Blue …

I came to a halt. He'd gone to a cat rescue center, he'd brought home a gorgeous cat, gifted her to me as my something blue. Why would he do something so sweet if he had another woman? He wouldn't, would he?

Maybe he wasn't having an affair. Maybe he was just placating some delusional woman who wanted him for herself.

Or maybe I was trying to think up excuses so I wouldn't have to face that he'd betrayed me.

Well, I wasn't going to get answers if I stayed in this spot.

I padded down the hallway toward his office, feeling a little like I was walking to my doom. I didn't knock on the door, I walked straight in. He wasn't at his desk, but the computer was on.

I looked at the private bathroom and saw that the door was shut. My eyes darted back to his desk. His phone was *right there*. I could check his messages. I could get the answers I wanted for myself … if it wasn't for the none too small matter that I'd probably need his fingerprint to unlock it.

Nonetheless, I hurried over to the desk and picked up the cell. I swiped my thumb over the screen.

Use your fingerprint or enter pin.

Fuck. Grinding my teeth, I set the phone back on the desk. A sheet of paper caught my eye. I frowned, tilting my head. Then I realized what I was looking at, and my world tipped upside down.

Plaintiff.

Dane Davenport.

Respondent.

Vienna Davenport.

Petition for Divorce.

My stomach sank, and my heart squeezed. He wanted to dissolve the marriage early? What, he wanted to get back to his girlfriend?

More tears pooled in my eyes. I stuck my tongue to the roof of my mouth to fight them off. It worked, but a horrible pressure built and built and built in my chest. A pressure to cry and scream and demand *why the fuck* he'd done this to me.

So Blue had been, what, a goodbye gift? Had he been trying to tell me it was over? Had I just not read the signs?

I heard a toilet flush followed by the creaking of hinges as the door to the private bathroom opened behind me.

"Vienna," he said, sounding surprised.

I slowly turned, still holding the first page of the divorce petition in my hand. "Something you want to tell me?" My voice sounded dead even to me.

He glanced at the sheet of paper I was holding. His eyes met mine again, and there was no emotion there. "I was going to talk to you about it today."

"Of course you were." I swallowed around the clog of emotion in my throat and, *shit*, it hurt. "Well, I'll sign it for you right now, shall I? It'll be easier for you."

"Vienna—"

"No, really, I might as well get it done." I slapped the paper onto the desk, snatched a pen from the holder, and scribbled my signature on the required line. "There. Now you can get back to your girlfriend. You obviously miss her."

He frowned. "My what?"

Oh God, the tears were going to fall. "Have a nice life, Dane." I made a beeline for the door, needing to get out, out, *out*. I wouldn't cry in front of him.

The bastard slid into my path. "Wait, we're going to talk."

I hissed. No, we were fucking not. "*Move*."

"You're upset, I get that, but—"

"I'm not upset. I'm pissed. Pissed that I bought your lies and let you play me."

His brows snapped together. "What are you talking about?"

"You sent me the message by mistake."

"What message?"

"Your reply to her text."

"Vienna, I have no fucking clue what you're talking about."

I brought up the message on my cell. "I'll read it out for you." I recited every word clearly, concisely, calmly … like I wasn't falling apart inside. I looked back at Dane, who was still frowning.

"Let me see."

"No." I stuffed my cell in my pocket and stared at his chest, refusing to meet his eyes. "I'm done here. Move."

"Look at me."

I didn't.

"*Look* at me."

Yeah, I still didn't.

"I did not send you that message, Vienna."

I snickered. "Oh, I received it by magic, did I?" His hand reached for my jaw, and I slapped it away. "Don't fucking touch me. I *believed* you about those pictures. God, I am such an idiot."

"Baby girl—"

"*Don't* call me that."

A muscle in his cheek ticked. "I didn't send the text, Vienna."

"Well it couldn't have been anyone else, could it? Your phone is right there."

"I'm a very careful man. Do you think I would accidentally send you a message of any sort? Is it something I've done before? Wouldn't I at least notice the fuck up?" He took a small step closer to me. "The message was spoofed."

I felt my brow pinch. "Spoofed?"

"There are websites people can sign up to that allow them to email, call, or text people while concealing their ID. All they'd have needed to do to send you this text was enter your number as the message receiver and then enter my number as the person they want you to *believe* sent it. It's that easy.

"A big tell-tale sign that a message has been spoofed is that the name of the apparent sender comes up as gray rather than the clickable blue. Look at all the other text messages you've received from me. I'll bet my name comes up as blue for them, and I'll bet it comes up as gray for the one you received just now. Check. Humor me."

I pulled out my cell and checked the past messages that I'd received from him. His name showed up blue every time. But, sure enough, it showed up gray for the incriminating text I'd just received. And that might have brought me some measure of relief if I hadn't found divorce papers on his desk.

I pocketed my cell and shrugged. "So the message was spoofed. Fine. Whatever. It doesn't even matter now. I signed your papers; I gave you your divorce. Whether you're with someone else is not my business and does not have to matter to me."

"I don't want a divorce, Vienna."

"What, you draft up shit like that for fun? Is that what you're saying? Oh my God, I can't deal with you right now."

"I don't want a divorce. Not now. Not ever. What I want is for you to stay with me. I made that pretty clear."

I stared at him, at a loss. "Are you high?"

"Why else do you think I got you that fucking cat?"

"Because she's all you *can* give me."

"That's what you think?" He exhaled heavily. "Jesus, Vienna. I made the decision that night in New York that I was keeping you. I could tell the next morning that you hadn't worked that out for yourself. But I said nothing, because I knew you'd doubt that I was capable of being in a relationship. And I was right to think that, wasn't I?"

I looked at him blankly. Wait, what?

"I knew I was going to have to show you that it could work; that this was truly what I wanted. I also knew that that might not be enough on its own; that you might balk at staying in a marriage that began as a sham, so I drafted up those divorce papers." He let out a long breath. "I don't want a divorce. I just wanted to give you the option. If you only want to be in a marriage that has been real from second one, I'll sign those bastard papers and then we'll remarry in whatever way you want."

I looked up at him, feeling like I'd been dealt a blow to the jaw. "You're serious?" The question came out in a whisper.

"Do I ever joke?"

"But … you'd lose your trust fund if we divorced now."

He cursed beneath his breath. "You're more important to me than a trust fund, Vienna." He seemed exasperated that I'd ever think differently. "There was another sheet of paper I was going to show you today." He crossed to the desk, opened a drawer, and pulled out a document of some sort. Returning to me, he held it out.

I carefully took it from him. It was a letter. A letter he'd received from a hospital. I quickly read it and frowned. "You … you've booked an appointment to have your vasectomy reversed?"

"You want kids, don't you?"

And then the tears fell. They just poured right down my face. There was no holding them back.

Dane softly cursed again and caught my face with his hands. He thumbed away the tears. "This was not how I imagined this conversation would go. I didn't think you'd be so shocked to hear I wanted you to stay. You heard the things I said to Owen yesterday. How could you then think I'd want a divorce?"

"I thought you were just playing the role of possessive husband."

He rested his forehead against mine. "No, baby girl. For me, this has been real for a while now. How did you not see that? I took you on dates, I got you that damn cat, I sleep in the same room as you."

"But never in *your* room. I thought that meant you were making it clear that it was just sex."

He lifted his head, frowning. "You love the room I chose for you, so why would I ask you to move? If you want us to move into the master bedroom, we can. But I don't think of it as my bedroom anymore. I go in there to dress—that's it. It's more like an oversized closet."

I took a shaky breath, hoping to center myself and stop the tears from falling. Thinking back, the signs that he wanted the marriage to be real were all there—I just hadn't read them right. Or maybe I'd been too scared to let myself believe they were signs of any sort, too scared to let myself hope.

Even now, despite how blunt and straightforward he was being, I found it hard to process that he was offering me the very thing I wanted most. Which was, quite simply, him. It didn't matter to me that I married him as part of a deal we made, because it was that deal that brought us together. I doubted we'd have found our way to each other without it.

I licked my lips. "You're *certain* you want this marriage to be real?" I needed to know he wouldn't change his mind at a later date. It would absolutely crush me.

His eyes hardened. "It *is* real. You are my wife in every way that matters. If you need me to sign those papers and remarry you, though, I'll do it. But let me be clear on something. If we divorce, it won't dissolve anything between us—it's just paperwork. You won't go back to being Vienna Stratton. You won't stop wearing my rings. You won't move out of this house. Nothing will change. It'll just mean we'll have the ceremony all over again."

I sniffed and shook my head. "I don't need that. I don't need another ceremony."

"You don't?"

"I kind of liked the one we had." Plus, our Vegas ceremony held its own kind of importance. It was the first time that he'd kissed me. The kiss had been *far* from fake, and it blurred the line between fact and fiction.

I looked at the letter in my hand. "I appreciate the gesture, but I don't want us to have kids if you don't actually want them, Dane." I placed the letter on a nearby shelf. "No child should ever feel unwanted."

He smoothed his hands up my arms. "I woke up early a few weeks ago. You were flat on your back, asleep, and your camisole had ridden up. I looked at your bare stomach, and I found myself picturing it all round with my baby. I don't know where the image came from—it just popped into my head. I can't really describe what I felt. I just know that baby wouldn't have been unwanted if it were real. I don't know if I'd make a good parent, though. I don't even know what does make a good parent. I'll Google it."

A chuckle bubbled up and burst out of me.

"I told you I could make you laugh if I wanted to," he reminded me.

I nodded. "You did."

"So, do I sign the papers or tear them up? Either way, you are mine, and you'll stay mine," he warned, his voice thick with ownership.

A pleasant chill skated down my spine. His possessiveness never failed to flick my switch.

A loving declaration would have been nice, but I wouldn't have believed it. I did think he *was* capable of feeling the emotion, but his willingness to connect with others had been oppressed by his father. That bastard had forced the people most important to Dane—his own siblings—to cause him physical harm. If you didn't properly bond with someone, it wouldn't hurt emotionally when they caned you, would it?

His bond with his twin had survived that shit, but then Dane had lost Oliver; lost the one person who mattered; the one person who anchored him. And what had that taught an emotionally stunted eight-year-old Dane? That caring for others only led to pain. So he'd shut down, becoming so self-reliant and self-focused that it pushed others away.

And yet, he'd opened up his world to me little by little. He'd let himself trust me—so much so that he slept beside me at night. He'd let himself care for me, even when taking that risk must have been *so hard.* And he'd grown to feel secure enough in what we had that he'd gone a daunting step further and made the decision to build a life with me.

The whole thing absolutely fucking humbled me. I didn't need the three little words people tossed around too lightly, too often. Not when the man in front of me had pushed past every self-protective measure he had to get to this point. Not when he stood here offering me all the things I wanted. That was *far* more profound than a declaration of undying love.

I inhaled deeply and replied, "Tear them up."

"Be certain, Vienna. I won't make this offer again—I'm too selfish for that. If you fully commit to me right now, I'll hold you to that. I won't let you go back on it."

"I'm certain." I tore up the single sheet I held and set the pieces on the shelf, right beside his hospital letter. "You can tear up the rest."

His steely eyes glittered with triumph.

"But you need to get rid of the idea that I'm trapped in this marriage," I quickly added. "Although I don't *want* to leave you and I wouldn't give up on us if we were experiencing a bad patch, I'm not someone who'd stay in an unhappy marriage, so you'd better pull your weight. And I *will* walk if you ever cheat—I'd lose all respect I had for you, and I wouldn't respect myself if I stayed."

He cocked his head. "Do you think I'd ever cheat?"

If for no other reason than it would make him feel like his adulterous father … "No. I don't believe you'd cheapen me or yourself that way. Which is good for you, because I wouldn't hesitate to scald your cock with boiling water if you ever strayed."

Dane winced. "Vengeful. I like it." He ate up the last bit of space between us. "You never have to worry that I'll cheat on you, Vienna." He dipped his head and kissed one side of my neck. "It would simply never happen." He pressed a kiss to the other side of my neck. "You're all I want. You're all I'll ever want." He brushed his lips over mine. "Got it?"

"Got it."

He hummed. "Good."

I went to kiss him, but he delved one hand into my hair and wrapped the other around my throat, holding me still. I gasped and gripped the sides of his shirt. My pulse began to quicken as—that easily—a delicious, electric energy started to build and crackle in the air between us.

His gaze drifted over my face, tracing every line, curve, feature, freckle. "All mine," he whispered.

I licked my lips when his eyes dropped to my mouth. But he didn't swoop down and claim it as I'd expected. Instead, he dabbed a soft kiss to the corner of my eyelid. It was sweet, sure, but I wanted his mouth on mine.

I didn't get it.

He breezed his lips over my eyelids and then began to whisper butterfly kisses along the sides of my face. Every touch was featherlight, even the nip to my jaw, awakening every nerve-ending and feeding the sexual tension that had snapped the air taut.

I sank into the moment, letting my body go soft and pliant against his. His low growl of approval tightened my nipples and made my blood thicken.

His cock, hardening fast, aggressively dug into my stomach. But he didn't grind against me. Didn't lay a demanding kiss on me. He hovered his mouth a mere inch above mine, stared deeply into my eyes, hiding nothing, seeing everything. Anticipation spiraled through me and wound me excruciatingly tight.

I sucked on his lower lip. He squeezed my throat and pulled back. Okay, I got the message. I was just supposed to take what he gave. But it didn't piss me off, because there was no bossiness there. It was like he meant it as a gift. Like he was communicating something and didn't want to be interrupted.

I parted my lips in invitation, half-expecting him to turn it down. He didn't. He dipped his tongue inside and ran it along the inside of my upper lip, but then he pulled back again. I checked the urge to chase his mouth, knowing it would get me nowhere. As if to reward me for that, he gently sucked my tongue. First slow, then fast, then slow again, ramping up the intensity.

Then, *finally,* he drove his tongue into my mouth and glided it against my own. He didn't rush or plunder. No, it was a slow-motion kiss. He lingered. Sampled. Relished. Savored. Treated my mouth like it was some kind of dessert that he wanted to slowly enjoy.

It was sensual. Electric. Magic. He made kissing a fucking art, subjecting me to a swirl of luscious sensation; sharpening my attention onto him. All I could feel was his mouth and hands. All I could taste was him. All I could smell was that intoxicating cologne he wore. Even my thoughts centered around him, freeing me of every worry. It felt like the world was spinning around me. Like he was the only thing standing still.

He roughly angled my head, letting me feel a nip of pain, and a full-body shiver skated over me. He didn't then finally devour my mouth as I expected. His kiss was slow and wet and lazy, but it was by no means tame or easy. It vibrated with the same addictive dominance that it always did.

His mouth was so soft and warm and skilled as it *ruled* my own. My breaths turned into shallow pants, and I felt a flush sweep up my chest, neck, and face.

His grip on my throat remained firm and possessive. His thumb occasionally breezed up and down my neck, which seemed hypersensitive. God, I didn't think my sensory awareness had ever been so acute. Everything felt enhanced. Every flick of his tongue, every graze of his teeth, every brush of his lips, every scrape of his blunt nails on my scalp.

I tried deepening the kiss, but the hand in my hair tightened enough to make me wince, warning me he was in control. I almost sobbed. My body was a mass of racing chemicals and pent up sexual frustration, hungry for more. No, I *needed* more.

He didn't give it to me. He swiped his tongue over my lip, prolonging the torture. Making me wait for another kiss. Making me *crave* more.

A whole bunch of emotions swam through me. Anticipation. Pleasure. Excitement. Want. Need. I couldn't take the teasing anymore. I couldn't.

"Dane," I rasped, my voice laced with desperation.

He growled and slammed his mouth down on mine, sinking his tongue inside. It was like tossing gunpowder on a naked flame. An atomic blast of raw need ignited us both.

He kissed me so hard and deep and hungrily I couldn't breathe. I didn't need to. He breathed for me. I breathed for him.

My mind and body felt drunk on sensation and the endorphins flooding me. My entire system went into maximum overdrive. I didn't know how I'd ever come down from it.

We pulled and yanked at each other's clothes, whipping them off piece by piece. We were both out of control. Both at the mercy of a viciously sexual need that *demanded* to be slaked.

Still eating at my mouth, he backed me into his desk. He swiped some things aside and then whirled me around. "Bend over."

I complied, gasping as my breasts rested on the cool surface, and gripped the edges of the desk.

"That's my girl."

One finger plunged inside me and swirled around. My inner muscles clamped down, determined to keep it.

"Already so wet." He slowly pumped his finger. "Four fucking years I imagined bending you over a desk—sometimes this one; sometimes the one at o-Verve. It's only gotten worse since I made you mine. I'm supposed to be concentrating on work. Instead, I'm thinking about how hot your pussy looks when it has my dick buried in it."

I jolted as his free hand came down sharply on my ass. "The fuck was that for?"

"Signing divorce papers; thinking of leaving me." He curled his body over mine and spoke into my ear. "For that, you don't get to make a sound until I tell you that you can."

I gaped. "You can't tell me to stay quiet."

"Wrong. I own your mouth. If I tell you to keep it closed, you do it."

"There's no way I'll—" I flinched as he slapped my ass again. "*Ow.* That one really hurt."

"The next one will hurt worse, so be quiet and I won't have to spank you again." Straightening, he withdrew his finger and replaced it with the broad head of his cock. "Remember, not a sound." He bunched my hair in his hand, snatched my head back, and slammed home.

The breath whooshed out of my lungs as I found myself stuffed full of every hard, thick inch of him. I could feel his dick throbbing against my inner walls; could feel every beat of his heart.

He groaned. "Love being in this pussy. Love filling it with my come." He began to mercilessly hammer into me at a frenzied pace.

I clamped my mouth shut to hold back my cries. Every hard lunge of his cock hit me so deliciously deep. I tried throwing back my hips to meet his thrusts, but his fingers dug into one globe of my ass and held me still for his possession. All I could do was cling to his desk and enjoy the ride.

His cock sliced through me over and over, stretching and rasping against my hypersensitive inner walls. Dane's grunts rang through the air, mingling with the sound of flesh smacking wet flesh.

He didn't relax his death grip on my hair, but I liked it. Liked how he held me in place as he took what he wanted from me, as if my pleasure didn't matter to him. Because I knew it *did* matter; knew he could make me come so hard I'd feel it in my teeth.

"That's it, baby girl, stay nice and quiet while I fuck you," he said, still driving hard and fast. "So good for me." The note of pride in his voice danced over my skin.

Friction coiled low in my stomach, and my pussy kept on quaking around him. I squeezed my eyes shut, as if it would help me hold in the moans that clogged my throat. I was determined not to make a sound. Not because I was scared of being spanked again, but because I liked hearing pride in his tone.

I gripped the edges of the desk harder as my orgasm hovered close, ready to rush through me any moment now. My pussy tightened and superheated. I felt his cock thicken and pulse, and I knew he was just as close to the edge as I was.

"Let me hear you, baby girl. Come when you're ready."

I moaned, long and loud, and a growl rumbled out of him. He upped his pace, drilling his cock into me so hard it jolted the desk. The pleasure made me burn hotter and hotter, winding me as tight as a fucking rubber band. The tension just kept on building and intensifying. Then the band snapped.

White-hot pleasure zipped up my spine, tore a scream out of my throat, and made my pussy clamp down on his cock. I heard him curse, felt his cock swell even more. He roughly rammed his dick impossibly deep and exploded.

He released my hair, and I slumped onto his desk, gasping for air.

After a few moments, he pressed a kiss to the spot between my shoulder blades and pulled out of me. "Wait here."

Like I had the energy to move. I was vaguely aware of him pottering around the private bathroom. He returned with a wet cloth and cleaned me up, as he often did.

He tapped my outer thigh. "Stand up for me."

I straightened, still panting a little, and turned to face him.

He drew me close and curved a hand around the back of my neck. "You good?"

"Surprised I can feel my legs. You?"

"Oh, I'm good." He softly sipped from my mouth. "We'll have to make use of that desk again in the future."

"I'm game. Though maybe we could skip the spanking next time."

"You deserved it after signing those papers." He stared into my eyes for a few moments. "I get why you didn't ask yourself if the message could have been spoofed, Vienna. I'm not a good man. I've never tried to be one. I manipulate people often. But you're the one person I'd never betray. If something happens that makes you question that, *talk* to me. Give me a chance to explain. Let me have the benefit of the doubt. Don't declare you're done and try to walk out on me."

"If I'd known you wanted this relationship to be real, I wouldn't have been so quick to believe you sent the message—I don't think you'd be disloyal to someone you made a true commitment to. But I didn't think I really meant anything to you."

"Well, you were wrong. Now that you know that, take a mental step back if you see or hear something that puts me in a bad light. Question it. Ask yourself if it really makes sense. Talk to me about it."

"I will. Promise."

He gave my nape a little squeeze. "Good girl. Now give me that mouth again."

CHAPTER THIRTY-ONE

"Is there a way to find out who sent that message?" I asked as we lay in bed facing each other. We'd gravitated to my room—well, I supposed it was *our* room now—after we left his office. Once he'd given a very disgruntled Blue a little attention, Dane had joined me in the shower before then slipping into bed with me.

He pursed his lips. "I would imagine that your carrier can tell you the origin carrier of the text message, but if the sender used a VPN or some random computer in a public place, your carrier might not be able to determine their ID. I'll do what I can to find out who sent you the message." He twirled a lock of my hair around his finger. "My money's on Heather."

I felt my brows dip. I'd personally been leaning toward Travis and Hope, since they'd been so uncharacteristically quiet lately. "Why her?"

"Because I still believe she sent you the flash drive. The pictures were mentioned in the text message. I didn't tell anyone about them. Did you?"

I shook my head. "No." I had to keep so many secrets about my marriage that it hadn't even occurred to me to confide in anyone about this.

"Then whoever sent the flash drive must have also sent the spoofed text."

"Heather was seriously pissed last night. She'd have wanted to get even, and she'd have been raring to do so. Especially since she'd soon lose her blackmail money."

Dane nodded. "Then again, Owen was just as furious. It's possible he's behind this."

I frowned. "He was angry at first, sure, but he looked resigned when he left. I think he'll back down now and let this whole thing go."

"Hmm."

"You don't think so?"

"If someone told me I couldn't have you, I wouldn't resign myself to that."

"Because you're like a dog with a bone. I suppose it's possible that he did the spoofing thing out of spite. I mean, his ego would have been smarting after some of the things you said—especially your claim that you'd have lured me from him, like he didn't have what it took to keep me."

Dane shrugged, skimming his fingers down my arm to curl them around my hand. "It was only the truth."

I snorted. "Um, no, it wasn't. You would not have bothered to lure me from him."

"Oh, I absolutely would have." He brought my hand to his mouth and nipped the tip of my finger. "Make no mistake about that."

"Bullshit. We're only together now because you dragged me into a fake marriage. If I'd already been married to someone else, you couldn't have used me as your fake wife, so we would never have gotten to this point. Things would have remained purely professional between us."

He lightly tapped my nose. "Wrong. I'd have made a move on you eventually whether you were single or not. If you'd been married, I'd have probably already done it by now. Because I would have hated the thought of you belonging to someone else."

"And you're so certain I'd have succumbed to your advances?"

"Yes."

"Arrogant bastard."

He raked his teeth over my palm. "You wouldn't have been unfaithful to him—you're too loyal for that. But you'd have left him and come to me. I would've made sure of it. I've told you many times before, I always get what I want. I wanted to make my business globally successful. I did. I wanted to purchase a house like this. I did. I wanted to make you my wife. I did."

"To get your hands on your trust fund," I pointed out, my stomach clenching when he sucked my finger into his mouth. "You fully intended to divorce me at a later date."

"Initially, yes, I did. But that changed. I decided to keep you, and I was resolute that I'd find a way to make you want to stay with me. I swore to myself I'd make you mine." He licked a circle around the pulse point on my wrist. "And I did."

"But are you truly sure you'll be happy in a relationship, Dane?" I asked, my voice low and soft. "You've been on your own for a long time."

"I like being alone—it helps me recharge; I don't think that will ever change. But I don't *prefer* it anymore. I don't prefer it over your company, anyway. Remember the day you went to visit Simon after work without giving me a heads-up? The same day that Heather later turned up here?"

"I remember." It was the day after he and I had fucked on his kitchen counter.

"Coming home to find that you weren't here … It was the first time that the house had ever felt empty to me. I'd gotten used to you being here. I hadn't realized how much I liked having you around until that moment. I knew then that I was in trouble. Especially since I'd lost control and fucked you the night before."

"You were pretty pissed at me that night."

"I was pissed at the thought of you leaving o-Verve." His dark eyes drifted over my face, hot and possessive. "I wanted you the second I first saw you, but I don't get involved with my employees, as you know. I had the option of firing you so that I'd be free to pursue you, but I knew you'd want nothing to do with a man who cost you your job. Besides, you seemed to be what I needed in a PA."

"And business always comes first to you."

"It did. Now *you* come first. But back then, yes, I put o-Verve before everything else. I normally don't hire women I'm attracted to, but I told myself it wouldn't be an issue. It turned out I was wrong. Even so, I kept you as my PA all those years because I liked having you close. I came to think of you as a permanent fixture in my life. One I could trust. One I could rely on. One that never let me down. One that never left when the going got tough."

I swallowed and bit my lip. I really never would have guessed he felt that way. I would never have even thought that he held me in more regard than he did his other employees. Dane just wasn't a person who let others matter. They had to somehow *make* themselves important to him. I hadn't realized I'd done that.

"It didn't occur to me that you'd leave o-Verve after the divorce," he went on. "I fucking hated the thought of you going anywhere. I didn't want to lose you. Then you started ranting about how no other man would want you if you worked for your ex-husband. I was furious that you'd even want another man touching you. So, yeah, I lost it."

"And you were determined that there wouldn't be a repeat of that. But then New York happened."

"When I walked into your hotel room and found you standing in your underwear, all I wanted to do was toss you on the bed and thrust deep inside you." He breezed his thumb over a tiny scar on the heel of my hand. "For me, sex was always just sex. Uncomplicated. Basic. Physical. Easy to resist. It never meant anything. It was just a release valve. But there was nothing uncomplicated about being inside you. It was … different. Better. So intense it was addictive. It meant something, because *you* mean something to me. And I knew if I took you again, I'd keep you.

"I wrestled with myself over it all day. I told myself I didn't want a real wife; that I didn't want the same things out of life that you did; that I was better off alone. But then you said something that sealed your fate."

I felt my brow furrow. "I did? What?"

"A woman at the conference asked you if you'd imagined when you first started working for me that we'd get married one day. You said, no, you hadn't seen it coming; that you never thought you'd ever get involved with your boss but that some things were just inevitable and fighting them was plain pointless."

I swallowed, touched that he remembered; that my words had affected him.

"Of course, I knew you were giving her what you thought would be a typical answer, but I also knew you were right. I knew that even if I resisted you that night, I'd take you again eventually. I didn't have it in me to keep on fighting it, just as I didn't have it in me to let you go when the time came. So I figured it was senseless to resist you anymore."

The guy really was a master at hiding his emotions, because I hadn't sensed any such struggle going on inside him. "That night in New York was stellar, so I'm glad you gave in."

His mouth curved. "Stellar?"

"Yep. I really wanted to hurt you when you wouldn't just let me come, though. But that's a regular thing."

"You come harder when I make you wait."

Yeah, I totally did. "Even so, I'd rather not wait. Or stay quiet—that was hard."

"It was meant to be. You were going to walk out on me." His gaze darkened and pinned mine. "You're lucky I'm not into doling out pain or you'd have received the spanking of your fucking life."

"In my defense, I thought you *wanted* a divorce."

"You should have known better."

"What was I supposed to think when I saw divorce papers on your desk?"

"I wouldn't have expected you to assume they were a gesture. But you should have at least been confused. You *shouldn't* have automatically thought I wanted you gone."

"Let me reiterate that *I didn't know you cared for me*."

"You didn't suspect it?"

I twisted my mouth. "Okay, I thought you might care for me *a little*. But I also think you care a little for the koi fish in your pond."

Dane sighed. "Yeah, I hold you in the same regard as I do my fish," he said, dryly. He grabbed me by my nape and tugged me closer. "Kiss me before any more stupid shit comes out of your mouth."

I frowned. "Hey, that was—"

"I said, kiss me."

I sniffed. "Maybe I don't want to."

"I don't care. Kiss me."

"You don't care?"

"No." He bit my lower lip. "Give me what I want."

"I'm not in the mood to—"

He took my mouth, tangling his tongue with mine, sweeping away any further objections I might have made.

I melted into him with a soft moan and slid my hands up his solid chest. Mine. He was really mine now. I still hadn't quite wrapped my head around it. I felt a little dizzy from all the little revelations he'd thrown my way.

Feeling pressure on my feet, I looked down to see Blue trying to wedge herself between my legs and his. I shuffled backwards slightly to give her some room. Tail up, she slinked her way between our bodies and rubbed the side of her neck over his chest.

I sucked in my lips to stifle a smile. "I think she's jealous that you're giving me attention."

Blue plonked her small furry self between us and curled up in a ball.

His mouth tightened. "She's not sleeping with us. If we let her do it once, she'll try doing it every night." He edged out of bed and picked up the cat. "Don't meow at me," he told her, heading for the closet. "You've got your own bed. Use it."

I heard him whispering something to her as he disappeared into the closet. I would bet my life he was nuzzling her and apologizing for moving her.

He returned to the bed with a sigh and sank his head into the pillow. "That damn cat's a pain in my ass. She's settled now. She'll stay in there."

"Hmm." I decided not to tell him that she'd just sprang onto the bed behind him. He'd find out as soon as she started scent-marking—

He flinched. "The fuck?" He looked behind him and let out a low growl … to which she started licking his face. His nostrils flared. "It's not funny, Vienna."

"I'm not laughing."

"You are. Just not out loud."

And knowing I shouldn't only made it harder to stop. "She just wants to snuggle her hero."

"I don't snuggle."

"You snuggle me."

"I'm a man. Men don't snuggle." Exhaling heavily, he rose from the bed, scooped her up, and disappeared into the closet again, lecturing her the entire time as if she could understand every word.

I rolled over and checked I'd put my phone on silent mode. The mattress dipped behind me as Dane returned and spooned me. I might have pointed out that he was pretty much snuggling me, but then he would have moved. Plus, I wasn't sure it counted, since he was cupping my breast.

Blue leapt onto the bed in front of me and tilted her head.

I felt my mouth quirk. "Um, Dane? We have company. Again."

"Tell me you're kidding." He lifted his head and cursed. "We're just going to have to shut her in the closet, because I'm not doing this dance with her all night long. Do you get me, cat? You're not staying in here."

Blue sat back, hiked up one leg, and began licking her ass hole.
"Oh, for fuck's sake."

CHAPTER THIRTY-TWO

The morning of the reception, I placed my pouch of bridal jewelry on the vanity dresser in one of the guest rooms. Satisfied that I could now tick the final item off the checklist, I let out a sigh. After breakfast, I'd moved my dress, shoes, and other garments in there, along with all the bits and bobs I'd need while getting ready.

I didn't want to dress in my room because several people would be with me this morning—all of whom were due to arrive any minute now. It wouldn't have bothered me to have them in my room if Dane hadn't officially moved his things in there the previous day. Now that it was also *his* space, I knew he wouldn't want other people entering it.

Putting a hand on my queasy stomach, I blew out a breath. I'd thought my nerves would be calm by now, but there was apparently no such luck.

Filled with last minute preparations for the reception, the previous day had gone past in a blur. I'd tried relaxing myself with a manicure, pedicure, and feel-good movie. Maybe it worked, or maybe I was just tired, but I slept surprisingly well. Then again, Dane had fucked me so hard and long last night that he'd sapped a lot of my energy, so that could have been the reason.

Now, I felt somewhat jumpy with anticipation. The reception was no longer simply a party, no longer part of a fake marriage routine. It would be meaningful. Special.

I wasn't just Dane's wife on paper now. I was his wife in every sense of the word. The marriage was officially real. And the reception was our chance to celebrate that.

"Everything ready in here?"

I whirled around to find Dane in the doorway. "Yes. I've gathered everything that Chris listed for me. If it turns out that something else is needed, I can blame him for the oversight."

Dane crossed to me. "Nervous?"

"My stomach's all fluttery, but in a good way. I can't quite believe the day is finally here. The past week has whizzed by." I eyed him. "You don't look in the least bit jittery."

He shrugged. "What is there to be stressed about? You're fine. I'm fine. Chris and Miley have all the details covered. No last-minute emergencies have cropped up." He stepped a little closer. "The only thing I'm worried about is you having one of your migraines. But you only have them in the evenings, so that's not something we need to watch out for until later."

I hadn't even considered that I might have a migraine. It was warming that he had.

He cupped my hip. "You're still not going to give me a peek of your dress?"

"Nope. You'll have to wait." I snickered at the petulant look on his face. "God, you are so spoiled."

He grunted. "You know I don't like to wait."

The buzzer sounded.

He whipped his phone out of his pocket and brought up the security app. "It's Chris and a few of his people." He pocketed his cell and then squeezed my hip. "I'll escort them up here to you and then I'll go get dressed in our room. Once I'm ready, I'll wait for you downstairs."

I nodded. "Okay."

He gave me a soft, languid, toe-curling kiss. "Breathe. Relax. Smile. All is fine." With that, he left the room.

He returned a minute later with Chris, the hairstylist, and the makeup artists. Chris gently ushered him away, insisting Dane not see me again until I was dressed and ready to leave. Dane shot him an unimpressed look but obligingly exited the room.

Chris crossed to me, smiling brightly. "How are you feeling, darling? Nervous?"

"A little. I can't quite shake it off."

"Oh, worry not, my dear girl. I know of something that will settle your nerves. First, you remember Phoebe, Jewel, and Sheena, right?"

"I do." I exchanged hellos with the three women, who then promptly set up their styling tools and cosmetic trolley.

The photographer, Floyd, turned up shortly after that. He was quickly followed by Melinda, Ashley, and Hanna, who brought their outfits with them. The three women greeted me with tight hugs, all smiley and giggly.

Hanna studied my face closely and then nodded in satisfaction. "There are no unsightly spots. Excellent."

"Unsightly spots?" I echoed.

"Hey, it happens to some brides," said Ashley. "I know you've already had your ceremony, but you're technically a bride again today. You don't want to have a crater on the tip of your nose on a day like this."

I snorted and turned to Melinda, both relieved and surprised to see that her smile didn't look strained. I knew she was hurting over Heather's behavior, so I'd expected that to have dimmed her excitement about the reception. "I don't think I've ever seen you look so giddy."

"I've been looking forward to this for *months*," said Melinda. "I'm so happy the day is finally here. I missed your ceremony, so this means a lot to me. And it's just fantastic that Junior will be at the reception."

I felt my brows lower. "Junior?"

"Heather called last night, told us about the blackmail situation, apologized for her behavior the other day, and said that she'd allow Junior to attend the reception. She's hoping it'll make up for some of the things she's done. Not only to me and Wyatt, but to you and Dane."

I barely bit back a *pfft* sound. Heather didn't make things up to people, and she wouldn't give a tinker's shit if I was upset about the crap she pulled. But it was possible that, now knowing Dane would stick to his word about threatening to fuck with her life, she'd done this as a gesture of peace. Either that or she simply refused to let me have her parents all to myself—that was how Heather would see it.

"Well that's great," was all I said.

"It is," agreed Melinda. "And I'm rather excited about having my hair and makeup done by professionals."

Chris did a little clap. "On that note, ladies, let's begin, shall we? Give me your outfits; I'll hang them in the closet. We don't want them getting creased."

While the hairstylist and makeup artists worked their magic on the other women and me, the photographer walked around snapping photos of us in various stages of unready.

My nerves settled a little after Chris gave me a mimosa. Having him around helped. Especially since he kept everyone focused on adhering to the timeline. He also plied us with snacks like granola bars, fruit, and sandwich wraps.

Hours later, we finally began to dress. Once I was ready, I stood in front of the full-length mirror. A smile instantly plucked at my mouth. I fucking *loved* my dress. The strapless, silk gown was a distinctive ivory shade. It was overlaid with French lace on which black roses had been sporadically embroidered, giving it an elegant yet gothic look.

The back of the ruched, corseted bodice was laced with black ribbon, and I just knew Dane would itch to untie it. Because the gown touched the floor, it would be impossible for him to notice my ivory lace, knee-high boots.

My hair had been loosely curled and looked silky smooth. Black and ivory roses had been cleverly weaved into the half up, half down hairstyle. Like the pendant on my necklace, the pearls of my earrings were set into flowers, making each of the bright pearls look like the bud of a rose.

Melinda waved at her face as if to fend off tears. "You look beautiful. Absolutely beautiful."

"You totally do," Ashley agreed, smiling at me. "I predict Simon and Wyatt will get all misty-eyed at seeing their girl this way."

"As for Dane," began Hanna, "he is going to melt. Inwardly, that is. On the outside, he'll look as collected as always, of course." She flicked her hand. "It's a psychopath thing."

I sighed. "Woman, he's not a psychopath."

Hanna chuckled. "You're so easy."

I rolled my eyes. "Well, all three of you look beyond amazing." I turned and thanked Phoebe, Jewel, and Sheena—all of whom were currently packing away their things.

"And now for the finishing touch," announced Chris, handing me my bouquet. "I clipped Melinda's pin to the ribbon for you."

I felt my lips part. He'd completely transformed the white-rose bouquet to match the theme of the reception, adding acorns, mini pumpkins, seasonal berries, black feathers, and also deep crimson and gold leaves. I grinned at him. "I love it, Chris."

He beamed. "Told you that you would."

Floyd took more shots, frowning whenever Chris tried bossing him. People then gradually began to leave so that they could head to the venue.

Alone, I grabbed my ivory clutch and left the room. I walked along the hallway but stopped upon realizing that Dane stood at the bottom of the stairs. My breath caught. Damn if he didn't look the epitome of deliciousness in that tux. Seriously, I just wanted to take a big bite.

His eyes—usually so hard and broody—were like dark velvet as they drank me in. A ghost of a smile touched one side of his mouth. "Get down here, baby girl."

I held tight to the bannister as I carefully descended the staircase. "You look rather dashing."

"You look stunning." He twirled his finger, gesturing for me to execute a full turn.

I slowly did so, smiling at his swift intake of breath when he got a flash of the back of my corset. "You like it?" I asked, facing him once more.

"Oh, I like it." Splaying one hand on my back, he cupped my neck with the other and lowered his mouth to mine. He kept the kiss soft and chaste, but I could *feel* the hunger in it. "I don't know what I want to do more. Whip this dress off or just hike it up around your waist while I fuck you."

Hmm, that was indeed a good reaction. I had the feeling he'd be just as turned-on by the boots.

He narrowed his eyes. "What's with the secret smile on your face?"

"You'll find out later," I said, lightly fingering the white rose revamped boutonniere he'd worn for our Vegas ceremony. "Is Sam outside?"

"He is." Dane took my hand. "Let's go."

Sam was one of our guests for the reception, so we hadn't meant for him to be our chauffeur. But he'd asked to have the "honor" of driving us to the venue.

The hotel wasn't too far away, so it wasn't long before we arrived. Miley met us at the door and informed us that all our guests were drinking cocktails in the large ballroom; they'd be escorted to the botanical garden once Dane and I were inside.

I was eager to get a good look at the indoor garden, but when we reached the grassy area that surrounded it, Floyd urged us from spot to spot while he took several shots of us in various poses.

I thought one in particular would turn out good. He'd directed Dane and I to indulge in another chaste kiss while Miley and Chris—who wouldn't be seen on the photos—tossed autumn leaves over us like they were confetti.

Once Floyd announced he was done, Dane turned to me and asked, "Are you okay?"

"No, there's a leaf stuck between my breasts."

"Lucky leaf."

Snickering, I pulled it out and let it flutter to the ground. "Better."

He flicked a look at the botanical garden. "Ready?"

I nodded. "More than ready." Linking arms with Dane, I crossed to the glass doors. Chris opened them and then stood back, allowing us to enter first. My breath caught in my throat. The place looked ... enchanted.

The strings of tiny lights, garlands of leaves, and amber candles gave the room a warm, autumn-y glow. There was the same foliage in the floral arrangements as in my bouquet—berries, mini pumpkins, acorns, feathers, and leaves.

Some larger pumpkins were scattered around, and some had been painted black to match the lace on my dress. Gold and champagne accents gave the décor a little glitz and glam, and the purple up-lighting gave it a dynamic, romantic ambience that made every other color "pop."

The tables were set up *beautifully*. Black glittering tablecloths, white draped chair covers, orange sashes on the chairs, autumn floral centerpieces, deep red napkins, and caramel apple favors.

And the two, tall escort card trees were just amazing. I wasn't sure if the black, gnarled, fairytale-looking trees were fake or not, but blossoms, crystals, and escort cards hung from the branches—each guest had a card telling them their table number.

All in all, it looked like a magical fairy garden in the midst of autumn.

My throat thickening, I looked up at Dane. "This is just ... I don't have words."

"Tell me you at least like it," begged Chris, standing a few feet away with

Miley.

I turned to the planners. "I love it. All of it. The pair of you are geniuses."

They both smiled and nudged each other playfully.

"Ready for your guests?" asked Miley.

Dane nodded. "Bring them in."

We weren't originally going to greet the guests as they entered, but I figured it was a good way of ensuring I spoke to every person. So I said hello, accepted kisses on the cheek, and thanked people for coming as they trickled into the botanical garden.

Chris and Miley directed people to the correct card tree and told them on which numbered branch they'd find their card. The system worked well.

When Simon entered and got a good look at me, he swallowed hard. "Sweetheart, you look beyond beautiful."

"And you look very smart in that tux," I told him.

He lifted his chin. "I do scrub up well, don't I?" He took my hands and gave them a little squeeze. "Maggie, Freddie, and even Deacon are all so happy for you."

I smiled. "Love you, Dad. And I love them, too."

He pressed a kiss to my forehead. "I'll want a dance later." With that, he moved along.

Wyatt stepped toward me. His mouth curved, and his eyes watered. "Melinda was right, you're a sight to behold," he said a little gruffly.

"And you look … uncomfortable," I said. "Handsome, but uncomfortable."

He tugged at his collar. "I hate suits. You know that. Hate tuxes even more. Tell me there's beer."

"There's beer." I strongly suspected he'd yank off the black tie and pull open a few buttons once he'd downed some drinks.

"Chris is giving me the stink eye, so I'll move along." He kissed my cheek and then put his mouth to my ear. "Proud of you." Then he disappeared.

Melinda and Junior came next. He gave me a cuddle and asked if there was cake. When I told him about the cookie bar, he flashed me the hugest grin.

I greeted several more people, including Hanna, Ashley, and Tucker. I also said my hellos to many of Dane's colleagues, including an insanely hot guy who I'd quickly learned was Blake Mercier; he'd brought along his wife, Kensey, and their two-year-old son.

Soon, Travis, Hope, Kent, and Jen walked in. I nearly gasped because, oh God, Hope was wearing white. Did she have no shame? Okay, it wasn't a wedding, but it was a wedding reception, so wearing white was in very poor taste.

I noted that she looked highly annoyed. I suspected that she'd thought *I'd* be wearing white and would, as such, be pissed at her choice of dress. Instead,

I could only cross my eyes. The woman was a waste of space, much like her husband.

Out of the four Davenports, Travis was first in line to greet us. After saying hello to Dane, Travis walked to me. "Congratulations, Vienna, you look beautiful." Smiling, he put his face closer to mine and whispered, "You'll eventually realize you made the biggest mistake of your life by not heeding what I said about Dane. Some people only learn their lessons the hard way, I guess."

I gave him a pitying smile and patted his arm. "It's an honest to God's shame you never learned yours. Now, if you don't want Dane to toss you out—and we both know he would—you'll get moving."

He might not have done, but then Kent accidentally-on-purpose knocked into him. Of course, Kent apologized to Travis, who walked off in a huff.

Kent gave me an "I got your back" wink. "You look striking, Vienna. My brother is a lucky man."

I smiled. "I'd say I'm the lucky one."

He kissed my cheek and then moved along.

Jen came next. The glassy look in her eyes told me she'd gone heavy on the cocktails. "The planners did a good job, I see."

"They did," I agreed.

She gave me a sweet smile. "Make him happy, Vienna. He deserves to be happy." That fast, she was gone.

I almost rolled my eyes when Hope appeared in front of me.

"Well, congratulations," she said to me, stiffly.

"Thank you."

"I figured you'd be wearing something a little more glamorous."

Knowing she was prompting me to comment on what *she* was wearing, I only said, "Thanks for coming, Hope." I turned to the person behind her and said hello, forcing Hope to either keep walking or make a scene. She kept walking.

Once all the guests were finally inside, Dane turned to me, his brows dipping. "What did Travis whisper to you?"

"That I'll eventually see I made a mistake in not heeding his warnings. Just ignore him, I did." I gave my head a little shake. "I can't believe Hope's wearing white. I suppose I should have expected the passive-aggressive jab. She's undoubtedly pissed that her games never paid off."

"She also doesn't like that you outshine her," he said. "If you want her gone, say the word, and I'll make it happen."

"Nah, let her stay. It'll be fun to watch people sneer at her for wearing white."

"Your call." Dane squeezed my hand. "Come on, let's go sit."

We settled at the head table. Simon and Wyatt sat on my side—mostly because they'd soon be making a speech together—while Melinda and Junior sat next to Dane. The little boy kept himself occupied using the small pack of coloring books that I'd asked Miley to place there for him. She'd done the same for all the children.

I took a moment to quickly scan the room. Everyone was now seated. Most were admiring the décor and snapping pictures. Others were chatting or laughing. Some guests were already shooting Hope looks of distaste. Her burning cheeks said that she was well-aware of it.

Shortly after, the food began to arrive. For starters, we had creamy soup served in small, artificial, hollowed-out pumpkins. I saw several people snapping photos of them, clearly appreciating the creativeness of it.

For the main meal, we enjoyed Thanksgiving-style platters of roast turkey, mashed potatoes, corn, dinner rolls, green beans, turkey stuffing, gravy, and cranberry sauce.

Dessert wasn't served, since we had a dessert table that included fruit pies, pumpkin spice cake, red velvet cupcakes, and a whole other selection of goodies. The kids mostly enjoyed themselves at the cookie bar and Trick-or-Treat candy buffet.

The wedding cake was smack bam in the middle of the dessert table on a tree trunk cake stand. The classic three-tiered cake was embellished with silk roses, fondant leaves, winding branches, and was topped with a bride and groom underneath a leafy arch. It was so gorgeous I wasn't sure I could cut into it—I didn't want to ruin it.

As the waiters began collecting the dishware, Simon leaned into me. "Have you noticed that Travis's wife keeps trying to pluck drinks out of his hand? I can't say I blame her. He's been knocking back champagne like it's his job."

I *had* noticed. "With any luck, he'll pass out right there at the table."

Simon snickered. "One can but hope."

At a cue from Miley, Dane rose from his seat with his champagne flute in hand. The room quieted in an instant. "First, on behalf of my wife and myself, I'd like to thank you all for coming," said Dane, smooth as glass. "Especially those who've travelled far to be here. And thank you Simon, Melinda, and Wyatt for making me feel so welcome into the family you've made together."

Warmed by that, I had to smile. Yeah, they'd been great with him from the start. There'd been a "bump," thanks to Travis, but my family had gotten past that.

Dane thanked a bunch of other people, including the wedding planners and venue organizers. He cast me a brief look and then added, "Anyone here who knows me is very aware that I always said I'd never marry. It's not that I have anything against marriage; I just simply never saw any appeal in it. Until Vienna."

There were a few *awws.*

"I first met my wife when she came to work at my company. I thought she was the most stunning creature I'd ever seen, but I have a hands-off policy when it comes to my employees, so I took a while to act on that. During the time she worked as my PA, I came to learn a lot about Vienna. I learned she's sweet. Loyal. Kind. Caring. Fearless. Honest. So honest she never once hesitated to flip me off or call me an asshole if need be."

My father muttered, "I can imagine."

Dane looked down at me. "You once asked if I thought I'd be the same in a relationship as I am in matters of business; if I'd always be pushing for more, never quite satisfied with what I had. The answer is absolutely no. You're the only person in my life who's ever made me feel content. The only person I'd ever want to share my life with. And the only person I'd never want to live without."

Sensing he meant every word, I swallowed hard. My throat felt thick. The bastard was good with words.

He turned back to the guests. "So I'd like everyone to stand and raise a glass to my wife, Vienna."

They all did, but I only had eyes for him.

"Now I'll hand you over to Vienna's father, Simon, and foster father, Wyatt," he said.

As Dane retook his seat, I leaned into him and smiled. "Dude, that was pretty sweet."

"It was pure truth." Dane pressed a kiss to my mouth. "If you keep looking at me like that, I'll have to drag you into a dark corner and have my way with you."

We looked up as Simon and Wyatt stood. They did a speech together, like a damn comedy duo. It was pretty funny, actually. There were smiles, laughs, and the occasional heckle from the other guests.

Kent also made a speech, which I wasn't expecting. It was short and sweet. No mention of dysfunctional family dynamics, Dane's old sex life, or any other awkward topics. As such, I was happy with it.

My stomach hardened when Travis grabbed his glass and went to stand. But his cousin put a hand on the asshole's shoulder and hissed something in his ear. Travis's mouth tightened, but he settled back into his chair. I breathed a sigh of relief. *Bullet dodged.*

When it came time for "the first dance," Dane and I made our way to the make-shift dance floor. He kept me flush against him, just like he had at the gala all those months ago, as we gently swayed to the song the band so expertly played.

"Are you good?" he asked, his hand splayed on my back, his thumb brushing over the ribbon of my corset.

"Yeah, just bloated after that huge meal. I'm surprised I'm not bursting out of this dress."

His eyes heated. "You'll be out of it later. I'm still not sure if it'll be before or after I've fucked you."

"Either is good with me." I snuggled closer to him. My lips parted when I realized he was rock hard. "My, my, my, that's a whole lot of quarters you're carrying in your pants right now."

"It's agonizing to know that with one tug on this ribbon, I can loosen that corset and have instant access to those pretty breasts."

"It's *supposed* to be agonizing for you."

He put his mouth to my ear. "My good girl's being bad, is she?"

I shivered at the feel of his breath on my earlobe. "You can punish me for it later."

"Don't think I won't."

Soon, the song reached its end. I would have headed straight back to my seat if Simon hadn't waylaid me and insisted on a dance. I chuckled when I saw that Melinda had done the same to Dane.

It didn't take long for the dance floor to fill up. Squealing kids ran in circles around the dancers and skidded on their knees, including Junior.

It wasn't until I'd danced with both Wyatt and Kent that I finally got the chance to return to my table and have a swig of my drink. I'd no sooner put down my glass than Ashley dragged me back on the dance floor.

A few songs later, Dane took my hand and led me over to his extended family, wanting me to have the opportunity to get to know them a little. I'd initially wondered if they would be as snobbish as Hope and Jen, but I quickly realized that they were very down to Earth.

After that, Dane and I walked from table to table, taking the time to briefly chat with our guests. I'd never received so many hugs or posed for so many photos. I'd smiled so often my jaw ached.

I wasn't so distracted that I didn't notice Travis having a few accidents. He knocked over a bottle of champagne, dropped a wine glass on the dance floor, tipped over a bowl of candy, and crashed into an elderly couple. I wasn't sure if he was wasted or just acting up like the precious little man child he was.

Standing at my table having yet another drink, I smiled when Ashley and Tucker approached. "Hey, you two. Enjoying yourselves?"

"I have a full bowl of candy to myself, what's not to like?" asked Ashley, clearly a little buzzed, cuddling the bowl to her chest like it was a newborn baby. "Melinda's sure enjoying herself." She gestured at my foster mother, who'd kicked off her heels and was dancing with her sisters, Hanna, and Junior.

"It would appear so," I said.

"Who are those guys?" Tucker asked me, pointing at two men who were breakdancing and appeared to believe they were a lot better at it than they truly were.

"Dane's cousins-by-marriage. You sure do look handsome in that suit,

Tucker."

Wearing a cocky smile, he adjusted his tie. "Well, I do try. I wore this suit for Ash's sister's wedding. The annoying one who calls me Tucky and hasn't sensed that I don't like it. The woman's not the brightest bulb, so it's a good thing for her that she's pretty."

Ashley's head snapped up. "You think my sister's pretty?"

Tucker stilled. "What?"

She rounded on him, her hand on her hip, her jaw hard. "You're hot for my sister? That's what you're saying?"

He jerked back. "I didn't say that."

"But you have a thing for her, don't you? God, I can't believe I didn't see it before. The clues were all right in front of me."

His face scrunched up. "Clues? There are no 'clues,' because I'm not hot for your sister. I don't even like her."

"Really? Well you compare us sometimes."

"You mean like when I say you're smarter, funnier, and not a fucking idiot?"

"You hate her husband."

"Because he keyed my car just to be a prick."

"You liked her Facebook post the other day."

"You mean the one that said, 'Happy Anniversary to Ashley and Tucker'? You liked it, too."

"That's not the point." Ashley lifted her chin. "Just admit it, you're in love with my sister."

He put a hand to his head. "Oh my God, how did you leap from me being attracted to her—which I'm *not*—to me being in love with her? I don't even *like* the woman, let alone want to sleep with her."

"I don't know if I believe you. Maybe we should go on a break or something."

"You said that yesterday because I didn't replace the toilet paper after the roll ran out."

Ashley's eyes flared. "Well, it's common courtesy."

Dane cleared his throat as he sidled up to us. "Sorry to interrupt, but I need to talk with my wife."

Ashley smiled at him. "Not a problem, Dane."

Tucker tipped his chin in greeting. "Yeah, no problem."

Then the couple began arguing again in low voices.

Dane guided me a short distance away, his hand cupping my elbow. "What's that all about?"

I sighed. "They're just having one of their mini fights."

"Will they need to be escorted out at some point?"

I waved that away. "Oh no, not at all. They'll be fine in a few minutes. They just need to argue it out."

"Hmm." Dane drew me close. "You should know that your father and Wyatt are in the photo-booth rental doing crazy shit with props. They tried to drag me in there."

I smiled, able to imagine it. "I'm looking forward to seeing those pictures." My smile faltered when Jen teetered to our side, her eyes glazed over.

"Hey, Dane," she said sweetly, a slight slur in her voice. "Aren't you going to dance with me?"

He sighed. "Go sit down, Jen."

She pouted. "But I want to dance. Now. With you." She put her hand on his arm and leaned a little *too* close. "Please, Dane?"

He moved his arm, making her hand slip away. "Go. Sit. Down."

She frowned. "Why are you being mean? You used to be so nice to me. Very, *very* nice." There was a wicked glint in her eyes. "Do you remember those times? Remember how good we were together?"

Skank. My nostrils flared. If he didn't deal with this bitch, I was going to wipe the floor with her face.

"You're drunk," spat Dane, "and you're embarrassing yourself."

Jen drew in a breath and straightened, her cheeks heating. "Asshole." She flounced off, a little unsteady on her feet.

"Not awkward at all," I muttered, seething but refusing to rant about some heifer at my wedding reception. I'd do that later. A lot.

Dane sighed again. "She'll hate herself for that in the morning."

Well, I was close to hating her right now. "At least Kent didn't hear her. He'd have been upset."

"Upset? He'd have been pissed. If I heard you talking like that to any man, I'd lose my shit. You know, I'm glad we eloped, because at least no one got to do stupid things at the ceremony itself."

"Aside from the officiant belching like crazy, you mean?"

Dane's jaw tightened. "All I could smell was the fucking onions he'd eaten."

I chuckled. "Same here. I don't care what you say, the whole thing was funny as hell."

"It wasn't in the least bit funny."

"How would you know? You don't 'get' humor."

Chris appeared, a fancy knife in hand. "It's time."

I moaned. "I can't do it."

"You can," he said, patting my arm. "Come on, it'll be over in seconds."

"I don't have it in me to ruin something so perfect."

Dane rolled his eyes and took the knife. "I'm quite sure your guilt will melt away once you have a piece of the cake in your mouth. Chris, lead the way."

CHAPTER THIRTY-THREE

Dane's prediction proved correct. It hurt my insides to slice into the beautiful wedding cake, but the taste did ease the pain. It was absolutely delicious with the frosting, butter cream, and jam. Dane seemed to enjoy his piece just as much.

Soon after that, trays of hot and cold finger foods were placed on a long table, providing late-night snacks for the guests. People practically descended on it, piling plates with rolls, shrimp cocktail, barbecue wings, dainty tea sandwiches, and mini quiche. The dessert table, cookie bar, and Trick or Treat buffet were also topped up, ensuring there were enough snacks for all ages.

I'd barely finished my food when Hanna and Melinda appeared, flushed and grinning. Each of them grabbed one of my hands.

"You have to come dance with us," insisted Hanna.

"I need to let my food digest first," I protested.

Melinda tugged on my hand. "It's your wedding reception. Get your ass on the dance floor where it belongs."

And so I ended up dancing again. I told myself I'd go rest after one song but, yeah, it didn't work out that way. I got caught up in having fun with my friends and family—hell, even Wyatt hit the dance floor. That did not happen often.

Dane didn't join me until another slow song came on. It was halfway through said song that the urge to pee hit me hard. Thankfully, my gown wasn't so long that I'd need someone to hold it while I did my business. I quickly excused myself, promising I wouldn't be long; happily accepting the kiss that Dane landed on me.

There were no restrooms in the venue, so I had to exit the building, cross the lawn, and use the restrooms inside the hotel. That done, I retraced my steps and headed back to the botanical garden. I'd almost reached it when a figure stepped out from behind a tree and blocked my path. It was dark out, but there was enough lighting for me to see their face clear enough. I could tell from their sour expression that this would be *far* from a pleasant conversation.

"I'd give you a round of applause, but then I might drop my glass," said Jen.

I felt my brow crease. "A round of applause?"

She took a sip from her champagne flute. "I've seen women pull all kinds of crap to try manipulating Dane into putting a ring on their finger. He never did it. Nope."

Ugh. "You really want to do this?"

"He always saw through their bullshit," she went on … so, yeah, she must really want to do this. "But you, Vienna? You fooled him *good.* You made him walk down a fucking aisle. How? I've got to know how you did it."

"Do you really believe I manipulated him into marrying me? Honestly? Because if so, you don't truly know him. Dane isn't someone who can be played."

"There's a first time for everything."

"You can't quite accept that he cares for me, can you?"

She snorted. "There isn't a single soul on this Earth he cares for. Not one."

"Just because he doesn't care for you doesn't mean he can't care for anyone."

Pain flashed across her face. "If you truly think that, I'd have to say that it's *you* who doesn't know him. But then, I don't suppose gold diggers give much of a shit if their marks care. That's all Dane is to you. A mark. People like you disgust me, selling yourselves for cash."

"Not just cash. I'll gladly take checks. Stocks. Shares."

She sneered. "He can do *far* better than you."

"I guess he felt like slumming it. Now if you're done making piss-poor attempts to insult me, Jenny—"

"Is it weird being married to a guy who won't sleep beside you at night?"

"No idea. Haven't found myself in that situation."

"Bull*shit*," she spat. "You know what's not fair?"

"That you're depriving a village of its prized idiot?"

Her lips thinned. "Think you're smart, don't you?"

"I do, actually. I also think—much like Dane, as it happens—that your opinions are irrelevant, so …" I went to step around her, but she planted herself in front of me again.

Her eyes flared. "Don't you dismiss me like I'm *nothing.*"

"Then don't act like a dumb fucking hoe bag."

She sucked in a breath and drew back.

"Now, as much as I appreciate you taking the time to entertain me like this, I'm gonna need you to move *the fuck* out of my way."

"I'm not done—"

"Yes, you are," a new voice cut in.

Jen jumped. Her face paled as Dane stepped out of the shadows, his eyes cold, his face diamond hard.

He slanted his head. "Tell me, Jen, why is it that you think you have the right to speak to my wife like that?"

Her mouth set into a bitter twist. "Your wife?" She sneered. "Never thought I'd see the day you let anyone fool you. It turns out that the infamous Dane Davenport can actually be conned. Because you honestly think she loves you, don't you?" Jen barked a laugh. "Wrong, my darling Dane. She's been manipulating you from the start, and you've been blind to it. I'm honestly embarrassed for you."

One of his brows hiked up. "Are you now?"

"Anyone can see she's leading you around by your dick. Well, anyone but *you*. Hell, she even somehow managed to talk you into spending all kinds of money on a party. You *hate* parties. You hate relationships. You hate the concept of marriage."

"What I hate is when people get the insane idea that they can treat Vienna like she's a piece of shit. Don't think being my brother's wife will protect you from the consequences, Jen. It won't. Now go home and sober the fuck up."

"She's only after your money," Jen persisted, gripping her glass so tight it was a wonder the flute didn't crack. "How do you not see that?"

"How do you not see that I don't give a shit what you think?"

Jen sucked in her cheeks. "I know a gold-digger when I see one, Dane. *That's* what she is. Did she play the victim of poverty so that you'd 'save' her?" Jen scoffed. "I bet she did. Hope doesn't think so. She thinks the whole thing is a farce, that you *paid* Vienna to marry you just so you could get that cushy trust fund. Maybe she's right. It would explain why Vienna didn't let the damn pictures chase her off."

"What did you just say?" asked Dane, his voice low and cold.

I felt my lips part. Oh, the *bitch*.

She blinked, the bluster leaving her in a rush. "I, um …"

"You said something about pictures," he prompted oh so calmly, but danger dripped from his tone. "What pictures might they be?"

Her eyes flickered, and she took a step back. "Dane …"

"You sent Vienna the flash drive?"

She shook her head fast. "No. Not me. *Hope*."

"Hope?"

"Yes. She told me she had photos that proved you'd cheated on Vienna. She said she sent them to her."

"What else did Hope say?"

Jen lifted her shoulders. "Nothing, really. She was just angry when Vienna didn't leave you."

"Hmm. And you had nothing to do with it?"

"No, nothing," she swore, her eyes wide.

"What about Travis? Was he in on it?"

Jen licked her lips. "No. He doesn't like that you're with Vienna, but he … he decided to let it go. Hope didn't want to. She *can't.* He's gambled away *so much* of their money. His share of your trust fund could fix the mess he's made."

"Yes, I can imagine why Hope did this. But why did you, Jen?"

"I told you, it was all Hope. It had nothing to do with me, I swear."

Dane crossed to her. "You're lying to me."

Blanching, she shook her head again. "I'm not, I wouldn't."

"The flash drive, the spoofed text, the phone call to the venue attempting to cancel the reception—you and Hope were behind it all. Why? I don't buy that you wanted to come between me and Vienna purely because you think she's a gold-digger."

Jen's eyes blazed at him. "She *is.* She's not good enough to be a Davenport. Hugh would say the same, if he was alive right now. He wouldn't have come here today. No, he wouldn't have given this marriage his blessing, and you know it. He wanted you to marry—" She cut off and snapped her mouth shut.

Dane lifted a brow. "Don't stop now. Who did he want me to marry? You?"

She swallowed. "He thought *I* was the one for you."

"And yet, he had no problem with you marrying Kent."

Her eyes teared. "I loved you. I would have been everything you needed if you'd just let me in. I would have fixed you; would have made you happy. But you wouldn't let me. I've never begged for anything in my life, but I *begged* you to give us a chance. You wouldn't."

"What the fuck does it matter? You're with Kent."

"I am. And I love him. I'm happy. I have a fucking great life."

"Which is considered the best kind of revenge, really, isn't it?" I cut in. "You wanted Dane to see you happy, to see that you're better off without him." I kind of understood. I'd felt the same when I realized I'd have to face Owen again.

"I *am* better off without him," she insisted. "And so are you. The only thing he ever cared about is that fucking trust fund."

"And that's why you don't want him to have it, isn't it? That's why you agreed to work with Hope. How very vindictive of you. I'll bet she recruited you. Yes, she'd have known how easy it would be to manipulate you into helping her."

Dane glared at Jen. "Tell me Vienna's wrong."

"She can't," I told him. "Some believe revenge is petty. Maybe it is. But it's often the way we work feelings out of our system. Especially betrayal, resentment, self-pity, and abandonment. You were her first crush—that's always powerful." I slid my gaze back to her. "All those years ago, he left you feeling helpless to make him love you. That was all you wanted him to do, wasn't it?"

She looked away, her eyes watering again.

"You told yourself that you could make him feel something for you. But you couldn't, and that was a blow your fragile young ego never forgot. There's more, though, isn't there, Jen? There's some other reason why you were so desperate to hurt him." My gut insisted on it. "What did he do that you can't forgive?"

Her lips trembled. "He already knows. I'm not surprised he didn't tell you. He wouldn't want you to know just what a cold bastard he really is." She swallowed. "I knew how resolute he was that he'd never have kids. I knew he'd never change his mind. Knew he didn't believe he'd find a woman who wouldn't care that he'd never give her children. And I knew it was because he needed to feel that he was the most important person in her life—he wouldn't want to share her attention or love."

I frowned because, yeah, that wasn't Dane at all.

"So I …" Jen took a shaky breath. "So I got sterilized. I wanted to prove to him that I could be what he needed; that I'd make him everything to me. But he didn't care, did you, Dane? It didn't matter that I'd given up so much for you. You turned your back on me yet again."

Dane glared at her, stone-faced. "You missed out the part where you offered to get sterilized and I told you not to do it; that it wouldn't make a difference to me because I wasn't interested in a relationship. But you went ahead and did it anyway."

"I thought you were testing me!"

"I'd never fuck with a woman that way, Jen. You should have known that. You've always been so sure you understand me, but you don't. You never did. How could you possibly have loved me when you didn't even really *know* me?"

Her eyes sparkled like chips of ice. "You think I would have gotten sterilized for someone I just *thought* I was in love with? You think I wouldn't have been damn certain of what I felt?"

"Either way, it is not my fault that you did what you did. I was clear that I was not interested in a relationship with you. I was brutally clear, in fact, because I needed you to really heed me. But you didn't want to hear that, so you didn't listen. You read something else into what I said."

"I think she knows, deep down, that the fault doesn't lie with you, Dane," I said. "I think she just needs to believe it does, or she has to face that she made this mess for herself."

Honestly, a part of me felt sorry for her. I'd always wanted kids, and it would gut me to be unable to bear them. But Dane was right: she'd *chosen* to be sterilized, even though he'd warned her that it would make no difference. "Can't you have the process reversed, Jen?"

"I tried," she gritted out. "It didn't work."

"You told me it did," said Dane. "Then again, you also told me that you no longer blamed me. You said that on the night you accepted Kent's proposal of marriage. Apparently, you lied."

"Because she needed you to believe she was happier without you," I pointed out. "Didn't you, Jen? I'm guessing Hope knew how you really felt about Dane. I'm guessing she capitalized on it."

"No need to guess," said Dane. "We can ask her. Why don't you come closer, Hope?"

I turned at the sound of a loud sigh. Hope stood off to the side, leaning against a tree, not even bothering to conceal her presence. "You're quite the puppet master, aren't you?" I said. "You certainly pulled Jen's strings, and it's damn shitty of you to play on something that's painful for her. I'd imagine you were quite the driving force behind Travis's insistence on getting his share of Dane's trust fund."

"Oh, Travis didn't need pushing," said Hope. "Not until Dane had him banned from all the local casinos anyway. Before that, he'd been happy to play the game. In fact, if he'd had his way, he'd have sold o-Verve secrets to the company's competitors, but you wouldn't let him into Dane's office, and Travis couldn't get access to your computer—he said you guarded your desk like a damn bulldog."

"What she's not telling you," began Jen, her eyes on Dane, "is that—inspired by Travis's idea—she had one of her boy-toy's try to steal Vienna's laptop so she'd get access to company secrets, only Vienna had taken it with her to Vegas."

Hope's face went rock hard as she turned to her sister-in-law. "Oh, trying to shove everyone's attention onto me, are you?"

"The burglary," I said, shocked, as the pieces came together. "You set that up." I looked at Dane, whose eyes now glittered with so much anger it was no wonder that Hope took a step back.

"She told the guy it was important that he make it look like a standard burglary," Jen added, the snitch.

Hope snickered at her. "It won't work, Jen. They're not going to let what you did *slide* just because you're giving up info on me." Hope sliced her gaze to Dane. "Go on. Swear you'll make me pay. Promise you'll ruin my life. It's already in ruins, thanks to your brother's gambling problem. You have no idea how much we need that money, Dane."

A muscle in his cheek flexed. "If you'd needed help, you could have asked for it. But you couldn't swallow your pride and come talk to me. You would rather have taken what was mine right from under me."

"Well, it's not like you need it."

"Neither do you," I told her. "Not really. Travis may be in debt, but the two of you still have a lot more than most people do. Sell some stuff. Downsize. Shop in cheaper stores."

Hope looked at me like I'd suggested she munch on dog shit. "And have everyone know about our debts? Have them laugh and ridicule us?" She shook her head. "Oh no, not a chance."

Then Dane was right. This was about pride. She wasn't prepared to lose face and have anyone know how far down she and Travis had fallen ... just like Barron hadn't been able to do.

"You wouldn't have helped us, Dane," said Hope. "You wouldn't have cared that we were close to losing everything. You would have told Travis it was his own mess and that he'd have to fix it on his own."

"I guess you'll never know if you were right or not," said Dane. "You can be sure of one thing, Hope. You really will feel like your life is in ruins by the time I'm done with you. You had countless warnings to leave Vienna alone."

Hope scoffed. "Like you really care. I'll admit, I fell for it in the beginning. I thought you two were serious. I thought she did indeed care for you."

"So you tried to make me doubt him," I said. "When that didn't work, you upped your game. And when that failed—"

"It became obvious that this marriage isn't real," Hope finished. "My warnings about him didn't send you running, the pictures didn't send you running, the text message didn't send you running."

"Because I trust Dane."

"No, because he's paying you to stay right where you are—it's the only thing that makes sense. You have no other reason to stick by him."

"Really? You stuck by Travis."

She shook her head. "I'm done trying to save that man from himself. He can't be helped. Neither can Dane. They're both too fucked up, thanks to Barron. I'm cutting my losses." She looked at Dane. "You truly are welcome to come at me with everything you have. But there won't be much for you to take from me—Travis will make sure I walk away from the marriage with little to nothing, the cunning bastard."

Dane cocked his head. "Have you so easily forgotten that I can bide my time when need be? There'll come a day when you have something important in your life again. I'll make sure you lose it, just like you tried to make me lose what's important to me."

Fear glimmered in Hope's eyes. "Even though my attempts came to nothing?"

"Even though," he confirmed. "You knew what you were risking when you played these games. You played them anyway. That was your mistake."

Hope gestured at Jen. "What about *her*? She wasn't so innocent in all this, no matter what she might say."

"Oh, I know that." Dane looked at Jen even as he said, "Vienna, call Kent. Tell him to meet us out here. Tell him to bring Travis."

I quickly did so and then rang off.

Tears welled up in Jen's eyes. "Please don't tell Kent, Dane. Please."

"I'm not going to tell him," said Dane. "*You* are. He's going to hear it from you. He deserves that much. You did all this behind his back. He has every right to know. I'd want to know, in his position. I'll be damned if I'll keep it a secret for you."

"I did something stupid, I know, but I don't deserve to have my marriage wrecked."

"Neither did I, but you tried to wreck mine. If you're lucky, he'll forgive you."

"He won't, and you know it. Do you think he'll thank you for making me tell him what I've done? He won't, Dane. He'll hate us both. Is that what you really want?"

"You won't change my mind, Jen."

"You'd really ruin your own brother's marriage?"

"*I* didn't do it. *You* did. Like Hope, you knew what you were risking. You obviously thought it was worth the risk; that *he* was worth risking. He deserves a lot fucking better."

Kent soon joined us. Travis staggered behind him, absolutely smashed. Their brows furrowed as they took in each of us.

"Is something wrong?" asked Kent.

"You could say that," replied Dane. "Tell him, Jen."

She looked at the floor instead, hunching in on herself.

"What is it?" Kent gently asked her, moving to her side. "Jen? Jen, come on, look at me." But she didn't.

"What's going on?" demanded Travis.

Hope sighed. "I tried to clean up your mess—*that's* what. You didn't have the guts to go up against Dane, so I did it. I pushed Vienna to leave him. And thanks to Jen, he now knows all about what she and I did. And now I'm screwed."

Well, at least she had the guts to own her fuck up. Unlike her accomplice.

Travis's jaw hardened. "I told you to drop it, Hope."

"Because you're too weak to stand up to him, just like you're too weak to stay away from the fucking casinos," she sneered. "Well, I'm done. Done with you and your family."

Travis stiffened. "What does that mean?"

"It means I want a divorce." Hope looked at Dane. "Come at me one day if you feel you must. But I'll be ready for it. You won't win; you won't get away with whatever you try to do."

"Of course I will," said Dane, his voice soft but flat. "I always do."

Her eyes flickering, she strode off.

Travis stalked after her, weaving all over the place. "Wait, we're not done talking."

"Oh, we're done in *every* way a couple can be done," she insisted.

As their voices faded away, Kent turned to his wife. "What did she mean, Jen? What did you and Hope do?"

Jen lifted her head, sniffling. "I made a mistake. A stupid, horrible mistake. You can't imagine how sorry I am; how I wish I could turn back time—"

"What did you and Hope do?" he demanded.

Jen looked to Dane, as if hoping he'd tell some bullshit story for her to cover up her sins, but he didn't. Closing her eyes, she turned back to Kent. "I … I let Hope rope me into her scheme to get Vienna out of the picture. I wanted to help Hope—Travis put them in *major* debt, and she was terrified they'd lose everything. Plus, I hated that Dane had been targeted by a freaking gold-digger. But I mainly did it for Hope and Travis. I knew it would hurt you to see your brother lose everything."

I snorted. "You really are good at buttering up the truth, aren't you?"

She shot me a narrow-eyed look but slid her attention back to Kent, frowning when he stepped away from her. "Kent, I know I messed up big time. I'm so sorry. You can't know how sorry I am."

Kent stared at her through empty eyes. "Like you were sorry for the things you said to Dane at his house when he got back from Vegas after marrying Vienna? You told me—all three of us—that you were *sorry*. But that was a lie, wasn't it?"

She shook her head madly. "No, no, it wasn't."

"It had to have been, or you wouldn't have teamed up with Hope," snapped Kent. "You didn't do all this for Hope and Travis."

"Yes, I did!"

"No, this isn't about them. You think I haven't noticed how much you've struggled to accept that Dane is married? It's not even jealousy. It's bitterness. You don't like that he's happy. And I realized you never really forgave him for refusing to try having a relationship with you. Give me one piece of honesty, Jen. Did you marry me to get back at him?"

Her eyes widened. "No, definitely not. I love *you*."

"But not enough. Not if you couldn't let this shit go and just be happy with me and what we have."

"Does he even know you got sterilized?" Dane asked her.

Kent stilled. "Sterilized?"

Dane tossed her a look of disbelief. "You never told him? Fucking hell."

I stared at her in open-mouthed shock. This just kept getting worse and worse.

She stepped toward Kent. "I was young and stupid and did something I can't take back. I didn't tell you because I was worried that you'd leave me."

Kent's nostrils flared. "At what point were you going to tell me that our attempts to try for a baby would never amount to anything?"

"Kent—"

"I told you I was worried I might be infertile. I offered to be tested. You told me not to do it; said it wouldn't matter to you, because you loved me anyway. You let me think the problem might be me."

Oh my God, what a fucking bitch.

She reached out to touch him. "I didn't want—"

"I can't talk to you right now." Kent backed away, his fists clenched, looking like he wanted nothing more than to stalk off. But then he stilled, as if remembering where he was. He turned to his brother. "Dane ..."

"Go," Dane said softly.

Kent didn't need to be told twice.

Jen hurried after him, calling out, "Kent, wait!"

He didn't wait or respond. He kept striding fast toward the hotel, and she kept on trailing after him.

I blew out a breath and turned to Dane. "Well, that was ... heavy."

He sighed. "Yeah." He crossed to me and cupped the side of my neck. "Are you okay?"

"That was going to be my question."

"I'm pissed, but fine. You?"

"Fine. Though my head is spinning." I rested my hands on his chest. "I'm sorry."

He frowned. "For what?"

"That you just found out two of your in-laws tried to fuck you over. I'm especially sorry that we couldn't have found this out *before* the reception, or even sometime after it." I bit my lip. "We can leave early, if you want."

"Leave? Why would I want to leave?"

"Well you can't be feeling good right now."

"I'm more pissed than anything else. I've never liked Hope, so her betrayal means nothing. Jen ... I considered her to be family. I thought she was good for Kent, even if they hadn't been as tight as they once were. That she so easily risked losing him infuriates me."

While I was glad that Dane didn't seem hurt by what either of his sisters-in-law had done, it saddened me that his emotional defenses were so extreme that not even a betrayal of this magnitude pierced them. It was one thing to have thick skin. It was another thing to feel so very little in the face of such duplicity.

Maybe, due to his childhood, he was so used to people trying to hurt him that it didn't have the same impact it would have on others. For him, it was the norm. Whatever the case ... yeah, I was just sad for him.

I leaned into him. "Do you want to go after Kent?"

Dane shook his head. "He likes to be alone when he's angry. Our father would seek us out and take out his rage on us when in a mood."

"So Kent does the opposite. He isolates himself."

"Yes." Dane brushed my bangs out of my face. "We can leave the reception, if you want. But I don't want to. Sure, we can let those bitches ruin it and have the last laugh. I'd rather carry on with our night and not give them the power to taint this for us. What about you?"

"I vote for the latter."

He squeezed the side of my neck. "Good. Then let's go back inside and enjoy the rest of our reception."

CHAPTER THIRTY-FOUR

We stumbled out of the hotel elevator later that night, sipping from each other's mouths. The mix of alcohol and sexual need swimming through me had my whole system buzzing. I felt warm and tingly and tipsy.

Dane took me by the wrist and led me to our room. Chris and Miley had booked us the honeymoon suite, so it was no surprise to see fresh flowers, champagne on ice, rose petals on the bed, and a tiered-stand of chocolates and strawberries.

Dane hauled me against him. "I spent pretty much the entire day thinking about what I'd do to you when I had you all to myself," he said, his voice low and vibrating with a need that equaled my own. "Now I finally have you where I want you."

And I really couldn't have been more pleased about that.

He splayed his hand on my throat. "I can feel your pulse racing against my thumb."

I expected him to claim my mouth, but he didn't. He just stared at it, his face cold, his eyes hot. I didn't realize I was holding my breath until I felt the strain in my chest.

Everything seemed to go still and quiet as I waited for him to move. My breathing picked up, and my pulse quickened even more. Anticipation was like a living thing inside me. Just when I thought I might explode, his mouth slammed on mine. That easily, the sexual buzz in my system amplified by a thousand. Hunger flared. Nerve-endings sparked. Chemicals raced. My heart began to pound like crazy.

Needing to touch him, I slipped off his jacket, pulled off his bow tie, and opened the top buttons of his shirt. I slid my hands inside and planted them on his chest, loving the feel of that hard muscle and barely leashed hunger.

He broke the kiss with a nip to my lower lip. "Stay right there." He moved to stand behind me and then, slowly and leisurely, undid the back of my corset. The material slumped forward, and he wasted no time in slipping his hands down the front of the corset to palm my breasts.

Closing my eyes, I arched into his warm, skilled hands as they shaped and squeezed. Each touch teased me. Inflamed me. Branded me.

Without turning to face him, I reached up and looped my arms around the back of his neck. "You still torn on whether to strip me naked or just flip up my dress?"

He pinched my taut nipples just right. "No." He kissed and suckled on my throat, humming in approval when I tilted my head to give him better access. "I've decided I'll take you while you're wearing this cock-tease of a dress. *Then* I'll get you naked and fuck you again."

That was a plan I could get behind.

He withdrew his hands from my corset. "Sit on the edge of the bed."

I complied and looked up at him, waiting for further direction, knowing how much that revved his engines.

His eyes went heavy-lidded. "Such a good girl. Now lift your dress and spread your legs; show me what's mine."

I very slowly peeled up the front of my dress while parting my legs.

His gaze dropped to my boots, and every muscle in his body seemed to tense. His dark eyes flew back to mine, glittering with need and promise. "So this is why you had that wicked little smile on your face earlier," he said, taking two predatory steps toward me.

"I wanted to surprise you."

"You succeeded. They stay on. All night."

"I really don't think I can sleep in them."

"I'll make it worth your while." He crossed to me, dropped to his knees, and snaked his hands up my inner thighs. "Such soft skin." He caught the waistband of my panties and slowly peeled them off. His eyes on my pussy, he said, "Spread your legs wider. That's it." He might be on his knees, but there was nothing submissive about him. Even then, he wore authority like a second skin. He was fully in command, held all the power and knew it.

"Lean back and brace yourself on your elbows, Vienna. Good girl."

I gasped as he buried his face in my pussy. He didn't tease me with little flicks or laps of his tongue. No, he *worked* me with his tongue, teeth, and lips; drove me up hard and fast into an orgasm that left me trembling and panting. Then he did it all over again. I collapsed onto the mattress, breathing hard.

He stood and deftly shed his clothes. "Hook your hands under your knees, pull your legs toward your chest, and then spread them wide for me. That's it. Keep them there like that." He slipped one hand beneath my ass, tilted my hips slightly, and then wedged the head of his dick in my pussy. "Hmm. My happy place."

I chuckled. "Feel free to—" My back bowed as he slammed home, ruthlessly burying himself balls-deep inside me. I let out a shaky breath. "Jesus, Dane. You could give a girl a little warning."

He gripped my ass. "Are you ready to be fucked?"

"Yes. Very, very yes."

He hummed and reared back. "Well that's a shame. Because I'm not ready just yet."

I frowned. "What? You are. You totally are."

He lazily sank his cock back inside me, hunger carved into every line of his face. "I love watching your pussy swallow my dick."

Dane kept his pace excruciatingly slow as he thrust inside me again and again. Occasionally, he'd pause to grind his pubic bone against my clit like the teasing little shit he was. My entire body was so hot I wouldn't have been surprised to see flames dancing over my skin.

Gasping and moaning, I urged him to move faster, to take me harder. He didn't. He seemed intent on driving me insane—something he came close to doing when he began to do some clever things with his hips. He'd circle them, move them side to side, or rub up and down, sending my clit and inner nerve-endings haywire.

"Dane—" I gasped as he yanked me closer, hooked my legs over his shoulders, and slid even deeper inside me. *Oh, God, yes.* I thought he'd then finally give me what I wanted, *needed*, but he kept his pace lazy and gentle.

"You are cruel," I croaked. "Just plain cruel."

His mouth curving, he bent over and lashed my nipple with his tongue. "You look like you hate me right now."

I could never hate him. Never. I loved the teasing bastard, and I wondered if he even knew it. Probably not. He wouldn't expect anyone to love him. He most likely doubted that anyone ever could. And that just wasn't acceptable to me.

I licked my lips. "I want you to know something."

He ground against my clit again. "What?"

I curled my hands around his nape. "I love you, Dane. I don't expect you to say it back. I don't even need to hear those words. I just want you to know."

He stared down at me, a whole array of emotions flickering in his eyes so fast I couldn't identify a single one of them. He swore under his breath, buried his face in my neck, and began fucking in and out of me. Hard. Fast. Brutally. Like he couldn't get deep enough.

I clung to his nape, moaning and scratching at his skin, loving every savage thrust. He went so deep it hurt a little, but I didn't care. Liked it. Especially since every stab of his cock hit my sweet spot, rubbed my clit, and made his balls slap against my ass.

After being teased for so freaking long, I was excruciatingly close to coming. I could feel my pussy tightening and spasming around his cock. I knew his own release was creeping up on him, because I could feel his shaft begin to swell and throb. "Dane—"

"Come for me." He sank his teeth into my neck, and I was gone. "That's my good girl." He fucked me through my orgasm, ramming harder, faster—almost feral. Then he punched his cock deep inside me and exploded.

The strength seemed to leave us both, and we sagged. The weight of his body made it hard for me to catch my breath, but I didn't care—I liked having him so close. So I breezed my fingers through his hair, lightly scratching his scalp.

Finally, Dane let my legs slip from his shoulders and down to my sides. He kissed his way up my neck and over to my mouth. His tongue swept inside and tangled with mine, tasting and savoring.

Pulling back, he brushed my bangs away from my face. "Love you, baby girl," he said, his voice low and soft. "You told me you don't need the words, but you deserve to hear them. I don't want you to ever be unsure of what I feel for you. I need you to know deep down to your bones that you're the most important thing in my world. I need you to know I could never love anything or anyone the way I love you."

My eyes stung, and my nose tingled. I had *not* expected that declaration. Hadn't been prepared for it. I didn't need to ask him if he was sure—Dane would never have said those words if he didn't mean them. "Right back at you. I don't know when it happened. I just know that it's true and it won't change."

"Same here. I haven't done anything at all to deserve you, but I'll never give you a reason to regret being mine. Not ever, Vienna. You can count on that. On me."

"I know, and I do. You were the best fake husband ever, so I have no doubts that you'll make the best real husband ever."

A low, rumbly chuckle vibrated his chest.

I gaped. "You just laughed. Sort of."

He nuzzled my neck. "It was a cough."

"It was not. Don't worry; I'll keep it between you and me."

"That I coughed?"

I play-punched his shoulder. "You laughed. I heard you." And I was determined to make sure it happened again. He deserved to have a home filled with laughter—not fear and anxiety the way his childhood home had been. I tilted my head as something occurred to me. "Are you going to want a bigger house when we have kids?"

His brow pinched. "Why would we need a bigger house? How many kids are you planning to have?"

"We won't *need* a bigger house unless you think you can't cope sharing your space with noisy little people."

He shrugged. "I'll manage. You didn't answer my question. How many do you want?"

"Two or three." Or maybe four.

"All right. We'll get started in a few years. I want to have you all to myself for a while first. I'm not ready to share you yet." He nibbled my lips with his own. "I'm greedy and selfish when it comes to you."

"You don't hear me complaining, do you?"

He skimmed his hand down my neck, over my breast, and down to my waist. "I love this dress on you. Do you remember the little black dress you wore on our first date?"

"I remember."

"I want you to wear it for me one night. I sat opposite you in the restaurant hard as a steel fucking spike. I kept picturing you bent over with that dress hiked around your waist. You've no idea how close you came to getting fucked in the car on the way home."

I would never have guessed he'd been going through the same sexual struggle as me. "Who says I'd have let you fuck me?"

One side of his mouth hitched up. "You'd have let me. You were just as hot for me as I was for you."

Totally true. "Oh, I was, was I?"

"Yes, you were. Which made it even harder to keep my hands off you. But I knew that if I touched you like that even once, there'd be no going back. And I was right."

"That you were."

"I always am."

I snorted. "You're an arrogant ass at times, but you somehow make it work for you. I don't even know how. It's like your superpower or something."

"When I was a kid, I wanted the power to teleport so I could go anywhere in the world. Which reminds me … I have a surprise for you."

"You do?"

"Yes. We're going on a trip next weekend."

I smiled. "We are? Where?"

"Venice. Hanna told me you always wanted to go there. It'll be our belated honeymoon."

I hugged him tight. "Thank you. I'm super excited. Wait, what about Blue?"

"She can come with us. We're not staying in a hotel. We're staying in my villa."

"Well of course you have a villa in Venice. Do you own houses anywhere else?"

"A few places. You'd like the lodge in the French Alps."

"Alps? I would not have pictured you as a skier."

He shrugged. "I might never have tried it, but ... Oliver always wanted to learn to ski."

And because the little boy had never had that chance, Dane had done it for him. "Can I ask you a question?"

"You just did."

I rolled my eyes. "You don't have to answer, I won't be upset if you don't. I just wondered ... Does the 'o' in o-Verve stand for Oliver?"

He nodded. "Yes."

"Why 'Verve?'"

"As a toddler, he couldn't correctly say 'Oliver.' He used to point at himself and say 'Verver.' But if people said, 'Oh, your name is Verver?' He'd scowl and say 'no, Verver.' In his mind, he was pronouncing it correctly."

A sad smile pulled at one corner of my mouth. "So, you added the 'O' and dropped one of the 'Rs'." And, in doing so, honored his brother.

"Yes."

I pressed a soft kiss to his lips. "Thank you for telling me that."

Dane hummed and sipped from my mouth again, tasting and tantalizing me. The kiss soon became hard and deep and wet. "Now I want you naked. Well, mostly naked. The boots can stay."

"Fine, but I'm not sleeping in them."

"All right," he said easily, so sure he'd get his way.

He did, actually.

EPILOGUE

Eight years later

"I don't like what this time of year does to you."

Dropping my paper plate into the kitchen trash can, I looked over my shoulder at Dane. "You don't like to see me happy?"

"I don't like to see you regress. Or to see the downstairs of our home looking like a spooky crypt."

"I didn't go *that* far." Okay, maybe I did. There were pumpkins, foam tombstones, synthetic spiderwebs, and fake skeletons all around. Rubber bats and strings of ghost lights dangled from the ceiling. I even had inflatable props like scarecrows, witches, and grim reapers. My favorite thing was the bubbling cauldron that occasionally let out a wicked cackle or other spooky sound.

The truth was … I went crazy with the decorations every Halloween. Turning to fully face him, I said, "I regret nothing."

"Was the smoke machine really necessary?" he griped.

I tilted my head. "You sure you're not just being whiny because you've spilled red juice all over your shirt?"

"I didn't spill it. Our daughter poured it on me because she thought it would be 'awesome' if it looked like I was covered in blood."

I clamped my lips together to stifle a smile. "I'm assuming you mean Alicia."

Our four-year-old daughter wasn't the most placid of children. She *insisted* she was a princess, fought with the soul of a reincarnated MMA fighter, and had a mischievous streak that seemed embedded in every bone.

"She just wants you to look, you know … Halloween-y," I defended.

"You never dress up."

"Because I'm not seven."

"Adults dress up, too," I reminded him, gesturing at my Maleficent outfit. I crossed to him and slid my hands up his chest. "It's a shame *you* won't. You'd look hot as a fireman." I hummed as he kissed me, curling his arms tight around me. "But this particular holiday *has* grown on you—I'll take that as a win."

He grunted. "Come on, you're missing this party you insisted on throwing."

"It's good to see you're enjoying it," I said dryly.

Dane kept one arm looped around my waist as he led me out of the kitchen. Walking into the living room, I had to smile at the sight of the kids dancing to the *Ghostbusters* theme song while playing Musical Statues.

Dane might not be too pleased by the effort I'd put into the party, but the children were sure enjoying themselves. They particularly liked the spread. Many of the foods were made to look like Halloween decorations such as ghosts, eyeballs, fingers, and mummies.

Drinking a glass of punch, Melinda frowned at the stain on Dane's shirt. "What happened to you?"

He sighed. "Alicia."

"Ah, I see," Melinda said. Because, to be honest, no further explanation was needed—the kid got up to all kinds of shit.

"It's a shame Junior didn't come," I said.

"He's thirteen now," she reminded me. "He considers himself too old to celebrate Halloween."

"You can never be too old to celebrate Halloween." I slid a meaningful look Dane's way, but he missed it—his gaze was on our two daughters.

I wouldn't say fatherhood changed Dane—he was still cold, ruthless, and calculating. But when around his children, those traits fell away. I'd initially worried that he'd struggle to allow himself to love and bond with them—such a thing wasn't reflexive for Dane. But I'd worried for nothing. He'd taken one look at them the moment they were born and fell hard each time. He was a protective, hands-on dad who never let his children feel second to his job.

"My money's on Addie," he said into my ear. "She'll win easy."

If he thought I'd bet against him, he was wrong. Our eldest daughter, who was a year older than Alicia, was much like Dane. Calm, serious, a deep thinker, and uber competitive. She also had his dark eyes, and her sleek medium-length hair was the same deep black as his. *Unlike* him, Addison was also sweet as pie and great with animals.

Wyatt paused the music. The dancing kids froze, apart from Ashley and Tucker's youngest boy, Cooper—he toddled around, too young to understand the game. He pulled hard on his older brother's leg, but Kellen didn't budge. Little Sabrina, however, wobbled and then stumbled back a step.

Beside Wyatt, Simon winced and said, "Sorry, Sabrina, you're out."

Her eyes went wide as saucers. "I didn't move. Mommy, tell him I didn't move."

"I would if it were true," said Hanna with a smile.

Hanna had become accidentally pregnant with Sabrina after a one-night stand six years ago. The kid's dad, Kyle, had been very involved during the pregnancy. He and Hanna had eventually become a couple, and they were cute as hell together—especially right now, dressed up as Mr. and Mrs. Incredible. Ashley and Tucker, who stood off to the side with them, had come dressed as Morticia and Gomez Adams.

The buzzer sounded just as the music restarted.

Dane checked his phone. "It's Kent and Emma."

I smiled. "Good, I was hoping they'd come."

"I'll let them in." He kissed my temple and then left the room.

Melinda leaned into me. "I really like Emma."

"So do I. She just 'fits' Kent in the best way." Unlike his ex-wife. He hadn't even tried to work things out with Jen, feeling too betrayed by all she'd done and concealed from him. She'd pestered him to forgive her for *months*. Hell, she'd even reached out to both Dane and I at one point, appealing for us to help her win Kent back.

"Emma's so sweet I was convinced it had to be an act at first—I couldn't see how anyone could truly be *that* nice," said Melinda.

"She's completely genuine. I'm glad he has her. I just wish he'd get over his hang-ups about marriage. Though I can understand why he's shy about taking another walk down the aisle. It didn't exactly end well last time."

"I think he'll make an honest woman of her at some point. I love how sweetly protective he is of her. He's even more so now that she's pregnant."

Yes, and I figured a *big* reason for that was that his ex-wife kept calling and sending Emma letters. Jen had popped back onto the scene when she heard that his girlfriend of three years was pregnant. Luckily, Emma had more staying power than to be scared off by Jen's antics.

I smiled as Dane re-entered the room with Kent and Emma. They weren't wearing costumes, but I hadn't expected them to. Kent was too serious for that. Emma wasn't so serious, but she'd never dress up unless he did too—she wouldn't want to make him feel bad.

"Thanks for coming," I said.

Emma grinned. "Thanks for inviting us."

Kent kissed my cheek and then scanned the room with his gaze. "Where are my girls? Ah."

Just then, the music stopped again. Moments later, Alicia stomped off the makeshift dance floor with a put-out sigh after being declared "out," making her blonde hair bop with each step. Spotting Kent, she dashed over and jumped into his arms. "Uncle Kent!"

"Don't you look pretty in your princess gown." He kissed her face and blew raspberries on her neck, making her giggle.

Kent was the doting uncle every kid wished they had, and I figured he'd make just as doting a father. He and Dane were somewhat closer these days and played a bigger part in each other's lives.

Travis kept a low profile. We received cards from him on the holidays, but he rarely visited. He had, however, cleaned up his ways. Sort of. He didn't gamble anymore, but he cheated on his oblivious fiancée, who I kind of liked and felt super sorry for.

Travis and Hope had divorced roughly the same time as Kent and Jen. Hope hadn't made contact with any of us again. Owen—true to his word—had stayed away and ceased trying to separate me and Dane. Similarly, Heather had stopped playing games, but she'd made no attempt to improve her life or change her ways.

I smiled as Alicia led Emma over to the sofa, declaring she should sit and rest. "She's a bossy little thing for sure," I said.

Dane hummed. "I wonder where she gets that trait from."

"I don't." I knew *exactly* who she got it from.

Ashley came over, her glass empty. "Anymore punch?"

"I'll get some for you," said Melinda, plucking the glass out of her hand. "I'm off to get more for myself."

"Thanks, Melinda," said Ashley.

Feeling something brush against my leg, I glanced down. "Dane, your owner's back."

He scowled as Blue then rubbed up against his leg. "Go to Addie," he told her gruffly, but the feline just blinked up at him.

Right then, a cry came over the baby monitor in my hand.

"I'll go," said Dane, giving my hip a little squeeze.

It did not surprise me that Blue followed him. Dane was still her favorite person in the house, but Blue also loved being around Addison.

The music again stopped. Only Addison and Kellen were left on the dance floor. Both were completely still, not even moving their eyes. But then Kellen, who was balancing on one leg, suddenly lost said balance.

"Addie wins!" Simon declared.

Everyone clapped, with the exception of Kellen.

"Uh-oh," muttered Ashley. "His face is going all red."

Because he *hated* to lose.

Kellen huffed. "*I* should have won, Wyatt." He jabbed a finger at Addison. "*She* kept moving—you just didn't see."

Apparently offended on behalf of her sister, Alicia got right up in his face—which wasn't easy to do, considering she was a good few inches shorter. "That's a lie!"

Ashley groaned and looked at me. "Do we step in?"

Once upon a time, we'd done it immediately, but nowadays … "I've kind of given up on trying to stop them from locking horns." The two did *not* get along. Honestly, they argued so often it was *unreal.*

"Take it back!" Alicia yelled at him, her hands balled up into fists.

"Or what, shorty?" he taunted.

Tucker quickly crossed to them and tried to smooth over the situation. He was such an optimist, bless him.

Kellen glared up at his father. "I should have won! Even Frodo knows that."

Alicia gasped at his nickname for her. And, yep, she leapt on him.

"Dammit." I crossed the room, intending to intervene, but my father beat me to it and pulled her away. I gave her my usual "it's wrong to hit people" talk while she gave me her usual "I know, I know, but he's such a loser" answer in justification.

After I sent her off to play with Sabrina, I turned to my father, who was shaking his head and smiling.

"Why is it that they always end up fighting?" he asked.

"Both want to be top dog," I said. "Kellen figures that, as the oldest, it should be him. Alicia sees no reason why being four should stop her from doing *anything*—even driving."

Simon snorted. "She's a Davenport through and through."

I nodded. "Pure truth."

Right then, Addison skipped over in her devil outfit. "I won, Mommy!" she told me, her eyes bright.

"I know, and I'm super proud of you." I scooped her up and kissed her cheek. "Well done."

She looped her arms around my neck. "Where's Daddy?"

"He went upstairs to get your brother. Ah, here he is now."

Dane walked into the room, carrying Oliver Hugh Davenport, who I'd dressed in a pumpkin suit, much to his father's consternation.

Addison's face lit up. "Can I hold him again? And feed him? And burp him?"

"Sure," I said.

"Yay!" Alicia shrieked, running over. "Ollie's here! Ollie's here! Ollie's here!"

Dane glanced at me. "No more sugar for her tonight."

Alicia curled her body around Dane's leg. "He's just so little, Daddy. I love how he smells. It makes me want to eat him."

"I'm glad you restrain yourself," said Dane.

Before I even had the chance to *try* to hold my son, my father carried him away—earning himself a frown from Wyatt, who'd also tried to take him.

Melinda shoved a glass in Ashley's hand and then followed them, clearly also wanting to get her hands on Oliver.

Sidling up to me again, Ashley cleared her throat. "Alicia, Kellen would like to apologize for calling you Frodo." She gently nudged her son. "Go on."

"Sorry," he bit out.

Alicia sniffed, releasing her father's leg. "Apology accepted," she said, as gracious and haughty as any royal.

"Now *you* apologize for hitting *him*," I told her.

She looked like she might argue, but then she turned to him and said, "Sorry."

"Fine," he mumbled.

Her eyes narrowed. "You're *supposed* to say, 'apology accepted.'"

Instead, he snickered.

She looked at me, her eyes flaring. "*Mommy,* he didn't accept my sorry."

"He did," Ashley cut in. "Didn't you, Kellen?"

He snorted. "No."

Alicia clenched her little fists and leaned toward him. "*Then I'm not sorry anymore.*"

"And I don't care," he yelled.

"Because you're a goof-trooper!"

I quickly separated the two. "You both have a choice. You can say one nice thing to each other, or you can say nothing at all."

Unsurprisingly, they both snapped their mouths shut.

Carrying Cooper, Tucker crossed to us. "Kellen, get over here and stop winding up four-year-old girls." With that, he led his son away.

Ashley smiled down at Alicia. "You look so beautiful in that dress. Which princess is your favorite?"

Alicia's face scrunched up, like the question was idiotic. "Me."

Ashley's lips parted. "Well of course."

"Aren't I the prettiest princess, Daddy?" she asked, either oblivious to or uncaring about the juice on her dress, the wonky tiara, the chocolate all over her face, and the fact that she only wore one shoe.

Dane nodded. "Of course you are, baby."

She beamed at him and lifted her arms. "Kisses!"

Dane obligingly lifted her and accepted the many kisses she feathered over his face, leaving smears of chocolate all over him.

Addison wriggled in my arms. "I want to go see Ollie."

"Me, too," declared Alicia.

Dane and I lowered our daughters to the floor, who both then skipped away.

He turned to me, wearing his classic unimpressed expression. "Just how much chocolate do I have on my face?"

"Only a little," I fibbed.

"It's not nice to lie, you know," he grumbled, wiping at his cheek.

I smiled. "You can't fool me. I know you're happy."

His expression softened, and he looked both sober and gentle at the same time. "I don't have a single reason not to be anymore, do I?"

ACKNOWLEDGMENTS

Firstly, I want to say a big thank you to my family - you're the best and most supportive bunch of people, and I know I'm unbelievably lucky to have you. My son was a big help when creating the book cover for THE FAVOR, so an additional thanks to you for that! Also, I want to thank my editor, Melody Guy, for all your advice, suggestions, and knack of spotting the dumbest errors I make. A big shout-out to my PA, Melissa Rice, because you're just the freaking best and help free up so much of my time so I can write. Last but not whatsoever least, thank you to everyone who took a chance on the book! I hope you enjoyed it, and I want you to know I super appreciate your support. I love every one of you.

All of you take care :)

ABOUT THE AUTHOR

Suzanne Wright lives in England with her husband, two children, and two Bengal cats. When she's not spending time with her family, she's writing, reading, or doing her version of housework—sweeping the house with a look.

TITLES BY SUZANNE WRIGHT

The Deep in Your Veins Series
Here Be Sexist Vampires
The Bite That Binds
Taste of Torment
Consumed
Fractured
Captivated
Touch of Rapture

The Phoenix Pack Series
Feral Sins
Wicked Cravings
Carnal Secrets
Dark Instincts
Savage Urges
Fierce Obsessions
Wild Hunger
Untamed Delights

The Dark in You Series
Burn
Blaze
Ashes
Embers
Shadows
Omens
Fallen

The Mercury Pack Series
Spiral of Need
Force of Temptation
Lure of Oblivion
Echoes of Fire
Shards of Frost

The Olympus Pride Series
When He's Dark
When He's An Alpha
When He's Sinful

Standalones
From Rags
Shiver
The Favor

Printed in Great Britain
by Amazon

42797629R00199